A
DARKNESS
FORGED
IN
FIRE

A DARKNESS FORGED IN FIRE

BOOK ONE OF THE IRON ELVES

Chris Evans

POCKET BOOKS

NEW YORK   LONDON   TORONTO   SYDNEY

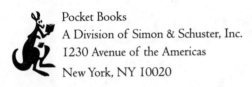
Pocket Books
A Division of Simon & Schuster, Inc.
1230 Avenue of the Americas
New York, NY 10020

First Pocket Books hardcover edition July 2008

POCKET and colophon are registered trademarks of Simon & Schuster, Inc.

For information about special discounts for bulk purchases,
please contact Simon & Schuster Special Sales at 1-800-456-6798
or business@simonandschuster.com.

Designed by Mary Austin Speaker

Manufactured in the United States of America

10 9 8 7 6 5 4 3 2 1

Library of Congress Cataloging-in-Publication Data is available.

ISBN-13: 978-1-4165-7051-6
ISBN-10:   1-4165-7051-9

To my parents, Robert and Barbara, for believing.

It means everything.

We're little black sheep who've gone astray,

Baa—aa—aa!

Gentlemen-rankers out on the spree,

Damned from here to Eternity,

God ha' mercy on such as we,

Baa! Yah! Bah!

~JOSEPH RUDYARD KIPLING, "GENTLEMEN RANKERS"

A
DARKNESS
FORGED
IN
FIRE

ONE

Mountains shouldn't scream, but this one did.

The agony of the rock vibrated beneath the paws of a small, brown squirrel crouched low behind a boulder near the summit. The frigid night air thrummed in sympathetic harmony with the mountain, blurring the light from a shooting star trailing crimson fire across the sky. Shadows shattered and reformed, their shapes subtly altered.

The squirrel sat up on its hind legs and looked to the sky, its glittering eyes following the path of the red star as it burned across the sky toward the east. Letting out a sigh, the squirrel shook its small head; no matter how many centuries you had to get ready, prophecies always caught you off guard. The Stars were returning to the world. It was a strange thought for a squirrel to have, but not for the elf-wizard that had taken squirrel form.

Remaining transformed for the time being, the wizard dropped to all fours and leaped to another boulder a few feet higher up, stretching out his arms and legs to take advantage of the loose folds of fur between them. He landed on the next boulder huffing for breath. It was definitely easier to fly going downhill. He looked up to the mountain summit and shivered in spite of the fur that currently covered his body. A group of trees dotted the peak. *And I'm just a squirrel,* the wizard thought, rubbing his paws together for warmth before continuing his climb.

The wizard's tail bushed as he scampered closer to the top. With each jump the ground felt increasingly wrong. Something was changing it from the inside, and he knew what. The roots of the trees on the summit were clawing their way deep into the heart of the mountain to feed on the rock. Until tonight, they had been contained, isolated on this mountaintop where they could be controlled, if not destroyed. The falling of the Red Star in the east signaled that was no longer the case. A power not known in the world since the beginning of time was returning. Power that could either save it, or destroy it.

He concentrated on the forest, wishing he was powerful enough to wipe it from the face of the earth himself, but knowing it was far beyond him. He hoped, however, that his plan might help the one who could. All the wizard had to do was steal one small thing. And survive. It's why he had transformed himself. A wizard going into this forest would never return. A squirrel, on the other hand, had the slimmest of chances of surviving by going unnoticed.

He hoped.

The wizard paused again in his climb to catch his breath, watching it turn to mist and rise in the icy air, drawing his eyes to the trees that clung to the rock.

No living thing should have found a home there, yet the forest survived, its roots boring ever deeper into the rock, suckling on the bitter ore it found. Leaves turned iron-black, the wind honing them to a razor edge. Bark crystallized, growing translucent to reveal the thick ichor pulsing beneath while branches withered needle thin, stabbing down at the ground in the vain search for something fleshier to consume.

It was a forest, of a kind.

The mountain shuddered and sent chunks of rock cartwheeling down its side, as if trying to shake the forest loose. Just in time the wizard hid in a crevice until the avalanche had passed. He poked his head up a moment later and prepared to make the final dash into the trees. It didn't look promising—arrowlike twigs splintered against rock with a sound of ringing iron as the trees now hunted among the shadows.

The wizard twitched his squirrel tail twice then darted between the crystal trunks in a wild dash for the center of the forest. Branches slashed down as he dodged and scrambled for his life.

Finally, out of breath and on the verge of exhaustion, he came to the very center of the forest.

There, on a ragged knuckle of granite, stood a silver Wolf Oak.

He knew the Wolf Oaks well, good nuts, but this one was wholly unlike the tall, majestic trees in the Great Forest of the Hyntaland on the plains below. Those trees were tall and proud, their limbs strong and supple in the nurturing sun. This tree shared none of those traits, growing low and wide across the rock, snaking its jagged limbs out in every direction to ensnare its progeny in a thicket of wild, dark hunger. Glinting, obsidian-shelled acorns covered the ground beneath it.

The forest was expanding.

The wizard felt the sudden urge to get off the ground and climb somewhere high. He looked at the trees around him and decided that the ground, as polluted as it was, was still preferable. It was as he feared. Being this close to the silver Wolf Oak was taking its toll; he was starting to think like a squirrel. Wolf Oaks were the natural conduits for the raw, elemental magic of nature, and among them the silvers had no equal. This one surpassed even them.

Five hundred rings ago, this silver Wolf Oak had been a sapling cub in the birthing meadow of the Great Forest, a new, young life full of promise. In time, it would have towered above the tallest trees, a singular being of incredible, if simple power, ruling and protecting the forest by influencing all living things around it. It had been that way since the beginning. Then the elves had come to the Hyntaland, and everything changed.

The wizard fought his most basic instincts—elf and squirrel—to flee down the mountain. Not yet though, not without getting what he came for. He placed one paw in front of the other and started to move cautiously toward the silver Wolf Oak, only to find his progress stopped because the more sensible squirrel part of his mind had wedged his tail between two rocks, saving his life.

Black, hoary frost sparkled on the rocks, radiating out from the tree in all directions. A moment later, a piece of night detached itself from the rest of the darkness.

The Shadow Monarch, elf witch of the high, dark forest, had come.

She stood beside the silver Wolf Oak, the reek of cold, metallic power filling the forest. He sensed more than saw. Her head turn and look toward him. His breath froze in his lungs, his vision darkening around the edges.

Her gaze moved on. He relaxed ever so slightly, drawing in the tiniest of breaths. Frost glistened off his whiskers.

The Shadow Monarch looked up to the sky, following the path of the fallen Red Star. She reached out to the tree. Anger, pain, desire, and something more infused the two, twisting the very air around them. Their madness wove together until their power was one and the same, staining everything. She then wrapped Her arms around the tree, a dark thing cradling a dark thing, and the wizard sensed what he had long feared: above all else, She wanted revenge.

The wizard raised his head, peering beyond his whiskers to the black tableau a few feet away. The Shadow Monarch was looking down at a pool of ichor beside the silver Wolf Oak. The pool shimmered, revealing an image of the Great Forest to the west of the mountain. Elves of the Long Watch, formed to protect the Great Forest from Her madness, patrolled among the trees. For centuries now they had kept Her at bay, forever vigilant, keeping Her and Her forest isolated high on the mountain.

It was a comforting vision. What happened next wasn't.

Black flame flickered in the Great Forest, and elves and trees began to shrivel and die. Stars fell, but wherever they landed Her forest was there, devouring the Stars' power and making it Her own. New trees burst forth from the cold earth like daggers of crystal and ore. These trees spread, covering more and more ground until no free space remained . . . blanketing mountain and desert, lake and ocean, in one dark forest.

The mountain shuddered anew. A different image formed in the dark pool. Soldiers now stood about, their green jackets and iron muskets the unmistakable hallmarks of the Calahrian Imperial Army, the sharp edge of the human empire across the ocean.

The image in the pool pulled back, revealing more. There was a small fortress on a hill, vaguely familiar to him. Power flowed from Her to the pool and the image grew larger as She searched for something there. The wizard gasped as Her magic suddenly washed over him. He struggled to keep control and remember why he was here, knowing he was slowly losing the fight as the magic of Her forest wreaked havoc with his mind.

The shooting star blazed across the sky above the small fort, then stopped, hanging there like a red sun. The brilliance of its light grew until the ichor turned completely crimson. And then the light was gone and no sign of the star remained, but something had changed.

Slowly, silently, he inched out of his hiding place and crept along the ground toward the thing he had come for. Every step was a cold needle in his paws, but there, just a foot away, lay one of the silver Wolf Oak's obsidian-shelled acorns. It was close, but he needed a distraction.

He concentrated, trying to draw magic from the foul power that coursed around him. Wincing with pain, he sifted it in his mind until he was able to cleanse enough to perform one small spell. It would have to do.

He focused his thoughts on a tree on the other side of the clearing, and for a moment it looked more like what it should have been; brown and green and healthy. The other trees attacked it at once, flailing and stabbing it in a flurry of branches. The wizard lunged, grabbing the acorn between his paws and stuffing it into his mouth. Cold lightning flashed through his head, but he managed to scamper back behind a rock before spitting the acorn out into his paws where it steamed in the air.

The mountain shuddered again, a deep, mournful sound. Rock sundered. Chasms opened deep into the mountain's core, laying bare its ancient past. Flames of black frost leaped from the darkness and high into the night sky. Her forest dug ever deeper, delving more than rock, reaching back to an age long past. Primal, red-throated roars not heard for hundreds of years filled the air, and they were hungry. Another voice rose above them, and the bit of the wizard that remained in control shivered at the words.

You shall feed, too, She told them. Roots pulled misshapen creatures from the depths. They spilled forth in black heaps, a shambling mass of crooked limbs and milky white eyes.

Go out in this world as you once did. Gather to me those that bear my mark. Those others that would harm My realm . . . destroy.

Every fiber in his body told him to run while his luck held, but he had to risk one last look in the pool. Like the Great Forest, tongues of frost fire were engulfing the fortress on the hill, burning everything. Her trees breached the earth, their roots clawing, searching for the star that had fallen there.

Enough. He stuffed the acorn back in his mouth and ran for his life.

The pain was overwhelming, but he had to get back down the mountain with his prize. Every leap took him further away from this infernal place and closer to the one who now had a chance to stop Her.

When he reached the bottom of the mountain he found a nearby cave and crawled into it, spitting the acorn out and collapsing in a heap, his body transforming to that of an elf again. He let the pain and exhaustion take him, drifting into unconsciousness with the satisfaction of knowing he had succeeded in the first part of his task. When he was fully recovered he would be able to deliver the prize in person.

High up on the mountain, the Shadow Monarch stood watching. She saw the elf-wizard collapse in the cave. Creatures stood beside Her, waiting. Some still bore the look of elves, though terribly twisted. They waited for the command to tear the wizard to shreds. The command did not come. Instead, the Shadow Monarch smiled.

Worlds shouldn't scream, but this one would.

TWO

A sentry leaned against an abandoned bullock cart, propping his musket against a shattered wheel. The faded painted letters on the side of the cart spelled out 35TH FOOT— CALAHRIAN IMPERIAL ARMY, not that he could read them, not that he cared. He took a quick glance around the other side of the cart and saw nothing, just a few dots of orange in the night where lanterns burned along the fortress walls. It was as run-down as the cart. Only in darkness did it still look fortlike, and even then the ragged line of lanterns showed where parts of the walls had collapsed through time and neglect.

He pushed his shako back on his head and ran a sleeve across his sweaty brow while undoing the top button of his uniform. *You could poach an egg in this heat,* he figured, then felt sick at the thought. There was a time when he'd scarf down a horse steak barely seared on the fire and ask for seconds, but the heat of this place robbed a man of appetite, and not just for food.

"Honor guard my arse," he grumbled to himself, pulling a small carved pipe and leather pouch of tobacco from a jacket pocket. "So the last Viceroy was daft enough to get himself killed here, so what? What honor do they think we're guarding now?" he asked, knowing he would not get a satisfactory answer, even if he wasn't just talking to himself. It was like that in the army. Ask away, the sergeants said, but you'll never like the answer. Made a soldier think there was little future in thinking much at all.

"Shoulda had a better guard two years ago, might have done him some good then," he said, chuckling at his own joke. He tamped a thick wad of leaf into the bowl of the pipe with his thumb then with his left hand patted his uniform for his flint and tinder box. He stole another look back up at the fortress. He had ten minutes, fifteen at the most, before the sergeant would come down to check on him. Time enough for a good smoke, if only he could find the flint. His hand fell on something hard and square in a pocket and he smiled. Pulling out the tinder box, he quickly slipped the piece of flint from inside and was about to strike it when a glitter in the sky made him stop. He looked up into a fiery light that roared into being directly above the fort.

He screamed, dropping the flint and throwing an arm across his eyes. Pure, red light radiated in every direction and then just as quickly, was gone. Slowly, he let his arm drop, blinking to get his vision back.

Everything looked the same as before. The fort still stood, the lanterns marking its walls. Had it been a spell? He patted himself all over and found that he felt the same, too. He remembered the flint and bent over to look for it. Was that frost?

He leaned closer, reaching down with his hand. The air felt cool on his fingertips nearer to the ground.

The grass shriveled before his eyes as the earth cracked like a plate thrown to the floor. Something black burst through the earth and latched on to his wrist. He tried to fall backward, but he couldn't break free of the icy grip. A shout froze in his throat as a dark shape emerged from the ground in front of him. Its face was a jagged puzzle of shadow, but something about it looked familiar.

". . . V-viceroy?" he managed, his breath a pale mist.

The thing that held him let go of his wrist and grabbed him by the throat, lifting him up until his boots no longer touched the ground. The small pipe and tinder box fell to the dirt and were immediately covered in a cold, black frost.

Not anymore," Her Emissary said, letting go of the dead body and moving toward the dots of orange light up the hill. A forest, of a kind, began to grow in its wake.

It began to hunt.

There were many places you didn't want to be in the middle of summer in the sweltering humidity of high noon on the southern coast of Elfkyna. The center of the bazaar of Port Ghamjal topped the list. Heat oozed through the streets like wet mortar, filling every crack and crevice and slowing the pace of life to a crawl.

Faltinald Elkhart Gwyn, recipient of the Order of the Amber Chalice, holder of the Blessed Garter of St. DiWynn, Member of the Royal Society of Thaumaturgy and Science, and Her Majesty's newly appointed Viceroy for the Protectorate of Greater Elfkyna of the Calahrian Empire, was not amused. He should have been in the viceroyal palace hours ago, but his carriage and procession were currently stopped dead.

"Malodorous cesspool," the Viceroy said, raising a scented handkerchief to his nose. Smells bubbled and oozed in the sweltering cauldron of five thousand merchant stalls jammed into an area originally intended to hold a fifth that number. Beasts of burden were as numerous as the flies that swarmed around them, buzzing black clouds surging several feet in the air with every swish of a dung-crusted tail. Cinnamon, raw meats, curdling milk, mustard, cardamom, and the bitterly sharp tungam nut assaulted the nose and watered the eyes and almost distracted the marketgoer from the underlying stench of sweat and raw sewage.

The carriage door swung open and a lieutenant in the green uniform of the Calahrian infantry saluted. The market smells washed into the cabin and the Viceroy fought the urge to gag.

"Sorry for the delay, your grace, but one of the outriders' horses knocked over an elfkynan's stall, and the merchant won't let us past until we pay."

The Viceroy sighed behind his handkerchief. "Is that all? Fine, shoot him."

The officer blinked and opened and closed his mouth. "Sir?"

"To delay the Viceroy is to delay the work of the Empire, which is tantamount to revolt." Of course, shooting a merchant in the bazaar as one of his first acts as newly appointed Viceroy would cause no little unrest in the country, he realized, and he was not unhappy at the thought. It was time for the Empire to forge a new path in the world even if Her Majesty did not agree, and to do so he would set Elfkyna aflame.

The lieutenant coughed, clearly lost on the word "tantamount." The word "revolt," however, registered with him like a cannon shot. "Your grace, I don't think it's as bad as all that!" The murmur of a growing crowd indicated that it wasn't yet, but could be if given the right provocation.

The Viceroy lowered his handkerchief and gave the officer a smile that showed teeth and not a hint of humanity. "Really? Bring me that news parchment," he said, pointing to a tattered scroll of paper pinned to the wall across from the open door. The lieutenant yelled at a sergeant, who quickly retrieved the parchment, handing it to the officer who in turn handed it to the Viceroy.

"Can you read this?" the Viceroy asked, pointing to the large black letters at the top of the scroll.

"It's the *Imperial Weekly Herald*, your grace," the lieutenant said slowly.

"Of the Calahrian Empire, yes. And below that?"

The lieutenant squinted. "NORTHERN TRIBES STAGE PEACEFUL PROTEST, a story by Her Majesty's Scribe Rallie Synjyn."

The first twinge of a headache blossomed behind the Viceroy's eyes. The very idea of a reporter of events struck the Viceroy as running counter to everything he believed in. Spies for those in power were one thing, but informing the governed was quite another. The masses did not need to know, only to obey. Clearly, Her Majesty's Scribe Rallie Synjyn was a thorn that needed plucking.

"The natives are growing restless. They have been without proper leadership for too long. Order must be restored." The state of affairs was indeed deplorable; things were not disorderly enough, a fact Synjyn and the *Imperial Weekly Herald* continued to convey.

Two years ago, in a sop to Imperial brotherhood, Her Majesty had appointed an elf from the Hyntaland to oversee Elfkyna. It did not turn out as Her Majesty wished. For one thing, the elfkynan weren't actually elves, and harbored a deep resentment of those that were. Three centuries before, an explorer looking for an eastern sea passage to the homeland of the real elves in the Hyntaland discovered a new land by mistake. Convinced he really had found the Hyntaland, the explorer insisted on proclaiming the natives elf-kind, despite the fact that the elfkynan were a somewhat short, stocky race that looked nothing like elves and far more like humans, though the Viceroy deplored the idea.

A second problem had been the previous Viceroy's capricious, brutal, and above all, bloody reign. An iron fist in an iron glove. *How . . . appropriate*, the new Viceroy thought, refusing to even entertain the pun—that the last Viceroy was murdered by the elf commanding the Iron Elves regiment, Her Majesty's colonial troops from the Hyntaland.

The scandal had rocked the Empire. The elves of the Hyntaland, once viewed as the Queen's most loyal colonial subjects, were now seen as the duplicitous beings they were. The Iron Elves were disbanded, their soldiers placed aboard a galley and sent south across the ocean to the desert wastes, while their officer was court-martialed and cashiered from the service, but not, unfortunately, executed. Evidence apparently existed that suggested the previous Viceroy had in fact been working for someone else. While Calahr was mortified by it all, the elfkynan rejoiced in the Viceroy's demise, and much of their growing resentment was deflated. The urgency to appoint a new Viceroy diminished, and it took considerable maneuvering within the royal court for Gwyn to finally secure the posting. In the meantime, the work of the last Viceroy had simmered in the heat with no one to stir it up.

Well, that was all about to change.

"I expect to be in my palace within the hour, Lieutenant. Someone is going to be shot in the next ten seconds; I'll leave it up to you who."

The lieutenant saluted and closed the door. Orders barked out and the sound of metal ramrods rattling in musket barrels sent up a cry among the crowd. The carriage swayed as people ran.

"Fire!" The musket volley echoed off the mud brick walls, followed by screaming. The carriage began to move forward again, the squelch of things beneath its wheels adding to the din. The Viceroy closed his eyes and allowed himself another smile. Things had indeed changed.

. . .

Four hours later the Viceroy stood among the ruins of his palace, looking for someone to blame. He took a calming breath and surveyed his new home. The palace was little more than a collection of tumbled blocks of sun-dried mud. It reminded him of a potter's wheel left unattended, the wet clay slumping and fracturing as it dried into soft, meaningless bits.

Shattered pieces of statues representing deities once venerated now suffocated under sheets of lichen, slowly eating away at them until not even the memory of their godliness remained. Had the previous Viceroy actually lived among this squalor? He considered that. The man *had* been an elf, one of the races close to nature and all that rubbish.

The lieutenant followed the Viceroy's gaze. "The last Viceroy never took up residence here, your grace," the lieutenant said, his voice quavering slightly.

"Always off on some kind of expedition or other. Searching for buried treasure, no doubt," the Viceroy said. It was a poorly kept secret that the previous Viceroy had spent the bulk of his time, when not antagonizing the elfkynan, tearing up the country in search of magical artifacts. The elf's search had ended, badly, at the little garrison fort of Luuguth Jor.

"They say he was looking for signs of the Stars, your grace, trying to find where they had once been. He had maps and wizards and everything to try and find them."

The Viceroy looked closely at the lieutenant for the first time. He had the look of a wax toy left too long in the sun. Everything about him drooped, from his eyes to his stance. Middle-aged, only a lieutenant, and assigned to guard duty in a backwater like Elfkyna, he was the epitome of the Empire today: soft.

The lieutenant blushed under the Viceroy's stare and continued. "You know, your grace, that old children's tale about how the Stars in the sky are really from the ground, and that one day, when a red star fell, the world would, well, end."

"The Eastern Star?" The Viceroy knew the legend, had heard the rumor about the elf's expeditions, and had thought it a case of too much sun and too little brain, but now . . . "The Stars are myth, points of light of no more power than that elf-witch in her forest across the sea."

The lieutenant shook his head, a not insignificant act of bravery for the man. "Oh, no, your grace, the Shadow Monarch is real. In fact, there's some who think, well, that the last Viceroy was working for Her, on account of him being an elf from over there, like Her . . ."

The Viceroy's eyes stared daggers, perfected from practicing the look in the mirror.

"Are you suggesting Her Majesty's representative was a traitor to the Empire?" The first rule he'd learned in the diplomatic corps was to never reveal your true thoughts to anyone. Ever.

The lieutenant stammered, so far out of his depth the pressure was making it hard to breathe. "I-I meant no disrespect, your grace! It's just that when Colonel Osveen killed him—"

"That will be all, Lieutenant," the Viceroy said, offering the man another tooth-filled smile. "I suggest you put your imagination to better use by wondering what will happen if this palace is not restored to a fitting state within two weeks."

"Two weeks?" the lieutenant managed to squeak, his face draining of all color.

"Sooner, if you prefer. Now, don't let me keep you from your work," he said, turning away as the man saluted and stumbled off into the dark.

The Viceroy walked toward what had been the throne room, or perhaps, he wondered, had they merely placed palm fronds on the floor and lounged there like so many dogs? Natives, he thought, they were the same the world over. The Empire was far too lenient in allowing them to keep their inferior cultures. It was long past time for the Empire to exert itself as it once had, bringing fire and steel and civilization to the unenlightened. Orcs, dwarves, elves, elfkynan, and the rest of the muddied races had been allowed to thrive in this age of peace, poisoning the Empire from within and without. The Queen's mercy would be the Empire's downfall if something wasn't done.

As he walked, he considered the rumors of the Red Star. He trusted rumors the way he trusted sharp knives, and sought a way to grasp the point without getting pricked. However, if the Stars were real . . .

Thoughts of the Stars were pushed aside as he entered his would-be throne room. Lanterns hung from iron poles in a circle. They cast a fluttering, yellow light, creating the impression of life where there was only crumbling mud and stone. The once ornate tile floor was spider-webbed with cracks and stained with splotches of fuzzy mold. Looking distinctly out of place in the center of the room was a long, oak conference table with two wicker chairs around it, the sum total of furnishings the palace had to offer. The chairs were of native design, far too rustic for his liking, but the table was unlike anything he had ever seen before. Its legs were carved to resemble those of a dragon, sinew and claw masterfully reproduced. It made the table look as if it were about to leap. The top gleamed with inlaid emerald leaves polished into the wood in the shape of a dragon's head, the mouth wide open and staring up at him with two black eyes. It made him feel he was being watched, a trick he suspected was created by more than a simple woodcarver's skill.

Viceroy Gwyn sat down in a chair in front of the table and ran his hands along the surface, marveling at the smooth, tingling sensation that ran up his arm. He deliberately placed his hand over the dragon's maw then chided himself for thinking anything might actually happen. It was a marvelous creation. He smiled. Well, well, it was the first positive thing the departed Viceroy had left him.

"Change is coming, wait and see," he said quietly. It might have been a breeze playing with the lantern flames, but for a moment, the table seemed to gleam a little brighter.

THREE

Konowa Swift Dragon didn't trust trees, not since he'd fallen out of one when he was a child of six years. His relationship with them had only gotten worse since then. He spun around quickly to face behind him, alert for any sign of movement. The game path he followed was bare, the trees to either side big, brown, green, and motionless. Good. Something buzzed by his ear and he slapped a hand against his neck then held it out in front of his face to examine the kill. He grunted with satisfaction; at least one black fly would no longer torment him.

"That'll teach you," he said, wiping his hand on the bark of a nearby tree. He grabbed the canteen slung across his shoulder and took a drink, looking around at this strange, sweltering forest that was now his home.

A miasma of sounds and smells assaulted him at every turn. Bugs, birds, and furred-beasts twittered, chittered, spewed, cawed, oozed, growled, yelped, and bit all day and most aggravatingly, all night. The trees secreted bucketfuls of cloying sap, the smell every bit as vile as a formal palace ball he'd once attended at the height of summer years ago in the Calahrian capital.

Between the stink and the racket there was enough to make him despise the forest, but fate, it seemed, wasn't satisfied with that. On top of everything else, Konowa was certain the trees were watching him. Worse, he had the growing suspicion that they were trying to tell him something. He walked up to one, even reaching out a hand to pat it, but it looked and acted just like a tree, being absolutely inscrutable as it stood there.

It's just the heat, he decided, wiping the sweat from his brow. Elfkyna was suffocatingly hot in the summer, humid in the snowless winter, and miserable the rest of the year.

He was, as he had been for the past year, alone in a forest.

It brought to mind the angry words he'd shouted all those years ago as he clutched his broken arm and kicked the trunk of the tree that had let him fall: *"I hate the forest and I don't want to be an elf anymore!"*

Decades later, that sentiment remained.

Sighing, Konowa dropped the canteen to his side and held his hands out before him, palms up, wondering if he would ever hold his own fate again. He looked closer at his hands. His natural tanned color was deepening to a hue close to the reddish-brown bark of the trees around him. *Great*, he thought, *I'm turning into a bloody tree.* He ran his hands through the tangled thatch of long black hair on his head, half expecting to feel leaves sprouting there. Instead, his fingers brushed against the tops of his ears, feeling the point on the right, and ragged scar tissue on the left where the point used to be. The mutilation hadn't been by choice, but he wasn't overly upset with the results. He had never been comfortable with his heritage.

Konowa closed his eyes and let the forest talk to him. Nothing. He opened one to see if anything had changed. A large, brightly colored snake wound its way up the trunk of an old, bent teak, using the tree's flaking pale-gray bark for grip. The snake paused, turning to look at him. Its tongue darted in and out of its mouth testing the air. Konowa closed his eyes again and focused his thoughts on the snake, but all he sensed was how foolish he was for trying. He gave up and sought out the trees themselves.

They were nothing like the lean, straight pines and firs or thick and limb-heavy oaks he had known as a child. Here, everything curved, from the trunks of the trees to the creatures and vines that crawled over them. Even the leaves were different, some wide and flat, others garishly green and bitter to the taste.

He tried a new approach. *You're an elf*, he reminded himself, *born of the natural world; you're supposed to be able to do this.* He slowed his breathing and willed his body to relax, trying to let the forest infuse him with its essence. Infuse? Essence? He shook his head. This was pointless. Everything teemed with life and all had voices, yet he heard only noise, felt only chaos.

It had been the same the day he walked into the birthing meadow to become an elf of the Long Watch. He remembered the mix of excitement and fear as he entered the most sacred realm of the *Hhar Vir*, the Deep Forest, seeking a sapling cub among the tender green shoots to become his *ryk faur*, his bond brother.

"Let your spirit walk among them, and one shall call to you," he was told, so he stayed in the meadow for five straight days without food or water, waiting, hoping. When the elves finally carried him out because he was too weak to walk, no sapling cub had yet called to him. The Wolf Oaks, the very embodiment of the natural world, had measured him, found him wanting, and rejected him. The thought still rankled. Even the elf-witch the elders told stories about to scare wayward children had found a sapling cub with which to bond.

Knowing it was fruitless but trying anyway, he now raised his arms high into the air and called again to the trees around him. His only answer was a swarm of gnats that flew into his mouth. Exasperated and spitting bugs, Konowa lowered his arms and squirmed inside the tattered and patched remnants of his uniform. The Calahrian Imperial Army green had faded to dirty white, and the knees and elbows sported ill-sewn patches of black leather from his knapsack. His musket, however, was in perfect condition. He let his left hand brush against the stock and smiled at the cold and lifeless feel of wood and steel entwined. The weapon would work if he kept his powder dry and the moving parts oiled, not if he "felt" in tune with it, as the oath weapons the Wolf Oaks bestowed on their *ryk faur* elves required.

A rumbling growl made Konowa turn. Jir, his companion of the last year, and probably the sole reason Konowa had not gone stark, raving mad out here, stood a foot away, having sneaked up on Konowa without the elf hearing a thing.

"You're better at this than me," he said, lightly rapping the bengar between the eyes with his knuckles. Jir snorted and shook his woolly head, staring up at him with big black eyes. Jir was larger than a dyre wolf, larger even than a tiger, sporting a coat of short, midnight-black fur streaked through with dull red stripes. His head featured a stubby, well-whiskered muzzle and a furry mantle of thick hair that ran halfway down his back. At the moment, he was marking his territory, forcing Konowa to jump back a pace. A swarm of black flies rose up from Jir's back as his long tail swished menacingly around his hindquarters. When he was done, Jir padded over on four big paws, rubbing against him and purring a deep, contented sound that made Konowa's body vibrate.

They were quite a pair, Konowa mused, scratching the bengar behind the ears. The feel of Jir's coarse fur reminded him of bark and he looked again at the forest that had become his home. Cathedral light fell like shafts of gold between the trunks as the sun dipped below the tops of the trees. It was the kind of moment his father had urged him to commune with, to find his center and become one with the forest. Konowa snorted. It was the kind of moment when he wanted a tankard of beer and a grilled sausage.

A light breeze sighed between the branches, evaporating the sweat from his forehead. After the heat of the past two weeks, it was a welcome change that would be even better once he and Jir were back in the hut with the door firmly in place. It was not wise to be out in the open when the moon climbed the sky.

Jir growled and shook his woolly head, indicating he'd had enough. Konowa lifted his hand and moved off. Lifting the stock of his musket out of the way, he squatted with some difficulty, his left knee twinging in protest, a souvenir from an orc lancer many years before. He grabbed a handful of dirt and sifted it through his hands, mimicking the actions of the Hynta-elves he'd watched all through his childhood years. His hand tingled with the power of the natural order, but he had no idea what to do with it. Konowa shivered in spite of the heat, dropping the dirt as if stung.

"Let's go home," he said.

Jir stared at him with apparent disdain. Konowa wasn't sure he didn't deserve it.

They walked for several minutes before he found a tree that he'd notched earlier that day with his small hunting hatchet. Cutting a tree was as much an act of defiance as an aid to navigation. The elves of his tribe would have been appalled to see him deface a tree with a steel ax, but they weren't here to guide him.

Feeling smug, Konowa lengthened his stride. He took one complete step and pitched forward into an unseen hollow.

"*Yirka umno!*" Konowa swore as he fell. He landed with a thud. As he lay there catching his breath, he realized with some surprise that he'd used a tribal curse, invoking summer lightning, the forest's most feared natural predator. *I'm going native*, he thought, pushing himself up to his hands and knees. He froze halfway up, coming face to rear with the hindquarters of one severely agitated skunk dragon.

"*Yirka!*" Konowa shouted, scrambling backward as the awful-smelling fire burst forth. He began to roll and beat at the flames, all the while gagging on the stench. Jir growled and wagged his tail furiously at the little black dragon and was no help at all. Konowa rolled and beat out the last of the foul-smelling flames, cursing all the while. He staggered to his feet, wielding his musket like a club, ready to dash the animal's brains onto the forest floor, but the dragon had already scampered off. Finally running out of breath, he leaned his musket against a tree, unstoppered his canteen, and poured the contents over his head.

He stood like that for several seconds, his face dripping, his chest heaving, and his eyes darting wildly from side to side like an elf possessed. When the roar of blood in his ears quieted enough for him to hear the perpetual hum of the forest, he flung the canteen away. No sooner had he thrown it away and watched it disappear among the trees than he realized he'd need it.

Konowa took stock of his situation. Aside from what felt like a bad case of sunburn, he was uninjured. His uniform, however, was absolutely ruined. He stripped off his cartridge pouch, shirt, boots and trousers, leaving only his loincloth on as he gingerly hopped from foot to foot on the carpet of nettles from the bushlike tree he found himself under.

After a few moments of that, Konowa decided it was time to try something new. Thoughts of the clean, cool water by the hut spurred him to action. Shooting a withering glance at Jir, he put his boots back on after carefully brushing any clinging nettles off his bare feet. Flies, gnats, and a dozen other bugs he couldn't identify were now buzzing about his head, but none dared land; the stench of the skunk dragon acting as the first effective remedy he'd found to keep them at bay. Picking up his musket, he hung his soiled clothes and pouches from the muzzle and rested the weapon on his shoulder.

"What else can go wrong?" he muttered, and started to walk for home with Jir padding alongside at a discreet distance.

The unmistakable sound of a tree falling carried in the twilight, and for the briefest of moments, Konowa sensed pain. It was gone so fast he wasn't sure it had happened, but when he looked over at Jir he knew something wasn't right. The bengar stood stiff-legged, his ears straight up, muzzle sniffing the air.

"It's nothing," Konowa lied, and kept walking, anxious to outpace the smell that clung to him. The light was fading quickly now, and he wanted to get back to the hut before it was completely dark. The sound of the forest changed at night, a subtle, gradual shift that crept up on the unsuspecting . . . along with things that made no sound at all.

Konowa turned to scold Jir to get a move on. The bengar was gone.

"Jir," he called softly. Jir had excellent hearing, but that wasn't why Konowa kept his voice low—the forest had gone silent. The constant hum of life that surged through the trees was absent, the forest was preternaturally still, as if time itself had ceased to exist.

"Not good," Konowa whispered to himself as he tipped the clothes from his musket and began to load the weapon, just to be safe.

Cradling the musket in front of his body, Konowa checked that the flint was still secure, then half-cocked the hammer as his old regiment's collect sounded in his ears.

Heavenly spirits, who watch over us . . .

He fished out a cartridge from his pouch with his right hand, bringing the waxed paper tube up to his mouth in one practiced motion and biting the end off.

. . . guide us into battle and make sure our hand . . .

The gunpowder mixed with his saliva and he grimaced at its familiar salty, bitter taste.

. . . that we might slay our enemy . . .

The weight of the small lead bullet pressed against his tongue, and he heard again the whip-crack of regimental pennants unfurled in a gusting wind, the creaking timber of gun carriages, the whinnying of horses, the pounding of their hooves, and the echoing barks of sergeants relaying their officers' commands.

. . . destroy them as those that went before us . . .

A tremor of anticipation coursed through Konowa's body.

. . . and keep our honored place as your faithful servants, your harbingers of death. We are the warriors of the Hynta. We fear nothing, for we are the Iron Elves!

"Amen," Konowa said out loud, no longer alone.

He prepared the musket for firing to the cadence of a sergeant long ago dead, killed by a swarm of battle-crazed orcs in a land even more foreign than this. Something cold and black touched Konowa then, and he felt the presence of the lost souls of his old regiment. He trickled a little gunpowder into the pan of the musket before closing the hammer. Keeping time with the past, he set the musket butt down in front of him and poured the remaining charge down the barrel before stuffing the lead ball and finally the paper cartridge after it. Without pause, he pulled out the ramrod slung beneath the barrel from the four brass pipes that held it in place and tamped down the wadding and bullet, all the while scanning the forest. He replaced the ramrod and brought the musket up to his hip, imagining the bristling line of soldiers to his left and right and drawing comfort from their stoic silence.

He nudged the cock all the way back, the chunk of flint held in its steel jaws glinting with purpose. He stood like that for several seconds, his hands growing slick on the wooden portions of the gun. All too quickly the nostalgia of the past bled away, leaving him alone again in a strange land very far from home.

Another sound came from somewhere to his left and Konowa moved toward it, allowing his senses to guide his feet as he kept his eyes searching the shadows ahead. The stillness of the forest hung like a veil from the branches, and the longer he walked the harder it seemed to push forward. He had decided he would only walk another fifty yards when he stepped into a clearing, and what had only been an exceptionally bad day became a waking nightmare.

FOUR

Not more than thirty yards away across the clearing crouched four rakkes around a fallen tree.

Four seven-foot-tall, boulder-shouldered, black, scraggly haired rakkes all staring at Konowa with milky eyes deep-set in scarred, leathery faces.

But rakkes were extinct.

What Konowa was seeing was impossible, yet he knew they were rakkes. He'd seen the drawings on stretched hides handed down from generation to generation, heard the ancient tales, even held a skull of one of the creatures in his hands. They had lived high in the mountain, coming down like nightfall to ravage the land below. The elves of the Long Watch had hunted them down and destroyed them. Centuries ago, and an ocean away.

Yet all of that meant nothing now. Four rakkes were only thirty yards away from him. They stood up as one, teetering slightly in this new bipedal stance, like drunks one round away from falling. Long, curving claws slid out from pawlike hands that hung down by their knees.

The largest of them opened its mouth to reveal long, yellow fangs glistening with saliva. It screamed a high, mewling cry and the other three responded in kind, shaking the forest floor.

It was a sound as cold and black as the depths of time it should have been lost in.

"*Cawwnnnawahhhh . . .*"

Konowa's chest heaved, his breath rushing out as forcefully as if he'd been hit with a cannonball.

The largest of the four rakkes had clearly said his name. The creature's mouth contorted with the effort as it struggled to pronounce it, its tongue more used to moving around lacerated flesh than words.

"*Cawwnnnawahhhh . . .*"

He should have run away. It was the sensible thing to do.

Konowa fired his musket, then ran straight at the rakkes, screaming for all he was worth.

There was a loud crack, followed by a huge billowing cloud of acrid-smelling smoke flecked with sparks as the musket bucked in his hands. The musket ball passing through the chest of the rakke saying his name with a wet thwack, blowing out chunks of eerily white spine through the now gaping hole in its back.

Running hard, Konowa grabbed the musket by its warm muzzle and swung the weapon in a smooth arc at a second rakke's head. The musket struck flesh and bone, jarring Konowa's arms and shoulders and cutting off his yell as he bit his tongue. The closest rakke went down whimpering, its skull crushed like an eggshell, one white eye pulped and oozing down its cheek. Konowa laughed then, a habit he had in battle, tasting the salty liquid of his own blood in his mouth. He swung a low backstroke at another rakke, feeling the satisfying crunch of bones travel up the musket and into his own.

A set of claws whistled by his head and Konowa dove forward, ducking underneath. His right shoulder slammed into the body of a rakke, and he pivoted onto his heels and brought the muzzle of the musket upward with all his strength.

The rakke screamed as the steel barrel slammed into its stomach, but without a bayonet on its end the musket only enraged the beast. The rakke wrapped both massive arms around Konowa and crushed him to its chest. Konowa was lifted off his feet and swung wildly through the air as he desperately tried to let go of the musket and reach for the hatchet strapped to his calf. He heard a crack—and a bolt of lightning exploded in his chest as one of his ribs snapped. His head growing lighter by the second, Konowa finally pried his hands free and reached for the hatchet. His fingers crawled along his leg in a weakening search as the grip around his chest tightened.

He found the handle, only to have it drop from his fingers as he was physically pounded into the ground. Konowa's breath rushed out of him in a scream, and he lay helpless on his back, waiting for the end to come.

A pair of milky eyes came down to hover inches from his, and he could smell the putrid raw meat of the rakke's last meal. Konowa smiled in one last act of defiance.

Jagged white teeth flashed in front of his eyes and hot, steaming blood splashed across his face.

When he focused his vision again, all he could see above him were stars. Konowa drew in a shuddering breath and propped himself up on one elbow.

Jir held the rakke by the throat, shaking the massive beast like wheat in a storm. When Jir was satisfied it was dead, he opened his mouth, letting the rakke's body fall to the ground with a thump.

Three more dark forms dotted the clearing, and the smell of blood and death thickened the air. Calling on the last reserves of his strength, Konowa staggered to his feet, using his musket as a crutch. Jir looked up at him and bared his fangs, a chunk of rakke flesh hanging out the side of his mouth.

"Easy, boy, I'll never be that hungry," he said, carefully sidestepping the feeding bengar to check that the other three rakkes were once again extinct. The large one that he had shot was clearly dead, the fist-sized hole in its back already swarming with flies. He could see the same was true of the second one he had hit, and Jir was making a meal of the third's innards. That meant Jir must have also killed the fourth one.

Konowa looked around for the body, spying one crumpled twenty yards away. He limped toward it, but immediately saw that something wasn't right.

As he got closer he realized it was an elfkynan woman. So where was the fourth rakke? He looked back at Jir, but the bengar showed no sign of unease as it ate. The fourth creature must have fled and never looked back.

Konowa let go of the musket and stumbled the last few feet to the woman's side, kneeling carefully while still holding his aching ribs. The woman lay facedown, dressed in huntsman's garb of toughened linen dyed brown and green. Like most of her people, she had dark skin, darker even than Konowa's. With only starlight and his own elvish eyes, Konowa could just make out the intricate pattern of tattoos that adorned her arms. A single plait of long brown hair with dull-looking bits of pearl woven in it snaked down her back and lay in a coil on the ground. Bracing himself for what he would find, he grabbed the body by the shoulders and gently turned it over.

Only the ingrained reactions of a warrior saved him as a thin stiletto dagger flew up. Konowa jerked forward so that the flat of her palm, and not the blade, hit the side of his neck. Before she could thrust again, Konowa butted the top of his head into the side of her face and rolled out of range.

A startled yell pierced the meadow and Jir growled in surprise, lifting his blood-stained muzzle into the air, spewing bits of meat. Konowa fought to stay conscious while he looked around for his musket. He finally spotted it, but it was too far away. The woman was already on her feet and advancing toward him when she suddenly wobbled and sat straight down, the stiletto tumbling from her hand.

Konowa's eyes went to the dagger. The blade gleamed unnaturally under the starlight, and he realized it was polished wood, not unlike the oath weapons of the Long Watch. He looked back at her and waited a moment to see if dropping the dagger was a ploy, but she just sat there, her eyes unfocused. The head butt must have done the trick after all. Choosing caution as the better part of valor, he sat perfectly still and concentrated on regaining his breath. While he did so, he studied the woman across from him.

She was definitely no elf. Konowa stared at her alluring face, drawn in by the almond-shaped eyes. He guessed she was no more than twenty, although the elfkynan's exotic look meant matrons in their fifties could look much younger. Whatever her age, her smooth, dark skin and full lips were a wonderful change after having only Jir's furry face to stare at. And then there was the matter of her rather quick reflexes. Konowa tried to chuckle, the absurdity of the day growing by the minute, but the effort sent stabbing knives through his chest and he gave up.

When the pain finally subsided to a more manageable level of agony, Konowa slowly stood. Speaking Gharsi, the most common of the twenty-three languages spoken in Elfkyna, Konowa hoped he could make himself understood. "I don't want to hurt you," he said, "well, again, anyway." Each word was a sharp stitch in his rib cage.

The sound of his voice jarred her back to sensibility and her eyes narrowed. She scooped the dagger from the ground in one swift motion. Konowa remained still, hoping she didn't have the strength to come at him again. He wasn't sure he had any left to fend her off if she did.

"Who are you?" she asked, answering in the common tongue of the Empire, marking her as educated. She risked a quick glance around the meadow. "And what are those things?"

"My name is Konowa," he said, slowly lowering his hands. "Those things . . . are rakkes. Creatures perverted by a dark magic. They were supposedly destroyed a long, long time ago." Suspicion made him cautious, despite the pain. "Their master was an elf-witch . . ."

Her eyes narrowed. "I saw no elf-witch," she said coldly. She looked over at the dead rakkes scattered about the clearing. "So why are these things here, now?"

Konowa stared at her for a long moment before answering, trying to gauge her sincerity. He finally decided she wasn't responsible for them . . . though he hoped his reasoning went deeper than his immediate attraction to her. "I couldn't begin to guess," he lied, refusing to contemplate why and how one of them called his name. "They shouldn't be. They're supposed to be extinct."

"So you keep saying," she said, the skepticism in her voice plain.

"Well, if something's extinct it should bloody well stay extinct, right?" Konowa said, suddenly exasperated by it all.

She opened her mouth to say something else, then paused, looking at him with renewed interest.

"Your name again?"

"Konowa," he said, feeling a sudden sense of dread.

"Colonel Konowa Heer Ul-Osveen of the Iron Elves?"

If blood could freeze in this steaming cauldron of a land, Konowa's did. Only minutes ago he'd thought his past was as dead as rakkes were supposed to be.

She looked up at him with eyes as green as the forest around him, and he saw his doom in them.

"The slayer of the Viceroy?" she asked again, finally sheathing her stiletto and rising slowly to her feet.

"Among others," he said, sinking to the forest floor.

She walked over and looked down at him. "I've been looking for you."

She took a deep breath, brushed a strand of hair from her eyes, and from within the hunting jacket she wore pulled a thin paper scroll bearing a large wax seal, which she expertly broke with a fingernail. Konowa closed his eyes and prayed for deliverance.

"Konowa Heer Ul-Osveen, by royal decree as dutifully witnessed this day in the Greater Protectorate of Elfkyna of the Calahrian Empire, you are hereby ordered to resume your commission as an officer in Her Majesty's Imperial Army effective immediately. Oh, and sir," she continued, a look of concern crossing her face, "I strongly suggest that at the first opportunity, you take a bath and put some clothes on. Your time of communing with nature is at an end."

Konowa sighed. If anything was to deliver him from this fate, it was probably out lost in the bloody forest.

FIVE

N o."

She let the scroll roll up with a snap and kicked a nettle with her foot, sending it bouncing toward Konowa and forcing him to turn over onto his side. He winced with pain as tiny flashes of light popped and winked before his eyes. Despite the fresh reminder of his ravaged rib cage, he noticed for the first time that she wore delicate-looking sandals of woven green grass revealing portions of her slender brown feet. *She couldn't have walked far at all in those,* he realized.

"You will report to the nearest encampment at once," she said as if speaking to a slightly dull child. "Besides, we'll be safer with the army than out here in the forest with those *extinct* creatures around."

He ignored the bait, focusing instead on the fact that there was no tremble in her voice, no hint of fear at all. Not even the sound of a bone snapping flustered her as Jir tore through a rakke's pelvis. *Perhaps,* he conceded, *what they say about women is true: They are tougher.*

"Is the army near?" Konowa asked.

"They were three days by horse to the south, on the other side of the Jhubbuvore," she said, naming a river Konowa vaguely remembered crossing years earlier. "But that was over a week ago. Where they are now I do not know. We should start at once—you are clearly in no condition to fight off any more of those beasts."

A tree cracked just outside the clearing.

Konowa jumped to his feet so fast it felt as if he broke another rib. He stumbled to his musket and picked it up, spinning in a slow circle as he searched the edges of the clearing. Jir raised his muzzle from the inside of a rakke and growled in response.

"What is it?" the woman whispered, the wicked-looking dagger magically reappearing in her right hand.

"There were four rakkes," Konowa said, pointing the muzzle of the musket at the bodies, "but we only killed three."

"Surely your bengar killed it somewhere nearby," the woman said, gesturing at Jir, who was looking questioningly at Konowa.

Turning to Jir, Konowa made a clenched fist then threw his arm out and opened his hand wide. "Hunt," he commanded. The animal rumbled a deep sound and disappeared into the forest in a single bound.

"Will he find it?" she asked, coming to stand next to Konowa even as she wrinkled her nose.

Konowa kept his eyes on the trees, but was very aware of her presence beside him. Heat roiled off her like the open door of a smithy's furnace. Then again, it might have been the pain of his rib cage.

"Maybe, maybe not. If that thing didn't look back it could be a long way from here." He spotted his cartridge pouch on the ground and walked over to it, deciding he'd better reload while he could.

"You're not like any messenger I've ever seen before," he remarked while gingerly ramming a new charge and ball into the musket.

The woman's eyes narrowed and the stiletto flashed as she twirled it in her hand.

"Messenger? I am Visyna Tekoy, daughter of Almak Tekoy, governor of Hijlla Province and supplier to Her Majesty's Imperial Army and the Outer Territories Trading Company in these lands."

"Ah, so your father's a sutler then?"

"A sutler! Do I look like the daughter of some rag and bone merchant?"

Konowa took a quick moment to run his eyes over her again. "Indeed you don't. Well, now, seeing as we've established how your father supports Her Majesty's troops, fair lady, pray tell in what manner do you service them?"

Visyna's retort remained unspoken as Jir suddenly leaped back into the clearing. He sniffed the air for a moment and stretched, sheathing and unsheathing great curving claws that reflected the starlight with lethal intent. When he was finished he walked over to where they were standing and lifted a hind leg.

Visyna yelled in protest, quickly stepping out of the way and into Konowa's arms.

"It means he likes you," he said. He reached over and patted Jir on the head. The bengar began to purr and Konowa relaxed; the fourth rakke was long gone.

"It's disgusting," she retorted.

Konowa nodded and took a deep breath of her dark hair, grimacing with the effort. He imagined it was wonderfully perfumed, but the lingering odor of the skunk dragon and Jir's enthusiastic attempts to make half the known lands his own defeated the exercise.

"I think you can let go now," she said. "Your musket is digging into me."

"That's not my musket," Konowa replied, brandishing the weapon in his right hand in front of her while he kept his left around her waist. He pulled her a little closer. "You know, I did save your life tonight. In some parts, that sort of thing engenders a certain amount of . . . gratitude."

Visyna stilled at the suggestion. *She's not so high and mighty after all*, Konowa thought, suddenly concerned that she might actually take him up on what had been no more than a bluff. A year in the forest or not, he was in no condition for *that*. Visyna turned around in his arm and faced him, her lips only inches from his. He was still wondering what they'd taste like when her fist slammed into his stomach, sitting him squarely on his backside.

"You filthy pig! I am no harlot! And you, sir, are no officer."

Tears streamed down Konowa's face as he gasped for breath and then he laughed, despite the pain.

"You're right there, m'lady. I'm no officer, not anymore." He picked himself up from the ground for the second time that night. He hurt from head to toe and suddenly there was nothing even remotely funny about anything. "You take that piece of parchment with you the next time you use the powder room, because that's all it's good for. The elf on that scroll no longer exists."

"You really are him, aren't you," Visyna said quietly. "You were the one who killed the Viceroy to save your people, and ours." She reached out a hand to touch his ruined left ear, but Konowa pulled away.

"You think I'm a hero? Do heroes end up exiled in a bloody forest? No, my lady, you have it all wrong. I am one of the *dyskara*, the tainted ones marked by the Shadow Monarch. Just good enough to fight for the Empire, but never, ever to be trusted." A year of bitter resentment flared up. "Be afraid, my lady. Molten ore flows through my veins and daisies are poison to me. I live in caves like dwarven folk and eat raw meat off the bone." He ignored her crossed arms and scrunched-up nose and pressed on, needing to vent his anger at someone. "You see before you a spiritual descendant of the Shadow Monarch, the *Horra Rikfa*—oath breaker, the forsaker of the forest, delver of the deep magic long ago lost to this world. Fear me, O pure and righteous one. I was marked by Her, ruler of the High Forest where trees grow in unnatural and vile ways, and elves have little patience for asinine conversations."

"*Jarahta Mysor!*" she yelled, swinging back her hand as if to slap him.

"Easy there, my lady, no need for that kind of language." As fast as the anger had come, it bled away. He tried a smile, but she wasn't having it. "You have no idea what it's like to suffer under the foolishness of myths and legends. I left the Hyntaland to get away from all of that, but it follows me around like a plague."

"Myths and legends?" she asked, shaking her head. "*They* don't look like either," she said, pointing to the dead rakkes.

"No, they don't, but it doesn't matter. You wouldn't understand."

"Really now?" Visyna said, her voice sharp, her eyes flashing. "The story of the elf-witch across the ocean is well known even here. The Empire brought more than oppression to my people, it also brought stories of the *Zargul Iraxa*, as we call Her, Seeker of the Darkness." She appeared to struggle for control of herself, then spoke again in a quieter voice. "Your ancestors forged a bond with the Wolf Oaks. They learned to harness the Wolf Oak's great power, using it to care for the natural order."

"I know the legend," Konowa said, sighing.

"Have you seen this forest realm of the Shadow Monarch?"

Konowa carefully let out a breath in exasperation. "No, I mean, yes, but it's just a bunch of trees."

"You went up there, then?"

Konowa wanted to say yes to end this conversation, but looking into her eyes he found himself suddenly unable to lie. "No, no one goes up there, but that doesn't mean the legend is true . . . entirely."

Visyna made a face then looked back at the rakkes. "And these creatures?"

"I honestly don't know," Konowa said, realizing just how true that was. How did they know his name? "Maybe She did send them after me, or," he said, suspicion flaring in his mind, "maybe She sent them after someone else."

Visyna's mouth formed a perfect O. "Me? You're mad. Clearly, some elves can be in the forest too long."

He took a step toward her. "My senses are clear enough to know something here doesn't make sense. How is it you just happen to have a scroll calling me back to service?"

"There are those who believe you can be of service again. Many of my people consider you a hero for what you did," she said, a note of admiration grudgingly modulating her voice.

"That still doesn't explain you."

Visyna looked as if she might take a swing at him, then relaxed. "Despite what you think, elves aren't the only people in tune with the natural world. I have . . . a gift, for finding things, so I was sent out to look for you."

"Alone?" Konowa asked, refusing to believe any of this.

"Not alone," she said quietly, lowering her eyes. "We were attacked by those things and I was captured, and you know the rest."

Konowa was certain that he didn't, not by a long cannon shot, but he decided to leave it alone for the moment.

"By the way, what did you call me there a moment ago? I haven't heard that one before."

Visyna pursed her lips. "*Jarahta Mysor*. It means bloodless shadow."

Konowa shrugged.

"A being without soul," she said, "an elf not of the natural world. You carry weapons forged in fire, were marked by Her, and serve the Empire that oppresses my people. You have forsaken your destiny and have turned your back on the *ruarmana*."

Konowa gave her a questioning look.

"Trees. They are the bridge between the sky and earth. Only trees reach both up to the heavens and down into the bones of the land." Visyna brushed another strand of hair from her face and stared at him with intense curiosity. "What is *your* native name for them?"

"Lumber."

Visyna's eyes flashed with anger. "You are more iron than elf!"

He held up his hands for a truce. "Look, as scintillating as our conversation is, perhaps we could save it for another time?" The pain in his ribs was now a steady throbbing that threatened to pound him right into the ground. "Who knows what other beasties besides rakkes are out here, and I don't want to be around when they smell all this."

Visyna looked as if she wanted to say a lot more, but held her tongue and began to pick up Konowa's belongings from the ground, careful to avoid any made of metal.

Konowa watched for a moment, then put the remnants of his uniform back on, grabbed those items she wouldn't touch, and tramped straight into the forest without looking to see if she would follow. He knew Jir would come along when he was done eating.

After several minutes he took a quick look over his shoulder and was surprised to see her only a couple of paces behind him. She moved with the assuredness of an elf of the Long Watch. Konowa wondered just what would make a woman so clearly enamored of nature serve the Empire, the largest single destructive force in the world. He chose not to dwell on his own reasons; he was in enough pain as it was.

It didn't take long for Konowa to realize he was hopelessly lost. Chances of finding his hut tonight were as remote as the chances of his figuring out just where this day had gone so terribly, horribly wrong. Only this morning he had had the forest to himself, with just Jir and the damn bugs for company.

Now he didn't know what to think about anything.

The reappearance of extinct creatures, Her extinct creatures, speaking one's name, along with a royal decree also with one's name, had a way of changing one's outlook on life.

Looking back to see that Visyna was still close behind, he pushed on through the trees, holding his ribs and cursing each step. He consoled himself that if this was the worst life could throw at him, things could only get better from here.

Konowa chose to believe that lie for as long as he could. He succeeded for an entire day.

SIX

Now don't tell me you didn't see that," Private Yimt Arkhorn whispered, peering into the night from around the trunk of a bulbous wahatti tree. Fat, broad leaves like the ends of paddles hung down from the wahatti's branches, providing perfect cover.

"I can't see my hand in front of my face," Private Alwyn Renwar said, feeling in the dirt for his spectacles, once again cursing his decision to join the Imperial Army. Deemed marginal for frontline duty, Renwar had been unceremoniously transferred to about the farthest-flung outpost one could draw—the Protectorate of Greater Elfkyna. As if that wasn't bad enough, when he got there he found he had been assigned to one of the rear-echelon guard battalions, with the noble task of watching over the wagon trains of the Outer Territories Trading Company. The food was terrible, the discipline ferocious, the duty alternating between long stretches of numbing boredom and short, sharp bits of sheer terror (like now), and women most certainly did not flock to his side.

Alwyn despised the army, all three months of it so far. He was thousands of miles from home, sweaty, miserable, and scared, and partnered with of all people a dwarf who appeared to be a couple of batwings short of a potion.

"I never should have taken the Queen's gold," Alwyn muttered, the enlistment coin long since spent, on what he couldn't remember.

"Quit your nattering and look," Yimt ordered, spitting a stream of crute juice onto the ground. The rock spice made a sizzling sound as it bubbled on the dirt. "It's a shadowy thing, real big like."

"I still can't find my specs."

"You don't need specs to see it. It's a sight bigger than Her Majesty's twin jewels and the cushion she rests them on," Yimt said with a lecherous grin.

"I shouldn't even be here," Alwyn said, patting the ground frantically. "Piquet duty for a month and for what? I didn't *do* anything. You're the one that 'accidentally' bayoneted then cooked *and* ate the officer's goose. All I had was a drumstick."

"Quit your griping, Ally," Yimt said. "Squad mates got to stick together. An' like I told that officer, that goose of his came at me with a right wicked look in its eye. I was defending myself, I was."

"They'll write you up in a dispatch for bravery uncommon," Alwyn said, now scrambling around on all fours.

"My mum would like that. Here," Yimt said, shaking his head in disgust, "it's for certain there ain't no elves in your family tree, with the pair of eyeballs you got." He reached out a thick-fingered hand and pushed a leaf to the side. "The thing is right there, seventy paces and no more. Have a swig o' this drake sweat and take another look."

Alwyn put his hand down and felt his spectacles . . . covered in gritty crute juice. He quickly buffed the lenses against his coat sleeve before the crute ruined them and put them on, staring with some trepidation at the proffered canteen.

The canteen was typical army issue, made of wood in the shape of a small drum, a large cork stopper at the top. What wasn't typical was that it appeared to be glowing.

"Go on then, it'll clear up your sight right proper," Yimt encouraged, shaking the canteen in front of Alwyn's face. Drops of the liquid sloshed out and hissed when they hit the ground. The sound reminded Alwyn of a snake and a new, horrifying thought occurred to him.

"You checked that we weren't over a viper nest, right?" Alwyn asked, his bowels clenching. He still woke up shaking sometimes, remembering the writhing mass of slick, black snakes that had come boiling out of a hole Yimt had assured him would serve perfectly well as a latrine.

"It's a wild land; you never know what's around the next tree, or down the next hole," Yimt said, still holding out the canteen. "You heard the news crier this morning . . . all that talk by the new Viceroy about the Empire shining the light of civility among the heathen. That's like taking a lit match into a powder room, and guess who they'll be sending."

Alwyn didn't know what to think. A rider in the employ of the *Imperial Weekly Herald* had come into their camp on the outskirts of Port Ghamjal just that morning, usually a cause for celebration because it meant news from home. This time had been different, however, the crier speaking in high, flowery language with veiled references to things Alwyn couldn't begin to understand, and none of it sounded good.

"You think the new Viceroy is up to something?" Alwyn asked, still staring at the canteen. "After all the problems with that elf they had before, I figured this one would calm things down."

"Ah, the naheeviteh of youth," Yimt said, shaking his head. "Things have been calm. There ain't a war going on anywhere, leastways not any big ones. Let me tell you, lad, I'll take peace and boredom any day."

"But you don't think anything really bad is going to happen, do you?" Alwyn asked.

Yimt's voice became grave. "Something bad always happens. The trick is being as far away from it as possible when it does. You stick with me and you'll be fine."

It was the closest to logic he was likely to get. Alwyn made the sign of the moon and stars, took the canteen from Yimt, brought it to his lips, and took a sip.

"Ack . . . ack," was all he could say for several seconds after the burning liquid roared down his throat.

"Flower sniffer," Yimt said, taking the canteen back and pouring a healthy dose of the stuff down his own throat without even swallowing. "Have another look then."

Alwyn felt as if the top of his head had been removed and molten lead poured straight into his stomach, but his vision did seem clearer. He inched his way around the other side of the tree and poked his head through the leaves. "What, that big thing by the fence?"

"That's one of them water buffaloes. Mercy, how many times did they drop you as a baby? Look to your left, there, see the shadow?"

Alwyn strained his eyes and thought maybe he did see something, but he couldn't tell what. Blast his eyes. He took off his spectacles and rubbed the lenses on his jacket some more then put them back on. "Right, I see it now. By the third post."

"By the quack in a duck's bill, you found it. All right, on the count of five we'll shoot," Yimt said, pulling back the heavy iron lever on his shatterbow, a two-and-a-half-foot-long crossbow with two musket barrels side by side. Each barrel was easily twice the diameter of a regular musket and fired an iron dart the size of a grown man's thumb. As if that wasn't destructive enough, each dart was filled with gunpowder and a tiny fuse that was lit when the shatterbow fired, in essence making each projectile a small cannon shell.

The dwarf grunted and let out a deep breath as he levered back the steel-reinforced wooden bow located halfway down the barrels. Alwyn edged away, hoping all the while that Yimt knew what he was doing.

"What, we're just gonna shoot?" Alwyn asked, his voice rising to a squeak. He'd heard about Yimt from other soldiers. The Little Mad One. He'd been in the army most of his life, starting out as a boy drummer at the age of thirteen. Back then, long before Alwyn was born, that was about the only way a dwarf could join the Imperial Army, that or the engineers, the artillery, or a flint knapper. And here it was today and Yimt was still only a private. Alwyn was beginning to see why.

"What if it's an officer out checking the piquets?" Alwyn asked.

"Good point. We'll shoot on three." Yimt brought his shatterbow up to his shoulder and took aim.

"Hang on, my musket isn't loaded," Alwyn whispered furiously, fishing for a cartridge in his pouch. "You really think it's an officer?"

Yimt turned and made a face at Alwyn. "Course it ain't no officer.

Them peacocks strut around like a whore on payday. Whoever that is don't want to be seen, which means we got every right to shoot. Still . . . it's nice to think it could be an officer."

Alwyn finished loading his musket and crawled forward so that his upper body was outside the mass of leaves. He took aim, his hands shaking so that the musket bobbed around like a dandelion in the wind. The shadow was moving along the fence line as if looking for something. It was large, very large.

"Ready . . . *fire!*" Yimt yelled.

There was the click of the trigger, the throaty twang of the strings propelling the darts up the barrels as the bow sprang forward from its bent position, followed by a double crack as the fuse on each dart was ignited by two embedded flints. A fraction of a second later, the two darts hurtled out of the barrels trailing a brilliant shower of sparks that turned the darkness into broad daylight.

"What happened to counting down?" Alwyn yelled back, then fired, too, the flash and bang of his musket rather puny in comparison to Yimt's cannonade.

Alwyn heard three heavy sounds, like a butcher slamming a hunk of raw meat onto a marble table, followed by a muffled explosion.

"We got him!" Yimt exclaimed, charging forward. He ran surprisingly fast on his stubby legs.

"Wait up," Alwyn cried, stumbling after him toward the fence.

Shouts rang up and down the line and the sound of running boots could be heard.

"So what did we hit?" Alwyn asked, slipping on something and having to grab Yimt's shoulder to keep from falling. Yimt said nothing, just stared down at the body before him.

Alwyn let go and knelt for a better look, then jumped back. Great chunks of flesh and bones littered the ground and dripped off the fence. The head, however, was still intact. "It's . . . it's a rakke! I don't believe it. I seen one once in a picture book my granny used to read to me."

"Your granny had one twisted way of showing affection if she was showing pictures of *that* to a youngster," Yimt said, handing his shatterbow to Alwyn and unsheathing his other weapon, a *drukar*. Like the shatterbow, the drukar was made for dwarves. The blade reflected no light at all, its blackened finish appearing like a darker shadow in the night. It was a foot and a half long, six inches wide, and angled down at the halfway point, giving it a distinctly talonlike appearance.

"Granny was from the old country," Alwyn said, slowly edging backward from the scattered remains of the monster spread out before him. "She used to tell me all kinds of stuff about magic, especially the stuff that was evil. And that thing was one of them."

"Ally, relax," Yimt said, hefting his drukar between his hands. "It's dead."

Alwyn shook his head. "But it always *was* dead—at least, long before you and I came along. Yimt, don't you understand, Granny said they died off ages ago."

Without another word, Yimt brought the weapon down hard, sending blood and gore flying everywhere.

"What'd you go and do that for? You said it was dead," Alwyn yelled, wiping his face with the sleeve of his jacket, his spectacles once again smeared.

Yimt kicked the rakke's head hard with his boot. "That's the army for you. You do your duty, you serve the high and mighty, put your life on the line, and what do you get? Monsters." He turned back to Alwyn. "What did I tell you? That news crier had it right with all that talk about darkness and vigilance for enemies of the Empire and whatnot." He struck the rakke again with the drukar. "Well, if we're going to be dumped in it, you might as well learn now. When in doubt, put cold steel in it. Kill it, and then kill it again."

"You were in doubt?" Alwyn asked. The dwarf really was mad if he thought that thing had still been alive.

Yimt cleaned his blade with a fistful of grass and shook his head. "Naw, it really was dead the first time," he remarked, the bitterness in his voice as acidic as the drake sweat.

Alwyn looked from Yimt to the rakke then back to Yimt again. "Then what's the problem?"

Yimt gave the head one more kick and spat. "There's never an officer around when you want one."

Swinging lanterns appeared out of the night as more soldiers arrived. One stepped forth and surveyed the scene.

"What have you done now?" Corporal Kritton asked, staring at the fleshy wreckage on the ground. He was an elf, one of the few still in the Imperial Army after the disbanding of the Iron Elves. His words were soft, yet they carried the weight of steel shot in them. "If you shot another water buffalo trying to infiltrate the line, you'll be marching with full packs all the way back to Calahr."

Alwyn's mouth went dry. The corporal absolutely terrified him. He was only the second elf he'd ever known, the first being the cobbler down the street from his home. Mr. Yuimi had been small, quiet, always bent over a piece of shoe leather whenever Alwyn had stopped in to see if he needed any chores done. No matter how silently Alwyn entered the shop, Mr. Yuimi always knew he was there, tossing a chunk of licorice to exactly where Alwyn was standing without ever looking. Corporal Kritton was equally good at knowing where his soldiers were, but unlike kind old Mr. Yuimi, Kritton never gave you a reason to smile when he found you.

"It ain't like that, Corp," Yimt said, sounding not at all intimidated by the elf's threats. "We was mindin' our own business, being the ever-vigilant eyes and ears of Her Majesty—"

"Silence." The elf turned his stare to Alwyn for a moment, then back to the dwarf. In the bright glow of the moon, his face was cast half in shadow, blurring the sharp features Alwyn knew were there. It was his eyes, though, that gave Alwyn the willies. They were green, shining in the night like a cat's.

"What did you shoot?"

"Wasn't no officer, not in the least," Yimt said, batting the head toward the elf with the flat of his drukar. "Course, shave its face and put it in a uniform and you might not be able to tell the diff—"

"*Ki rakke . . .*" Corporal Kritton said.

Yimt looked at Alwyn and made a face that was most unflattering to the elf before turning back.

"Er, right you are, Corp, it's a rakke," Yimt said, lowering his voice an octave. "Ally here's been going on about them being extinct and all, but I never believed it. You know the stories, how that elf-witch twisted creatures to her will and all. Well, last time I heard, that Shadow Monarch was still perched on that little mountain of hers, so the way I figure it, as long as she's there, these things will be, too."

Corporal Kritton turned so fast to look at the dwarf that Alwyn thought he was going to attack Yimt. For several seconds Kritton said absolutely nothing, then he smiled, and the contents of Alwyn's stomach froze solid.

"Her Majesty doesn't pay you for your opinions. I think what we have here is a case of dereliction of duty, allowing an enemy of the Empire to get this close to the lines," he said. "I could have you flogged for this."

"Flogged?" Yimt said, puffing out his chest and looking at the rest of the soldiers now gathered around them. "All we did was save lives tonight, same as we do any time we get piquet duty, ain't that right, Ally?"

Alwyn tried to speak, but though his mouth opened and closed, no words would come out. An off-kilter dwarf, a monster from a storybook, and a maniacal elf for a corporal, and all because he thought wearing a uniform would impress women.

"See, Ally's so shocked that you'd think we wasn't doing our duty that he can't even speak," Yimt said, looking up at Alwyn with genuine concern in his eyes. "Tell you what, Corp, Her Majesty can keep Her medal. We'll take our reward in beer and call it square."

If I'm really lucky, Alwyn decided, *I'll pass out before they start to flog me.*

SEVEN

Konowa chose to believe he was leading Visyna through the forest as the sun was setting on their second day together. It helped keep his mind off his rib cage. And it soothed his ego to believe, as usual, that he wasn't lost

In the not-too-distant past, he'd led the Calahrian Imperial Army's finest regiment of soldiers into battle, and most important, brought them back out again each and every time. Killing the Viceroy then had been just one more battle for him, one more threat to the Empire destroyed.

The Viceroy had been in league with Her, and of all the things on this earth that Konowa despised—and the list was long—serving the Shadow Monarch was the most foul. Her very existence tainted every elf of the Hyntaland, especially those like Konowa. His hand drifted up by his ruined ear tip before he realized what he was doing.

What he hadn't realized was that while killing a hundred enemies in battle would earn you a medal, killing in peacetime got you court-martialed.

"Does it hurt?" Visyna asked, bringing him back to the here and now.

He quickly brought his hand down. "What? Oh . . . no, not really. They call it 'ghost pain.' You forget it's no longer there," he lied, wishing he could stop remembering.

She tilted her head to one side in a manner that suggested she didn't quite believe him, but let it be. They hadn't been together two full days and already Konowa found himself interpreting her moods by the way she held herself. Flashes of anger were always signaled by a stiffening of her body, a sight Konowa found enticing. Of course, it also meant enduring several minutes of an opinion that wasn't his own, but after a year alone it was refreshing to hear *any* voice that wasn't his own.

"I think I see a clearing up ahead," she said, pushing through a wall of vines.

"Fine, I'll have a look," he started to say as she disappeared through them without waiting. That was the other thing about her. Soldiers obeyed orders. Miss Visyna Tekoy, daughter of Almak Tekoy, most certainly did not—

"Konowa!"

Her shout came from the other side of the vines.

"Are you all right?" He unslung his musket and ran after her without waiting for her reply, ducking under low-hanging branches and holding his injured ribs tight with one arm. A moment later he burst through the same wall of vines Visyna had, and found himself in a clearing, and in trouble.

The ground shook beneath his feet. Konowa had stepped into a field of low scrub and directly into the path of a galloping horse.

Its human rider wore the pale blue of the Imperial Army cavalry with bright silver epaulets of chain mail on each shoulder. A gleaming helm of burnished steel wrapped with a band of spotted leopard pelt and topped by a flowing plume of red-dyed horsehair adorned his head. The horse itself was brown with a single white star on its chest, which was growing at an alarming rate as animal and rider charged straight for him.

Konowa leaped aside as man and horse whipped past, his shouted cry to hold up going unheard. He was still watching the rider when he felt a presence behind him and turned to see another trooper spurring his mount in his direction.

The second trooper stood high in his stirrups and reached across his body to pull his saber free. The horse galloped forward and veered to

Konowa's right, giving the trooper ample room to skewer Konowa on the end of his wicked-looking blade. Konowa remembered the proper tactic: Stay still, then jump to the right and bayonet the horse as it galloped past. Without a bayonet, Konowa's options were few.

When the horse's muzzle was just feet away, he leaped to his right to keep the man's saber arm on the far side of the horse and swung the stock of the musket at the charging horse's face. The musket missed, but its continued stroke caught the trooper a glancing blow off the top of his knee. The man howled in pain and tumbled from his saddle in a billowing cloud of dust.

Using the dust as a screen, Konowa ran forward another few steps and surprised yet another trooper, who had expected him to be standing over his fallen comrade. Konowa screamed and faked a blow at the horse's head, hoping instead to smash the stock into the metal chest plate of its rider. The horse lifted its head in surprise and stutter-stepped, causing its rider to pitch forward over its neck. Konowa let go of the musket and grabbed the temporarily off-balance man by the arm and belt, pulling with all his strength. The muscles along his ribs seared in protest, but Konowa held on, and a moment later was rewarded, as the trooper fell from his saddle to land flat on his back.

A flash of light caught Konowa's eye and he turned to see a cavalry saber arcing gracefully toward his head. Time seemed to slow—Konowa saw everything perfectly, realizing with calm detachment that there was nothing he could do. The trooper was crouched low in his stirrups, the reins clenched between the gloved fingers of his left hand while his right swung the heavy blade downward. One large brown eye of the roan the man rode was just inches from Konowa's face, and he saw his own reflection in it. Then the eye was past and the shoulder of the horse brushed against him and he prepared to feel the bite of the cold steel.

A rush of wind like a scythe through ripe hay whistled in front of Konowa's face and then the horse was gone and he could see the open countryside in front of him. He waited, wondering if the slightest movement would topple his head from his shoulders. Nothing seemed out of place aside from the erratic pounding of his own heart, so he carefully raised a hand and placed it against his neck. He felt sweat and grime, but no blood or cut. Amazed, Konowa turned his head to see the trooper reining in his horse and staring awestruck at the hilt guard of his saber. The blade was gone.

Konowa looked around and saw the flat chunk of steel lying several feet away in the grass. Everything had now gone eerily quiet. He looked up to see that a group of cavalry, perhaps ten, had hauled in their steeds and were staring not at Konowa, but at Visyna. She was standing near the edge of the forest, holding a branch in front of her like a weapon. The air shimmered around her and Konowa blinked, uncertain that it wasn't sweat in his eyes. When he looked again, the air was normal and Visyna began yelling about frightening a lady and did they know who her father was?

Before the cavalry could recover from her assault, Konowa bent over, nearly toppling to the ground as more lightning raced through his chest, and picked up the blade portion of the saber. Gritting his teeth, he walked the few paces to the sergeant who only a moment ago had tried to decapitate him.

The shabraque over the sergeant's saddle was made of a dark-blue cloth with ornately embroidered crests in gold stitching on the rearmost portion. It depicted an arrow in flight aided by a pair of eagle's wings. Konowa recognized it at once as the emblem of the Fourteenth Household Cavalry, commanded by the Duke of Rakestraw, Colonel Jaal Edrahar.

"You always greet strangers that way?" Konowa asked, holding out the piece of steel.

"There's been some unrest lately, bandits and such," the sergeant said, letting go of the reins and taking back the blade. "Who are you?" His eyes took in the ragged remains of Konowa's uniform with extreme skepticism.

"I'm just lost in the woods," Konowa said, "but that is Ms. Visyna Tekoy, daughter of Almak Tekoy. We need to get to a military outpost at once."

As he talked, the sergeant's roan started to nuzzle Konowa's shirt. It took a big sniff, its eyes went wide, then it whinnied and stepped back.

"And I need a flagon of beer and a wench to rub my back," the sergeant said, reining in his mount. "You aren't going anywhere until I know more."

"I've never known Colonel Edrahar's troops to refuse aide to a damsel in distress," Konowa said, looking over at Visyna, who was still menacing the troopers with her branch.

At the sound of the Duke's name the sergeant looked down at Konowa with a wary expression on his face.

"You know the Duke, then?" he asked.

"Know him? Sergeant, six years ago I saved that sorry excuse for nobility at Khundarr Ridge."

The sergeant sat back in his saddle and pushed his helmet up from his brow, revealing a tanned face dominated by a large, blond mustache, the ends twirled into complete circles. "I was at Khundarr Ridge. The Duke wasn't saved by no savage, it was that officer of the Hynta-elves . . . bloody hell." Like all good noncommissioned officers, the sergeant covered his shock by shouting. "Right, you two," he yelled, pointing to the two unhorsed troopers who were dusting themselves off. "Seeing as you were daft enough to get your arses knocked off, you can walk back. And right smartly, too," he growled before the troopers could utter a complaint.

"Can't have an officer walking, now can we, sir?" the sergeant said, gesturing with the now-useless hilt of his saber. "Sir, you take the gelding and your woman can ride the gray mare."

Konowa smiled and thought of correcting the sergeant. Visyna was most certainly not his woman.

"Name's Lorian, sir, Sergeant Dhareg Lorian. Sorry for that crack about savages, didn't mean nothing by it. I'll get you and the missus to the Duke by morning. We're bivouacked just over the next hill, a few miles north of Port Ghamjal. We'll have you there in no time."

Konowa nodded. "I appreciate the offer, but I'm not sure it's wise to leave the troopers out here alone. We came across some—" He started to say rakkes, then thought better of it.

Sergeant Lorian tipped the helmet a little farther back on his head. "Across some what, sir?"

"Bandits," Konowa said, "lots of bandits. I'd suggest you don't leave anyone behind." It was strange, but after a year, it was hard to make it an order.

Sergeant Lorian didn't look as if he believed Konowa, but he finally shrugged and motioned to the unseated troopers. "All right, you lucky buggers, double up on the mare, the officer and his lady will ride the gelding. Now be quick about it."

Konowa walked over to the gelding, remembering to mount from the left. He placed his musket muzzle-down in the leather container strapped to the side of the saddle that had only moments before held a trooper's musket. Visyna walked over, her face flushed with shouting. He decided to be a gentleman and offer her his hand.

"Thank you, no. I think of the two of us it's *you* who needs assistance," she said, holding out her hand to him.

Konowa decided the snickers he heard were from the horses, and reluctantly took Visyna's hand. With his left hand he grabbed a chunk of the horse's mane, then placed his left foot in the stirrup, said a little prayer, and jumped. As it was, he barely got up into the saddle, his ribs crying out in protest as he swung his right leg over. Visyna had no such trouble, hopping up behind him with delicate ease. She chose to ride sidesaddle on the rolled blanket strapped to the saddle.

The elves of the Hynta were not known for riding, staying mostly within the confines of the Great Forest. Still, they had an affinity with horses, as they did with most things in the natural order, and took to it with grace and ease when required. Konowa, on the other hand, found riding a horse as enjoyable as sitting on a rockslide at the top of a very steep cliff. Horses were huge, all steel-shod hooves and sharp teeth, and worst of all, had minds of their own.

He gave the one beneath him a good long look. To his surprise, the horse appeared thin, its ribs showing from beneath the shabraque. Tufts of hair seemed to be falling out, too, but then Konowa knew military life was never easy on horses, or any other living creature. Still, he'd remembered the Duke's mounts as being among the finest in the army.

"Easy now, easy, it's just a short trip," Konowa said, slowly gathering up the reins that had fallen to the ground.

The horse started stamping its hooves and tried to back up, tugging hard on the reins in an effort to unseat Konowa. "I know, I know," he muttered, "but you'll just have to get used to the smell." He pulled back on the reins and leaned forward, almost falling. The horse swung its head around and nipped at him with a set of huge yellow teeth.

"Problem, sir?" Sergeant Lorian asked, riding up to a few feet from where Konowa was struggling to keep the gelding in check.

"No," Konowa lied, noticing that the sergeant seemed to be looking more at Visyna than at him. The horse jittered to the right and Konowa reached down to pat its withers. He pulled his hand back a second later as the horse's head whipped around again. "We're just getting to know one another," he said. The horse shifted about beneath him, perhaps hoping he might fall off if it kept trying, but Konowa squeezed his knees to its sides and pulled back hard on the reins to show the animal who was boss. There was the stamp of a hoof and a few swishes of its tail and then it calmed, ceding, at least for the moment, superiority to Konowa. Visyna said nothing the whole time, but he could feel her stare on the back of his neck.

It was a strange sensation to be on a horse again—the feel of the leather in his hands, the rhythmic breathing of the horse beneath him. Konowa slackened his grip on the reins and forced himself to look up. Everything seemed different on top of a horse. He was struck by how remote and distant the last year of his life had suddenly become, and all that from gaining a few feet of perspective. Things were clearly changing. He was beginning to allow himself to imagine that they might even be changing for the better when the horse swung its head around and managed to nip him on the knee.

The more things changed, the more they hurt like hell.

EIGHT

T he cavalry troop wheeled about, placing Konowa and Visyna at the front of their formation. Konowa turned his head slightly to speak to Visyna.

"I thought I saw the air shimmering back there," he said, turning around a bit more. "If I didn't know better, I'd say it was some kind of mag—" He didn't get to complete his sentence as the horse suddenly shifted underneath him, knocking his left foot out of the stirrup. He started to slide off, then felt her hands wrap around his waist and pull him back.

"You should pay more attention to your riding," she said. Her hands stayed around his waist even after he had his foot back in the stirrup, and he decided keeping his mouth shut was the better course.

Movement far off to the right pulled his eyes away, and Konowa caught a glimpse of black and red fur. He smiled. Jir could trail them from a safe distance and had the speed and stamina to keep up, as long as he didn't try to mark too many trees along the way. Konowa was still watching the forest when the sergeant steered his horse in front of Konowa's, causing him to pull up.

"Um, it's a bit dangerous out here, sir, m'lady, and I was wondering if you wouldn't mind taking the rear of the column? It would ease my mind to know we had an officer of your caliber back there watching out for us, sir." He doffed his helmet to Visyna and smiled.

"You think that's necessary?" Konowa asked, puzzled by the request. Visyna gave his waist the smallest of squeezes, but it was enough to lighten his heart. "Good idea," Konowa said before the sergeant could change his mind.

He was in such a good mood he decided he might have misjudged the cavalry all these years, their most recent attempt to kill him notwithstanding. To be fair, that was everyone's reaction until they got to know him. He was thinking of telling the Duke how impressed he was with his men when he overheard one of the troopers talking to a mate.

"Bloody hell, I thought the sarge would never get that bugger downwind."

"You there," Konowa said loudly, startling the man who had just spoken.

"Yes, sir," he said, reining in his mount to ride alongside them.

"I've been away from the civilized world for a while, perhaps you'd be so kind as to catch me up on what has transpired in the Empire this past year."

The man's eyes widened even as his nose twitched. Before the trooper could answer, Visyna whispered in Konowa's ear. "Sergeant Lorian has a rather large horse, I could always ride with him if you'd prefer."

"On the other hand, I'm sure Ms. Tekoy will be able to fill me in. Dismissed," he said, finding that giving an order after all this time wasn't so hard after all. The trooper saluted and quickly cantered up to the front of the column, leaving Konowa and Visyna alone.

"You really do have a way with people, don't you?" she said.

Konowa tried turning again the saddle, but gave up when more pain lanced across his chest. "It started at a young age. The point is, or rather, was," he said, waving at the lost point of his own ear, "that if you were born with a black tip, Her taint was believed to run deep in the blood. To the elves of the Hynta, especially the Long Watch, it doesn't get much worse than that. Not that long ago, they just abandoned a marked baby on the plains beyond the forest to die. So no, if I don't get along well with others, it might be because most have always wanted me dead. It tends to make one a little . . . antisocial."

"But why mark babes? Why would the Shadow Monarch do such a thing?"

Konowa shrugged. "Only She knows, and She isn't saying. All I know is that's the hand I and the other Iron Elves were dealt, and we've played it as best we can."

"I was dealt a different hand," Visyna said, moving her hands underneath his shirt and resting them on his ribs. "Perhaps I can change your outlook on things in some small way."

Konowa raised an eyebrow, but said nothing. Her hands probed along his rib cage with care, but it still hurt.

"Easy, woman, they're bruised enough already," he said.

She pulled her hands away from his chest and began rummaging in a small cloth bag she carried. "Your name, Heer Ul-Osveen, it sounds Calahrian."

"One of the finest in the Calahrian Empire," Konowa said. He shifted his behind in the saddle, trying to find the right up-and-down rhythm with the horse. "Lieutenant Osveen held off a force of a thousand orcs with only ten men at the battle of Yacat Gorge. That was during the Border Troubles a century ago."

"Is there a time in the Empire's history that it didn't have border troubles?" Visyna asked.

Konowa let the barb slide. "The orcs could have gone around the gorge and taken the small outpost the lieutenant and his men were guarding, but the hairy buggers were compelled to fight, and Osveen and his men slaughtered them."

"Compelled?" Visyna asked, leaning forward to rest her chin against his right shoulder.

"Osveen had been a playwright before joining the army. His greatest claim to fame was creating amusing limericks for his plays. Ah, but you're the daughter of the great Almak Tekoy. Perhaps your ears are a bit too tender for something like that."

Konowa swore he could feel the skin of her cheek turn hot.

"My ears are in fitter shape than yours," she said.

"You wound me, madam."

Visyna went back to rummaging. "So tell me one of these limericks."

Konowa readjusted again in the saddle and gave it some thought. "Let me see . . .

> *A witch had a useless new suitor.*
> *His device was unable to suit her.*
> *So she went to her potions,*
> *set a new spell in motion*
> *and inserted a newt instead of a neuter."*

Visyna stopped what she was doing. "And this would make orcs want to fight?"

Konowa shook his head. "No, Osveen came up with a bunch of limericks and other insults to draw the orcs into a fight."

"Newts have no intrinsic magical properties, you know," Visyna continued. "I don't understand why a witch would have any around in the first place."

"It's just a— I mean it's supposed to be funny," Konowa said.

"But it isn't, is it? Ah!" Visyna exclaimed, patting his arm, "now I understand. You chose his name because like you, he's not very funny either, right?"

Konowa tried to remember why he'd hated being alone in the forest and was having a hard time doing it.

"I chose it because Osveen was a rogue, taking on overwhelming odds with little more than a sword and his wits. Besides, I had to. Elves who leave their tribe and are rejec—who choose not to join the Long Watch must leave behind their *pulchta*, their dream-name."

"Not really funny at all," she said, completely ignoring his explanation. "Raise your arms again." A pungent smell filled the air, at once musky and acidic.

"What are you doing back there?" Konowa asked, doing as he was told nonetheless. A moment later something wet and cold attached itself to his chest. He opened his eyes and, looking down through the wide neck of his shirt, saw Visyna plastering leaves over the broken rib, a brown goo holding them in place.

"Not so tight," he muttered, but the feeling was surprisingly good. "You're very good with your hands," he said, closing his eyes as the pain began to subside.

"Not just my hands," she said, beginning to squeeze the leaves tighter against his skin. The wet poultice on his chest grew fire hot, and he began to sweat. His breathing slowed and he felt himself falling off the horse.

"What the—" was all he managed before she pulled him upright as if he weighed no more than a baby. The air shimmered as his vision blurred and every muscle in his body flowed like water. A moment later, Konowa was standing in the birthing meadow of the Wolf Oaks, which meant he was dreaming, which annoyed him no end. *I know how this goes already*, he told himself, frustrated that his own mind would betray him by making him relive the first great humiliation of his life. He tried to race through the scene so that he could move on to something else, but the view before him refused to change.

Accepting the inevitable, he walked to the center of the birthing meadow, brushing past the young sapling cubs stretching themselves skyward. The sun was high overhead, yet with each step the air got noticeably colder, and the grass beneath his feet began to crackle. Strange, he thought, remembering his time in the meadow as quite warm. Now, however, frost was spreading out to cover everything. Most of the sapling cubs were big enough that the frost had no effect on them, but one tiny Wolf Oak began to bow, its slender trunk slowly curving toward the earth as its leaves started to blacken.

He walked toward the little sapling cub and then stopped short. It was silver. Only once in many decades was a silver born to the Wolf Oaks, and not without cost. Even as he recalled that there had been no silver when he had gone to the birthing meadow, another elf entered the meadow and walked toward the sapling cub. She was young, and beautiful, her eyes filled with love and concern for the little tree. A voice sounded in his head then, a scared, weak voice begging for help. It was the sapling cub, and it was dying.

Konowa swayed on his feet, overcome with the power in that small, fragile voice. It yearned for life, for the chance to grow its roots deep into the earth and stretch its branches high into the open sky. Never in his life had he felt such need, such desire to live.

More elves filled the meadow, and it was clear that unlike the elf before Konowa, the silver Wolf Oak's pleas would find no solace with them.

"*Pwik tola misk jin*—to life the strongest," said the elves of the Long Watch, turning and leaving the birthing meadow.

Tears of sorrow and rage welled up in the elf woman's eyes as she stared after the departing elves. Konowa understood her anger and her grief.

"We must save it," he said, hoping there might yet be a way. "We have to save it."

The scene before him suddenly changed, and he was now standing on top of a black, bare mountain, the wind tearing at his clothes. He shivered with the cold, his breath coming in painful bursts. The little sapling cub was now a full-grown Wolf Oak, but twisted and jagged, its roots stabbing the rocky ground beneath it while its branches flailed at the sky. Thick, black ichor oozed from its trunk, staining the once-silver bark, and the voice that had cried out for life now raged with an insane, consuming fury.

The elf from the meadow was there, too, stepping between the slashing branches, which parted for her. She rested a hand on its trunk, uncaring of the ichor that ran over her skin, lighting it afire in a blaze of black frost. She was no longer young and beautiful, age and something more having carved great lines into her features. Her eyes, however, were still filled with concern and love, but with an intensity that froze Konowa to the bone when he looked into them.

'Now, I will save you, too,' the Shadow Monarch said, reaching out with her burning, cold hand and touching the tip of his left ear.

In his nightmare, Konowa burned.

NINE

A steward entered the throne room and quietly placed a
cup of evening tea before the Viceroy. Gwyn clasped it
prayerlike in both hands, curling his fingers around the cup.
He had changed from his traveling clothes. The light from
the lanterns bounced crazily off the coronet that now rested on his head,
a delicately worked crown of white gold studded with jewels representative
of every foreign land he had visited as part of the diplomatic corps, and
incorporated into the Empire.

Protocol demanded that the crown be smaller than Her Majesty's,
and it was, barely. No fool though, he wore a second, much smaller and
more modest coronet when traveling to Calahr, or on the rare occasions the
Queen ventured forth to survey Her lands.

The light also highlighted his exceptionally pale skin, stretched taut
across a delicate bone structure that bespoke his pure heritage, something
many in the High Court were sadly lacking. That was the problem with
empires—the bloodlines of the conquered lands mixed with that of their
masters, polluting everything. In time, he would deal with them. For now,
though, he focused his thoughts on his immediate situation.

Within the starched precision of his uniform, he forced his body to
relax until no outward sign of movement could be detected. It was a trick

he'd picked up early in the diplomatic corps and had used to great effect on many occasions. Without need of a mirror he saw himself perfectly: velvet-green jacket with gold facings, his slender shoulders made larger by two wide epaulets, blood-red aiguillettes of fine silk braid hanging down from each, gold-plated buttons in double rows running the length of the jacket's front, and around his waist a brilliant white belt from which a thin rapier hung in a scabbard of wrought silver. It was like looking at a painting, an effect Gwyn desired, for under the table his legs shook nervously in their riding breeches and calf-high leather boots.

He had scheduled a meeting with the commander of the cavalry forces in Elfkyna to commence an hour ago, but the Duke had not yet arrived. Gwyn knew it was deliberate. Why the Queen had allowed a despicable lower-caste peasant to rise so high in her army escaped him, but it was indisputable that the bastard knew how to fight.

Gwyn sipped sparingly at his tea until the voice of a retainer telling someone "this way" signaled the arrival of the Duke. The Viceroy turned slightly in his chair to offer a chiseled profile to the scoundrel.

"Good evening, my dear—" Gwyn started to say, then stopped. A green-uniformed corporal wearing the distinctive "Crown and Wagon" patch from one of the Outer Territories Trading Company's regiments stood just outside the ring of lanterns.

The elf came to attention and saluted.

"What is the meaning of this? Who are you?" Gwyn demanded.

The corporal lowered his hand. "Corporal Takoli Kritton, part of the piquet detail, your grace. There was a disturbance in front of one of the posts tonight. A rakke, sir."

"Are you drunk, Corporal? I've always found a firing squad a quick cure for that." So, the rumors about the last Viceroy were perhaps not the idle chatter he'd once thought.

The corporal didn't blink. "I am not drunk, your grace."

Gywn considered the elf. His voice was soft, his movements slow and deferential, but something told Gwyn you wouldn't turn your back on him. It was the eyes, or more precisely, the fact that they revealed nothing at all, and Gwyn prided himself on being able to plumb the depths of souls and learn their weaknesses.

"Really?" Gwyn said, affecting boredom. "Yet you interrupt me with stories of extinct creatures. Very well, if what you say is true, bring it to me."

The corporal took several steps forward and placed a large haversack on the table. A dark stain grew at its bottom, and an oily fluid began seeping onto the table.

"What's this?" the Viceroy asked, recoiling from the bag.

"Its head."

The Viceroy didn't bother opening the haversack. He didn't need to. Wheels began to turn in his head as he worked through the ramifications. The last Viceroy had been in Her service, and Her power was clearly expanding.

Yes, he could use this.

The Viceroy allowed himself to feel a moment of joy before he reined himself in and looked back at the corporal, making a more thorough appraisal. The elf slouched slightly, as if trying to make himself appear less than he was. He wore his long black hair tied in a queue, but again, it was his eyes that gave Gwyn pause. A Hynta-elf, Gwyn decided, his complexion as dark as that of some of the elfkynan. You never could tell how old these elves were, unless they looked ancient, and even then one never really knew. This one appeared to be in his midtwenties, not that that meant anything to him.

Gwyn needed to know more. "And how is it you came to have its head while still retaining your own?" He motioned for an elfkynan to place the haversack on the floor beside him and mop up the mess.

"I personally ordered my men to be on the watch for anything peculiar tonight, your grace. I felt something wasn't right."

The Viceroy smiled, an act without any intent to put the elf at ease. "Elves and their senses. It's like having bloodhounds, and house-trained at that," he said, peering down at the floor by the elf's boots as if to verify his own statement.

"Sir," the elf said, his cheeks coloring.

The Viceroy smiled. Elves were rare in the army, rarer still in the days since the Iron Elves were disbanded. This one was clearly a remnant of that disgraced horde. He wore his shako set at just enough of an angle that it marked him a veteran of more than one campaign, but not so tilted that it would catch the ire of an officer. It almost served to hide the fact that the point of one ear was missing, another telltale mark of a former Iron Elf. Seven wound stripes were sewn above the cuff of his left sleeve, a rarity among the cannon fodder they assigned to the Trading Company—typically the bastion of drunkards, fools, and cowards.

Gwyn was certain the elf before him was none of those. No, he was something far more dangerous.

The only other obvious flaw was an irregular dark band that ran the full way around the left sleeve of his uniform. "That dark mark, there, on your coat, what's that?"

"Just a stain," the elf said, his eyes looking everywhere but at the Viceroy.

Gwyn suppressed a smile. "Actually, it looks to me like a patch was once sewn there, a very specific patch, I think, one of leaves, if I had to take a guess. Tell me, Kritton . . . is it?"

"Sir," the elf said, refusing to take the bait.

"Corporal, what unit were you with before joining the company? A wizard's assistant perhaps, or a scout? Hmmm, no, you carry a musket so you certainly aren't a pureblood. No self-respecting elf would carry metal, would they?"

The elf's body grew even more rigid, but his voice remained neutral. "Regular light infantry, sir."

"Come now, Corporal," the Viceroy said, enjoying himself immensely, "the army spends a great deal of time and money instilling pride in one's regiment. Are you saying you don't remember which one?"

"The Iron Elves, sir."

"Ah, the *shamed* regiment," Gwyn said triumphantly. "Must have been a terrible blow, having the regiment dishonored like that. Your commanding officer turning out to be a traitor to the Empire. Cast all elves in a rather poor light."

"Sir," the corporal said, clearly restraining himself.

"Quite," Gwyn said, suddenly growing tired of the sport. He had bigger fish to fry tonight. "Job well done, Corporal. I'll make sure to circulate a note regarding it tomorrow, might help your officers see you in a better light. Dismissed."

The corporal threw a parade-ground salute at Gwyn, then wheeled about and marched away, forcing several elfkynan to scramble out of his path.

Gwyn raised his cup to his lips but stopped short of drinking, considering how he might use this latest incident to his advantage. The mind of the masses was a simple thing to manipulate. Play to their beliefs, invoke their various gods and deities, then vanquish their foes, real or imagined, and claim righteous benediction from said god or spirit and reap the rewards.

"It's all too easy, isn't it?" he said out loud. The table shimmered in the lanterns' glow in reply. He brought the cup to his lips and stopped in horror. Bits of gore from the haversack floated in the tea. A sly one. He might have a use for this elf yet. He was debating whether to have him called back when the sound of boots echoed off the ruined walls of the palace.

"Ah, the popinjay has a new roost. Interesting aroma, Viceroy," the Duke of Rakestraw said, striding into the light.

Red hair fluttered around his head like ribbons of blood, framing a face so scarred that it was difficult to pick out the line of his mouth unless it was open. A heavy, curved cavalry saber, known by friend and foe alike as Wolf's Tooth, hung from a sabertache slung down over one enormous shoulder and was of no more cumbrance to the duke than fleas on a dog.

Dull silver spurs sparked against the stones as the Duke quickly crossed the floor, his black riding boots flashing as only polished leather cavalry boots could. His pale-blue surcoat was open at his midsection, revealing a black sash wound around his stomach—Rogolth's Banner. The gall, Gwyn fumed, to wear a fallen orc king's personal standard. Did Rakestraw think showing off the spoils of one of his cavalry's murderous rampages would influence the events of the evening?

"My dear Duke, how good of you to make an appearance," Gwyn said, releasing his grasp on the cup and giving the soldier a measured wave.

The Duke smiled, a jagged crease across his face that looked as vicious as the blue eyes that glared back at Gwyn.

"I haven't all night, Viceroy," he said, walking a complete circuit around the rubble-strewn throne room before choosing a chair directly opposite Gwyn. He sat down with a thump, then rested his boots on the edge of the table.

Gwyn grabbed for the cup and succeeded in spilling more on the table, ruining the effect of the light across the dragon's maw.

"The days of quietude in the Empire are at an end, I'm afraid," Gwyn began, motioning at an adjutant to clean the table again. "Her Majesty's long and benevolent reign over the masses is being challenged. It falls to us to stop it."

The Duke flashed a ragged smile. "Her reign, or the challenge to it?"

"Very droll, my lord Duke, but I do not find this the least bit amusing. I came to Elfkyna expecting to find order, and instead am shocked to find chaos." He decided not to mention the rakke.

"Chaos?" the Duke asked, his voice rising. "The only chaos I know of was the riot you caused in the bazaar this afternoon. Fifteen dead. What are you playing at, Viceroy?"

Gwyn spread his arms wide. "I assure you, this is no game. Rebelliousness is spreading like a plague, and I have begun what you and the rest of the Imperial Army have been unable to do. The natives will learn to stay in line, or suffer the consequences."

The Duke's head was already shaking before Gwyn finished. "You think slaughtering a bunch of civilians is going to cow them? All you've done is stirred things up. I'm already hearing about unrest across the city. When news of this reaches the northern tribes, they're bound to react."

"They already have, weeks ago as it turns out. My information indicates an army from the northern tribes has moved down the Shalpurud River and begun building a series of small outposts. These forces are disrupting our trade routes and making it difficult to take out material to the coast."

The Duke huffed. "Your information comes from my scouts. This army is more mob than anything else. They hardly pose a real threat to the Empire."

Gwyn allowed the smallest of sighs to escape his lips. "That is why diplomacy is best left to those who understand the finer points of things."

The Duke motioned as if to leave and Gwyn hurriedly continued.

"The *Imperial Weekly Herald* is reporting that all foreign powers should leave Elfkyna. That is nothing less than a call to arms against the Empire."

"Over a period of fifty years! Frankly, I think they're a bit timid about it all."

Gwyn couldn't believe anyone could be this obtuse. "The elfkyna are not at all capable of self-government. Not now, not fifty years from now, not ever. I've studied their history. Tribal warfare racked this land for centuries. Only under the benevolent rule of this Empire has peace and stability existed long enough for real progress to be made, and this talk of rebellion threatens it all." A part of Gwyn listened rapturously to his own performance, marveling at his skill.

"The only talk of rebellion appears to be coming from you," the Duke said, his eyes drilling holes into Gwyn.

Gwyn sat up a little straighter. The Duke was perhaps not as obtuse as he had first suspected. "I don't think you appreciate the severity of this." He motioned to another adjutant. The elfkynan stepped forward carrying a long, leather tube which he upended on the table. A beautifully tanned sheepskin hide slid out, which the adjutant carefully unrolled.

"Fortresses have sprouted up along the river," Gwyn began, standing to better point to the map, "here, here, and here. Worse, my spies report that elfkynan rebels have occupied the fortress Taga Nor and are rebuilding its walls. Truly, the situation is grave."

The Duke leaned forward slightly to get a better look at the multi-hued sheepskin and snorted loudly.

Peasant, Gwyn thought, staring lovingly at the map.

The entire Calahrian Empire was laid out like a jeweler's wares. Strips of real gold foil delineated the outer boundaries of the territory controlled by the Empire, while beaten silver represented the major rivers. Mountain ranges made of crushed rubies gleamed and Celwyn, the Calahrian capital, sparkled with all four carats of a rare obsidian diamond.

"You could feed a village for a year with the baubles on this thing," the Duke murmured.

"Whatever for?" Gwyn asked. Diplomacy was art, something the Duke clearly didn't understand. Monarchs had broken down and wept as they looked at the map and realized the wealth and power arrayed against them. Often it was enough to offer the map as a gift, making sure that a particularly impressive jewel, though never as large as the one representing Celwyn, was placed on the capital of the ruler in question. *Her Majesty wishes to assuage any concerns you have that your voice will not be heard within the Imperial Empire. You can see the importance She gives to your voice . . .*

The map was oriented so that Celwyn was perfectly centered, the seat of power around which the world turned. That it was in reality several thousand miles north of the equator had been easily fixed by the royal cartographers.

"Pretty. Can I get one of those for my daughter? She's turning five next month," the Duke remarked.

"It's no laughing matter," Gwyn continued, scanning the faces of the elfkynan. *If even one of them smiled . . .* "The Empire is facing a significant threat."

"I'm still waiting for the part where you tell me why I'm here," the Duke said. He began tapping the table with his boots, dislodging bits of material that Gwyn chose to believe were mud.

Gwyn motioned for his retainers to leave and the elfkynan quietly exited the ruined throne room, leaving him alone with the Duke.

"Tell me, how is your land these days?"

The Duke said nothing, but his eyes flashed bluer than any gem on the map.

"I've heard stories of pastures lying fallow and a disease infecting the herds," Gwyn continued, careful to keep the smugness out of his voice. "A most disconcerting event for Her Majesty's primary supplier of fine horses, is it not?"

"It's nothing," the Duke said through clenched teeth.

"Really?" Gwyn asked, with what he knew sounded like genuine empathy. He'd certainly practiced the tone enough. "I was concerned that so many sick and dying horses would unduly affect your fortunes. Still, rumor has it Her Majesty has been forced to seek mounts for her cavalry units from more far-flung parts of the Empire. I shudder to think what that would mean should the trend continue. What a terrible shame it would be to have to sell off Greendale Manor," Gwyn said, knowing damn well the Duke had put the manor and most of his land up as collateral to borrow against his losses.

The Duke's right hand slid slowly across his body until his hand rested on the pommel of Wolf's Tooth. Gwyn judged his distance. He was well within the arc of that vicious blade. He pressed on quickly.

"Strange days. I only mention it because I've received reports that a magnificent herd of horses roams the plains to the west, near Linma," he said, pointing at a sparkling sapphire on the map. "Hundreds, perhaps thousands of fine specimens. True, they aren't the royal stock of your purebloods, but then again, they aren't dying either. Quite a windfall for the man who captures them. Enough to pay off one's debts, I would think? With a bit left over for sport."

The Duke's hand remained on the pommel.

"Go on," the Duke said, clearly unconvinced.

"The orcs, as always, are proving troublesome. If you were to mount an expedition and head west, really just a show of force, the sort you used against the former orc king, I think we could secure that border for the foreseeable future. And while you're in the area . . ."

Gwyn slowed his breathing and waited. It was pitiful, really, to watch the Duke struggle with his sense of honor. Rakestraw's family fortune was gone, pilfered away while he was out galloping at everything. Less time in the saddle and more with an accounting ledger would have served the man well, but he was too much the adventurer, and for that he would pay. Only the constant sales from the Duke's stables had kept the gold flowing in, but now, with disease decimating his herds, there was nothing.

"The orcs?" The Duke laughed, shaking his head. "Someone's having you on. Those hairy buggers have kept their heads down for the last ten years."

This was not going the way the Viceroy had planned.

Gwyn reached down beside him and picked up the haversack, holding it out for the Duke.

The Duke leaned forward to have a look inside, then jerked backward, his hand clutching at the pommel of his sword.

"Where did that come from? Those things are dead."

Gwyn smiled pleasantly. Now this was more like it. "I see nothing gets by you. Yes, it is dead, now, but it appears the orcs have been playing with magic best left alone."

The Duke slowly released his grip on his sword, never taking his eyes off the haversack. "Orcs? You're wrong. That's the work of that elf-witch."

Gwyn nodded solemnly, sliding his argument along this new line of thought. "I can see you understand things perfectly. You are right, of course, it is Her work, and my informants tell me the orcs have struck a deal with Her. Reports are coming in of more of these things to the west, near the orc border. Would you rather hunt them here, or wait until they are roaming the fields of Greendale Manor?" Gwyn put the haversack back down. Things were once again as they should be; the Duke was off guard.

The Duke warily looked back at Gwyn, as if trusting him were the most dangerous thing he could ever do.

"The orcs in league with Her? Are you sure?"

Gwyn pointed casually to the black banner around the Duke's midriff. "The Empire has long thwarted their expansionist aims. Why, you yourself decapitated their King and routed their army with but a handful of cavalry. A truly heroic deed that saved Elfkyna from being overrun years ago, but one that served to box the orcs in. Clearly, they have not forgotten."

"Have you spoken to the elves of the Long Watch about it? Word should be sent to them at once," the Duke said, but his voice was quieter now.

Gwyn rolled his eyes. "Really, I have better things to do than bandy words with skittish elves who see dark intent behind every squirrel that burrows into a tree. I assure you, my dear Duke, the creatures are here. I had rather hoped the solution would be found here, too."

"What of these rebels to the east?" the Duke asked, so obviously stalling that Gwyn had to pinch the bridge of his nose to keep from smiling. "If I'm off to the west, what then?"

Gwyn nodded solemnly and clasped his hands together. It was like toying with a child. "Rest assured they will be dealt with. In the meantime, the orcs and their terrible conjuring must be stopped, and who better than you and your gallant men to do it?"

"How terribly bloody convenient," the Duke growled, looking down at the map again. "I don't trust you, Viceroy."

Gwyn waved his hand. "Be that as it may, your orders are clear, and the benefits of following them far outweigh the costs of disobeying them, wouldn't you say? Now, I suggest you prepare to depart with all due haste. Good evening."

The Duke rose slowly from his chair and stood for a moment looking down at the table. When he raised his head to look at Gwyn, the Viceroy took a step back before catching himself. The man was smiling, a grin so wide and so fierce that as the Duke turned and walked through the circle of light and was swallowed up by the darkness, Gwyn wondered if it was possible he might have underestimated the warrior.

"You're in my palace."

Years of training were still not enough to keep the Viceroy from jumping. He shivered in spite of the heat. A writhing mass of shadows stood just outside the circle of lanterns not an arm's length from where the Duke had just passed. Frost sparkled on the edges of the table.

The Viceroy regained his composure, forcing a slow, deep breath through his nose before he spoke. He repeated the Calahrian diplomatic mantra in his mind. *When negotiating, you don't represent the Empire, you* are *the Empire.*

"Your statement lacks factual corroboration. This palace, such as it is, is property of Her Majesty the Queen of Calahr. Now, if you'd care to lodge a formal—"

"Fool! You would test Her Emissary thus? I once served your Queen, but now I serve a true monarch."

The voice sounded like tearing sheets of iron. The shadows that made up its form moved into the light, scraping over the stone like glacier over rock. Gwyn expected to see a body, but there was only the seething black-ness in the shape of the former Viceroy.

"Of course . . . Emissary," Gwyn said, unable to keep the tremor out of his voice. "My apologies. I was under the impression that you were underground, as it were."

The shadows grew blacker for a moment and the temperature in the throne room dropped.

"She has brought me back to serve Her. You will serve Her, too."

A shadow snaked toward Gwyn, a brilliant red light shining where the palm of a hand would have been.

Gwyn leaned forward. "A red star? *The* red star, the Eastern Star? You've discovered it?"

The light vanished. *"Not yet, but it has returned, and they dig for it even now. Serve Her, and your reward will be power beyond measure."*

Every syllable was like an ice pick in Gwyn's flesh. He allowed his eyes to stray away from the shadow, unable to keep it in proper focus. He waited for the threat, but when none was forthcoming, he realized it had no reason to articulate the obvious. Not serving Her had only one consequence, and it would be swift.

"What is it She requires?" The question itself wasn't treasonous. Gwyn needed power in order to move the Empire in the proper direction. If trading one monarch for another furthered that aim, then it was his duty to obey.

"Keep your forces away from Luuguth Jor."

Gwyn feigned shock. "But word of revolt in the east is spreading. Her Majesty will expect me to send men at once to put it down."

The shadows writhed faster, a black blur sucking the very warmth from the air. *"You must not. They need time to grow, and to dig."*

Gwyn struck his most regal pose and turned to look straight at the shadow. "Her power, it seems, is not as strong as I was led to believe. I could divert the Imperial Army, for a time, but I take a great risk in doing so. I begin to wonder . . . why should I bother?"

There was a sudden gust of wind and the lanterns flared and went out, shuttering the throne room in darkness. Gwyn took a step back and was stopped by something terribly cold and heavy standing behind him. He couldn't move, and he didn't know if it was the will of Her Emissary or abject terror that kept him rooted to the spot. Breath flowed down on his shoulder and neck as if straight from the frigid peak of a mountain, Her mountain. And then a voice was in his ear, each word a crystal sliver.

"Because dying is only the beginning."

The lanterns flared again. Gwyn was alone.

It was a long time before he called for his retainers, long enough for his heart to start beating again at a dignified, controlled pace, and the wetness in his trousers to dry.

TEN

Konowa awoke to a gentle kiss. He smiled, the nightmare already a distant memory. Warm breath caressed his skin as soft lips brushed against his cheek, the sweet smell of oats—

"Get away!" he shouted, opening his eyes and batting away the muzzle of the gelding. The horse bared its teeth and stamped a hoof and Konowa rolled out of the way, jumping to his feet in one motion.

"Making a new friend, I see," Visyna said lightly, walking up to pat the horse. Sergeant Lorian followed her.

"You, too," he replied. He started to brush the dirt off his clothes, then stopped. The pain in his ribs was gone. "What happened?"

Sergeant Lorian looked puzzled. "We rode all night, sir, although I gather you slept most of the way. We stopped a couple of hours before dawn for a short break for the rest of us. We're heading out now—the encampment isn't more than an hour or two away."

"Why stop so close to the encampment, then? Why didn't we ride on through?"

"The horses needed rest, too," Lorian said. "Push them too hard for too far and you'll push them straight into the ground. Not even unicorns can go forever, and these horses are far from that."

"Have you ever ridden a unicorn, Sergeant?" Visyna asked. She was rubbing the gelding's coat with a handful of grass. The horse looked back and started eating the grass out of her hand.

"Couldn't ride one since I was fifteen," he said, smiling. "Besides, they pretty much stick to women. Temperamental sort."

"Unicorns or women?" Konowa asked.

Visyna huffed and the sergeant looked suddenly embarrassed. "Right, better get things squared away. We mount in five minutes," he said, and walked over to see to his troops.

"He seems nice," Visyna said, picking some more grass for the gelding to eat.

"Charming," Konowa said, staring after the sergeant. The gelding looked at Konowa and stamped a front hoof.

"I think someone is trying to get your attention." Visyna laughed, holding the grass out to the horse. The horse sniffed at her hand, then whinnied, taking the offering in its large, yellow teeth.

"You appear to get along with everyone," Konowa said, grabbing a fistful of dry leaves and absently rubbing the gelding with them.

"And you, on the other hand, do not."

"I bring out the worst in people," he said, rubbing the horse harder. Tufts of hair fell out, revealing red splotches covering the animal's skin. The horse waved its head from side to side and shook its body. "Did we get saddled with a sick horse?" he asked, looking over to Visyna.

She shook her head. "These horses were born and bred in Calahr—they are not suited to this land. It is one more affront to the natural order to transport animals so far from their native home."

"I know what you mean," Konowa said. "Two-legged animals don't fare much better."

Visyna clicked her teeth. "But you had a choice, these creatures did not. This is why my people hate . . ." She paused, clearly reconsidering her next words. "Why your Empire upsets the balance of life."

Konowa decided he didn't feel like sparring with her again. He went back to rubbing the gelding.

"Here, do it like this," Visyna said, walking around to his side of the horse. She took the leaves from his hand and replaced them with grass, then placed her hand on top of his. "Gentle strokes. You aren't trying to skin it."

She stood close to Konowa and the touch of her hand was warm and soft. He quietly drew in a deep breath, but this time she smelled more like the horse.

"You're right," she said after several moments.

"About what?"

"This horse . . . in fact, most of these horses. This climate is not ideal for them, but there is something else, a malaise."

"Maybe they're homesick," Konowa said.

Visyna continued to hold his hand. "That is part of it, but there is more, something I don't understand . . ."

"Speaking of things unexplained, what did you do to me? That was more than just leaves and herbs you used," he said. Her grip tightened on his hand then loosened again.

"No more than understanding the natural order," she replied.

"Ah, I thought maybe there was more to it than that."

"You thought wrong," she said, letting go of his hand and pointing to the saddle. "It's time to go."

Konowa sighed and nodded, gathering up the reins and climbing up without her help this time. He found the stirrups without looking and settled down on the horse, cringing as his muscles protested at being back in the saddle. She jumped up behind him and they joined the already moving line of horses. The rhythmic *clip-clop* of hooves on the roadway grew to a steady drumbeat that, he thought despairingly, would be tattooed into his brain forever.

Fortunately, this leg of their journey was mercifully short, and before Konowa was prepared for it, a shout up ahead signaled they had reached the forward piquet of the army encampment.

Passing through the line felt like being swallowed whole. The orange glow of cook fires was already fading as the sun came up. As its first rays stretched out across the land, they revealed a white-capped sea, the frothy waves coalescing into fields of canvas tents set in neat rows for thousands of yards in every direction. Men moved about them in that slow, stilted gait of having spent a night bedded down on the earth. Konowa rubbed his own backside in empathy.

A pungent tang caught the back of his throat and he gagged for a moment.

"Anything wrong, sir?" a trooper asked.

"Quite the opposite. I forgot what an army in the field smelled like, that's all."

Meat, most likely goat and rat dragon, roasted on spits and bubbled in pots. Somewhere nearby an armory sergeant had opened a barrel of black powder, the distinctive foul-egg odor hanging heavy in the air. And over it all were the more earthy scents of bootblack and pipe clay mingling with the ever-pervasive aroma of manure and animal sweat, of both the two- and four-legged variety. It was a world away from the dank mold of the forest.

"Companeeeeee! By the wheel, form square!"

Konowa twisted in his saddle. Two rows of Imperial infantry, more commonly called siggers, a bastardized nickname picked up long ago for the silver-green color of their coats, wheeled smartly into a four-sided square. Each side faced out, their bayonet-tipped muskets glinting in the sun. It was the time-honored defense against cavalry, and almost always successful, if done properly. More sounds vied for his attention, and he looked away as a building surge of shouted orders, smithies' hammers, and lowing oxen grew as the camp came alive.

A line of horses bent their necks to drink from a trough made of sailcloth fashioned by a stand of bushy-looking trees covered in moss. Farriers took the opportunity to examine the animals, and any lame or in need of shoeing were selected out. In a grass square surrounded by canvas tents another company of soldiers paraded with bayonets fixed so that they looked like a large, bristling porcupine trundling about in search of an exit.

"It must be strange to be around so many people again," Visyna said, behind him.

"I'm getting used to one, at least."

He felt a gentle squeeze around his stomach and smiled. He turned in the saddle to face her, but before he could respond a trooper rode up with a riderless horse in tow.

"If you'll get on this horse, ma'am, the Trading Company has a headquarters over yonder where you can get a message to your father."

"And you, sir, can follow me," Sergeant Lorian said, his face betraying obvious disappointment that Visyna was going with the troops. "The Duke's quarters are this way." Without waiting for Konowa to acknowledge Lorian, he spurred his horse into a trot.

Visyna slid over to the other horse without touching the ground. "Perhaps you'll stop by?" she asked.

"I'll find you," Konowa said, reluctantly urging the gelding after Sergeant Lorian. After a few yards he turned in the saddle to look back at her, but she was already trotting away.

"Major, the Duke is waiting."

"I've been gone over a year, what's a couple more minutes?" he muttered, and gently kicked the gelding in the ribs to get it moving.

They rode through the camp faster than Konowa would have liked. He noticed several troopers pointing, and he recognized the uniforms of several regiments. A murmur swelled in their wake, and by the time they rode up to the Duke's tent it was a dull roar. Pennants on the end of lances stuck in the ground on either side of the tent fluttered in a stiff breeze. They were the colors of enemy regiments, captured in battle and now displayed as trophies, but a few were unknown to Konowa. Clearly, the Duke had been busy.

Konowa wasn't so sure he wanted to dismount, but he followed the lead of the sergeant and climbed gingerly to the ground.

A crowd of soldiers jogged up to surround the tent, jostling each other for a look. "It *is* him," a voice said from the crowd. "Like hell," said another, "they sent him south with the rest of them." More claims and counterclaims flew back and forth. Konowa was considering taking bets on the matter when the Duke's tent flaps flew open and a man of singular distinction stepped into the light.

The crowd of soldiers disappeared faster than mead on payday.

Konowa was tall, close to six feet, but the Duke made him look like a child. No one dared question the Duke's parentage within earshot, but popular rumor supposed that there had been a mountain troll in the family woodpile. Dressed in riding boots and breeches and wearing an undershirt that might have been white in the distant past, he did nothing to dispel that notion. Wolf's Tooth, naturally, was slung over his shoulder.

Konowa threw the reins of his horse to a trooper and walked forward to stand in front of the red-haired giant. He searched the man's face, looking for a sign, but the blue eyes gave nothing away. Silence radiated out from them like ripples in a pond.

All at once the Duke lunged forward and wrapped Konowa in his arms, lifting him off the ground. "You sorry excuse for a soldier! I'd given you up for dead!"

The grip was as strong as the rakke's, albeit with friendlier purpose. Konowa struggled to breathe and finally had to pry the massive arms open enough to regain his footing and take a step backward to look up at his old friend. "It's great to see you too, Jaal," he said, smiling at the Duke. A row of white teeth beamed back at him from the scarred visage of his friend, and Konowa realized how much he'd missed him.

A scream sounded from off to the right and several horses spooked. Two privates, a dwarf and a man, came running toward the tent followed by a large bengar. Konowa shook his head. Jir cornered the two soldiers against the side of the tent and was advancing on them, his snout high in the air, sniffing.

"Jir! They're not for eating," Konowa yelled.

"Sweet knobby-kneed nuns! Is this monster yours?" the dwarf yelled. The other soldier kept wiping at his spectacles as if he couldn't believe what he was seeing.

Konowa briefly considered asserting his officer status, but the dwarf was already having a bad day and there was no good reason to make it worse.

"In a manner of speaking. He doesn't normally react like this. The last time I saw him this agitated was a few nights ago, when he ate some rakkes."

The dwarf's eyes bulged. His companion stopped rubbing his specs and looked ready to faint.

"Ate? Ate! We ain't no rakkes," the dwarf cried. "We just killed one of the critters ourselves."

Konowa felt the blood drain from his face. Could it have been the fourth rakke? Why would it come here?

"Where is the body?" he asked.

The dwarf spat a stream of crute juice at Jir, who started growling and sank down on his haunches, never a good sign. "Call off your beast and maybe I'll tell you, elfie."

"You'll tell him now, Private," the Duke of Rakestraw thundered, his voice a hammer poised to fall.

"Colonel, sir! I didn't see you there what with this monster attempting to eat a couple of Her Majesty's finest, and if I may say so, sir, bravest siggers in service in the far-flung reaches of Her Empire and the dominions it contains."

"As wagon nannies for the Outer Territories Trading Company?" Jaal asked, a hint of skepticism in his voice. He looked over at Konowa and rolled his eyes. "Private! While we're still young, and you're in one piece."

"Right," the dwarf said, carefully saluting the Duke. "As I was about to say, we burned the brute, sir, sent it back to the fires it came from, nothing but ash and bone now. Vital service we performed, no doubt about it." He finished, casting a glance at Konowa as he said the last part.

"Did it say anything?" Konowa asked, his hopes of solving this diminishing now.

"No offense, sir, but we weren't exactly interested in engaging it in chit-chat," the dwarf said, his eyebrows high with indignation.

"I think this has gone on long enough," Jaal whispered. Konowa looked around and saw that a crowd had started to gather again. He nodded.

"Curb that mutt of yours and let's go inside," Jaal said, taking his hand off of the hilt of Wolf's Tooth. "You're still a disruption to good order and conduct." He turned and went into the tent.

"Jir, heel," Konowa ordered, pointing to a spot by the tent flaps. To his immense surprise, Jir obeyed, slinking away from the frightened soldiers, but never turning his back to them.

"I suggest you two take a bath and get rid of the smell," Konowa said, addressing the dwarf and his bespectacled companion. He stared in turn at the other soldiers, watching until they suddenly remembered they had better places to be.

"Look who's talkin'," he heard the dwarf mutter, pulling his counterpart after him. They edged away from the tent before breaking into a run in the opposite direction.

Konowa let out a sigh and stepped into the tent after the Duke. The décor was typical Jaal; sparse, ordered and without a whiff of pretension. A simple wood-framed cot occupied a quarter of the tent. A saddle, its leather polished to a parade-ground finish, its stirrups cinched tight and high, sat at the bottom end. At the head of the cot was a folding wooden chair, with Jaal's blue cavalry jacket draped over its back and his red-crested helmet perched on top of that. A second pair of riding boots, a small travel chest, a board laid across two wicker ammunition crates for a table, and a lantern hanging from the center pole completed the furnishings.

"Being a Duke doesn't appear to have that many advantages," Konowa said, admiring the cobwebs in a corner.

A look that Konowa couldn't interpret crossed his friend's face, but it was quickly replaced with a smile.

"And neither does being a savage, I see," Jaal replied, "well, except for your pet out there." He offered Konowa the chair while he sat down on the cot, its canvas sheet sagging to just an inch above the ground. "I seem to recall you having something less than a tender affinity for the forest. 'Filthy, nasty place filled with bugs' was your usual refrain, was it not?"

The smile on Konowa's face lessened. "Things changed."

Jaal nodded. "They did at that. Well, you're back now. The whole camp knows it, and very soon the entire army will know it. Trouble is definitely in the wind. I only just received a messenger from Marshal Ruwl about detaining you on behalf of no less a personage than the Prince himself. Damn me though if I know what's going on. They're both due here in a few days on some silly inspection tour, so I guess you'll find out then."

"You mean *we* will," Konowa said.

For a long moment the Duke said nothing, and Konowa wondered if Jaal had heard him.

"I'm going hunting to the west," Jaal said at last.

It had been a while, but Konowa could tell his friend was troubled. "Orcs? You'll be back in a fortnight. They aren't our problem and you know it. I thought I'd put an end to Her ideas in this part of the world, but it seems ridding the world of one of Her servants only got me a whole lot of trouble."

Jaal smiled at his friend. "You did the world a favor when you killed the Viceroy, I'm sorry I wasn't able to—"

Konowa waved him off. "I wasn't going to have you throw away your career for something I did. Besides, I know what you did for my boys. If some in the royal court had had their way, the Iron Elves would have been scattered throughout the army. You kept them together."

Now it was the Duke's turn to motion Konowa to stop. "I'm not sure it was much of a favor. They sent them to garrison the forts in the southern wastes across the Midea Sea. Just sand, camels, and not a tree for hundreds of miles. Pretty damn harsh, especially for elves born in the forest."

"Not elves," Konowa said, "Iron Elves. We don't have quite the same affinity for trees as the others. Still, I imagine it's been rough for them."

"They won't hate you, if that's what you're thinking. You did what had to be done, they know that."

Konowa bowed his head. "Maybe. I've had a year to think about it myself. I sometimes wonder . . ." He lifted his head, pushing those dark thoughts from his mind. "Enough of that. So, I hear there's a new Viceroy in town."

Jaal nodded, but did not smile. "Faltinald Gwyn, career weasel, pardon me, *diplomat*. Invited me over to his palace the other night. He claims the orcs are meddling in magics and other sorcery that they can't possibly understand, in league with Her and those rakke things."

"Orcs working with an elf-witch? Is he mad?" That was about as likely as a dwarf voluntarily shaving his beard.

"I don't know. What I do know is I'm leaving and taking the cavalry with me just as you return. There's unrest in the north that the Viceroy's convinced is the start of a rebellion, but he's ordered me west." Jaal winked at Konowa. "So naturally I sent some scouts up north to check things out, but they won't be back before I have to leave."

"Maybe he's a treasure hunter like the last one," Konowa said, his fists clenching as an image of the last Viceroy flashed through his mind. The elf had disgraced them all—if Konowa had to do it all over again, it would have ended the same.

"This one is full weasel. I don't know what he's up to," Jaal said, this time looking away from Konowa's glance.

Konowa smiled at his old friend. There was a wary, sad look to Jaal. Did he feel guilty about what had happened to him? Jaal had always been like an older brother, even though Konowa had decades on him. Jaal had threatened to resign his commission and go with Konowa after his court-martial—and Konowa knew he would have if he had let him. Alone in the forest, Konowa had been the one to carry guilt around, with only Jir by his side; never judging, never condemning. He would never have the bengar's stoicism, but he could sure as hell match its loyalty.

"You have been more friend to me than any elf has a right to," Konowa said. He winked at Jaal, spread his arms out wide, closed his eyes, and began speaking in a deep voice. "*Lim rokna re rika, ti rokna se rika, gev esig lo werta oxul, ki rika yinja.*"

Jaal shook his head, sending his red hair flying about his face. "I'm a bit rusty. May my cullions be squeezed by a maiden fair?"

Konowa opened his eyes and fixed Jaal with a look of mock disdain. "You fight your battles, I'll fight mine, and we will find our enemy is the same, and fight as one."

Jaal bowed his head. Konowa took it for relief.

"So," Konowa said, "my banishment is over, and Marshal Ruwl is still days away. What do we do now?"

The Duke of Rakestraw took a deep breath and sat up straight, looking around the tent for a few moments before returning his gaze to Konowa.

"Swift Dragon, you may have been hugging trees for companionship for the past year, but you aren't that addled yet. We do what soldiers the world over have done when awaiting their orders." He leaned forward and reached into one of the spare riding boots, pulling out a large black bottle. "We drink!"

ELEVEN

Despite what felt like a lifetime of virtual isolation in a sweltering, bug-biting, foul-smelling forest with little else to do but think, Konowa Swift Dragon remained at a loss about how one really found inner peace. Was it knowing which question to ask, or merely the act of searching for the answer? With considerable effort he considered his current predicament and gave it a try.

His head pounded like a kettledrum on a sun-baked parade square. Even the long-gone tip of his left ear hurt. It wasn't a result of his battle with the rakkes, nor Visyna's attempt on his life . . . before she got to know him, of course. It wasn't almost getting decapitated by Her Majesty's over-eager cavalry or even the simple insidious torture of riding a horse. It was, and of this he was absolutely sure, the Sala brandy he had been drinking with the Duke of Rakestraw for the past forty-eight hours.

"The commander of Her Majesty's forces in the Greater Protectorate of Elfkyna asked you a question," Marshal Ruwl's wizard was saying.

And that. A fire deep within Konowa rekindled. There were six officers on Ruwl's staff in the Duke's tent, though Jaal had departed earlier that morning without even saying good-bye. Something was bothering his old friend, but as drunk as they had gotten Jaal refused to discuss it, instead finding more bottles and flasks tucked away in sleeves and pockets and regaling him with the events of the past year.

"Did he now?" Konowa replied, turning his attention back to the group crowded around him.

They glittered and sparkled like a flock of magpie dragons, their chests adorned with bright baubles, there to impress other males and woo females. Konowa read their faces and saw their disdain. He yawned and scratched his head, then lurched forward as if he was going to leap at them. They all flinched, all except the old elven wizard, Jurwan Leaf Talker. He calmly stared at Konowa while munching on a bag of nuts. His eyes sparkled with annoying intelligence in a weather-tanned face so craggy it might have been bark. Leaf Talker leaned on a halberd with a burnished, sharpened point on one end, a string of leaves wrapped around the base of the point like a garland. Clad as he was in a many-colored robe of animal skins and wearing an intricate feather headdress of gray, black, and red plumage that drooped down over the tops of his ears, the wizard looked more like a vagabond than the wielder of powerful magic that Konowa knew him to be.

"I did," the marshal said, "and you will be so kind as to reply."

Konowa broke the wizard's stare and finally looked at Marshal Ruwl. He was a hollow caricature of the man Konowa had once known. Despite the light that glowed through the canvas tent the marshal appeared faded. His silver-green coatee hung loose from his shoulders and his bicorn wobbled on his head as if it had shrunk. What surprised Konowa the most, though, were his eyes; rheumy and red-rimmed, too weak to hold a stare for more than a moment.

"No," Konowa said.

"No?" replied the marshal. Several of the officers gasped, while Leaf Talker smiled.

"Are you deaf now, too?" Konowa asked.

At least three sabers rattled in their scabbards as the marshal's staff surged forward at the insult.

A small cough from the wizard caught everyone's attention.

"Gentlemen," Ruwl said, "please vacate this tent so that we may speak alone."

"But, sir—"

The marshal raised a slim hand and quieted his retinue.

"Now."

They left reluctantly. Leaf Talker, however, remained.

"You're drunk," the marshal said without preamble.

"And you're a coward, but at least I'll be sober in a few hours," Konowa said, collapsing onto the Duke's chair.

If the insult affected the marshal, he didn't show it. "You don't like me, do you?"

Konowa stared at him for several seconds. "You wonder if I *like* you? I *despise* you. The Iron Elves were *disbanded* because of you. Fine, court-martial me for saving the Empire, but they did nothing wrong."

The marshal's sword whistled from its scabbard and was pressing against Konowa's throat in a flash. The eyes that had looked so old and tired a moment ago now burned with a fury that caught Konowa's breath. He glanced over at the wizard, who was busy stuffing several nuts into this mouth at once and showed no signs of intervening.

"You . . . don't . . . know . . . anything!" the marshal whispered hoarsely. "I had no choice."

Konowa glared back at Ruwl. "Like hell. You know damn well the Viceroy was in league with the Shadow Monarch. He was doing everything in his power to stir up revolt in this country. I did the world a favor when I killed him, and what did I get for it? A court-martial and my regiment taken away. Tell me, how do you sleep at night?"

"I don't sleep anymore," Ruwl said absently, lowering his sword. He looked at Konowa with eyes that were once again those of a very tired, very old man. Resheathing the blade, Ruwl walked over to the cot and lowered himself to sit. It barely sagged under his weight.

Something deep inside Konowa stirred, and he was shocked to realize it was pity. "Are you looking for sympathy?"

"No, and neither will you get any from me," Ruwl said. "Command is about making difficult choices. Of course I knew who the Viceroy really served. He was as artless as he was ruthless."

Hearing the admission left Konowa speechless.

"I knew," Ruwl continued, "Her Majesty knew, and I suspect most of the Empire knew, but that was beside the point. You took matters into your own hands by going to Luuguth Jor and killing him before there could be a trial. An officer of the crown cannot simply take matters into his own hands. You gave me no choice."

Konowa found his voice. "A *trial*? He was killing the elfkynan like flies, robbing their temples, digging up sacred relics in search of something for the Shadow Monarch. That mad elf was trying to put Her on the Queen's throne! He had to be stopped. Talking him to death wasn't an option."

"So he didn't tell you what he was searching for?" Ruwl asked. The look of surprise on his face appeared genuine.

"We didn't chat," Konowa said grimly.

Ruwl paused as he considered this, then continued. "When you were at Luuguth Jor, did you see . . . anything out of the ordinary?"

Konowa threw up his hands. "I saw a sad excuse for a fort, a few mud huts, a river, and an elf who was a disgrace to all the Hynta."

"And what did you do with the Viceroy's body?"

Konowa's next outburst froze on his lips. "We buried it outside the fort. Why?"

Ruwl looked over at Leaf Talker, who swallowed the nuts in his mouth and shook his head, sending the feathers in his headdress dancing. "All things that will be, will be, unless they are destined to be . . . different."

The pain behind Konowa's eyes increased. "What?"

"Quite," Leaf Talker said, thumping his halberd on the ground. Vibrations hummed through the air; for a moment it was as if a door to another world had opened, and then closed again. "Despite your time among the trees, you have learned very little from them."

Konowa wasn't sure if he should laugh or cry. "My patience was at an end before this conversation started. You sent for me, not the other way around. In the few days I've been back in civilization, I've been attacked by extinct creatures, heard enough rumors to last several lifetimes, and still I don't have the first clue what is going on."

Marshal Ruwl stood and withdrew a thin scroll of parchment from his jacket, handing it to Konowa. "We know why the rakkes have returned. They are but the first. More will come. Unless we find a way to stop Her."

Konowa gripped the scroll hard. The dream he'd tried very hard to forget flashed vividly before his eyes. The Shadow Monarch's cold hand reached out to him from the shadows. He could feel the paper softening with the sweat of his own hand. The marshal and the wizard stared at him, waiting.

Konowa had no choice. He was going to accept no matter what they had planned. She had to be stopped, and he needed to belong again. It was like standing on a mountain peak; there was nowhere to go but back down.

Konowa nodded and slackened his grip on the scroll, prying open the wax seal and pulling the rolled paper to its full length. When he finished reading it, the strength in his body gave out and he sank into the chair, the scroll sliding from his hand.

"You're reforming the Iron Elves . . ."

"I really rather expected you to have pieced that together before now," Ruwl stated, his tone bringing Konowa back to his senses.

Konowa's mind raced with the possibilities. "To do what, lead them on a death march? Her mountain is well guarded, Her power too great for a single regiment, not that the men wouldn't try. But no one who enters Her realm comes back."

There was a small, dry noise from the wizard that sounded an awful lot like laughter, but when Konowa looked, the elf was busy stuffing still more of the endless supply of nuts into his mouth.

Ruwl looked annoyed. "No one is asking you to attack Her directly. There isn't the time or the resources to mount an expedition to travel across the ocean and lay siege to Her mountain. No, you are to take the regiment north following the Baynama River as far as Luuguth Jor."

"You said before you knew why the rakkes had returned. What's that got to do with Luuguth Jor?" For no reason Konowa could explain, he pictured the fort smothered in a sea of twisted trees.

Ruwl looked again to Leaf Talker, who nodded. "We believe more than just rakkes have returned."

Konowa put it together. "You can't be serious . . . I *killed* him. I put my saber through his heart. You court-martialed me for it."

"For disobeying orders," Ruwl said in an entirely matter-of-fact tone. "Killing him was beside the point. In any event, it seems he, or something like him, has returned. An apparition has been sighted in more than one place. It looks like the departed Viceroy, but claims to be Her Emissary."

"You have proof of this?"

Ruwl sighed, a pained look crossing his face. "No, at least, little more than rumor. Seers, shamans, and wizards among others say they have seen or felt something amiss, and it all points to Luuguth Jor. The garrison there has not been heard from in almost a fortnight. Strange stories are beginning to drift down from the north, but the new Viceroy has convinced Her Majesty that the cavalry should be pulled back to go after the orcs in the west. With them out of the north, we've had no way to confirm anything."

Konowa remembered the feel of his saber sliding into the elf's chest. He couldn't be alive, could he? "Jaal—the Duke—told me about this move to the west. Is the Viceroy now in charge of the military here?"

The marshal rose slightly from the cot, then regained his composure. "He is Her Majesty's representative in this country, and his orders are the Queen's orders."

"Why us? Why go to all this trouble to reform the Iron Elves just to check out a rumor?"

"Simply put, we have no other choice. The Viceroy's orders apply to all Calahrian regiments in Elfkyna, and he wants them all focused on the western border and the orcs." The disdain in the marshal's voice was obvious.

"You don't suspect this new one, do you?" Konowa asked.

"He serves Her Majesty and has yet to show divided loyalties. Still, the Iron Elves are being raised by personal fiat of the Prince and as such do not fall under the orders of the Viceroy."

Konowa's head began to pound even harder as he tried to pick his way through the gambits within machinations. He looked at Leaf Talker, who smiled back as if nothing the least bit strange was happening, but then, wizards never played it straight . . . or monarchs or generals, for that matter.

"So the Queen allows her Viceroy to move all her forces in Elfkyna to the west, while at the same time allowing her son the Prince to raise a regiment to head east? What am I missing?"

"A head for politics," Ruwl said. "It is both naïve and dangerous to view the Empire as being of one mind. The Queen, in her long reign, has developed that most delicate of royal traits: holding contradictory views at the same time."

"Then she suspects the new Viceroy." Konowa had only met the Queen once, several years before at an award ceremony for several officers, himself one of the recipients. She'd smiled and been pleasant, laughing and making small talk, yet Konowa came away from that meeting with the distinct impression he'd been a mouse in the presence of a very charming cat.

Ruwl offered Konowa the briefest of smiles. "Her Majesty is prudent in all matters. Therefore, the regiment will proceed to Luuguth Jor and ascertain whether the Red Star has indeed fallen back to earth. If the Star is there, you will retrieve it."

"*That* prophecy?" Konowa said, looking straight at the wizard. "Shooting stars fall from the skies like rain. What about the old Viceroy?"

"Kill him, again. And this time, do a proper job of it."

Konowa blinked. "Kill a dead elf, again, and find a mythical magical object. Anything else?"

Ruwl pinched the bridge of his nose. "It is obvious that trees make poor intellectual companions. Your grasp of the greater import of things is not what it used to be. I would have thought the rakkes would be enough to convince you things have changed. If they can come back from the dead, why not the Viceroy, and if him, why not others? The Star, whether real or myth, is a significant threat, and must be kept from Her."

"It's still a faery tale," Konowa said. "Like the Ice Queen of the Julg orcs. The return of Stars from the heavens in the world's time of need is just legend."

"That matters little," Ruwl said, absently brushing at his sleeve. "To the elfkynan, and for that matter, to a great many in the Empire, the legend of the Star is the very foundation on which their faith is built. The Star's power is incalculable. The people believe it to be true, therefore it is true."

"It'll be a hunk of crystal," Konowa said, rolling his eyes, "a shiny gem that reflects the light in pretty colors."

The marshal tapped his foot. "Perception is reality. He, or she, who holds the Star commands the legend. What if the other Stars turn up? Magic or glass, we need this one. With it, we convince the elfkynan that the Empire remains strong, and thoughts of rebellion drift away. With it, we convince the Shadow Monarch to stay on Her mountain and not interfere in the affairs of the Empire. Without it, She and many more will grow to believe the opposite, even perhaps that they can defeat us."

"Maybe they can," Konowa said.

"Indeed," the marshal replied, "but to oust the Imperial Army from Elfkyna would cost untold thousands, tens of thousands, of lives. They are a proud people, but they do not have the weapons or the army to challenge us at anything close to parity. The bloodshed would be horrendous and Her Majesty would send reinforcements. Is that what you want?"

Konowa's shoulders slumped. "Fine. Let's suppose for a moment all of this is true. It will take weeks to bring the regiment back from the southern wastes, and even longer to re-equip and prepare for this. Do we have that much time?"

Ruwl stood up. The blanket on the cot wasn't creased at all. "Arrangements are being made. The Prince has ordered you commissioned as a captain." The marshal raised a hand to Konowa before he could react. "I informed the Prince that your abilities to lead men into battle were not in question, but a rank of only captain would compromise this. He was unmoved by my argument. His Highness takes a dim view of officers who kill Her Majesty's representatives. However, the Duke of Rakestraw saw fit to purchase your commission to major, and the Prince has allowed it to stand, for now."

Konowa slapped his knee. Jaal hadn't said a thing the entire time. "So who's been assigned my second in command to make sure I adhere to this vision of yours?"

The marshal coughed. "It is my duty to inform you that as of this date you are granted the commission of brevet major, subknight commander and second in command of Her Majesty's Light Infantry Regiment of the Hynta, the Iron Elves."

Konowa blinked. "Second in command?"

"In order to ensure that the Viceroy cannot interfere, Prince Tykkin will personally lead the regiment as its knight superior, and will be here shortly to officially take command of the regiment."

"And you think I'll accept this?" Konowa said, his voice rising as he looked from the marshal to the wizard, the blood pounding in his ears.

"You will, and you will conduct yourself *in a manner befitting an officer and gentleman!*" The marshal paused, then continued in a quieter tone. "Life is all about making the best of a . . . challenging situation. Princes become Kings, and won't always have the inclination to lead a regiment into the darker places of the Empire."

Konowa thought about that for a moment. Of course Ruwl was right. But Tykkin?

Suddenly something came to him, a ditty: ". . . bottles and batwings, spells to make bees sing, it's all for the book, the lists of Prince Tykkin. Hell," he said, finally remembering. "He's the bloody compendiast!"

The wizard actually chuckled. Marshal Ruwl pursed his lips. "If you mean the Prince is fond of the study of natural history and artifacts of rare and special significance, then yes, he is."

"Like the fabled Eastern Star, Red Star, whatever-you-call-it Star of Sillra," Konowa said, fitting at least one of the pieces of this puzzle in place.

"The Star, as I mentioned, is far more important politically, and the Prince has been made aware of this. He assures me his interest is in matters more pertinent to the state of the empire."

Konowa thought he understood, and the knowledge made him sick to his stomach. "Aha. The Queen's feeling her age so she's preparing the young snot to sit on the throne. Time to trade in the scrolls and telescopes for a sword and scepter. Crush a rebellion, debunk some legends, find a pretty bauble in the process. And I get the distinct honor of nursemaiding him through the whole damn coming-of-age exercise."

Ruwl flushed red. His hand strayed toward his saber, but only grabbed the sword knot. When he spoke, it was in a whisper that carried like an arrow through silk. "A year is a long time to live alone in the wild, especially in this land. It would be easy for an elf to forget the greater world and its rules of conduct, so I will grant you this impertinence here, now. When you leave this tent, however, you are an officer in Her Majesty's Army and you will act like one, or so help me I will return you to the forest myself, one piece at a time." The marshal removed his hand from the sword knot and, pivoting on one heel, parted the tent flaps and stepped outside, leaving Konowa alone with the wizard.

Konowa stared after Ruwl, wholly unsatisfied with the way events were developing. Things were moving too fast, too fast by half.

"It's been a long time, my boy," Leaf Talker said, offering Konowa a nut.

"Maybe not long enough," Konowa said, still staring at the tent flaps.

"Ah, then perhaps your time with nature was more beneficial than your current attitude and appearance would suggest?" he asked, ignoring Konowa's rudeness.

Konowa said nothing for several seconds, then turned to fix the wizard with a cold stare. "I still hate the forest, Father."

TWELVE

Visyna rode her horse into the tree line along the western edge of the encampment. The noise and smell of so many soldiers in one place was overwhelming, and the bitter tang of metal filled the air. She took the first opportunity she could to get away. After her disappearance of last week, her father's men were not at all inclined to let her go anywhere unescorted, which is why four cavalry troopers rode a few hundred yards behind her.

"Stay in the open, please, my lady," one of the troopers shouted.

Visyna turned on her horse and cast a withering glare back at him. "A lady sometimes needs privacy, especially after morning tea."

The soldier reined in his horse as if he'd come to the edge of a cliff. "Yes, of course, my lady. My apologies."

Visyna turned away to hide her smile from the blushing trooper. She clicked her tongue and her horse edged farther into the trees until they were hidden from view. She figured she had ten, maybe fifteen minutes at the most before they would come looking for her. It would have to be enough.

She continued deeper into the woods for another minute, then halted her horse, lightly jumping from its back to the forest floor. The horse whinnied, and she ran a hand along its neck, enjoying the trembling wave of muscle that greeted her touch.

"Stay," she whispered, and walked deeper into the woods.

The smells here were wonderful. She took a deep breath and luxuriated in the beauty and freshness of new growth. Birds chirped and sang gaily, while beneath it was the steady hum of insects. How, she wondered, could he not love this?

Konowa. He excited her and frustrated her as no other had, and suitors had always been as plentiful as the leaves on a tree. So why did she find this elf so intriguing? He was *Jarahta Mysor*, a tainted one. And even though she knew it couldn't be true, she swore she could smell metal in his blood when he was near her. He was loud, quick to anger, obstinate, and worst of all . . . apparently not the least bit interested in her. Not once had he come to visit her since they arrived in camp, instead spending all his time drinking with the Duke. Sergeant Lorian, on the other hand, was most certainly interested—the four troopers with her today had been hand-picked by him to guard her. Lorian was considering buying a commission and becoming an officer, a fact that would raise his prospects with her father, and, she realized, impressed her, too.

But he wasn't Konowa.

Enough, she chided herself, there would be time later for that. Looking around once to make sure she was alone, Visyna walked a little farther until she found a small bare patch of dirt under a large soap nut tree. She closed her eyes for a moment and let her senses explore the area, questing for a sign, but as usual, she detected nothing.

Opening her eyes, she sat down cross-legged on the earth and began the breathing ritual. The birdsong faded, followed by the hum of insects, and soon not even the leaves rustled. With each intake of breath, her hands wove intricate designs in the air in front of her. With each exhalation, she drew her hands across an imaginary plane, erasing the designs suspended before her. She coaxed her senses to delve deeper into the fabric of the forest and felt herself stretched and pulled as if great wings bore her aloft, her ethereal being soaring ever higher. Time was running out.

As her breathing slowed, the designs became more detailed, her fingers stitching brilliant patterns that no seamstress could hope to match. Filigrees of silver light began to flow from them and she smiled and closed her eyes. The earth fell away beneath her as her body quivered and swayed, its very essence being shifted and rearranged like water within water.

When she opened her eyes again, the forest was filled with light. A glowing Star floated in front of her wreathed in silver light. The air bent and shattered around it in refractions of brilliant emptiness. Visyna trembled and wondered again at the feelings that flooded through her. She felt at peace, and in awe, but something else that she could never quite place.

The Star spoke. Its voice, unlike the brilliance of the light around it, was thick and slow, each word tumbling forth like a mountain crashing to the ground:

"Save me, my child, and I will set your people free."

". . . the sawbones puts a cream on it, see, and it clears right up," Yimt said, scratching himself in contradiction.

"Sssh," Alwyn said out of the corner of his mouth, "the corporal will nick you for talking in ranks. I want to hear what they're saying."

Alwyn kept his stare on the temporary dais placed in the middle of camp. The sun boiled high above the assembled troops, rolling down wave after wave of furnace heat to create a fetid stew of sweat and funk that simmered among the gathered ranks and kept the medical orderlies busy picking up fainters. Royal banners hung limp from lances held by equally wilted troops of the palace horse guard decked out in gleaming white fur shakos and high-collared jackets of a deep silver-green. Their struggle with heatstroke signified the presence of no less a personage than the heir to the throne: Prince Tykkin.

"That one there, all puffed up like, that's the prince," Yimt said, peering between the ranks of troops in front.

Alwyn squinted through the drops of sweat swimming across his specs at the man Yimt was nodding toward. Short and a little doughy, Alwyn thought, recognizing Prince Tykkin from a painted miniature he'd once seen of the Royal family. Like the painting, the Prince was wearing a staggeringly tall shako with a jeweled band around its base, so that his brow sparkled. Several other officers lined the dais, but none shone as brightly as the Prince. Alwyn shifted his musket and tried to hear what was being said.

". . . and by decree of Her Majesty on this date, the eighth month in the sixty-fourth year of her reign, the Hynta Light Infantry, the Iron Elves, are once again added to the rolls of the Imperial Army. His Royal Highness, The Prince of Calahr, will speak to you all shortly. The regimental colors will now be consecrated, Father NuKol . . ."

"What he say?" Yimt asked, elbowing Alwyn in the hip.

"They've reformed the Iron Elves," Alwyn hissed back. He was beginning to feel trapped and took in a deep breath to calm his nerves. He started gagging.

"Reform the Steel Faeries, eh? Won't be the same this time around," Yimt said, but there was respect in his voice. He spat out a stream of crute juice from the clump jammed in his right cheek. The grayish liquid started steaming as soon as it hit the ground. "They've gone and stripped all the battle honors from them, I'll wager. Poor buggers, they deserved better. Just 'cause that officer of theirs went off his rocker don't mean they had to pay for it, you know? Officers, you can't trust a one of them."

"But why disband them when it was just the officer who killed the Viceroy?" Alwyn asked.

"Miniature politics, Ally," Yimt said.

This was new. "Miniature politics?"

Yimt nodded. "See, you got your largority, that's you humans, and then us smallority, elves and dwarves, that make up the Empire, not counting the extra-miniature races. Well, the largority never trust the smallority on account the smallority are always wanting to be in the largority, if you follow. When that Iron Elf officer killed the Viceroy, they figured it was a power play for control of all the elves in the Empire . . . you know, revolt from within kind of thing to take over the largority. All that business with that elf-witch of theirs, but that's more insidinal politics between the elves."

Alwyn's stomach started to roil. "Wait, so if the Iron Elves were disbanded because they can't be trusted, why are they reforming them now?"

Yimt crunched some crute between his teeth while he considered that. "Well, to understand that you have to reckon with diplomatic new-auntsays. Sort of the doily to the political table if you get my meaning. No doubt a whole lot of teat-a-teat and mashinations went on behind the scenes. I expect they needed some time to go by after they got rid of that officer, you know, to let bygones go by."

"But isn't that the officer up there beside the Prince?"

"That tall, dark-looking elf?" Yimt asked, placing a hand on Alwyn's arm and using his shatterbow as a small ladder to climb higher to see over the shoulder of the rank in front of him. "Kind of the same look as our Corp, come to think on it, bit swarthy and earthy like." Another stream of crute splashed to the ground. "In fact, if my memory hasn't melted in this heat, I'd say he was the spittin' image of that savage we saw the other day when we was about near ate by that beast."

Alwyn squinted even harder. "You sure? He looked more like a rakke to me. And the smell."

"Like I was telling you," Yimt replied, spitting another stream. "You wait till we get in the field proper and see if those officers don't start looking and smelling like the rest of us. Even the Prince there would wilt." He let go of Alwyn's arm and jumped down from his shatterbow, the weapon none the worse for wear, although he did have to heave to pull the butt out of the ground.

"The Prince? I can't imagine him getting dirty, but that elf is easy enough to see." Alwyn lowered his voice and scrunched down to be a few inches closer to the dwarf. "I heard tell that animal that almost ate us is really his lady, turned into beast form by a sorcerer. Hrem in B Company swears he saw a woman come into camp with him, but she ain't been seen since, then that bengar thing showed up. Makes you think."

"Can't imagine what the kids'll look like," Yimt said, shaking his head slightly.

Alwyn licked his lips, the skin dry and easily flaked into strips. "Hrem also said it was a sign of some kind, like that rakke we killed. He said they're bringing back the Iron Elves to fight the Shadow Monarch."

"Did he now?" Yimt asked. "You know, I always thought Hrem had a good head on his shoulders, bit large, but good. Might be something to that."

"So where are they anyway? The only elves I've seen are the corporal and that officer up there."

"Guess their boat hasn't put in yet. Long way to come back from the southern wastes only to send them off again. Say, where did they say they're sending them? Back to the Hynta?"

"North to Luuguth Jor, where the Viceroy was killed," Alwyn said.

"Odd. The Thirty-fifth Foot Guard garrisons that fort," Yimt said. "Had to make sure the elfkynan didn't take the place over and turn it into some kind of shrine to celebrate the death of the Viceroy."

"Well, that's what I heard," Alwyn said. How bloody appropriate— he'd known more about what the army did listening to news criers back home than he did now that he was in it. "Maybe they're going to show the flag, give the elfkynan something to think about."

Yimt spat another stream of crute and laughed. "Something to think about all right. The elfkynan will be thinkin', if that boat don't show up where are they gonna get troops dumb enough to fill the ranks?"

"From volunteers," came the silky voice of Corporal Kritton standing behind them, "and you two just did."

THIRTEEN

"There will be changes, of course," Prince Tykkin said without preamble.

Konowa stood at attention under the awning of the Prince's marquee and said nothing. He'd been summoned after the ceremony for an immediate audience with the Prince. That had been over an hour ago, the Prince only now deigning to see him.

Konowa waited. A feeble breeze tried and failed to move the ludicrously large section of canvas that kept the sun at bay. The awning looked to be the mainsail for a ship of the line, making Konowa wonder if somewhere there was a vessel adrift at sea. He hoped the Prince had enough sense not to bring such an extravagance on the expedition.

"Your previous conduct was a disgrace, a stain on the collective glory of the Imperial Army," the Prince said, coming to stand in front of Konowa. "Now that I see you in person, I wonder if it might have been better to leave you in the woods. I've had reports that your conduct since rejoining the army has been less than exemplary and that troubles me. I will have nothing but the finest, Major, the finest soldiers, the finest uniforms, the finest drill, and the finest quality of character in those that serve me."

If the Prince was waiting for a reply, Konowa wasn't going to give one. He kept his eyes unfocused, a trick he'd learned years before when standing in the ranks. It kept you from staring straight at something, usually trouble. He focused instead on the various indignities his new uniform was subjecting his body to.

His neck was already red and itching from the high leather stock that ringed the jacket's collar. It kept a man's head up and made the ranks look stiff and proud when marching past a reviewing stand, but it was a dangerous nuisance in battle when freedom of movement counted. The leather ankle boots that replaced his soft hide ones were tight and hard against his feet, while his pants chafed and his shako felt like a cannonball perched on his head. His left hip ached from the saber he now carried strapped to his waist, a gift from Jaal. The three-foot-long blade had a bright white enameled hand guard with gold inlay to signify his officer status and was no doubt worth a pretty penny, but he'd take his old musket in its place any day. He willed his body to go numb and prayed that the Prince would hurry up.

"Still, I believe you will be of some small value," the Prince continued, his voice sounding a bit nasal. "But you will follow my example of how an officer in Her Majesty's Army should conduct himself from this point on."

The smell of pomade drifted from beneath the Prince's ridiculously tall shako, reminding Konowa of the cloying sap of the forest. A single ponytail of white-powdered hair hung down the Prince's back, the end tipped by a diamond brooch. Up close, the Prince's eyes only reached Konowa's chin, the reason, perhaps, that he wore tall hats. His eyes were a pale green kept in permanent shadow by a heavy brow. An equine nose jutted over thin lips, but for all of that he wasn't unhandsome, and a few weeks in the field would melt twenty pounds off his paunchy frame, giving him a warrior's build. What, if anything, would give him the intelligence to command men Konowa didn't know.

Konowa glanced over at a large folding table set up in the tent and was disheartened to see it cluttered with books. He read a few of the titles and grew even more despairing:

Basic Manual for Officers on Disciplining Troops in the Field, Be They Deemed Light Infantry or Regular, Pursuant to All Occasions They May Encounter.

Legends, Myths, and Fables of the Peoples of Greater Elfkyna and Territories of the Masua Subcontinent.

The Royal Society of Calahr's Large and Exceptional Collection of Specimens of the Animal, Vegetable, Mineral, and Thaumaturgical Worlds With Lavish Illustrations and Appendices, Volume IV.

Perfect, Konowa thought, *just perfect. He's going to lead a regiment with one eye in a manual and the other looking for pretty flowers and treasure-hoarding dragons.*

"Her Majesty speaks highly of you, did you know that?" the Prince asked. Something in his tone triggered a warning deep inside Konowa.

The Prince stepped closer to him, peering up at him, watching. "She followed your exploits with great interest. *My gallant rogue* were Her exact words," Tykkin said, searching Konowa's face for some kind of sign.

He's jealous, Konowa realized. The Queen's son, the future King, had had to listen to his mother praise another—him, of all people. It must have been especially galling. *And now I've been made his second in command. This just gets better and better.*

"I wasn't aware," Konowa said, quickly adding, "sir."

"Not aware?" The Prince seemed to struggle with his breathing. "Not . . . no, of course you wouldn't be, would you?" Whatever internal battle the Prince had waged was over, for now. "In any event, you have been made my subordinate and I expect total and instant compliance with every order. The loyalty of the Iron Elves will not fail again."

The last part was said with the Prince's face mere inches from Konowa's. When Konowa still did not move, the Prince stepped back and turned away from him. There was the sound of a stopper being pulled from a bottle and then the tinkling gurgle of wine being poured into a glass. Konowa licked his lips and chided himself for being little more than a salivating dog. Damn the Prince!

"Begging Your Highness's pardon," Konowa said at last, his voice sounding like a cannon salvo under the tent, "time is of the essence. We should discuss the matter of reforming the regiment. Marshal Ruwl informed me that arrangements had been made. When can we expect the elves?"

The Prince tilted his head to one side as he looked at Konowa. "He didn't tell you, did he? Well, well. The marshal may be wary of your temper, but I am not. The elves are in the southern wastes, and that is exactly where they'll stay. I have dispatched men from my personal staff to purchase the necessary troops and supplies from the regiments in camp. The regiment will form from the very cream of the army located here."

It felt like a blow to the stomach. "Here, sir?" The cream of the army was most certainly not sweltering in the stinking sun of this camp. "But I thought the lads—the regiment was being called back. How can the Iron Elves be reformed without them?"

The Prince did not turn around, but Konowa heard the smirk in his voice. "The Iron Elves will henceforth be a regiment more agreeably integrated with men from the Empire."

"With all due respect, your Highness—"

"*It is done!*" the Prince shouted, spinning around to face him. "This regiment is *mine*, and I will command it as I see fit. Reconcile yourself to that, Major." He let out a slow breath and composed himself. "Now, the matter is closed. A toast," he said, motioning to a filled lead crystal glass on the table.

Konowa looked at the drink as if it were poison, but finally stepped forward and took it.

"To the glorious future of the Light Infantry of the Hynta," the Prince said.

Konowa stared at the Prince, his own glass stopped awkwardly halfway up to the sky.

"Do you dare challenge me thus?" the Prince asked, his eyes narrowing to slits.

This fool knows nothing. "No, sir, but one never toasts the regiment in that manner. We did not seek glory—quite the opposite. The proper toast is only given at midnight, sir, under a black moon," Konowa said, looking down at a stupid little man who would one day be King. *One quick blow to the neck would solve so many problems.*

"I knew that," the Prince said, looking at him with suspicion. "However, today we start a new tradition."

"Yes, of course, sir," Konowa said. Acting on an impulse before his better judgment could stop him, Konowa gulped his drink in a flick of the wrist. "To the glorious future of the Light Infantry of the Hynta. Long live the Iron Elves . . . and Men. May our enemies crumble before us!" he shouted, then threw his glass to the ground. The crystal shattered into hundreds of glittering pieces.

The Prince's eyes went wide and his mouth dropped open. He said nothing for a long moment. Konowa looked at him with the closest he could manage to complete innocence. A grin now would likely find him hanging from a noose.

The Prince finally downed his own drink and followed suit, breaking his own glass on the hard-packed dirt.

"You will explain to me later the traditional toast," the Prince said.

"Of course, Your Highness," Konowa said.

"Go collect my men."

"Yes, sir, at once," Konowa said, coming to attention. He offered the Prince a crisp salute before turning and stepping out of the tent, and into a whole new problem.

FOURTEEN

Konowa walked in a straight line, prepared to bludgeon the first person who crossed his path. Unfortunately, the first person was a horse, and Konowa's anger subsided into a crushing weight. This fool of a Prince was going to get them all killed.

"You appear to gravitate toward the more pungent these days," Jurwan Leaf Talker said, smiling broadly and startling Konowa as the wizard came around the other side of the horse.

Konowa shook his head. Too many musket salvos had permanently damaged his hearing.

"And you don't know when to leave well enough alone," Konowa said, walking past his father.

Jurwan reached out a hand, his fingertips brushing Konowa's arm. The touch was as light as a leaf floating on a stream, but it stopped him like a cannon firing canister shot at twenty yards. Bloody wizards.

"Judging by the color of your face and the tone of your voice, I'd say you've met the Prince," Jurwan said, chuckling softly, removing his hand to pat the horse's neck. His other hand reached into his hides and pulled out bits of keela fruit, which he offered to the animal. The red pulp dribbled down Jurwan's fingers as the horse nibbled at it, and Konowa felt a queasiness in his stomach.

"He is an arrogant little poppet who cares more about finding purple-winged moths and pleasing his mother than leading a regiment." Konowa kicked at a weed near his boot. "*Regiment.* It won't be anything close to what it was before. And when were you going to tell me the Iron Elves wouldn't actually have any elves in it?"

Jurwan slowly shook his head and clucked his tongue. He walked over to Konowa and bent down by his feet, gently straightening the weed. For an old elf, he still moved with fluid ease, a skill Konowa had long ago given up trying to master.

"The past is gone, my son, or at least, it used to be. For now, you must embrace the present, so that you may walk with a clear mind and free heart into the future, while being ever vigilant for that which went before you, for it may yet come again."

Konowa looked down at his father with wide eyes. "Is this mystical pap the counsel you give Ruwl? I mean, in between tending to blades of grass and injured mice?"

Jurwan stood up and smiled. "No, I only say it to annoy you, and because it's true. As for Ruwl, I tell him he needs to adapt to his surroundings, be open and malleable, not hard and stubborn, as some are wont to be. Oh, and that he should have more Tremkaberry tea shipped over from home. I find the local tea here rather bitter. Which reminds me," he continued, grabbing Konowa by the arm and steering him around the horse. "I am making dinner and am in need of a pair of strong hands to help me."

"I'm really not in the mood for roasted worms and grass soup, Father," Konowa said, allowing himself to be propelled along nonetheless.

"Wrong season for worms," Jurwan said absently, casting a quick glance down at the ground. "The earth is too dry at the moment; she waits for Sky Sister to cry."

Konowa looked up to the sky and sighed. "Rain, it's called rain. Look, is your tent much farther? I have many things to do before the regiment sets out on this mad adventure."

"And one of them is to eat a meal with your father, if that isn't too much to ask," Jurwan said, squeezing Konowa's arm as they walked. "Ah, here we are!"

"Where?" Konowa asked. Jurwan had taken him to the edge of the camp where an old willow tree bent over a stream. Its branches were thick with leaves and draped on the ground.

"*Muh ko ji,*" Jurwan said, and the branches parted. For a moment, Konowa's body tingled and he heard, or thought he heard, a very old, very wise voice answer his father. He pushed his senses outward and listened, but there was nothing more to hear.

"Come, we have arrived just in time," Jurwan called from inside.

Konowa shrugged and stepped through the hanging branches. They closed behind him with a soft swish, and he was inside a cozy and surprisingly cool dwelling that was not at all obvious from the outside.

A large bowl, sanded and carved to a fluid smoothness, floated above a small fire in the center of the floor. Konowa couldn't help but smile. His father had mastery, not that the old elf would call it that, over the elements of life, yet used his great skills to cook with a wooden pot. The flames curled around it, trying to feed on the wood, yet the bowl remained a beautiful satin brown, its surface completely unblemished. Inside it, water was just starting to boil, thin beads of air bubbles winding their way to the surface to release tiny wisps of steam.

"A fire within the confines of a tree, Father?" Konowa asked, walking around the small area and marveling at the coolness of the air. He undid the chinstrap of his shako and took it off, running a hand through his sweat-soaked hair.

"Balance in all things, my son," Jurwan said, sitting cross-legged on the grass floor in front of the fire and motioning for Konowa to do the same. "The fuel is dead wood, and I have ensured the flames do not feed on more than that."

"Black Spike would not have been impressed," Konowa said, regretting it immediately. Jurwan's bond brother, one of the mightiest Wolf Oaks to have grown in the deep forest, had been killed many years ago, and it was a loss Konowa knew the old elf felt deeply.

Jurwan shook his head. "Not at all. My *ryk faur,* like most of the Wolf Oaks, was far more pragmatic than the Long Watch make them out to be. Fire, like all elementals, is necessary, even desired at times. Should an elf shun water because he might drown, and so die of thirst? My bond brother would not begrudge me a warm meal, may his ashes bring life to those that follow."

"Sounds more reasonable than the woman I just met," Konowa said. His heartbeat quickened at the thought of her, but he wasn't sure if it was passion or frustration.

Jurwan's eyebrows rose in exaggerated surprise. "You're courting then? Well. Perhaps she can knock some sense into that thick head of yours."

Konowa waved the thought away. "She's elfkynan, some kind of witch, too, for that matter. Our views on the world aren't exactly in harmony."

"A witch," Jurwan said, his voice taking on a dreamy quality. "I do hope the grandchildren take after her."

"Easy, Father, she hasn't even bothered to see me since we arrived in camp," Konowa said, pacing around the fire. "Not that it matters."

Jurwan shook his head slowly, letting a small sigh escape his lips. "Be not so sure of what matters and what does not. Drops of rain become an ocean. And if courting hasn't changed completely since I was your age, I think she might be waiting for *you* to visit *her*."

"I've been rather busy, what with this lunacy I've been dragged into," he said, putting a halt to his pacing and choosing a fallen log as a seat.

"The grass would be better, my son," Jurwan said.

And the lessons in life begin. "You can burn wood but I can't sit on it?" Konowa asked, throwing his shako to the ground beside him. "Or is it only that I am in touch with nature if my backside is flat on the earth?"

Jurwan began unfolding a cloth-wrapped bundle. "Don't be silly. But you may wish to reconsider your seat, as it is full of ants—a type of biting ant, actually."

The log soared through the branches as Konowa jumped to his feet and began to beat at his trousers.

Jurwan made a tut-tut sound and shook his head. "A whole year alone in the forest. It's a wonder *you* didn't burn it down."

Konowa glared at his father, but the old elf was busy arranging a group of vegetables for the cooking pot. He sighed and walked around to the other side of the fire to sit down, checking the ground carefully before he did so.

Jurwan handed him a thin wooden blade and a potato. Konowa hefted the knife and was pleased with its balance and weight. He twirled it between his fingers, faster and faster. It felt warm and comfortable in his hand and the edge gleamed with a sharpness to match any fire-forged blade.

"The potato will not hurt you," Jurwan said, peering down his nose at Konowa.

Konowa stopped twirling the knife and began cutting slices of the potato into the pot, gently sliding each chunk into the water.

"You haven't told me what you think about all of this," Konowa said.

"There is only one world," Jurwan replied, passing Konowa two carrots and a small pouch filled with a tangy-smelling spice. "All of us, from the smallest insect to the largest mountain, must live within it, and in harmony with one another."

"You missed your calling, Father—you should have been a courtier. You manage to say something and nothing at the same time." Konowa sighed dramatically as he diced the carrots with quick, smooth flicks of the knife. When he was done, he upended the pouch with the spice into the bowl, turning the water a rich brown color and filling the air with a tantalizing aroma.

Jurwan wasn't paying attention, handing Konowa a red kelsa root and some bright-green sprigs of reimoni. "Stir the water, keep everything moving," Jurwan said. He rocked back on his heels, looking up at the hanging branches, which suddenly parted to allow a thin shaft of sunlight to shine down in front of him. "The Empire thinks like the bull dragon. Exert enough force and it can impose its will. Bite, and bite hard, and it can kill anything. In this the Empire believes, so it seeks out that which it does not understand but nonetheless fears, and in finding it, would control it, or kill it."

"Yes, but the bull dragon, when using its wings, can walk across a frozen lake, fishing between the cracks without falling in." Konowa sat up a little straighter, pleased to be able to use one of the old elf's homilies against him for a change.

"More than fish swim beneath the ice, my son, but the dragon only sees its own reflection."

"Is there a moral to this story anywhere in the near future?"

Jurwan looked at his son with raised eyebrows and motioned for him to get back to the pot. "Only young bulls seek out opponents. The older, wiser ones lie in wait."

Konowa thought about that as he used the knife to stir the pot, adding more carrots and herbs between swirls. A chunk of potato bobbed to the surface, its already golden-brown hue a clear sign the soup was nearly done.

"If I didn't know better, Father, I'd say you were trying to warn me." Konowa watched the potato bob on the surface. He stabbed it with the tip of the knife and brought it to his mouth.

"Patience!" Jurwan scolded, slapping Konowa's hand down and sending the potato flying back into the pot. "And if you would open your mind as wide as you do your mouth, you might benefit from it."

Konowa rubbed his hand and looked at his father. "I've been heeding warnings all my life," he said, pointing to his ruined ear.

Jurwan looked at him and for a moment Konowa saw not the always-sage wizard, but a very worried parent.

"Your destiny is your own," Jurwan said at last.

When had that ever been true? Konowa wondered. "I know our history, Father. Somehow, in the world before this one, Her hand touched me as it did so many others, and I was marked, an elf destined for the Shadow Monarch's realm. *Tokma ka æri.*"

Jurwan's voice grew louder and the wizard was back. "*Nothing forged in fire* is the mantra of the Long Watch, but it is not the only way. Do not think you know everything you think you know."

Konowa's head was already in too much pain to work that all the way through. "The Iron Elves were the tainted ones, Father, and we did our best to prove everyone wrong. We joined the Empire to fight against our destiny, and for a better future, and what did we get for it?"

"So this is your excuse for all you've done to yourself these last few years? Self-pity?"

Konowa pounded the ground beside him with his fist. "I didn't choose to be born with a black ear tip! I didn't court-martial myself! I didn't banish myself to the forest, and I certainly didn't volunteer to be an outcast!" he shouted.

"And yet you live as if you did," Jurwan said, motioning for Konowa to keep stirring.

Riddles and tests, always a new challenge. Growing up, Father had been like a shadow at dusk, teaching with questions, guiding with silence, never scolding, and never praising. His mother, on the other hand . . .

"Would not approve of either of us at the moment," Jurwan remarked.

"Damn it, Father!" Konowa said, the hairs on the back of his neck shivering. "I hate it when you do that."

Jurwan stared at his son in mock surprise. "My dear boy, you are as obvious as the night after the setting sun. It is no great feat to listen to the flow of life around you and follow its natural course." He held up his hands and waggled his fingers at Konowa, gently mocking him. "I can see you took the stories of the Long Watch a little closer to your heart than I imagined. I blame myself for letting your mother teach you that, but she was determined you would join us as *ryk fauri* and prove the birth omen wrong."

"And you?" Konowa asked, wondering where this was all leading. "You adhere to the old ways. This shelter, the cooking pot, the hides you wear, even the way you talk. If I didn't know better, I'd say you had a change of heart about steering me toward the Empire."

Konowa said it in jest, and was completely unprepared for Jurwan's response.

"Perhaps. If you had stayed with the tribe, we would not be in this land, and you would not be embarking on this quest for the Eastern Star."

The two sat in sudden silence, both staring at the fire.

"Father," Konowa finally said, "do you really believe it is true? A red shooting star falling in the east here? And now buried under some dung heap in Luuguth Jor, and the Viceroy come back to life?"

Jurwan's answer shook Konowa to his bones. "The rakkes are real enough, and I have seen things that make me believe the rest is true as well. And though you have chosen not to tell me, you have dreamed of Her recently."

"How did you know that?"

For an answer, Jurwan looked up to the branches overhead and whispered something. A moment later a single willow leaf came fluttering down to land in his outstretched hand. As Konowa stared, the leaf stood perfectly upright in his father's palm, slowly turning. Jurwan studied the leaf for several seconds, then closed his eyes. There was a rustle of wind in the branches above their heads and suddenly dozens of leaves were falling, but many were from different trees. Konowa pushed apart the wall of willow branches to look outside. A strong wind was snapping banners and chasing dust clouds high into the air.

"The rakke knew your name," Jurwan said.

Konowa turned back to his father, now surrounded by a pile of leaves on the ground.

"It doesn't anymore."

Jurwan nodded. "She's reaching out far and wide, beckoning to those who would serve Her. A black, cold flame in the night, invisible to most, but not all."

Konowa stirred the pot so hard he splashed some of the soup into the fire. "Serve the Shadow Monarch? I'd kill Her just like I killed Her servant."

"Not quite the threat it was a year ago," Jurwan said, winking at his son, "but I have no doubt you would oppose the Shadow Monarch with every fiber of your being."

Konowa was in no mood to be placated. How could his father not see the only course of action open to them? "The Iron Elves should be called back and then the entire Imperial Army should be sent against Her mountain. What will killing the Viceroy all over again achieve? We should go after *Her*."

Jurwan shook his head. "She is strong now, much stronger than She has ever been. Her trees have dug deep into the mountain, feeding on a power they were never meant to taste. A direct assault would end in disaster. No, Luuguth Jor is where you must go, and quickly."

"With the Prince in command?" Konowa asked. Thoughts of the man made him grip the knife harder, his knuckles whitening. "What does His Highness know about fighting?"

"Consider that this is the Queen's son, the future King and ruler of the Empire," Jurwan said, reaching over and tapping Konowa on the hand so that his grip relaxed. "You have an opportunity to shape the monarch-in-waiting. Think what it would mean if you could convince him that the lands of the Hynta elves were best left to us."

Konowa looked at his father with genuine surprise. "The past is gone, Father. The Hynta's only hope is in embracing the future. You know I think this idea of the Queen's, if it really is Her idea, to be a complete farce, but this Empire isn't going away, and with each passing year it grows stronger. The Long Watch will have precious little to watch over if they don't accept that."

"The Long Watch have seen the rise and fall of more than one empire. Do not be so sure it won't bear witness to the demise of this one, too."

"Then help me, Father, help me to destroy Her. Convince Ruwl to call back the Iron Elves before it's too late."

Jurwan shook his head. "The more I think on this, the more I am happy that they are far away. She would try to turn them, too. No, better they stay where they are for now."

"Then what should I do?" Konowa asked.

Jurwan acted as if he had not heard him. "I received a message from your mother. The Long Watch are very worried."

Konowa sighed. "The Long Watch are always worried; it's their nature. They fight for a past that is gone. I'm worried about the here and now."

"It is the here and now that is *becoming* the past that has them worried," Jurwan said. "Many said we should burn everything and put an end to Her."

Konowa leaned forward. "Burn it? I can't imagine the Elves of the Long Watch burning a forest, not even Her forest."

"Probably not. Their compassion for all living things is a heavy burden. I fear before long we will reap a bitter harvest from this." He hesitated for a moment, then reached out his hand and gave Konowa a small pouch.

"More spice? Unless you want me to kill rakkes with my cooking, I'll need more than this."

The pouch felt heavy and cold. Konowa undid the leather thong and looked inside.

There was only blackness. Without pausing, he reached down with a finger to see what trickery was going on. His finger touched something freezing and hard.

"Wh—" was all he had time to say before a stabbing pain entered his finger like a thin stiletto of ice. He pulled it away and brought his finger to his lips. Immediately a bolt of lightning surged through his body, leaving him trembling and panting. He watched with open-mouthed amazement as Jurwan reached over and took the pouch from his other hand, tied up the thong, and set it down on the ground.

"It's an acorn from Her *ryk faur*, the silver Wolf Oak She would not let die," Jurwan said, his face giving nothing away. "You have carried a great burden all these years, my son, bearing the mark of otherness with a strength and pride that has served our people well, though they choose not to see it. You did not bond with a Wolf Oak and join the ranks of the Long Watch, yet you, and those elves like you, have protected the Hynta and its forests at a great cost. The Iron Elves live again, and I think this time, they deserve more than the scorn of their people."

"But this is—"

Jurwan held up his hand. "Help, I believe, when you need it most. Until then, leave it be. Now," Jurwan said, smiling again, "stir the soup, my son. Adventures, however ill-advised, are better met on a full stomach . . . and you'll need your strength if I'm to have grandchildren any time soon."

Konowa did as he was asked, but he was no longer hungry. He stared down at the leather pouch on the ground. The full import of what he was embarking on was only just starting to seep into his understanding, the chances of success slim to remote.

"But real all the same," Jurwan said, taking the knife from his son's hand and stirring the soup himself. "Let us hope it is enough."

FIFTEEN

Konowa crumpled the leaflet in his hand and let it fall to the ground. The only path they were likely to tread in the coming days was one washed with blood. He looked up and started walking toward the parade square where the new regiment was being formed.

Everything was moving too fast, and all in the wrong direction.

Just a week ago, his biggest concern had been getting smothered by mosquitoes in the forest. Now he was enmeshed in a web of events he didn't begin to understand, but he knew he'd better if he and the regiment were going to survive. Nothing that had happened to him so far gave him much hope, especially the notion that there was a shadowy hand guiding things as his father suggested. He instinctively patted his coat, where the pouch Jurwan had given him was tucked away. He was constantly reaching for it, a little worried that he should suddenly feel so attached to the blackness held within. Every so often he would feel a sensation as if the leather had been worn away, allowing the cold smoothness of the acorn's shell to rub against his skin, sending a sudden chill coursing through his body. Despite the heat, it was a feeling he could have done without. Each time it happened, he felt tempted to open it up and look inside, and each time he fought it. His life was growing increasingly more complicated by the day without adding to its difficulties by ignoring a wizard's warning. Perhaps, he mused, his newfound restraint boded well.

"Get your hard head back to the wagons. The regiment isn't accepting any dwarves!"

As usual, Konowa was dead wrong. He looked up to see a large group of soldiers milling about the parade square as a sergeant yelled at a dwarf soldier. Konowa recognized the dwarf as the one Jir had taken an interest in.

"Trouble?" Konowa asked. Jaal had recommended Sergeant Lorian be promoted as the Iron Elves' regimental sergeant major and Konowa had happily agreed. As with most of the details, the Prince had neglected to find an RSM and no regiments would give theirs up. Konowa came to a halt in front of the troops and returned Lorian's salute while the soldiers came to attention. It was still taking Konowa by surprise—the only salute he'd received in the forest had been Jir lifting his leg.

"No, sir, I was just culling the herd. The Prince's leaflet has attracted quite a few volunteers, including this dwarf."

It was said evenly enough, but Lorian clearly disapproved of the soldiers gathered around them. Not that Konowa blamed the man, a career soldier and proud of his service. The collection of troops before them *was* appalling. Every regiment, regular army, and those assigned to protect the Trading Company had taken the Prince's gold and selected the very worst from within its ranks. It appeared that every corner of the Empire was represented. There was a group of black-skinned warriors from the southern islands, the number of battles they had participated in marked in scarring lines on their cheekbones, and even a pair of pale, pasty fellows with corn-yellow hair who could only be from the northern fishing enclaves of the Dirilza. Konowa knew there wasn't a weedier, rougher-looking group of soldiers assembled anywhere within the Empire at that very moment.

Of course, there was one bright exception. Before he'd left, the Duke of Rakestraw had convinced five of his hussars to transfer to the reformed Iron Elves: four veteran troopers and, of course, Sergeant now Regimental Sergeant Major Dhareg Lorian, the latest in a growing list of those who had tried to kill Konowa on first meeting. They weren't elves, but they were first-class soldiers, and that was rare enough.

Konowa turned his attention to the dwarf.

"A dwarf, you say? Well, that would certainly explain his height," Konowa said, giving the soldier a quick appraisal. Little more than four feet tall, he was as broad as any two elves across the shoulders. Obvious intelligence sparkled in a pair of clear blue eyes, about the only feature of his face besides a squashed nose that his beard of tangled black hair, in which the remnants of his breakfast still clung, didn't obscure. His uniform looked like a collection of rags held together by spells instead of stitching, but his boots were sturdy and well polished and his double-barreled shatterbow and the scabbard for his drukar gleamed with obvious care.

The dwarf's mouth opened and closed, but then he nodded and smiled. "You have a keen mind you have, sir. I was tellin' my mate Alwyn here that very thing I was. That officer there, I said, he's a bright one. I like to be forthright an' honest like a good sigger should in explaining to these youngsters the ways and means of the world, keeping in mind the vagaries of service to her Blessed Majesty all the while—"

"Can you read, Private?" Konowa asked, cutting him off.

"Oh, yes, sir, Major. See my pay book," he said, lifting the top of his shako and pulling out a small red booklet and opening it to the first page. "Says Private Yimt Arkhorn right across the top there."

Konowa looked. There were a multitude of marks and notations for transgressions of military law and good order, most falling under the infamous four-letter rubric BWTD—Brawling-Whoring-Thieving-Drinking. The area for rank had clearly been erased and rewritten several times. "It appears that it used to say Sergeant Arkhorn, Royal Engineers. That's a long way from nursemaiding wagon trains."

Private Arkhorn coughed. "Misunderstandings and out-and-out jealousy, sir. Some folk just aren't as keen to serve Her Majesty as others, you see, and they resent those of us like you and me who excel, if you take my meaning. You can't make a spell without breaking a few crystal balls, as me grandmare used to say, but alas, not everyone holds to that philosophy."

"Impertinent little rat," Lorian growled, taking a step closer. "He's been busted more times than I've had hot dinners, Major."

Konowa flipped through the pay book and was astounded to see paymaster stamps dating back over thirty years, from virtually every major campaign and battle the Imperial Army had fought in. He handed back the pay book and raised his hand. "And seen more fighting, too. However, that doesn't address our problem. If you can read, Private, then you'd know the call for troops excluded dwarves."

"Begging the Major's pardon, but that's not true," he said. To prove his point, he lifted the top of his shako again and pulled out one of the leaflets, turned it upside down, and pointed to the part about dwarves. "See here, in black ink it says dwarves need not apply? Well, that's as plain as the wart on a witch's teat. Means dwarves are automatically accepted; we don't even *need* to apply."

Konowa looked away momentarily to hide the smile on his face. Lorian, however, had just about lost it.

"This is absurd, sir," Lorian interrupted. "The dwarf is making a mockery of the call for volunteers. The Iron Elves—"

"Is now made up of humans," Konowa said calmly, looking at the sergeant, "so adding a dwarf doesn't seem all that troublesome."

"But his teeth, sir, look at them. He's one of them rock eaters."

"Eat rocks?" the dwarf roared. "What kind of mad-hatter do you take me for, begging your pardon, sir. You don't eat them, you *chew* them."

Konowa had indeed noticed the pewter-colored set of teeth in the dwarf's mouth.

"Grew up in the mines did you, Urilian Mountains?" Konowa asked.

The dwarf nodded. "That I did, sir. Was noshing my first bit of crute afore I was even weaned. Bit tough on me dear old ma'am. But not to worry, I ain't lit off a cartridge yet on account I use Lil' Nipper here," he said, patting the shatterbow affectionately. "The range is a tad shorter than a musket, but she makes up for it in wallop. Been in the family for years. It was my aunt's, you know." He smiled, his metal-impregnated teeth glinting like newly minted coins.

Konowa turned to Lorian. "He could probably ignite every cartridge and shell from here to Calahr with that silver tongue of his, so I don't think there's much point worrying about his teeth. We're going to need every able-bodied soldier we can get. He can stay. In fact," Konowa said, stepping away from the troops so they could all see him, "any sigger that wants to tread that path of glory and prove himself can stay. I don't care what you've done up to this point, and I don't care who you are. From this moment on, you are Iron Elves, and if you aren't the finest troops in all the lands right now, you will be." Konowa refrained from adding the postscript: *or you'll be dead.*

A bugle call sounded from over by the Prince's marquee, three long, two short, two long. Konowa grimaced then resumed a look of nonchalance as he turned and headed back to see what the Prince wanted now. The voice of Private Arkhorn carried on the air like the squawk of a nattering magpie.

"See that, I told you I'd convince him!"

"But you were complaining ever since Corporal Kritton volunteered us. You said that joining the Hintys was a one-way ticket to death and glory," another soldier said.

"Glory and death, Ally," the dwarf corrected him, "glory and death. The key is to get them in the right order, and make sure there is a lot of space between them so you can enjoy the first."

"You think we'll get a chance for that?"

"Ally," Arkhorn said, his voice dropping low so that Konowa could barely hear it, "I think we'll get more chances than we can use in a lifetime."

"They are absolutely despicable!"

Konowa barely nodded. The air was already thick with heat and his head still ached from his overindulgence with Jaal. He'd never fully appreciated the relative coolness of the forests of this land, as well as their lack of Sala brandy and persuasive friends.

Prince Tykkin stamped a boot on the ground, sending up a lazy cloud of dust. "The colonels have taken advantage of my generosity and given me nothing but dregs. These soldiers are a disgrace." He paused and took a deep breath. "Major?"

"Yes, sir?"

"Is that a dwarf?"

Konowa followed the Prince's stare and saw Private Yimt Arkhorn at the end of it, all four blustery, roguish feet of him.

"Yes, sir, a veteran, sir, twelve campaigns. He was in Rewland with your father thirty years ago. I asked around, and he's as good a sigger as you're likely to find."

The Prince sniffed at the word *sigger*, and it occurred to Konowa that in His Highness's refined circles nicknames, especially crude ones, were not in vogue.

"What's he doing here?" the Prince asked. His voice had climbed an octave and his cheeks were blushing like a pair of polished apples.

"The regiment needs veterans who know one end of a bayonet from the other, no matter what their race. When the spell is cast and we're in the thick of it, all that matters is balls, sir, musket and soldier. We'll need both."

Prince Tykkin's eyes opened wider at Konowa's analogy, but the words apparently had an effect, because he remained quiet for several moments.

"Major?"

Konowa surveyed the troops and tried to anticipate which one had drawn the Prince's attention this time. The possibilities were too great. "Sir?"

"There's a soldier wearing spectacles. And that one over there has only one eye."

Konowa looked to where the Prince was pointing and sure enough, one of the new soldiers had a black patch over the socket of his right eye. The entire side of his face look ravaged from disease, but Konowa knew better.

"A misfire from his firelock," Konowa said, "the powder went off in his face. It happens when the metal gets hot from steady firing, especially with inferior muskets. The metal weakens and instead of sending the blast down the barrel, it bursts it at the lock, right where the soldier puts his cheek."

"The man should be invalided home, or placed in the commissary division," the Prince said. "How am I to build a regiment with material like that?"

"RSM!" Konowa shouted, pointing at Lorian. "Bring me that man at once."

The one-eyed soldier was unceremoniously yanked out of ranks and double-timed over to stand panting in front of the Prince and Konowa.

"Private Meri Fwynd, Y-your Highness, sir, Major," he said, bringing his right hand up to his ruined eye in salute.

"Private, the Iron Elves were once, and will be again, the finest regiment in Her Majesty's Army," Konowa said. "Why should Prince Tykkin have a cripple such as yourself in the ranks?"

"I ain't no cripple, sir," he said, his face flushing red. "Sure, I lost an eye an' the ladies don't look at me the same no more, but I can still put a ball through a piece of meat at two hundred paces and I can march till my feet are bloody stumps, sir! I won't let you or the Prince down, I promise you that."

"We'll see," Konowa said noncommittally, secretly proud of the soldier's outburst. "Return to the ranks; dismissed."

As the man saluted again and double-timed it back to the regiment, the Prince turned to face Konowa.

"What answers am I likely to get if we poll the rest of the soldiers?" he asked, the sarcasm in his voice noticeably absent this time.

"Versions of Private Fwynd. The dwarf has teeth worth a lieutenant's commission, but he knows his business. Damn near—pardon me, sir—darn near talked the point off my other ear. In fact, he and the one with spectacles shot and killed that rakke the other night at the piquet lines. Of course, they're not all good lads. We have more than our fair share of louts, thieves, ruffians, and wastrels, but I'd bet my life that they'll hold when the time comes."

For several moments the Prince said nothing, staring at Konowa without really seeing him. Finally, he spoke.

"They had better. If they run, it won't be an enemy bayonet they have to worry about, but an Imperial noose." With that he turned and walked away.

"And all you'll have to worry about is them deciding whether to run you through before the enemy does," Konowa said under his breath.

He stood there for a long time, watching the soldiers who would once again carry the name Iron Elves into battle.

SIXTEEN

The following morning, the soldiers were on the point of mutiny.

Lorian had formed them into a hollow square and was issuing new uniforms and equipment out of two wagons. Konowa didn't need to be there, but something told him he should, just in case.

"I'm not wearing no dress!" Yimt yelled, tossing the offending item to the ground.

"Hold your tongue, you poxy dog!" Lorian roared back, stepping between Konowa and the soldiers. "You'll do exactly as you're told or it'll be the taste of rawhide on your back! You were eager enough yesterday to join."

"That was afore I knew you had to wear a dress!"

Konowa reached down and picked up the cloth, a rough, black wool overlaid with a dark-green vine and leaf pattern, and gently brushed the dirt from it. Another brilliant idea of the Prince's. "This is a *caerna*, a broad cloth worn wrapped around the waist. It's cut so that it's as long as a soldier is tall, which allows it to be wrapped around your waist two and a half times, and wide enough to cover from waist to knee. It was the fashion in Calahr some two hundred years ago and was considered a sign of honor, for only warriors could wear it."

"That's all well and good, sir," Yimt said, keeping a wary eye on Lorian, "but it looks like a dress to me."

The other soldiers chimed in, nodding and voicing their agreement.

"Besides, the Hintys didn't wear no dresses, er, caernas, afore when you were in charge, sir."

Konowa paused a moment before responding. The troops grew quiet, recognizing that they had reached the limit of an officer's indulgence. "Let's be perfectly clear," Konawa said, staring down any lingering resentment, "the colonel of this regiment, its knight superior, is His Highness the Prince. It is completely within his prerogative to attire the regiment as he sees fit, and he has done so. He has decreed that the Iron Elves adopt a new tradition in keeping with its resurrection, and in order to ensure a glorious future," he said. He hoped his sarcasm wasn't obvious; the men needed to trust their leaders. Without that, the regiment was doomed. "Some of this will no doubt seem odd at first, but you will get used to it . . . and you *will* follow orders."

"Will the Prince and the major be wearing them then?" Yimt asked. The silence was palpable as the men waited for Konowa's reply.

"The Prince has also decreed that all officers are to be mounted, and therefore will wear a trousered version of the caerna." The reaction he got wasn't a full-on revolt.

Private Arkhorn scratched his beard. "On horses? But what about when we form line and go into battle? Surely you'll come down then? You'll be as obvious as dragons in a pigeon coop up there."

Lorian snorted. "I've been in my share of cavalry charges with barely a scratch on me."

"That's all well and good, sir," the dwarf said, "but I'd wager you were going a mite faster than a foot regiment formed in line. The major here will be head and shoulders above us and moving at a snail's pace. The bastards in the enemy line will be drawn to him like flies to blood."

Konowa could have done without that particular analogy, especially as the dwarf was right. Sitting on a horse with a line regiment was akin to painting a target on yourself. Perhaps the Prince was trying to prove something to mother dearest back home.

"You just look after the boys to your left and right, and the officers will take care of themselves," Konowa said, with far more conviction than he felt. In fact, the more he thought about things, the less sure he felt about any of it. They were leaving in less than an hour, woefully unprepared to do so. They barely had enough "volunteers" to make up three companies of ninety men each plus the regimental staff and a handful of artificers. They had no surgeon and a colonel with no experience. Worse, they had no wizard. Konowa had thought his father would accompany them, but Jurwan had said he had other matters to attend to. What could be more important than this? Whatever it was, it meant the regiment was 313 souls, less than half of what the first battalion of a regiment should have. The leather pouch his father had given him now felt as light and insubstantial as the hope they had of surviving.

"A few tricks hidden away then, Major?" Yimt asked. The other soldiers visibly relaxed when they heard this. They were eager to believe the Iron Elves were imbued with mystical powers, ignoring the fact that the regiment had been unceremoniously disbanded and sent packing without so much as a puff of magical smoke, unless vanishing without a trace had been magic.

Konowa was nonplussed for a moment, his hand halfway to the pouch before he caught himself. "Here, here, and here," he said, recovering his composure and pointing to his head, heart, and crotch. "Think with your head and fight with your heart and you'll be fine."

"Uh, Major, sir?" the private with spectacles asked. He was pale, skinny, and scared, not exactly the Empire's finest. "What about the, um, third bit?"

Konowa looked around at the soldiers and smiled. "Find a willing lady, she'll show you," he said, to a great roar of approval. He turned to Lorian. "RSM, we move out in an hour. I expect to see every last man, elf, and dwarf in full uniform, no exceptions."

"Yes, sir!" Lorian said, saluting Konowa before turning back to the troops. "You heard the major. I want a pile of all your old kit over here, now! You there, four-eyes, any idea how to wear this thing? Look, someone find someone who can show me how to put this on!"

Konowa walked away, leaving Lorian to work it out. He chose a route behind a row of tents bordering a thick copse of tall, sharp-edged jimik. If there had been any kind of breeze he wouldn't have dared walk near a patch of sword grass. Each blade was over four feet tall and as sharp as any forged weapon. He'd once seen a panicked ox charge straight into a stand of jimik. The poor beast had bled out in less than two minutes, but the men had eaten well that night.

As Konowa continued on his way, the immutable truth of the situation hit him: The Shadow Monárch was looking for him. He'd always believed there was more than a little truth to the legends, but until the rakkes it had been easy to push the thought aside. Less easy to dismiss was the question of why She was interested in him and why so many Hynta elves had been born with black ear tips. He tried to recall moments in his life when he'd felt drawn to commit evil, and while there was much blood on his hands, he couldn't say that he'd ever felt anything call to him with black intent, certainly not Her.

He walked on, trying to puzzle it through, and realized something else was vying for his attention. Konowa slowed, trying to make sense of what he felt. The back of his neck tingled and his skin had grown cold again. He reached up and shifted the pouch under his jacket. The feeling got stronger. Konowa stopped walking and closed his eyes, letting his senses flow out around him. There was the usual chaos of smells and sounds, voices and sensations that swirled together into a maelstrom of everything and nothing at once. This time however, he didn't give up, but pushed himself to keep trying. The cacophony of life remained, but now he could feel a path through it, as if a force were parting the fog in front of him. In a sudden burst of red emotion he saw, or rather felt, a figure moving toward him. He opened his eyes, and for perhaps the first time in over a week, was not surprised to find someone wanting to kill him.

"It's been a long time, *ruij-ki*," hissed a voice, one that transported Konowa back to the night he had killed the Viceroy.

Corporal Kritton stood before him. It *had* been a long time since Konowa last saw his face, but there was no mistaking the twisted mask of rage that glared at him now. It was the same look he'd worn at Luuguth Jor when he threatened to kill Konowa if he attacked the Viceroy. Kritton had seen the repercussions Konowa hadn't, but killing the Viceroy had been the right thing to do, no matter the cost.

"You call me leader in our native tongue yet I hear no honor in it," Konowa said, breaking eye contact in hopes of averting the inevitable. Kritton's knuckles were white as he gripped his musket, giving Konowa little hope he could. The elf had emerged from between the tents, pinning Konowa with his back to the jimik. The only way out was through him.

"Do you expect it?" Kritton asked, saying each word through clenched teeth. Drops of spittle dribbled down his chin. "Do you believe I would honor the elf who betrayed us all? We followed you, we trusted you. Save our tribe, and our people, you said. Join the Empire, change it from the inside." He turned his head slightly to show his own ruined ear. "It was our destiny, you said, the fate of the marked ones unfit to become *ryk faur*."

The contents of the pouch in Konowa's jacket trembled as if frantic to be released. "And I believe it still."

The expression on Kritton's face finally changed, to one of surprise. "You have the gall to say that after allowing *pwal gor* into the Iron Elves?"

Konowa winced at the slur. *Impure.* Throughout his youth, it had been used against him and those like him. "Humans and dwarves are part of the greater world. If we are to preserve the Hynta, we must learn to deal with them, and the other races, too."

Kritton sneered. "Is the regiment to be nothing more than a collection of refuse then?"

The hilt of his saber was in his hand before Konowa had realized it. He forced his hand to release its grip. "Times have changed. The Prince himself has raised the regiment and thus will fill its ranks as he sees fit." That wasn't entirely true. Konowa had taken the dwarf both because he was a tough veteran and because it pleased him to know it annoyed the Prince. "But surely you could have stopped the dwarf; he was assigned to the Trading Company like you."

This time Kritton looked away, and Konowa made the connection. "You put him up to it," he said, unable to keep the surprise from his voice. "A test to see what I would do."

Kritton clearly was like many of the marked ones, never having come to terms with who they were. For them, the shame and guilt of being impure was a consuming force. Unable to join the Long Watch, they had created a belief that if they fought hard enough in service to the Hynta, the Wolf Oaks would one day accept them and purify their tainted souls of Her touch. To this end, they chose to serve the very Empire that threatened their ancestral home and a way of life that they could not wholly participate in, and fought like demons in the hope that one day they could. Having suffered from prejudice their whole lives, they were nonetheless eager to form a pure regiment of marked elves alone, and for its part, the Empire had welcomed these fierce warriors and used their rage against her enemies.

"A test, and you failed," Kritton said. His grip on his musket never loosened, but his voice began to shake. "The Iron Elves were once proud and noble. Now the regiment is no different from any other."

Konowa shook his head. The blackness resting against his chest pulsed in time with his heart, pumping cold ichor through his veins. "You are wrong, Takoli," Konowa said, using Kritton's Hynta name. "The regiment is very different. You'll have to trust me."

Kritton's eyes grew wide and his head pulled back as if he had been slapped. "Trust you? We trusted you once and where are the others now?"

"I am doing everything I can to get them back. But how is it that you are not among them?" Konowa asked.

"My attempts to stop you from killing the Viceroy were viewed as proving my loyalty to the crown, and for that I was spared the fate of the others. I was allowed to remain as a shining example," Kritton said. His mouth twisted as if the very words were bitter on his tongue.

"I am truly sorry, Takoli."

The elf's eyes glared. "Takoli is dead! I should have killed you when I had the chance."

"I expected it," Konowa said truthfully. "And after I was court-martialed, I waited in the forest for one of you to find me, but no one came. Perhaps the real reason elves like you can't join the Long Watch is that your forest craft is not good enough."

Kritton bared his teeth and stepped a few inches closer. "I could track you down anywhere, even if you fled to Her forest. But I am no fool. Your father is Ruwl's pet wizard. He walks in the spirit world, wields great power. He would protect you."

Konowa snorted. "My father could have done nothing even if he had wanted to, which he wouldn't. Some battles are an elf's to fight alone." The cold burned him as no fire ever had. He knew in a way that both thrilled and terrified him that he could reach out and kill Kritton with a single touch, and it was becoming increasingly difficult to fight that urge.

"Easily said when all the other elves are banished."

Konowa bristled at the words and took a step forward. "Enough! I offer you no more than what I offered you the first time: the opportunity to serve Her Majesty and this Empire. Do it with honor, and with conviction, and we will serve the Hynta as well. Now, either attack and accept the consequences or learn your place. I do not have time for the weak-willed."

The sound of boots heralded the approach of many troops, cutting off Kritton's reply.

"Is there a problem, Major?" Lorian said, coming around a tent with several soldiers behind him.

Konowa looked at Kritton, who returned his gaze with one of pure hatred before turning away. The acorn was no longer cold against Konowa's breast. It was as if a string holding him upright had been cut, and he had to concentrate on not falling down. Sweat beaded on his face and everything appeared blurred around the edges.

"No, no trouble at all. I was just getting reacquainted with an old friend."

Lorian didn't look as if he was buying it, but he knew enough to let it go. "Well, if you're done with the reunion I could really use the corporal's help in getting the new troops squared away."

Konowa nodded. "We're done, for now. I'll see you on the parade square," he said, not waiting for a salute. He turned and walked away, the blades of jimik looming mere inches from his side.

Konowa walked as fast as he could, but not fast enough to escape the cold, black warning that pressed against his heart.

SEVENTEEN

Now this is a sendoff," Yimt said as he marched beside Alwyn. "The Duke of Rakestraw is all right, even if he is a higher-than-thou."

Alwyn looked over and down to see the dwarf's head turned to the right, watching the band of the Fourteenth Household Cavalry play them out of camp. Their instruments gleamed under a pale blue sky dominated by the fiery white sun. Alwyn didn't recognize the tune, and couldn't tell if it was for good luck or good riddance, but it was bouncy and loud and it felt good, especially as it took his mind off the heat.

"I thought the cavalry had gone west," Alwyn said, mopping sweat from his face with the back of a sleeve. He then ran a hand over his face and held it out in front of him, pleased to see that the jacket's dye hadn't run. *Maybe there were benefits to being in a regiment with a Prince as its colonel.*

Yimt turned back to face straight ahead, the wings on his shako flapping slightly as he strode along. "Charging around at their own shadows like a flock of witless pigeons," he said.

Alwyn nodded, his eyes drawn to the sound of fluttering cloth up ahead. They had unfurled the Colors. Perhaps only the Queen Herself commanded more loyalty than the pair of square flags each regiment was given. The flags, always cotton with fine wool stitching (silk was for ladies' unmentionables, the recruiting sergeant had said, buying Alwyn another beer and pushing the enlistment parchment in front of him), hung from eight-foot-tall halberds carried by two color sergeants designated to protect them with their lives. Six very tough-looking soldiers, and that was saying something considering the recruiting pool, marched beside them, tasked in turn with protecting the color sergeants. It wasn't much of a walk to say that in turn the regiment looked after them. To lose a Color on the field of battle was worse even than running in the face of the enemy, so long as you took the Colors with you.

The dominant flag was the Queen's Colors, replete with the royal cypher of intricately woven letters and leafy garlands on a shimmering silver-green background. Rumor had it that the silver in the flag was real spun metal, but its worth as a symbol far outweighed however many ounces of precious metal might have been contained in it. The second was the Regimental Colors, a black flag with the national ensign of Calahr in the top left corner, while the main body of the flag featured a mountain range outlined in silver above a dark-green forest. Elvish script arced across this in steel-colored embroidery, which read *Æri Mekah*—Into the Fire. Alwyn felt both pride and fear at those words.

"Blast, the music stopped already," Yimt said.

Alwyn listened and realized the band wasn't playing anymore, but a new and exceedingly unpleasant sound had taken its place.

"Them ain't the Iron Elves! Look more like the Rusty Remains to me!"

"Hey you! You, the short, fat elf. What happened, did you fall out of a tree on your head?"

"We can relax now, boys, the Steel Faeries are here to save us."

Alwyn gripped his musket and glared back at the soldiers.

Yimt chuckled and patted Alwyn on the hand. "Pay them no mind, Ally, they're just jealous. Besides, remember that notion, sticks and stones and all that? There ain't nothing they can say that should bother you."

"Nice dresses, ladies!"

Yimt was a small, fast blur as he charged out of the ranks. "It's a caerna, you flea-bitten jockey!" he yelled, shaking his fist in the air to shouts of laughter.

Several band members dabbed at their eyes with handkerchiefs and clutched their sides as Yimt stomped around shouting curses that involved physical acts of self-pleasure that Alwyn figured not even a wizard using all his powers could accomplish.

"Why don't you play us a song under a full moon!" Yimt yelled, turning and bending over to reveal his fleshy dwarf posterior to the startled cavalrymen.

It was the Iron Elves' turn to laugh as several of them followed suit, offering their own cheeky salute.

Yimt darted back into the ranks and resumed his place beside Alwyn. "I stand corrected," he said, laughing merrily as he marched along. "Now *that* was a sendoff! Here, how about a song?"

" 'The Warlock's Lament'!" someone shouted.

"I don't know that one," Alwyn said.

"No worries, Ally, just follow along."

With that, the dwarf burst forth in what Alwyn could only assume he thought was singing, immediately joined by the rest of the regiment:

There once was a warlock old and randy
Who fancied a witch sweeter than candy
Beware old graybeard, watch out what you wish for!

May I take a dip in your cauldron sometime
Asked the warlock slyly pouring some wine
Beware old graybeard, watch out what you wish for!

If you polish my jugs, I'll grant you a wish
Rub my wand, said he, and I'll eat from your dish
Beware old graybeard, watch out what you wish for!

So he ate what she served, and she rubbed what he had
And nine months later his new name was Dad!
Beware old graybeard, beware!

New stanzas were added, with Yimt supplying most of the more col-
orful ones. Alwyn could only shake his head and wonder how high the
dwarf might have risen in the army if he had put his creative energy to
better use. Still, Yimt seemed happy, even if his crystal ball had a few cracks
in it. The dwarf sure knew the ins and outs of army life better than anyone
Alwyn had ever met. All in all, it was better having Yimt as a friend than
an enemy.

"Now that's got the blood up," Yimt said, taking a break from singing
to grab his canteen and have a drink. Alwyn took a quick look around, but
no corporal or sergeant was in sight.

"Relax, Ally, we're in the field now," the dwarf said, running a sleeve
across his mouth after downing a prodigious slug. "The first rule out here
is to keep yourself fit to fight. Button polishers and crease keepers don't
amount to much when you're in the line and there's a horde of screamin'
natives comin' at you. This is the last time in a long time we'll shine like
this.

"Take a look at our new kit, would you?" Yimt directed, waving his
right hand around, his left cradling his shatterbow against his shoulder.
"Sure, looks all fancy now; the silver-green as fresh as spring clover, all the
leather bits polished, the shako badge a-glittering, bright silver piping on
our jackets, not a frayed bastion loop, and every pewter button in place
with nary a chunk of wood as a replacement . . . yet. Even these fancy
socks look spiffy without any holes in them." He raised his legs higher as
he marched so Alwyn could get a good look at the black wool stockings
with their band of embroidered green leaves circling the top just below the
knee.

"Yup, take a good look, Ally, and remember this. Won't none of it
stop a musket ball or a spear point. You can shine like a crystal ball in
moonlight, but it ain't going to make a spit of difference to that arrow shot
from two hundred yards away."

Alwyn felt a sudden nostalgia for his old, worn uniform. "So are you
saying I shouldn't care about taking care of my stuff? The corporal would
have my head."

Yimt looked up at Ally as if he'd sprouted tusks. "Is there not enough air up there? I'm saying you got to focus on the important things: musket, powder, boots, blades, water, and victuals. Sure, you take care of your kit, but just so's a corporal don't write you up, see? Look," he said, pointing to his chest, "see how the cross belts cover up most of the buttons? Well, when you're out here, if you have to polish, you only polish the ones that the corporal can see, see?"

Alwyn did, though he thought he'd still polish every button just in case. "And that's the key to surviving out here?"

Yimt marched along in silence for a minute, and Alwyn was going to repeat the question when the dwarf finally answered.

"Ally, the key to that is simple," Yimt said. There wasn't a trace of humor in his voice. "Wherever Death is swinging his scythe, you be somewhere else."

"But, we're infantry, we're always going to be where Death is."

"Then carry a bigger scythe," Yimt said, patting his shatterbow.

Alwyn gripped his musket a little tighter and hoped it would be big enough.

The plain simmered like a skillet over an open fire. The sun was shining off the ebony spikes of cactus thorns sprinkled throughout the vines, causing them to twinkle with something close to malevolence at the approaching flesh. Prince Tykkin had decided on this route, deeming it the least likely to be watched by enemy scouts. Konowa could see why.

The Prince led the regiment on a magnificent charger named Rolling Thunder, a silvery-gray, four-year-old Mernian gelding, a breed rare and much sought after among royalty and wealth for their precious-metal coloring. That Konowa knew this much about a horse was thanks entirely to the lengthy lectures Jaal had subjected him to over the years about the qualities and temperament of various horse breeds. It bordered on criminal in Konowa's eyes that a soldier got little more than a piece of silver a month in service to the Empire, while a horse like the Prince's could be worth hundreds of pieces of gold.

It was a bloody great waste of money, as far as Konowa could tell. Dust from the road had already dulled the animal's coat to pewter, and a large spotted animal skin made into a shabraque covered a large portion of its body, leaving very little of the horse's coat to be seen. More gold down the well cushioned the future King's behind. His saddle was wrapped in a thick, red fur from a bear the Prince himself had dispatched on an earlier expedition, which probably meant the Prince had been allowed to walk up and stab it with his sword after the poor animal had been dead for a day. And just in case that bit of tack didn't woo the damsels, the Prince had had the bridle and reins fitted with ornately decorated wrought silver and burnished brass. Konowa gave it less than a week before some enterprising soldier had pocketed a few bits of the finery.

Konowa squirmed in his saddle and looked over his shoulder at the troops marching behind them, then quickly faced front again. His embarrassment at riding when the soldiers had only their feet to move them was galling, but the Prince was adamant that they ride as befit the station of officers, so Konowa found himself bouncing along most unhappily on a large black gelding named Zwindarra, a loan from the Duke of Rakestraw. Unlike the glittering Prince and his steed, Konowa's tack was simple, sturdy brown leather, the shabraque a quickly converted caerna with the regimental crest sewn on either side. The saddle itself was covered with the softened hide of an animal Konowa thought might just be skunk dragon, no doubt a parting jest of Jaal's.

Konowa looked ahead to their chosen path with barely concealed dread. Everywhere he looked, vines lay across the plain like one great slithering mass heaped on top of itself in looping coils of green sinew. In places the stems were as thick as banyan trees, creating impenetrable walls every bit as daunting as those of a stone-and-mortar castle. The fortress at Luuguth Jor lay two hundred miles to the east through this morass, a journey of at least two weeks with no further impediments beyond what nasty surprises the land itself could spring. Konowa doubted, however, that nature would be their only foe.

"I think I'll check on the troops, sir," Konowa said, motioning back at the regiment.

"I won't have them mothered, Major," the Prince said, but waved him away all the same.

"Sir," Konowa replied, and swung Zwindarra in a short arc to allow the regiment to march past.

"Pasty twit," Konowa muttered, watching the Prince ride on. Unlike His Highness, he worried about the morale of the troops, but after the initial shock of the caerna, their sense of pride in their new regiment began to take over. He'd sensed as much as he'd seen their backs grow a little straighter, their chins lift until they were marching with purpose, only beginning to feel the mystique of belonging to the Iron Elves, no matter that most of them had never even seen an elf up close before in their lives.

Konowa readjusted himself in the saddle, patted the spot on his jacket where the pouch lay underneath, and watched the regiment pass. They marched in column, six elves—men, he corrected himself—abreast, their winged shakos bobbing in time. White flashes of knee sparkled where legs not normally exposed to the sun now gleamed between the hems of caernas and the edge of stockings.

A few shouted greetings to him as they marched past and Konowa nodded and smiled. Seeing soldiers once again wearing the uniform of the Iron Elves stirred mixed emotions in him, his mind seeing elves he once knew where a new and unfamiliar face now marched. *I won't fail you again,* he silently vowed.

"You almost look like you belong in a saddle, Swift Dragon," said the Duke of Rakestraw, sidling up to Konowa on a huge roan.

"Jaal! What are you doing here?"

"You didn't think I'd let you slip away without saying good-bye, now did you?" the Duke asked, smiling.

"I thought maybe you were here to check on your investment," Konowa said. "You let me drink your wine, bought my commission to major, and loaned me one of your own horses. I've only been out of the forest for a week and already my debt to you knows no bounds."

Jaal slapped his knee and both horses started. "Bah! You'd do the same for me; think nothing of it. Besides, Zwindarra here is no ordinary steed. His great-great-mare was a unicorn, and he's got a bit of the mystic about him. If you get into a bind, he'll stand firm and won't veer."

"Just like his master, then," Konowa said, leaning down to pat the horse on the neck. Zwindarra swung his head back and tried to bite Konowa's hand.

Jaal roared and shook his head, his red hair flying madly from underneath his helmet. "Oh, and he's a tad temperamental, but I figure you two should cancel each other out."

"Your kindness will not be forgotten."

The Duke laughed some more. "Just bring yourself and this motley crew back again and I'll consider your debt paid in full."

Konowa felt the sting, even though it wasn't Jaal's intention.

"It's a new day, my friend, a new beginning. They'll shape up, you'll see. By the way," the Duke said casually, "Lorian tells me you had a meeting with a veteran of the regiment."

For a long moment, all that could be heard was the creak of the saddle and the clomping of hooves. "I don't blame him, Jaal. I hate me, too."

The Duke's gloved hand came down hard on the front of Konowa's saddle as he leaned close to whisper in his ear. "You listen to me, laddie. You take that guilt and you shoot it, stab it, and bury it deep. The past is done. There's three hundred soldiers that are alive and would like to stay that way. Don't matter if they're elves or not. Don't matter if they like you or not. You don't have the luxury of feeling sorry for yourself or letting others carry around thoughts of revenge. First chance you get, you deal with him, hard."

He let go of the saddle and straightened up, smiling once again. "But look on the bright side. Those elfkynan get one look at your lads and their shapely legs and they'll die of laughter and everyone will come back a hero."

There was a sudden blaring of trumpets. The noise rattled around Konowa's head like marbles in an empty iron pot. Both he and Jaal turned in their saddles to look back over the path they had come.

A group of large brown animals with huge flapping ears, long trunks, and great curving tusks of black ivory trundled through the vines with no concern for where the path might be. "Muraphants," Konowa said, already feeling the ground shake beneath Zwindarra.

"Ten of them," the Duke said, shaking his head in clear amazement. "I passed them on my way out here. They're loaded with enough supplies for this little mission to last a year, or until His Highness gets bored."

"As long as none of them are carrying Sala brandy," Konowa remarked. As the animals drew closer, he was able to make out the huge wicker panniers strapped to the muraphants' sides and saw that they were absolutely bulging.

"Still room enough to bring back a bit of treasure, though," Jaal said casually.

Konowa looked closely at his friend. "Do you think a Star could really be there?"

Jaal shrugged his shoulders. "Who knows. I've had a devil of a time trying to get any scouts up north with this new Viceroy in place, but I've heard enough to tell me a myth about a Star is the least of your worries."

Konowa nodded, further talk pointless as the muraphants rumbled past. Atop each beast, just behind its head, sat a rider wielding a long feather. Whenever the rider wanted the animal to turn, the elfkynan would touch the feather to the muraphant's appropriate ear and the animal would respond by walking in that direction.

Zwindarra began to prance and Konowa had to squeeze hard with his knees to keep his balance. Jaal leaned over and whispered something into the gelding's ear, and he immediately calmed down.

"You'll have to show me how to do that," Konowa said.

Jaal looked absolutely shocked, lurching in his saddle as if struck by lightning. "You're the elf—aren't you in tune with nature? Speaking with animals, making magical weapons from trees and all that?"

Konowa took a hand off the reins and pointed at his chest, raising his eyebrows at his friend as he did so. "*Iron* elf. I . . . R . . . O . . . N. You're thinking of one of those squirrelly elves that eats berries and wears bark undergarments."

The Duke laughed, his eyes watering with the effort. A muraphant trumpeted in response, and the two friends nudged their horses out of the way as the massive beasts of burden rumbled past toward the marching column of soldiers up ahead.

Konowa craned his neck to take a look at the riders as they went by and recognized one.

"Visyna!"

She looked down at him but did not wave, instead tapping her muraphant with her feather and steering it toward him.

Konowa pulled back on the reins—Zwindarra whinnied and turned a baleful eye on him, but allowed himself to be nudged forward toward the huge animal and its waving trunk.

"What are you doing here?" Konowa yelled up at her when she was alongside.

She brushed the hair out of her face before answering, and Konowa was struck again by her beauty. She was dressed much the same as she had been in the forest, but instead of sandals wore toughened canvas boots. Her hands and arms were covered by wide-cuffed gauntlets of a silky material that looked like skillfully woven leaves. And there was something else, a coldness in her look that he didn't understand.

"The Prince commandeered these animals and supplies for this expedition," she said, not really looking at him, "and as my father's representative, I am coming along to safeguard our property. Besides, you have no surgeon, and I know how to treat the sick and wounded."

"This is hardly the kind of expedition a woman should be on," Konowa said. "We're sure to see battle."

"Then all the more reason for my coming along," she said, giving the feather a snap so that the muraphant veered closer, startling Zwindarra. The horse took a nip at its trunk, eliciting a bellowing roar from the beast.

"He always was the charmer," the Duke said, sidling his horse up to Zwindarra and giving the horse a pat. "Jaal Edrahar, Duke of Rakestraw, my lady," he said, looking up at Visyna. He doffed his helm and bowed low in the saddle in a single fluid motion that never failed to impress the ladies.

"Ah yes, the drinking partner. Shouldn't you be leading an expedition in the other direction?" she said, giving the feather a swish and swinging the muraphant back toward the rest of the herd as it followed after the regiment.

"A pleasure, my lady!" the Duke called after her, laughing loudly as he put his helmet back on. "And she only tried to kill you once, you say?" he asked Konowa.

"I didn't get a chance to turn on the charm," Konowa said, watching the muraphants disappear in a cloud of dust.

"Good lord, man, you had better start soon! I'm beginning to think there isn't a soul in this regiment who doesn't want to have a go at you."

"And my mother always said I played well with others."

"They weren't children, they were wolves. Didn't you wonder why the other tykes had furry tails?"

"I never did fit in with the tribe," Konowa said, a feeling of melancholy washing over him.

"You don't fit in anywhere, but when has that ever stopped you?"

It was Konowa's turn to laugh. "When I was seven, I was out running the hills when I came across a traveling bomak. He said he would tell me my future if I would pick him some apples high up in a tree. I did as he asked, he thanked me, and then he said, 'One day, you are going to die.'"

"You should listen to your father," Jaal said, "get in touch with nature. Maybe that will give you a better attitude about things."

"Take my word for it, Jaal," Konowa said, "up close it's just a whole lot of dirt."

The Duke smiled ruefully at his friend and held out his hand. "Swift Dragon, you are without a doubt the least elvish elf I have ever met."

Konowa took the Duke's hand. "And you're the prettiest man I know."

For a long time after the Duke had ridden away to the west, Konowa held on to a smile, the sound of his friend's laughter ringing in his ears.

EIGHTEEN

The regiment marched all morning until the sun burned directly overhead, heating the trapped air inside their shakos to furnace-like temperatures. Dust leaped from the ground with each footfall, covering their once-immaculate uniforms in a thick coating. When the order was given to halt, the soldiers quickly sought what shade they could find beside the trunks of the twisting vines. A particular stink wafted up from the vegetation, but it was still preferable to standing in the heat.

"Sweet goblin-gonads," Yimt gasped, collapsing with his back against a springy mass of vines. He spat out the leaf he'd kept clenched in his teeth to keep his bottom lip from burning under the glare of the sun and uncorked one of his canteens. In a single motion, he poured a long draught down his throat, then closed his eyes and sighed. He was the picture of contentment; sprawled on his back, head resting against his pack, drukar by his side, and the wicked-looking shatterbow lying across his lap. He pulled his "splinter" from its sheath in his stocking and started cleaning his fingernails, then used it to prop up his shako. He opened his eyes and stared at Alwyn.

"How far did they say we was going today?" he asked.

Alwyn tried to answer, but his mouth was so dry from inhaling dust that all he could manage was a cough.

"Something about some river," the soldier with one eye offered, sitting down beside them to rest his back against the vine. "We was making for a river."

Yimt shook his head, then undid the leather chinstrap on his shako, twisting the wings so he could set it upside-down beside him. He ran a hand through his greasy black hair and Alwyn noticed that the air above his head actually shimmered.

"Normally, a river sounds nice, but not in this despicable land. Nasty things, all thick and brown and not fit to drink for neither dwarf nor beast," Yimt said. He paused in his head-scratching to pull out a squirming bug between thumb and forefinger. "Would you say that's a flea or a louse?"

"Louse," Meri said, assessing the bug with his one eye.

Yimt looked down at the tiny bug and scratched his head with his other hand. "I don't know about that. No offense now, lad, but you are only giving it half an appraisal."

"I know I've been feeling weird since we got into these vines. Something don't feel right," Alwyn said, wriggling his shoulders inside his uniform. "I've got this creepy-crawly feeling like my skin isn't my own, you know?"

Yimt nodded. "Definitely ticks, they're a lot more energetic than lice. Course, fleas can get right jumpy at times, too." He struggled to sit up a little, then squished the tiny bug between thumb and forefinger. "First kill of the expedition. Whatever it was, it's dead now. Feel better?"

Alwyn shrugged and tried to think of something else.

"Oh, where are me manners?" Yimt suddenly said. "Say, Meri, is it? This here pile of complaints is Ally."

Meri stuck out his hand and shook Alwyn's. "Pleased to meet you. So, what do you think of our new regiment so far?"

Alwyn took a drink from his own canteen, the warm water turning the dust in his mouth to mud. "I don't know, I got some strange feelings about it."

"I know what you mean," Meri said. "Things ain't entirely right, if you get my meaning."

"Troll pudding," Yimt said, unbuttoning his jacket to scratch his chest. "I been thinking more about it, and you know, we are some lucky elves, especially for some skinny men and an old dwarf like me. Our knight superior is none other than the Queen's son himself. You think the old bird would send him out to get killed? After all the educating and training they put into his noggin? She ain't about to have it dashed in by some native chucking a spear. I figure we're just out here to show the flag, let the Prince play at soldier for a bit then back we go to a nice safe camp. And you notice how airy things feel marching in these caernas?" Yimt asked, moving his scratching in a southerly direction. "It's freedom it is, specially in this infernal place. Feels darn right to me."

"I think I'm blind," Alwyn said in mock horror, turning away as Yimt continued to scratch. He caught Meri staring at him with his one good eye and suddenly felt ashamed. "Er, I didn't mean nothing by it, Meri," he said.

"That's all right. There are a few advantages, you know."

"Really, like what?" Alwyn asked, ignoring Yimt, who was making a big display of rearranging his caerna.

For an answer, Meri lifted the patch over his eye and pulled a small snuff box out of the socket. "Only place I ever found to keep it dry," he said, holding the little silver box out to Yimt and Alwyn.

"That's okay, thanks," Alwyn said, struggling to keep the water in his stomach from charging back up his throat.

"Don't mind if I do," Yimt said, taking a pinch and sticking it between his steel-colored teeth and lower lip. "Adds a bit of extra kick to the crute."

Alwyn was wondering if anything bothered Yimt when he sensed a presence and turned to see Corporal Kritton standing nearby. Ever since they'd killed the rakke the other night, the corporal had withdrawn into himself, barely talking to anyone. Normally, Alwyn would have enjoyed that, but there was something unsettling about the look in the elf's eyes, something not quite right. Before Alwyn knew what he was doing, he found himself calling out to him.

"Hey, Corporal, how far we going today?"

The elf turned toward Alwyn with a look of pure hatred. Kritton's upper lip twitched and his fists balled up, then he abruptly spun on his heel and walked away, disappearing from sight behind a large vine. Alwyn found his mouth was half open and closed it with care, taking a deep breath as his heart started beating again.

"Well that's just rude, that is," Yimt said. He'd reached over and taken the ramrod from Alwyn's musket and was busy scratching himself underneath his stockings. "A nice lad like yourself tries to be social and engage in polite conversation and what do you get for it? Our Corp just ain't the same he ain't, not since he met up with the major."

Meri leaned closer. "I heard that he has it in for the major on account of the regiment being disbanded, but that's not the half of it. Hrem over in B Company said that we're not going to relieve the garrison at Luuguth Jor at all. There's some kind of treasure buried there, some jewel called the Star of something, and the Prince is going to dig it up and take it back to Celwyn. All the talk about rakkes and the Shadow Monarch is just a smokescreen."

Yimt stopped scratching. "Smokescreen my aunt's hairy chest. Ally and I killed one of them beasts sure as I'm sitting here now. They're real, and that means that elf-witch across the ocean is, too, and She's up to something."

"But why reform the Iron Elves?" Alwyn asked. A terrible thought came to him. "You don't think they mean for us to fight Her?"

Before Yimt or Meri could answer, sergeants were shouting for the regiment to fall in.

Alwyn grabbed his musket and levered himself up. He turned to give a hand to Yimt, who was struggling to rise.

"This heat too much for you?" Alwyn asked jokingly, secretly worried that the old dwarf might not be up to the rigors of a long march. Light infantry regiments typically marched at a pace of 120 steps per minute, significantly faster than the 75 of a regular regiment. The Iron Elves, when they had been all elves, were reported to have sustained 150 steps a minute for a full day's march, but Alwyn knew that was impossible . . . at least, he knew there was no way *he* could do it.

"I'll march you young pups straight into the ground," Yimt grunted, finally getting to his feet.

"You were caught in the vine. Look," Meri said, pulling a long strand of vegetation from Yimt's belts.

"Well I'll be boiled in a witch's pot," Yimt said, holding the vine up to get a better look. "If I didn't know better I'd say the bugger was trying to keep us here." He threw it to the dirt and ground it in with the heel of his boot. Yimt bent down and grabbed his shako, taking a quick peek inside before jamming it on his head. "They don't pay us enough, not by half," he said, stepping quickly away from their temporary shelter.

As they walked back toward the dusty road where the companies were forming up, Alwyn couldn't help looking over his shoulder. The vines remained where they were, a tangled green mass of rotten-smelling vegetation. So why did he feel that if he turned his back on them, they'd pounce like a dragon on a goat?

NINETEEN

The regiment resumed its march, tramping ever eastward in a choking white haze. After the steamy wet confines of the forest, Konowa felt completely exposed and constantly scanned the surrounding plain for signs of danger. The view was better from atop Zwindarra, but his legs were aching from standing up in the saddle to save the muscles of his backside from further insult. He had finally decided to try sitting again when he spotted a dust plume rapidly gaining on the column from the west.

"Prince Tykkin," Konowa said, pointing back down the trail.

"Likely more supplies," the Prince remarked, and rode on, his eyes scanning the ground in front of them. *Probably looking for some damn insect,* Konowa thought.

"I'll just check it out then, sir," Konowa said, saluting and cantering Zwindarra back toward the oncoming visitor. "You four," he said, pointing to a group of soldiers as they marched past, "fall out and follow me." He was pleased to see they began loading their muskets without being told to do so.

Konowa tried to find Kritton as the rest of the column marched past, but the dust and the bobbing horse made it difficult and he soon gave it up. He did see Visyna's muraphant and nodded, but he was past before he could see if she responded.

By the time he came to the end of the column, the dust cloud was upon him. From out of the swirling dirt came a covered wagon driven by a figure in a gray cloak and drawn by four of the ugliest horses Konowa had ever seen.

"Glad I finally caught up with you," the stranger said, hauling in the steeds.

Two wizened hands pushed back the hood of the cloak to reveal an old human woman.

Konowa motioned for the soldiers who had accompanied him to catch up with the column. He turned back to the woman and doffed his shako and bowed—temporarily losing his balance before righting himself.

"Major Konowa Ul-Osveen, sub knight commander, the Hynta Light Infantry," he said, trying and failing to nudge Zwindarra closer to the wagon.

"The Iron Elves," she replied, taking a large cigar and clamping it between exceptionally yellow teeth. "Commanded by His Royal Arseness the Prince." Her face crinkled like a sun-dried prune, and she smiled at him through a wreath of dark blue smoke. "But I'm guessing from the politely stunned look on your face that you haven't the foggiest crystal ball who I am."

Konowa was hot, his backside felt alternately numb and on fire, and the cursed high collar on his jacket was rubbing his neck raw. He really didn't feel up to a guessing game, but something held the insult between his teeth. After all, she was the first new person he'd met in some time who hadn't tried to kill him on sight.

"I must confess, dear lady, that you have the advantage."

Her laugh sounded like a flock of startled crows, and Zwindarra's head reared up in surprise.

"You are a charmer. Name's Rallie Synjyn."

Konowa leaned forward in his saddle for a closer look. "I'm sorry, you're *the* Rallie Synjyn?" Her Majesty's Scribe of the *Imperial Weekly Herald* was famous the Empire over, and only partly because of her incredible knack for being at the right place at the right time. Almost as many stories had been written about Rallie as she had written herself, and most were so outlandish, involving strange sightings and bizarre happenings, that no one, least of all Konowa, knew what to believe. Naturally, it sold a lot of parchment.

"One and the same," she said. "Of course, I used to be Rallina, but folks don't want to read about battles and adventure from someone quite so girly sounding, and you know, it's all about getting paid. Fortunately, the Queen understands that better than most, plus," she said, giving him a wink, "the old gal recognizes a good quill when she sees one."

Konowa decided he liked Rallie Synjyn, a lot. "What brings you out here?" he asked, opting to reveal nothing he didn't want to hear a news crier yelling a week later.

Rallie started laughing and slapped her knee with her hand, sending up a cloud of dust that combined with the cigar smoke to hide her from sight. It took a moment before she reappeared. "Certainly not to document the meanderings of Prince Precious up there. The reformation of the Iron Elves is news, Major, *big* news. It was a pity what happened to you and your boys, a right shame. Putting cold steel in that bastard was a favor for the world over. Up to no good, that one. I am glad to see you back in the saddle again, although I can only imagine what it's like to not have your elves with you."

Konowa suddenly found it hard to see. Rallie chose to fiddle with something behind her for a few moments, giving him time to compose himself.

"I can't imagine the Imperial Army will be thrilled that you're here," he finally said, "whatever the Queen thinks."

Rallie turned back to him, her shoulders shaking with laughter. "The General Staff think I'm more of a threat than a herd of dragons, but the Queen likes the idea of keeping her generals honest by having at least one newt in the potion." She took another puff of her cigar and let out a slow, long breath, eyeing Konowa up and down. "Actually, I'd make that two newts."

Konowa tried to look innocent. "Me? I'm a paragon of virtue. I follow orders."

Rallie laughed so hard tiny smoke rings popped out of her nose.

Shaking her head as she regained her composure, she fixed him with a hard stare. "Not too strenuously, I hope. I think a time is soon coming when you'll need to take matters into your own hands."

He imagined his hands wrapped around the Prince's neck—a tempting proposition. "My job is to bring this regiment back, and in one piece. I'll see it done, no matter what."

"Best to let the Prince think he had something to do with it," she said, motioning toward the head of the column. She clucked at her steeds, who were straying toward the vines. "He thinks I'm here to write glowing stories about him for the court. You know the stuff; he leads a regiment into a deep, dark corner of the Empire, slaughters a few natives, grabs some baubles and magic totems, stubs a toe getting off his horse, and goes back home a hero, replete with wound stripe on his sleeve and war stories to woo the courtesans out of their hoop skirts."

"Surely the Queen wouldn't let you write that?" Konowa asked, spurring Zwindarra to keep up.

Rallie placed a finger against the side of her nose and winked, her eye disappearing in flaps of tanned, leathery skin. "The day you assume you know the mind of a monarch, *any* monarch, is the day you likely lose your own, along with the skull that holds it. There's more to this than meets the eye, Major, you can count on that."

"You're not the first person to say so."

"Your father is an astute old bugger," Rallie replied. "You should listen to him. Strange things are afoot. That's why I'm here. There's a story coming like a Star from the heavens. The key is to not stand directly underneath it when it falls."

Konowa couldn't hide the surprise on his face.

"The ears may not be elven, but they suffice," she responded. Shaking her head with glee, she drew another great puff on the cigar so that its tip glowed bright orange.

"Then it's true? There really is a Star there? What about the Viceroy?"

Rallie shook her head. "I suspect much, but at the moment can prove little. I hate to sound like a daft old bat, but I feel something deep in my bones, something terribly wrong in the world. It's as if everything is slowly being twisted out of focus." She suddenly looked embarrassed. "The questions are many. The answers, I think, will be found in Luuguth Jor."

Konowa tipped his shako to her and rode in silence for a while, thinking.

The first elven Viceroy of the Calahrian Empire turned out to be a traitor in the service of the Shadow Monarch, and Konowa, as commanding officer of the only elven regiment in the Imperial Army, killed him. Simple enough. Only the Viceroy didn't die, or did die and has now come back as Her Emissary, looking for what should have been just a children's tale—a red shooting star. Not so simple. Myths becoming reality and the dead becoming, well, less so. Like the rakkes, extinct for hundreds of years, suddenly reappearing and knowing his name. That was no coincidence, of that much he was sure. The Shadow Monarch was looking for him. He gripped the reins tighter. She wouldn't have to look much longer. If Her Emissary was prowling around that miserable little fort at Luuguth Jor, She'd soon find out exactly where Konowa Swift Dragon was, and what he was capable of.

Far up ahead, a muraphant trumpeted, setting off the rest of them in a chorus of deep, rumbling blasts. Not to be outdone, the animals pulling Rallie's wagon lifted their heads in the air and honked, making a long sonorous sound that reminded Konowa of the after-echo of cannon fire. A voice from within the column that sounded suspiciously like the dwarf's suggested in no uncertain terms that they should all stuff it or wind up as steaks.

Konowa chuckled and coaxed Zwindarra closer to the wagon so he could get a good look at the beasts pulling it. What he had taken for especially monstrous horses were in fact brindos, a native species of deer that looked more like the ill-advised union of rhinoceros and horse.

"I call the big one there Baby, but they're all my babies really," Rallie said, smiling benevolently at her animals.

Baby was neither small nor cute, standing as tall as Zwindarra, but sporting a dull black hide of interlocking plates. It looked like a jigsaw puzzle in motion. Its hooves were cloven, its tail a stubby whip that thrashed vigorously to no effect that Konowa could discern, and its head was a wedge-shaped block featuring a pair of enormous floppy ears and two small, evil-looking green eyes. As it called out to the muraphants farther ahead, Konowa got a good look at its teeth and was surprised to see large flat molars. He wasn't sure why, but somehow he had expected brindos to be fanged like Jir.

Konowa realized he hadn't seen the bengar in some time. He'd never admit it, not to anyone, but Jir had saved his life out there, and not just from rakkes. Without the company of that furry, territory-marking carnivore, Konowa would have gone mad. Undercurrents of life in the forest had ebbed and flowed through his dreams, leaving susurrous after-echoes of something he didn't understand. *What must the elves of the Long Watch endure?* he wondered, feeling thankful that he had been rejected that day in the birthing meadow.

"A piece of gold for your thoughts," Rallie said, bringing Konowa back to the present with a jolt.

"You'll get a lot of change then," Konowa said, smiling to cover his sudden unease. Might Rallie possess his father's uncanny ability to know another's thoughts?

"I very much doubt that, Konowa Swift Dragon," Rallie said with a huge grin, "not if you told me your true thoughts."

Konowa forced a smile and rode on in silence, musing there was little chance of that.

TWENTY

The sun's rays beat down on the regiment like bricks of light as it marched east across the vine-covered plain of Qundi. The trail they followed meandered like an old river, its bed a silty carpet of dust inches thick that spumed into the air with every footstep, plastering the soldiers until they were as gray as the earth. With each step they saw the effects of the endless battle to keep the trail open; great swathes of blackened, shriveled vegetation lined the trail and trunks lay hacked apart, the ends brown and desiccated. But wherever flame had burned or blade had cut, new growth had burst forth, sending tendrils back across the trail, forcing the regiment to employ ten soldiers and a pair of muraphants at a time to hack and trample a clear way forward.

It was a slow, exhausting march. Soldiers stumbled and fell, their skin as dry as parchment, their eyes rolled back in their heads. By late afternoon, one muraphant had had its supplies redistributed to other animals so that it could carry soldiers too weak to walk. Konowa had first asked Rallie if he might put some of the troops in the back of her wagon, but she had politely declined, suggesting they would be far more comfortable on the muraphants. After the twentieth soldier collapsed, the Prince was finally forced to order a halt and make camp for the night.

"Can they not even march a day's distance?" the Prince asked, pacing under the awning of his marquee and sipping wine from a crystal goblet.

Konowa forced his balled fists to unclench. "It is exceedingly hot during the day with no shade for cover, sir . . . and no horse to ride," he said, barely keeping his anger in check.

"They are soldiers of the Calahrian Empire, part of the finest army in the world. Do they need to be coddled? Should I call for carriages for all of them so that they may ride in comfort, growing soft and idle in the process?"

Like you? Konowa wanted to say, but instead shook his head. "I would merely suggest that we alter our marching schedule so that we rest during the heat of the day. We can march during the night and the early morning when it's cooler. It will do us little good to come to battle with soldiers dazed and weak and unable to fire a musket."

Prince Tykkin appeared to give this some thought, continuing to pace about, pausing only to refill his goblet. He didn't bother to offer any to Konowa, whether out of spite or from concern that more of his lead-cut crystal would wind up shattered on the ground.

"Very well, we shall rest until nightfall, then resume the march. Ah," the Prince said, his face brightening as he looked past Konowa, "here comes my scribe."

Konowa turned to see Rallie making her way toward the tent, her large gray cloak wrapped around her like a shroud. He wondered how it was that she didn't suffocate from the heat, but appeared to step as sprightly as if it were a cool, winter day.

"What weighty things does this war council discuss?" she asked, helping herself to a goblet and filling it to the brim.

The Prince beamed at what he interpreted as a compliment. "I was just telling my second in command that in order to better preserve the men's health and keep them fit for battle, we will henceforth march at night." He turned slightly away from Konowa as he said it.

Rallie pushed back the hood on her cloak, revealing a tangled mess of frizzy gray hair to which the concept of a comb was clearly foreign. "A compassionate and wise decision, Your Highness," she said, giving Konowa a wink. "Tell me, what provision have you made for drinkables out here on the plain?"

"I have several casks of that wine, as well as barrels of water," the Prince said, motioning for Rallie to take a seat on one of the wicker chairs set out.

"I meant for the men," she said.

"Yes, of course. They'll make use of the rivers we cross, no doubt," he said, clearly uninterested in the conversation.

"Make sure they boil it first, or the only story I'll be sending home will be a rather watery discourse," she said, a loud, throaty laugh spilling out from her mouth.

"Indeed," the Prince said, struggling to get the conversation on track. "I imagine you'll want my views on the raising of the regiment and our progress thus far. I know Her Majesty and Her loyal subjects will be interested to hear of it," he said pointedly.

"Absolutely, Prince Tykkin. In fact, Her Majesty seemed particularly interested in hearing about the major's resurrection," she said, downing the goblet with a practiced flick of her wrist.

Konowa kept his stare even and concentrated on forcing the corners of his mouth to remain still.

The Prince's cheeks turned bright red. "Unfortunately, he has other business he must attend to. Isn't that right, Major?"

"Actually, sir, everything is in order. I think I have the time."

"The initiation," the Prince said suddenly, giving Konowa a triumphant smile. "You were going to initiate the men into the regiment the traditional way, if I recall." He eyed his crystal and visibly relaxed. "Yes, I think it critical that you do it. Tonight. Perform whatever rites or ceremonies need to be done. I trust that I do not need to be involved."

Konowa knew when he'd been defeated. "Not at all, sir. Your Highness, ma'am," he said, saluting and marching out of the tent and into the thickening night.

He walked aimlessly among the impromptu camp, not at all happy with the arrangement. Swirling offshoots of leaves rose well above men's heads in several places, limiting visibility to a few feet at most, while the trunks themselves made walking about the camp more like navigating the great royal maze in Celwyn, or a bloody forest.

Cooking fires winked to life, and Konowa marveled that anyone could be hungry in this heat. Then again, soldiers—especially the old hands—knew that you ate while you could, never knowing when the next chance might present itself.

He hated to interrupt them now, but even though the Prince thought he was getting Konowa out of the way, Tykkin had unwittingly given him an opportunity to address the men directly and explain the heritage of the Iron Elves to them. It wasn't the way he would have liked to do it, but fools wait in vain for the perfect time.

He buttonholed the first sergeant he saw and told him what he wanted.

Twenty minutes later the regiment was squeezed into the largest open area they had.

Sergeant Lorian stood beside Konowa and kept twirling his halberd between his hands. "The Prince should be here for this."

"The Prince has other plans," Konowa said, hoping now that the Prince didn't reconsider and suddenly show up. The Iron Elves were Konowa's, not the property of that sorry excuse for nobility. "Just do what I say," he said, jumping up onto an overturned cooking pot. The murmur of voices quieted as he raised his hand to speak.

"I know you're tired after a long day's march, so I'll keep this brief."

Cheers rose up from the men, and then all was quiet again.

"The Iron Elves have a long and storied past in the Imperial Army, and in that past, the regiment recruited from my native land of the Hynta. Times have changed. What hasn't changed is the honor and pride that every soldier in the Iron Elves should feel. You are now part of the finest regiment that ever walked the face of the earth." It was hyperbole of a sort. The Iron Elves *had* been the finest regiment. This collection of soldiers was something else again.

"Many might ask why reform the Iron Elves at all? The answer, gentlemen, is out there," he said, waving his arm to the blackness beyond. "The Empire has many enemies, and those enemies are on the march. You'll have heard rumors, and I'll be straight with you, I don't know what to believe myself, but I do know this: The Iron Elves once again stand ready to defend the Empire, and that is no small thing."

There was the obligatory roar of approval.

"But to be in the Iron Elves and fight under its Colors is more than just wearing the uniform. There are traditions, an initiation that bonds you to the regiment, and to each other, a bond that may not be sundered no matter what enemy we face!"

The roar was louder now. Konowa had made sure a couple of wine casks had been tapped before he started talking. One should know one's crowd.

"So I ask you now to pledge yourself to this regiment and accept what fate awaits us, not just as soldiers, not even as elite soldiers, but as the *Iron Elves!*"

Shakos flew high and fists pumped the air. Konowa waved them quiet and pulled his saber from its scabbard. The troops followed suit, grabbing their bayonets and holding them in their right hands.

He leaped off the cooking pot and knelt on one knee. The regiment followed suit. Quiet reigned. A singular clarity gripped Konowa and he saw his regiment again, his Iron Elves, about to be reborn.

Konowa turned to Lorian and nodded for him to begin.

"Iron Elves! Ground your weapons!"

Konowa thrust his saber into the earth as the soldiers did the same with their bayonets. A sensation, one of crystal purity of purpose, washed over Konowa.

The regiment spoke with one voice:

> *"We do not fear the flame, though it burns us.*
> *We do not fear the fire, though it consumes us.*
> *And we do not fear its light, though it reveals the*
>   *darkness of our souls,*
> *For therein lies our power!"*

The silence that followed reverberated like the aftereffects of a cannon firing. In the stillness Konowa was whole again—he was home. He looked out at the soldiers before him. These were his brothers, his Iron Elves. Something greater than geography or even race united them, and nothing would break that bond. Not this time.

He was about to stand and draw his saber from the earth when the faintest of breezes brushed along the ruined top of his left ear. A sliver of cold pricked his chest where the acorn lay in its pouch. He looked down at the ground around the saber. It was surrounded by a thin crust of frost. He watched, amazed, as the frost spiderwebbed out to race across the ground and touch each bayonet at the same time, and for the briefest of moments, each soldier disappeared into shadow. It happened so fast that he wasn't sure it had happened at all. He blinked and looked again. Now there was no frost anywhere, no breeze.

"Uh, Major, how long do we need to do this?" Lorian whispered in his ear.

Konowa shook his head and stood, drawing his saber from the earth. Lorian ordered the regiment to do the same.

"You are now, all of you, Iron Elves! *You are the fire-forged!*"

The troops roared their approval one last time, whether in agreement with him or just happy to be done and be able to get back to their cook fires he didn't know. Konowa cleaned off his blade and sheathed it, staring at the ground.

"You didn't see anything odd?" Konowa asked Lorian.

Lorian looked angry. "Odd, sir? Why, was one of the men fooling around? I'll deal with him, sir, just point him out to me."

Konowa waved him down. "No, nothing like that—the men were splendid. Never mind, I think I just need some sleep." He saluted and watched Lorian walk off into the dark.

Sleep. He'd said it to cover for his own foolishness, but he could use a good night's worth. He patted the area over his chest and was surprised that he felt nothing. Funny, maybe it really was his imagination.

He had started walking toward his tent when something tugged at the edges of his awareness. He stopped, cocking his head to one side to listen. He spun slowly where he stood and tried to listen, to feel the ebb and flow of life around him. It was pointless. The camp was once again awash with noise and commotion, mixing with the more natural rhythm of the land around them so that he could discern nothing but the typical chaos. Except for the all-too-rare moments like the one of a minute ago, it had been that way his entire life, feeling adrift among a people that saw, and felt, the world differently than he, whether it was elves or men. The more he thought about it, the more he came to believe he was trying to see more than there really was.

Konowa kicked at the dirt and began walking again. Sleep could wait. He considered searching out Kritton, but quickly decided against it. After the grueling march of today and the initiation of so many into the Iron Elves, his mood would hardly be improved. He heard laughter and looked around, spotting the muraphants clustered near Rallie's wagon. Despite the abundance of vegetation, the animals were reluctant to stray far from the cook fires and instead huddled in a single mass near the brindos, who for their part circled around the muraphants in what appeared to be a guard-dog posture.

He looked back to the fire and spotted Visyna sitting with Lorian and a group of soldiers. *Well, that didn't take long.* Seeing her tonight was perhaps not a great idea either, but after all that time alone, he was ready for change. Besides, majors outranked regimental sergeant majors—he'd find something to keep Lorian busy with.

He started toward Visyna, shouting out and waving as he went. Lorian stiffened, pulled back from her, and began talking to a soldier nearby. Konowa wasn't sure if he wanted to feel jealous or not. *Later,* he scolded himself. For now he would tell Lorian to double the watch. That would get him out of the way and take care of Konowa's nagging suspicion that something just wasn't right. He ran the back of a hand across his forehead and realized he was no longer sweating.

The acorn under his jacket felt like a block of ice pressed against his skin and he gasped. There was something out there, just outside the glow of the fires.

He was almost right. The first scream came from inside the camp as hell opened up and engulfed them whole.

TWENTY-ONE

Konowa turned and came face to face with horror.

Black-carapaced creatures the size of small dogs were emerging from the sides of hollow vines. The insects, if that's what they were, made a chittering noise by clacking together a pair of curving pincers that jutted out from diamond-shaped heads. Feelers waved frantically where eyes should have been as they scurried forward on eight spindly legs covered with coarse black hair.

There was a tremendous bellow and Konowa jumped to the side as panicked muraphants thundered past, their trunks held high in the air. The black insects leaped at the animals as they stampeded, but the four brindos ran alongside, head-butting and trampling the eight-legged horrors at every turn.

"*To arms!*" Konowa shouted, drawing his saber from its scabbard.

"*Faeraugs!*" Visyna screamed, running to stand beside him. She saw the incomprehension on his face and shouted again. "Dog-spiders! They haven't been seen in these parts in years! This makes no sense!"

Like rakkes, he thought to himself, taking a step forward to keep her behind him. He felt naked without his musket, furious that he'd left it with his saddle and other baggage.

"They'll try to drag people back into their vines—we have to stop them," Visyna yelled, her thin stiletto flashing in her hand.

"Stay here," Konowa said, starting forward to attack the nearest faer-augs as more boiled out of the vines.

"Major! Your orders?"

Konowa spotted Lorian twenty yards away, already directing a group of soldiers. *The men! I'm an officer again*, Konowa chided himself, responsible for the lives of hundreds, not just his own. He took another step forward, then forced himself to stop.

"Don't bother loading. Fix bayonets! A and B companies fall back to the road, don't leave anyone behind! C Company on me!" he cried, slowly walking back toward the wagons as the faeraugs scrambled closer.

"No!" Visyna screamed, grabbing him by the arm. "They need to stay by the fires. You need light!"

"I can see well enough," Konowa said, shrugging loose from her grasp.

"But *they* can't! They're not elves, they're *men*."

Konowa realized his mistake too late. "Damn it!" He tried shouting again for the men to go back toward the campfires, but the chittering noise had risen to such a high pitch that he couldn't make himself heard.

Suddenly, a faeraug lunged at Konowa's leg and he cut down with the saber, severing the monster in two. His arm tingled; the faeraug's body was like wood. Something surged inside him, a feeling of cold power, but there was no time to puzzle it out. Another came at him from the left and he pivoted, stabbing it between its pincers. This time the blade slid in easily. A gush of oily black fluid spurted from the dying creature's mouth as he withdrew the saber. Frost appeared to briefly glitter along the blade.

He became aware of the noise and chaos beyond him and looked up.

Soldiers thrashed madly, stabbing with bayonets and smashing at their attackers with the butts of their muskets. Screams and yells punctuated the horrible chittering noise. Here and there a bright flash was seen, followed by the sharp crack of a musket firing, indicating some of the men had been able to load and fire. There was a roar and whoosh and two fiery trails arced across the black to detonate a second later, sending parts of faeraugs flying high into the air. But for every shot there were a hundred chittering shrieks—the odds were not in their favor.

"Visyna, tell the muraphant drivers to take burning brands from the fire and move forward to give the soldiers light. Visyna!" He whirled around but couldn't see her anywhere. He started to run toward the fire, and several faeraugs pounced on him at once, their combined weight knocking him to the ground. Instead of bracing for the fall, Konowa curled and rolled as he hit, shaking the creatures from his back and jumping back onto his feet before they could attack again. He swung his saber in a smooth arc and felt it slice through their thick flesh three times. Jolts of lightning raced through his arm and shoulder, but he managed to hold on to his saber. Konowa stumbled backward as another faeraug bore down on him. A soldier stepped in front of him and cleaved it in two. Four more were quickly dispatched and the bugs skittered into the dark, looking for easier prey.

"Thanks," Konowa said, reaching out his free hand to clasp the shoulder of his savior.

"If you are to die, it will be by my hand and no other," Kritton replied, glaring at Konowa before moving off into the night.

There was no time to debate the matter, as a new cry caught Konowa's attention.

"The Prince! Rally to the Prince!"

A seething mass of the creatures was crawling over the Prince's marquee, pulling it down by sheer weight of numbers. Their pincers cut through the cloth with ease, allowing still more of the monsters to pour through the gaps like water into a sinking ship. A group of soldiers led by the drukar-wielding dwarf, Private Arkhorn, were hacking and stabbing their way toward the marquee even as screams came from inside.

They aren't going to make it in time, Konowa realized, unsure if that troubled him or not. He took a tentative step toward the tent and was immediately set on by several more faeraugs, ending any thoughts he had of rendering aid to the Prince. Konowa had time for one more glance just as the tent collapsed completely, with the soldiers still several yards away, before the pincers of the faeraugs close at hand drew his attention back.

Konowa swung his saber back and forth to keep a circle of clear ground around him as he edged backward toward the fire. It suddenly dawned on him that he'd misheard the warning. It wasn't rally to the Prince, it had been *Rallie* and the Prince—she was still in there.

• • •

Alwyn clenched his musket in both hands like a club and swung it wildly. He missed the faeraug he was aiming for and knocked Yimt's shako off the dwarf's head.

"Watch where you're swinging that bloody thing!" Yimt shouted, managing to duck out of the way just in time as Alwyn took aim at another creature. The two of them were pressed back to back fending off the dog-spiders.

"There are too many of them," Alwyn cried, swinging his musket again. It connected, and he felt the satisfying crunch of a faeraug's head being caved in, but in the next instant three more latched on to his musket and tore it from his hands. Another jumped at his face and Alwyn threw up his arms as a last defense.

He suddenly found himself lifted off his feet. Alwyn lowered his arm to see Yimt had picked him up with one hand while wielding his drukar with the other. Alwyn tried and failed to follow the course of the dwarf's blade as it slashed through the faeraugs. Wind whistled past Alwyn's ears as Yimt swung his drukar. The black blade was a whistling blur of death.

Faeraugs lunged and skittered all around them, looking for an opening, but whenever one leaped, Yimt's drukar met it head-on. A red, pulpy mist soon surrounded them, and Alwyn's specs were completely covered in blood.

"Yimt, put me down and I can help," Alwyn shouted, not really sure how true that was.

The dwarf kept swinging his drukar. "Naw, you're doing fine as my shield."

"What?"

"Just teasing, but you are getting a bit heavy," Yimt said as he set Alwyn back on the ground. "Find a weapon and watch my back."

Alwyn ran a quick hand across his specs and picked up the first musket he could find. It was slimy with faeraug guts and the stock was shattered, but it was better than nothing. He risked a quick look at Yimt and was horrified at what he saw.

Yimt held his drukar in his right hand and a bayonet in his left. Both were slick with blood. But it was Yimt's face that startled Alwyn. He'd expected to see the Little Mad One in all his fury, but instead the dwarf looked as calm as a still pond. Alwyn realized then that Yimt wasn't just a soldier. He was a professional killer, and he was in his element.

Unfortunately, so were the faeraugs.

Konowa looked back to the tent, but could no longer tell where it was. Soldiers milled about everywhere, and the dwarf, if he still lived, was nowhere in sight. A faeraug scrambled into the cleared circle and Konowa impaled it with a two-handed stab, pinning it and his saber to the ground.

When he tried to remove the blade he found it was stuck.

The dog-spiders seemed to sense his problem and started creeping toward him.

Konowa looked around frantically for something to fend them off with. In complete desperation, he grabbed hold of one of the pincers from the dead faeraug and ripped it free to use as a weapon. Black slime oozed from the torn end, covering Konowa's hands and making it difficult to keep a good grip.

The faeraugs continued to close, their feelers waving madly, as if to say *we have you now*. Konowa was preparing to charge straight at them when a sensation of cold needles stabbing his chest brought him to his knees. He opened his mouth to scream but nothing, not a sound, not even a breath passed his lips. *Am I dead?* he wondered, watching the faeraugs move ever closer.

A faeraug scrabbled forward on its eight spindly legs to mere inches in front of him. Its pincers opened and closed and then it squatted, preparing to lunge straight for his throat. Konowa tried to lift his hand, but his body would not respond. Other faeraugs were moving in, getting ready to swarm.

The acorn from Her Wolf Oak pressing against his chest beat like his own heart.

The faeraug jumped.

It all happened in an instant.

The faeraug leaped into the air and was skewered on the point of a sword. It squirmed frantically as a black frost spread over it. A moment later, it burst into black flame and was utterly consumed. Konowa shook his head, not sure what he was seeing. The other faeraugs scattered as a group of soldiers suddenly loomed from the darkness, hacking their way through the creatures with a cold precision that Konowa could never hope to emulate. In a rush of sound and heat, the world came back to Konowa, and his senses were once again assaulted by the battle around him.

The soldiers had formed a protective ring around Konowa with their backs to him, their swords rising and falling with grim determination. He was unable to see any of their faces, their bodies always cloaked in shadow no matter which way they turned. Konowa clutched at his chest as he gulped in air and tried to stand.

A whistling noise made him look up. A silver light was arcing across the night sky. When it reached its apex it stopped, and then burst with a ferocious concussion. His ears buzzed with pain and his sight went completely white even as he closed his eyes. When he opened them again, it looked like broad daylight. Scattered groups of soldiers cheered, their muskets rising and falling like scythe-men walking through a field of grain. The faeraugs, so terrifying in the dark, now appeared smaller, more vulnerable. The light confused them, and they started to flee toward the vines.

The soldiers who had saved him were gone.

A presence approached Konowa from behind. He grabbed for his blade and wrenched it free, then spun around to defend himself. A cold, burning sensation stung his hands, and when he risked a look down he saw that they were clean, the blood of the faeraug completely gone, a few crystals of frost winking along the hilt of the saber before they, too, vanished.

"They only hunt at night—we will be safe now," Visyna said. Her clothes were torn and she had a thin red cut along one cheek, but otherwise she appeared unhurt.

"You did that?" Konowa asked, pointing up at the sky with his saber.

"It's little more than a conjurer's trick," Visyna said, a look in her eyes saying otherwise.

"Can you burn the vines?" Konowa asked. He was looking for signs of the dwarf and Rallie, but there was still too much chaos to make out anything clearly.

"Yes, but the muraphants are still out there, and a fire would only panic them further. Besides, the light will be enough for your men to defend themselves now. The faeraugs are fleeing."

"To hell with that!" Konowa rasped, rounding on her and bringing his face inches from hers. "If you have the power to destroy these things, then do it!"

Visyna glared back at him and stood her ground. "You would have me lay waste to this entire area even though you are now protected?"

Konowa opened his eyes in surprise. "You're just like the elves of the Long Watch. They'd sit idly by and watch men freeze before they'd fell a tree to make a fire. This isn't a game, Visyna. Torch the vines, that's an order."

It was her turn to look surprised. "I will not kill indiscriminately, and I most certainly am not a soldier for you to command. I have provided you light—defend your men by it as you see fit, but I will not do more to aid in this slaughter."

Konowa clenched the pommel of his saber and gritted his teeth. Visyna's eyes glinted with the reflected light that still burned above them, and it was clear she wasn't going to listen to him. Without another word, Konowa spun on his heel and sprinted toward the Prince's tent. Dead faeraugs lay everywhere, their black blood churned into the earth by the boots of the soldiers, the massive foot pads of the muraphants creating a grotesque mud.

"Has anyone seen the colonel?" Konowa shouted, fully expecting to find the Prince in a hundred pieces.

A bent blade swung up in the air, dripping blood. "He's over here, Major, and none the worse for wear, I'd wager," Private Arkhorn said.

Konowa jogged the last few yards and stopped in amazement. The dwarf was covered in the black blood of the faeraugs, their bodies piled up around him to his waist. In fact, the dwarf was actually stuck, and using his drukar to chop his way out of the entanglement.

"Get that man out of there," Konowa ordered. Several soldiers began spearing the bodies on the end of their bayonets and heaving them away.

"Easy lads, easy," the dwarf yelled, menacing them with his blade. "Not all the meat in here is bug."

Shouts to his left drew Konowa's attention and he prepared for another attack, but relaxed as Jir bounded into the light, the body of a faeraug clamped firmly between his teeth. The dog-spider's legs were still twitching.

"There you are," Konowa said, reaching out to pat the bengar on the head. Jir growled and dropped his muzzle toward the ground so that he could stare up at Konowa through the fur of his bushy eyebrows.

Konowa slowly pulled his hand back and broke eye contact. "And here I am, over here, nowhere near your dinner."

Jir sniffed once and quietly padded across the open ground toward the darkness, his eyes never straying from Konowa. All the while, the eight legs of the faeraug twitched and convulsed in Jir's mouth. The soldiers gave him a wide berth.

"This is not at all how I expected the evening to turn out."

Konowa whirled around at the sound of the voice. "You're alive."

"I am pleased to see you in a like state." Rallie stood among the tattered remains of the tent, her cloak as pristine as when she'd first entered it. Her hair, however, was even frizzier.

"And the Prince?" Konowa asked.

"Still in one piece," he called out, hobbling out of the dark to stand in front of her. "No thanks to the guard detail for my tent." He made an effort to stand up straight and brush at the many rents in his uniform. "Secure this camp and put every man on watch, then flog the soldier in charge of protecting me!"

Konowa wanted to strike Prince Tykkin right across the mouth. "Sir? Surely you don't blame the men for this?" He took a step forward—this fool couldn't really mean it. "There was no way to know these creatures were going to attack."

Several soldiers gasped and the Prince's eyes grew wide. He took one step backward and placed his hands on his hips. "Are you threatening me, Major?"

Konowa raised his hands in confusion and only then realized he still held his saber in his hand. He reached down to grab a couple of vine leaves to clean the blade before sheathing it, but stopped when he saw the steel was perfectly clean. "My apologies, Colonel . . . the heat of battle, you understand."

"I'm sure the Prince understands—" Rallie started to say, but was cut off as the Prince surged past her.

"I want a name, Major, and I want it right now."

"Sir, perhaps we could discuss this in private," Konowa said, motioning toward the soldiers grouped around. The dwarf had been set free and had come up to stand close by, as if guarding Konowa's back. Surprisingly, it was a definite comfort.

"No need, Major, it's my fault," Lorian said, coming forward. He had lost his shako and his hair was plastered to his skull, the sweat still dripping down his face. The steel tip of his eight-foot-long halberd glistened with black blood and he leaned on it to catch his breath before straightening up and saluting the Prince. "Colonel, as acting regimental sergeant major, the responsibility was mine. If anyone is to be flogged, it should be me."

The Prince smiled, a humorless one no doubt refined in Her Majesty's court, maintaining pretense without any actual warmth behind it. "A noble gesture, but no, I want the man *responsible*. Who was in charge of my guard detail?"

The muscles in Lorian's jaw trembled and he looked at Konowa beseechingly.

"Tell me!" Prince Tykkin ordered.

Lorian let out a small sigh. "Corporal Kritton, sir, the elf. He was assigned to guard your tent."

"An *elf*," the Prince spat out, fixing Konowa with a baleful stare. "Very well, I want him broken to private and given twenty lashes at dawn. Is that clear? Major, you will see to it personally."

Konowa's protest died on his lips. Dozens of soldiers were now standing around them, the flickering light of burning brands shooting shadows back and forth across the blood-soaked earth. Musket fire still crackled and the cries of wounded punctuated the night and Konowa knew he had more important things to attend to.

"Yes, sir," Konowa said, saluting and leaving. He headed for the nearest fire, where a group of soldiers were tending to the wounded.

"The Prince survived?" Visyna asked, appearing suddenly in front of Konowa, halting him in his tracks.

"Thanks in large part to the dwarf. When a day or two has passed, I'm going to recommend him for a medal. The Prince won't agree, of course, but it should make promoting Private Arkhorn to Corporal significantly easier."

Visyna shook her head. "Surely you see the folly in this. This regiment is anathema to everything natural. I fear that the faeraugs were but the first of many tribulations to come."

"Wrapping ourselves in leaves and chewing grass won't change that," Konowa said, moving to step past Visyna. She surprised him by reaching out a hand and grabbing his arm.

"Get rid of it."

Konowa was nonplussed. "Get rid of what?"

Visyna gripped his arm harder. "You know what I'm talking about. I can feel it as if I held it in my hand. Your father was wrong to give it to you. It will not provide you with the help you need."

"And I suppose you will? Like the way you burned the vines when I asked you?"

She let go of his arm. "And what then? Would you have me burn every piece of land that holds shadows? This regiment is no different from the Empire that spawned it. Wherever it goes, it will leave a scar."

"Better the land than us," Konowa said.

Visyna shook her head. "Do you not see? You are already wounded," she said, pointing not to his ear, but to the place where the pouch lay under his jacket. "You risk everything for nothing. When we were in the forest, I sensed that you were starting to connect with the power around you. Don't give up now."

Konowa felt his face flush. "Stay out of my mind, Visyna. You don't know anything about it."

"Then help me to understand, and let me help you."

"And what, go back to the forest and live among the bloody trees?"

Konowa asked. "Have you ever met an elf of the Long Watch? They live in a world that has little to do with the one the rest of us inhabit. They will sit for days in a field of grass just to listen to the wind play among the blades and think nothing of food. I've seen them weep like babies when a tree is struck by lightning, yet when a wagon full of human homesteaders foundered and drowned in a fast-flowing river their only concern was that the wood of the wagon was pierced with iron nails!"

"And what would these humans have done except cut the trees to clear the land for farming, built roads, and dug up the earth in search of metal?" Her face was taut with an inner struggle, as if every fiber of her being was restraining the desire to call a bolt of lightning down on him. "If the elves of the Long Watch don't care for this world, who will? Your precious Empire that brings *civilization* at the point of a bayonet? Your master's way is the way of fire and violence. Burn it if it won't change to meet your needs. Slash it down if it won't bow to your will. Great rifts are being carved in the natural order of the world. Do you think that can go on forever without consequence?"

Konowa wasn't sure what he would have said next, as a soldier came running up and interrupted them.

"Begging the major's pardon, but we've got a man in a bad way. We need the witch, sir." He was breathing heavily, his eyes still wide with the exertion of fighting just a few moments ago.

"Take me to him," Visyna said, turning her back on Konowa and moving off into the night. The soldier looked from her to Konowa.

"Show her!" Konowa barked, following them as the soldier tore off through the shattered camp.

Faeraugs lay dead everywhere he looked. He saw bits of uniforms, broken muskets, and overturned cook pots interspersed among the carnage, and tried to picture what the camp had looked like just a short time ago.

"Make a hole, the major and his witch coming through!"

A group of soldiers parted, revealing a man lying flat on his back, his right arm draped over his stomach. Konowa kneeled on one side and Visyna on the other.

"E-evening, Major . . ."

"I remember you," Konowa said, looking into the man's one good eye. Blood covered the soldier's face and a rattling sound emanated from his chest.

"Yes . . . yes, sir, Meri. Hell of a night, sir, if you'll pardon my swearing. I did my best, Major. I didn't let you down—" Meri was suddenly racked with coughing, and blood trickled out of the corner of his mouth. His right arm slid off his body and Konowa gently grabbed him by the hand, placing it back over the gaping wound in his stomach. Meri's skin already felt cold.

"I know you did. You just rest, Meri, save your strength," Konowa said, looking over at Visyna. "Miss Tekoy here will fix you right up."

". . . best news I've heard all day," Meri managed before another coughing fit.

Konowa leaned over him and whispered to Visyna, "Can you help him?"

Visyna shook her head.

"But you healed me. Surely there is something you can do?" he asked. In battle, he could always fight harder, but now, in its aftermath, he felt helpless. He had no weapon, no skill to combat this. Soldiers were dying again and there was nothing he could do.

Visyna rose from beside Meri and walked several yards away, motioning for Konowa to follow her. When they were out of earshot of the soldiers around the dying man, she whispered to him.

"Do you know nothing of the arts? In healing you, I tapped your own strength and that of the land around us." She looked over at Meri and her face softened. "He hasn't the strength to begin to repair the wound, and this land," she said, kicking her boot in the dust, "has little to offer. Surely you feel it? The natural order is poisoned here. Something is changing the land. Faeraugs have not been seen in years, and even then they were never that big. All I can do is ease his suffering."

A cold stabbing pain flared in Konowa's chest and he reached reflexively for it, his hand closing around the shape of the acorn. He took his hand away and looked at Visyna.

"No!" Visyna shouted, causing several soldiers to look over at them. She lowered her voice as she continued. "Would you pour water on a drowning man? Can you not feel what it is?"

"My father wouldn't have given this to me if it was that dangerous. Surely you can use it somehow to help Meri?" he asked, pulling the pouch out of his jacket and holding it out to her. "I'm not asking you to destroy anything this time, but to help."

She stared at the small leather pouch in his hand for a long time, then looked back at him with regret and something close to fear in her eyes. "I cannot do this."

"You don't need to," Lorian said from behind, startling both of them. "He's dead."

TWENTY-TWO

Don't blame her, Major—there's nothing anyone could have done for him," Lorian said.

Konowa continued to look straight ahead as the two of them walked through the camp. Troops milled about in groups, some laughing and passing around bottles he chose not to notice, others staring out into the dark, their muskets clutched tightly in trembling hands.

"I want the men kept busy," he said. "Don't give them a chance to think about this. I don't care if you have them digging latrines from now until sunrise, just don't let them think."

"I'll see to it, Major, but they're going to wonder what's going on, and if it's connected to what we're doing out here . . ."

Konowa nodded. "You don't think this was a coincidence, then?"

Lorian shook his head.

"Good. If you did, I'd think the Duke had pawned a slow wit off on me."

A series of honks answered by low, rumbling bellows signaled the return of the brindos and muraphants. *At least the regiment still has a food source,* Konowa thought viciously.

A soldier marched up holding a lantern and handed Lorian a piece of parchment. Lorian gave it a quick look and grimaced.

"Three dead in A Company, five in B, and one in C, along with twenty-two wounded, three serious," Lorian said.

"How many faeraugs did we kill?" Konowa asked, but he already knew the number would never be high enough.

"Five, maybe six hundred," Lorian replied. "It's not much compensation, but once the lads got over their shock, they performed well."

Konowa nodded, stepping around an overturned kettle and a shredded haversack, its contents spilled on the ground and trampled in the dirt. "I'd like several soldiers written up for commendations. Private Arkhorn for one." He paused before saying the next bit. "And there was a group who used swords. They saved me when I fell."

Lorian looked puzzled. "You were right about the dwarf, sir, he's one hell of a fighter. But I don't know what other soldiers you mean. The men have their muskets, bayonets, and small daggers. I've no doubt a couple of them have a few other weapons stashed away, but other than Arkhorn with his drukar, and me and the other sergeants with our halberds, only officers carry swords, sir."

Konowa laid his right hand across his chest, then quickly removed it when he saw Lorian watching him. "It must have been muskets, then. Very well, check with the other sergeants and have the list for me by dawn."

A commotion up beyond the next patch of vines halted further conversation. Konowa drew his saber and Sergeant Lorian brought his halberd to the ready. Sharing a silent look, they stepped around a mass of leafy stems expecting another attack. Instead, they found a cloaked figure holding a lantern, kicking dead faeraugs into a pile.

"Rallie?" Konowa said.

"Ah, Major, Sergeant Major," she said, looking up from her exertions to give them a friendly smile. "Pardon the mess, and mind your step—a few still have a bit of life left in them." She laughed and gave a still-twitching faeraug a swift kick, sending its body tumbling into the growing pile.

"I could have some soldiers take care of this," Konowa said, noticing the wagon behind her appeared to have suffered no ill effects from the attack.

"Not at all," she said, "you two will be fine. Major, you can start over there, Sergeant Major, that group to your left, if you please. Tear off their legs, but leave them alive, would you?"

Lorian appeared ready to object, but Konowa shook his head and began helping her move the bodies. Lorian looked around as if still expecting an attack, then joined in, spearing the dead bodies on the end of his halberd and adding them to the one pile, ripping off the legs of those still with life in them and adding them to another.

"The Prince was most upset," Rallie said as she dragged two more bodies forward from under the wagon. "He was hoping his first battle would be against two-legged enemies."

"We'll have that soon enough," Konowa replied, looking over at Lorian, who nodded in agreement. Konowa moved closer to Rallie and lowered his voice. "I thought the little nit was upset because the faeraugs ruined his tent."

Rallie stood up straight, holding her back and walking over to lean against the wagon. She pulled a cigar from beneath her cloak and had it lit in an instant, the glowing orange dot illuminating her face with devilish hues. "He's soft, self-centered, and scared—a dangerous combination out here. First blood has been spilled, and he was buried under a tent with me when it happened. His ego is rather fragile at the moment."

"His ego? I don't give two shakes of a gryphon's tail how fragile his ego is." Was Rallie actually defending him? "This was only the first of what we're going to face. Nine men have already paid the price, and more will surely follow."

Rallie took the cigar out of her mouth and pointed to a spot behind Konowa. He turned and hacked at a faeraug crawling toward him from out of the pile. Its carapace cracked and split open on the second blow. Lorian walked over and speared it back on top of the other bodies.

"The Prince will learn, and you two will be the ones to teach him, with a little help from me," Rallie said, chuckling as she stuck the cigar back in her mouth. "In fact, his lessons have already begun." She reached into her cloak and drew forth a rolled piece of parchment. "My interview with His Highness where he expresses his personal condolences to the families of those slain."

"He actually expressed feeling for the lives of common soldiers?" Konowa asked. Lorian stopped spearing bodies and walked over to stand beside Konowa.

"He will once the news criers start repeating it," Rallie said, her face breaking out into a huge grin from behind a cloud of dense smoke. She reached down to grab a body and then jumped back when it started to wriggle. She motioned to Lorian. "Be a dear . . ."

Lorian stepped forward and stuck the faeraug, swung it over to the pile, then used his boot to knock it off the end of his halberd.

"Now, in order to show the public that the Prince is indeed maturing into a thoughtful leader, I need to feed my darlings and send one of them on its way." Rallie walked toward the heap of bodies and selected a particularly juicy-looking faeraug. A shiny dagger materialized from within the folds of a sleeve and Rallie quickly had a dripping hunk of thorax in her hand. She carried it over to her wagon and lifted the flap of the canvas tarp covering the contents. There was an immediate frenzy inside, which set the wagon rocking violently on its wheels. Loud squawks emanated from under the tarp, and Konowa could just make out a row of wooden cages. Rallie tossed the meat through the bars of the first cage and the squawking got even louder.

"There you are, my darlings, nice fresh meat for a change." She had Lorian pass her more hunks of faeraug, a task he clearly found unpleasant, as she continued the feeding for each cage, tossing in flesh and speaking soothingly to whatever was inside.

"What are they, ma'am?" Lorian asked, holding out a dripping piece of meat at arm's length.

"My messengers," she replied, opening the door to one of the cages and sticking her arm inside. "I used to use carrier pigeons to deliver my reports, but they got eaten more than they made it through. So far, these little beauties have avoided that fate." She pulled her arm out and with it a dark form perched on it. "They're sreexes. Aren't they adorable?"

Konowa stared with barely concealed disgust at the creature perched on Rallie's arm. The bird, if that's what it was, flexed its wings, spreading leathery feathers that covered its entire body except for its huge, curving talons, iridescent red eyes, and fanged, whiskered muzzle. He guessed it must weigh twenty pounds. Stringy bits of flesh still hung from its incongruous mouth as Rallie stroked its back and cooed to it.

"You're my precious, aren't you, Martimis?" she said, nuzzling the sreex with her nose. The sreex responded by closing its red eyes, then raising its snout in the air, howling. "Lovely, aren't they?" Rallie asked, walking over to Konowa and Lorian to let them have a better look.

Lorian clenched his halberd a little tighter and quietly moved back to a safer distance. Konowa was tempted to do the same, but held his ground. "Never seen anything like it," he said truthfully, noticing for the first time a pungent aroma emanating from the beast.

"I'm not surprised," Rallie said, holding out her arm and motioning for Konowa to do the same. "I purchased a pair of these in a very special market a long, long way from here. Breed like rabbits. The Royal Zoological Society is still trying to classify them."

Konowa reluctantly held out his arm as Rallie coaxed Martimis over to him. It leaned forward to grab the cloth of his jacket in its teeth, then hopped, both claws easily wrapping around his forearm as its full weight came to rest. Konowa found himself in a staring contest with the creature, its red eyes growing brighter.

"Oh, don't do that, Major, or it'll think you want to mate," Rallie said, walking back to her wagon, where she began rolling up a piece of parchment and stuffing it into a small tube that looked suspiciously like bone.

Konowa looked away and saw Lorian trying not to stare himself.

"Miss Synjyn, do you know what's going on?" Lorian asked, finally tearing his eyes away from the sreex. "How can rakkes and dog-spiders come back again?"

"That is the question, isn't it?" Rallie said, walking back with the tube. "I have my theories, none of them particularly hopeful. It's not by chance, I think, that all these creatures should gravitate toward the Iron Elves and their mission."

Lorian looked quickly at Konowa, then back to her. "You know about the Star?"

Rallie chuckled and shook her head. "Well, if I didn't, I do now."

Lorian blushed.

Rallie waved away his embarrassment. "I piece together puzzles for a living, Sergeant Major," she said, holding up the bone for Martimis. The sreex opened his mouth and Rallie threw it in. He swallowed it in one gulp, his claws digging into Konowa's arm with increased pressure as he did so.

"All right then, my darling, time to earn your keep." Rallie called Martimis back to her arm and whispered something to it, then flung her arm in the air, propelling the sreex into the night sky. It opened its wings wide and flapped, the sound reverberating in the clearing like a musket shot. The animal circled once, howled, and then disappeared into the night.

"How long to reach Calahr?" Konowa asked. The feeling rushed back into his hand and he rubbed it casually, noticing that Rallie showed no signs of discomfort.

"Two weeks, maybe more. Depends as much on the weather as any other danger. Now," Rallie said, clapping her hands, "I need to feed Dandy."

Konowa took another look at the wagon. There was a much larger cage behind the smaller ones under the tarp.

"Short for Dandelion. Only eats live meat, that one."

"What is he?" Lorian asked, the worry in his voice plain.

"Special," she said, a sly smile on her lips. "Would you like to see him?"

Konowa bowed his head and started to back away. "Thank you, Rallie, but Lorian and I should get back. Another time, perhaps?"

"It's a date," Rallie said, grabbing up some of the legless faeraugs and carrying them back to the wagon. "Good evening, gentlemen."

Konowa and Lorian bade Rallie a good night and quickly walked away.

"Dandy?" Lorian asked after they were out of earshot.

"Better not to think about it," Konowa said, trying very hard to follow his own advice.

"Yes, sir," Lorian said, then cleared his throat. "I have to be honest with you, sir, all these creatures coming back . . . I don't like it."

Konowa looked over to see if Lorian was trying to be funny. "I can't imagine many would, which is why I need you to keep it together. The boys are going to look to you, Lorian, and they need to see you take this in your stride. Tell them you heard the dog-spiders broke out of a wizard's private menagerie—sounds believable enough. Remember a few years back when that ice dragon started building a nest in the Royal Maze in Celwyn? Turns out a tavern keeper had kept the thing as a pet to keep his wares cold and the thing got loose."

"But ice dragons are real, sir, just rare and from the far north. Those dog-spiders were supposed to be extinct, and they didn't escape from any zoo."

"I know that, and you know that, and the troops probably know that, too, but if we act as if it's no big thing, they'll take their cue from that. Now, anything else?"

Lorian looked as if he wanted to pursue the issue further, but knew when to let it go. "About Corporal Kritton. The Prince wants him flogged at sunup and we don't have any drummer boys on roll."

Konowa stopped and let out a deep breath. Traditionally, flogging was carried out by the youngest and smallest members of a regiment. That way, a soldier would feel the sting, but the lash wouldn't cut too deep. If his wounds didn't get infected, he would heal and perhaps become a better soldier for it. At least, that was the theory. Konowa thought flogging a cruel and fool-headed way to discipline soldiers. He had never resorted to it when he had commanded the Iron Elves.

"Find the weakest, sickliest soldier you can and make sure he understands what I want. This is for the Prince, so make it look good. And try and let it slip that this is for show. We're trying to stop one rebellion, we don't need to be creating another one in our own ranks."

Lorian nodded. "I'll take care of it. Anyway, it's a lousy charge, sir— the men know it. And they know you're doing everything you can for them. They won't blame you."

"Kritton will," Konowa said, looking up at the stars. The acorn against his chest grew a little colder at the thought.

TWENTY-THREE

Ten mounds of dirt marked the graves of the soldiers killed by the faeraug attack, the tenth having succumbed to his wounds during the night. It had been tough digging, the soil dry and hard-packed and shot through with roots. After a bit of enterprising bartering by the troops assigned to dig the graves, three muraphants were enlisted to gouge the area with their tusks. Even with their help, it took several hours and the graves were only just finished in time to lay the first casualties of the Iron Elves to rest before another first for the newly reformed regiment began.

Alwyn said a silent prayer for Meri and then in spite of himself another one for Corporal-now-Private Kritton as the elf was marched out to a clearing in the vines past the fresh graves. The regiment stood around the clearing in a three-sided hollow U facing inward. The elfkynan drivers and the correspondent, Miss Synjyn, stood off to one side just behind the troops. A brindo honked and was answered by a muraphant's trumpet, breaking the silence that smothered the clearing.

A sergeant held Kritton at each elbow, but the prisoner gave no indication of wanting to escape. He'd already removed, or had removed, his jacket and shako, so that all that covered his upper body was a brown cotton undershirt. His long black hair was tied in a queue at the back of his neck by a simple leather thong. He kept his head up and straight, showing no sign of what he was thinking as the three walked toward the center of the U where four halberds were lashed together forming an inverted pyramid. Their steps stirred up plumes of black ash, the remnants of the burning faeraugs, their smell still thick in the air.

On reaching the halberds the sergeants stripped off his shirt, and then tied his hands above his head to the wooden staffs. They quickly tied his ankles to the shafts and then stepped away. One of the sergeants pulled a piece of leather from his pocket and offered it to Kritton to bite on, but the elf only glared at him. Shrugging, the sergeant put it back and walked away, announcing in a loud voice that the prisoner was secure and ready for his sentence to be carried out.

Prince Tykkin stepped forward and looked around at the assembled soldiers. He was dressed in a new uniform, his silver-green coatee a bright exception among the dust- and ash-covered uniforms of the regiment. It was a matter of course that officers should look better than their men, and Alwyn supposed a Prince should look better than his officers, too. The major stood a few feet away from him and appeared even darker and wilder than he had when Alwyn had first laid eyes on him back at the camp just a few short days ago. The major kept reaching up to adjust his left lapel and then rest his hand on the pommel of his saber. Alwyn wondered if it was some kind of ritual.

"The Iron Elves have been blooded," the Prince said without preamble. His voice was a bit high, as if he was unsure how loudly to speak. "We have suffered death and injury, as is to be expected in battle. What is not to be expected, or tolerated, however, is disobedience in the face of a direct order. No matter who, or what, your enemy is, you will perform your duty to the fullest at all times." He paused and looked around again at the troops. "This regiment was written off the rolls of the Imperial Army once, to its great shame. That will not happen again! Any soldier, no matter what his rank, will follow my orders and those passed down through the chain of command without question, or pay the price." With that he turned on his heel and walked out of the U, never once looking back.

Sergeant Major Lorian stepped forward. "The prisoner will now receive his punishment. And I don't want no fainters in the ranks or you'll feel the sting of the lash next."

The troops stiffened at the threat. Alwyn swallowed and looked straight ahead.

"Private Renwar, step forward."

Alwyn couldn't move. A murmur rose up in the ranks and was quickly silenced by the glare of the sergeant major.

"Renwar, step forward!"

Alwyn hesitantly took a step, then another.

Lorian walked over to him and handed him a rawhide whip. "Easy does it now, boy," Lorian whispered. "Aim for his shoulders and don't lay it on too heavy."

Alwyn looked back to Yimt, who shook his head helplessly. Alwyn nodded and walked toward Kritton without being able to feel his legs. His entire body had gone numb. His heart thudded in his ears like a berserk muraphant stampeding across a flagstone floor. He knew the regiment was still standing all around him, but he couldn't see anyone. It was as if his entire being had been boiled down to the rawhide whip held in his right hand and the bare panel of brown skin that was Corporal Kritton's back five yards in front of him.

Alwyn squeezed the handle hard, knowing the rough braid was creating a patchwork of red-and-white flesh in his hand, yet no feeling passed through into his skin. He continued to stare at Kritton's back and was utterly mesmerized by it. Ribbons of muscle flowed over shoulder blades, sweeping down toward the valley of his spine like water-polished rocks. He was looking at the very essence of nature, seeing in one elf's back the simple majesty of the natural world, and now he had to destroy it. It didn't matter that Kritton was a despicable person, probably even deserved to be flogged for a thousand other crimes, if not this one. Alwyn, for the first time in his life, was going to deliberately inflict harm on another creature. He'd fought for his life against the faeraugs, but this, this was different. This was cold-blooded.

The full realization of that hit Alwyn like a lightning bolt and he staggered for a step before regaining his balance. This was the army. This was life. Whatever was clean would be made dirty. Whatever was whole would be broken. It was a revelation Alwyn was entirely unprepared for.

You'll look sharp in a uniform, lad, the recruiting sergeant had said, and Alwyn had believed it, wanted to believe it. Alwyn's father had agreed, noting the prize every young boy yearns for: *It'll make a man out of you.* Mr. Yuimi, the little elf tailor down the road, however, had shaken his head very sadly when Alwyn had told him the news. That single, silent head shake had hurt more than anything else. Only now did he begin to understand what the little elf had known.

The RSM cleared his throat and looked at Alwyn, who could only nod in response. "On my count, twenty lashes and not one more . . . begin!"

As Alwyn drew his hand back he tried to imagine the small cobbler's shop and the joy his visits had elicited in both the cobbler and himself, but it had disappeared from his mind. All that remained was the small, stooped figure of a gray-haired elf shaking his head sadly. Alwyn looked at Kritton's back through tear-blurred eyes and brought his arm forward.

TWENTY-FOUR

Visyna turned her head as the first stroke whistled through the air and cut into the soldier's back. There was an audible intake of breath from the ranks, but no man moved. She could stop it if she wanted to. It would take little effort to call forth a wind to swirl the ash and dust so that it was all but impossible to see, and to keep it that way until sense prevailed. She allowed herself a moment to enjoy that thought, knowing full well that she would do nothing.

"One!"

It was Dhareg—Regimental Sergeant Major Lorian, she corrected herself bitterly—calling out the lashes. She thought her anger with Konowa intense, but now she found herself growing more furious as the other man who had expressed interest in her affections compounded his culpability in this atrocity.

"Don't be too hard on them, dear," a gravelly voice said in her ear, "they all follow orders."

Visyna started and turned to see Rallie standing right beside her. She was adept at sensing the presence of others, yet the old woman had walked up beside her as insubstantial as a shadow on a moonless night.

"Hard on who?" Visyna asked, flinching as the second lash left a pink welt running diagonally across the soldier's back. His shoulders rose for a second and his head rocked back and forth, but no sound escaped his lips. The flogger appeared more affected, weaving on his feet and looking increasingly ill.

"Them, all of them," Rallie said, casting a hand toward the regiment. "It's a hard life being a soldier. Most of them are illiterate louts, thieves, drunkards, and worse, and that's just the officers, mind you."

A tiny laugh escaped Visyna's lips before she could stop it. Several of her father's muraphant drivers looked at her in shock.

"This is no laughing matter," Visyna said, glaring first at the drivers, then at Rallie.

The old woman had pulled her hood down so that her wild gray hair wreathed her head like a cloud, revealing portions of a weatherbeaten face as tough as any bark. She held a small, leather-bound booklet open in one hand and a quill in the other. She didn't smile, but the amusement in her voice was unmistakable.

"It never is, yet it's one of the most absurd contradictions in the world today. Look at them," Rallie said, pointing with the quill toward the regiment. "Boys, most of them. I'd wager more have seen the inside of a man's skull than have seen the inside of a woman's bedchamber. They're trained to kill, to rip and rend, and it sometimes takes rough measures to keep them in check. We create monsters of a sort, but we need them, and we need them to be vile and heartless at times because it's them, boys and rogues all, that stand between us and the monsters we didn't create." Rallie nodded to herself and began writing.

"So you condone this?" Visyna asked, genuinely surprised. She had heard many of Rallie's stories and always thought her more concerned with the well-being of the troops than this.

Rallie looked up from her writing and shrugged her shoulders. "It doesn't matter if I do or don't. My job is to record what I see so my readers understand what happens out here." She peered out at Visyna from a tangle of hair, her blue eyes clear and unblinking. "The quill, after all, is mightier than the musket. It may just be that my readers will decide that there are better ways than this," Rallie said, turning away from the flogging and heading away from the spectacle, "and I would not be disappointed if they did."

"Does that include enlightening them to the injustices of oppressing other people?" Visyna asked as another lash bit into flesh. The pain of the elf being whipped was palpable, even without her heightened abilities. She felt compelled to watch the next stroke, but willed herself to follow the old woman instead.

"A lesser of two evils I should think," Rallie said as she put distance between them and the regiment. "The Empire, for all its arrogance and greed, is at its core concerned with the welfare of all the races." She raised her hand before Visyna could object. "Yes, dear, that still doesn't make it right, I know, and were it a simpler time I would support you fully in your endeavors, but this is not that time."

"Support me in my endeavors?" Visyna asked, a sudden chill racing through her body. She looked to see who might have heard, but of course, they were alone among the vines.

Now Rallie did smile and rubbed her nose with her quill. "My little witch, you have a good heart and a strong mind, but you have much to learn about subtlety. The Prince is oblivious to most things, and Konowa has his own concerns, but if you continue shouting about the evils of the Empire, I suspect someone will eventually take an interest in you, and it won't be friendly."

Visyna's heart raced, but she forced herself to stay calm. The flogging that had so disturbed her was now just one more indignity brought about by a corrupt power. "There is a rebellion growing in the north. If the Star of Sillra is there, then it is the Empire that should worry."

Rallie cackled softly and placed a hand on Visyna's arm. It was cool and light, and gave away nothing of her emotions. "The Empire *is* worried, or the Iron Elves wouldn't be here now, but the refinding of the Star is but a small piece of the puzzle. The Shadow Monarch has delved deep in her High Forest, too deep even for the elves of the Long Watch to contain whatever she's done. Everything is coming back, the good, the bad, and the very, very bad. With the Star and the Iron Elves come rakkes and faeraugs and who knows what else? It is a dangerous time to be politicking."

All this confirmed Visyna's suspicions, yet she was still taken aback. "The Star is ours. With it, my people can be free. It is a risk worth taking."

Rallie turned away for a moment as a groan carried to them from the prisoner. She made a clucking sound with her tongue and began walking again, writing furiously in her book as she did so.

Visyna tried to read what she was writing, but the script was neither Empire nor any other she recognized.

Rallie spoke while still writing. "The Prince means to take it for himself, and from him, it will find its way to Her."

Visyna kicked a vine out of their way and then put a hand to her mouth in surprise at what she had done. "So he'll run back to the Queen with it so She can add it to their larder of stolen treasure?"

Rallie stopped walking, closing her book with a snap and tucking it away within the folds of her cloak. "The other Her, dear, the other Her." She turned and began walking back toward the U, the sound of another lash punctuating the air as she did so.

Visyna hurried to catch up. Sweat was already rolling down her face and the nape of her neck was steaming beneath the thick coil of her hair. Rallie, she noticed with annoyance, was unaffected. "Konowa carries with him a piece of Her mountain. I feel the Shadow Monarch's presence here, and it is growing. Konowa should never have accepted it. It is a trap."

Rallie stuck the quill behind her right ear and spread her arms wide as if addressing a congregation. "If you'll forgive an old hack her purple prose, dark clouds are gathering, and She is at the eye of the coming storm." She tilted her head toward Visyna and lowered her voice. "Yes, it *is* a trap. It never ceases to amaze me that people should choose to be so blind. You are a rare one, my dear, a true child of the earth and the life force within it, in tune with all living things in a way most are not. You see what so many choose not to, that opposites exist everywhere—the sun and the moon, summer and winter, predator and prey. If God, the Devil. If the Stars, then a Shadow Monarch seeking to quench their light."

The whip cracked again, tightening the air until Visyna thought she could physically feel the bite of the lash. "Then what do we do?" Visyna finally asked.

"For now, we bide our time, and do what we can to keep these lads safe from harm. They'll be needed for more than faeraugs before too long," Rallie answered.

They were now back to where they had stood before, and Visyna cast a quick look at the elfkynan nearby. They were all transfixed by the flogging, unused to such deliberate and cold violence.

Rallie placed a hand on her arm again. "Steady on, child, there are many miles to go yet, and I, for one, have a few tricks up my sleeve. All the same, be careful whom you listen to—the brightness of a star is in part a reflection of the darkness that surrounds it."

Before Visyna could reply, a gasp rose from the regiment and there was the sound of a sack of flour being thrown to a flagstone floor.

"The poor thing has fainted," Rallie said, clucking again. "He didn't even last the twenty lashes."

The dragon leaned over him, its sulfurous breath bringing tears to his eyes. He tried to move, to run, but its great claws pinned him to the ground. The weight was crushing him, but the smell was worse. He opened his mouth to scream, but his cry was cut short as the dragon spewed a jet of molten flame down his throat.

"Told you that would see him on his pegs again."

Alwyn stumbled to his feet, knocking someone to the side, a canteen filled with drake sweat tumbling to the ground, its contents gurgling obscenely onto the dirt. His senses fought with each other over which felt more pain, and the effect almost canceled each nauseating sensation out . . . almost. His stomach roiled, his eyes watered, his head pounded, his legs wobbled, and his right shoulder and arm trembled with raw pain.

The flogging. As if reading his mind, a hand grabbed hold of his left arm and steered him to a thick vine. Alwyn collapsed in front of it, leaned his back against it, and let his head hang down between his knees.

"You might want to adjust yourself there, Ally—there're womenfolk present," Yimt said.

"Wh-what?" Alwyn croaked, not recognizing his own voice.

"Fix your caerna, lad, you're showing your wares."

Alwyn focused his eyes and saw his bare legs and the cloth of the caerna bunched up by his waist. He used his left hand to tug the cloth back into place and then looked up at the blurry figure of Yimt.

"I can't do this, Yimt, I can't be a soldier." This time he knew the voice to be his; it spoke from his heart.

The dwarf seemed taken aback for a second, then shook his head and knelt beside him. His knee bones cracked as the dwarf settled into a squat using his shatterbow as a rest while he handed Alwyn his specs and a canteen.

"This one is just water," Yimt said, tilting the canteen up and letting its contents dribble into Alwyn's mouth.

It was warm and scummy, but it helped.

"Now you listen to me, Ally. I don't want to be hearing no more talk like that. You're shaping up to be a fine soldier. Flogging's a lousy task, that's all. I made sure everyone knew you had a case of the trots something fierce, and that's why you keeled over like you did."

"So the entire regiment thinks I have the runs?" Alwyn asked, pulling his caerna down a little more.

"Sure," Yimt said, beaming at Alwyn. "The lads already knew you had one of them delicate constitutions. Better they think you can't keep anything in than . . ." The dwarf looked suddenly embarrassed, pulling on his beard and looking everywhere but at Alwyn.

So he thinks I'm a coward, too, Alwyn realized. He lowered his head as another wave of nausea swept over him. The flogging was just one more example of what he should have known all along. The little elf tailor had known, and Yimt knew it, too—he was too weak to be a soldier. He actually thought he had been getting the hang of soldiering; the marching and the yelling, the lousy food and long hours standing guard, but it had all been schoolyard games compared to this. Now that the potion was in the pot, he couldn't take it. He couldn't even swing a whip twenty times at the back of an elf he had hated and feared. It was all too damn hard. He raised his head to tell Yimt so and instead saw the major standing over him.

"How are you feeling, Private?"

Alwyn's self-pity vanished in a flare of white-hot anger. He lurched to his feet, raising his right arm in salute even though it shot needles into his shoulder. "The private is fine, sir. Shall I continue whipping the prisoner?"

The major blinked and looked over at Yimt, who shrugged from a position of attention. "You completed fifteen of the twenty lashes allotted for Private Kritton's punishment. I have deemed that enough."

"Really, sir? Only fifteen?" Rage gave Alwyn a courage he never thought possible. He stood up a little straighter and looked the elf right in the eye. "The corporal failed to protect the Prince's tent, after all, surely that deserves the full twenty?"

For a long moment, the major held Alwyn's stare, then he turned his back to him. "Arkhorn," the major said, "we move out in twenty minutes. You know the drill—see to it that the troops in your section have all their equipment. I don't want them shucking something they might need later just because it's heavy and the weather is hot. And make sure they all drink a full canteen of water. It's easy for a soldier to lose his head in this heat."

Alwyn glared at the officer's back and something inside him snapped. To hell with all of it! He reached out a hand to grab the major by the sleeve and was hit in the stomach by a full canteen of water, knocking the breath out of him and collapsing him to his knees.

"Not a problem, Major," Yimt said, walking over to stand between Alwyn and the elf. "I'll make sure they all stay cool."

The major turned slightly and looked past Yimt and down at Alwyn, his face giving nothing away. His one hand clutched at his chest as if holding something against his heart, then he spun on his heel and walked away. Alwyn was still gasping for breath when Yimt turned around and hit him on the forehead with the palm of his hand, knocking him backward onto his butt.

"What'd you do that for?" Alwyn asked, tears coming to his eyes. That angered him even more, and he propped himself up on his elbows, ready to stand up and take a swing at the dwarf.

Yimt leaned down and brought his face in close to Alwyn's. The eyes that had seemed forever twinkling with mirth and mischief were now cold and clear.

"That was to knock some sense into you," Yimt said, his voice cool. "What do you think, you can just quit? We're out in the middle of the wilds now, lad. Oh, I know what they say about the 'Little Mad One,' but let me tell you something, I've survived a lot worse than this when others around me got put in the ground. Life's bloody tough," Yimt continued, jabbing a stout finger into Alwyn's chest. "It's about time you grew up and got used to that. Out here, you don't just turn in your kit and scamper off to mother. Out here, you're either one of us, or you're one of them."

"One of who?" Alwyn asked.

Yimt shook his head in disgust and stood up. He shouldered his shatterbow and rested his hand on the hilt of his drukar. "The dead. Ask Meri." With that, he turned and walked away, leaving Alwyn feeling more alone and unsure of anything than he ever had in his life.

TWENTY-FIVE

The regiment marched because it was ordered to, but it was clear from the outset that they weren't going to get far.

They were mentally and physically exhausted, a fraying rope unraveling before a coming storm.

Soldiers saw faeraugs in every shadow. So many leaves and vines were bayoneted that someone, probably the dwarf, quipped their new nickname should be the Iron Gardeners. Derisive shouts of "prune the bastard" echoed up and down the line. The elfkynan atop the muraphants had their hands full keeping the beasts in check, waving their feather goads furiously and no doubt wishing they had something a bit more substantial like a good piece of wood. Soldiers shied away from the clearly agitated animals, and the column was continually stalling. Even then, Konowa thought things would soon calm down until he watched Jir stalk and pounce on a waving leaf, his hackles raised and an unsettling growl emanating from deep within the beast.

"We'll lose more men if we keep this up, sir," Konowa finally said, waiting for the Prince to explode in anger. To his surprise, the Prince only nodded, his thoughts clearly somewhere else.

Konowa ordered the regiment into laager. The remains of the afternoon were used to slash and burn vines to a hundred yards out on all points of the compass. A single, large bonfire of dead undergrowth was lit in the center of the camp, and several smaller ones spread out on the perimeter as darkness fell. No faeraug was going to get anywhere near them, not tonight.

Satisfied that all was in order, Konowa found the tent some soldiers had erected for him and crawled into it. He pulled the shako from his head, undid the top button on his jacket, and gave in to exhaustion.

Konowa stood before a single silver Wolf Oak in a forest. The tree stretched so high above the other trees that he had to crane his neck to look up at it. Its leaves swayed gently in a cool breeze while a fat, glowing moon sparkled across its bark.

Oh, hell, he thought, *another bloody dream.*

It wasn't the birthing meadow this time, but it was somewhere within the Great Forest, and it was night. He tensed, knowing it would only be downhill from here.

A year alone with only a bengar to talk to had not been easy. A lesser elf would have gone insane confronting the horrors he faced night after night, both real and imagined. Then again, a lesser elf would not likely have started hunting the hunters, slaying them in his sleep with such force that he often woke with his throat raw from screaming his battle cry.

Thunder shook the leaves, flickering the moonlight over the forest floor. A single strand of lightning stitched its way across the night sky, heralding the coming storm. The forest flooded with fear. The trees cried out, filling his mind with their terror. It was chaos, so many voices all clamoring to be heard, to be understood, that he despaired of ever making sense of them, so he tried to shut them out.

A new voice entered his mind, but unlike the others, it was calm. More lightning lanced the darkness, but the voice soothed the storm of voices. Konowa relaxed. He looked again at the great silver Wolf Oak before him and knew it to be the little sapling cub from the birthing meadow. *How is that possible?* he wondered. Even as he watched, its branches spread out like a great web above the forest, shielding the lesser trees from the fury of the storm.

Lightning stabbed down. Crackling white showers of sparks flew high into the air wherever a bolt struck home, tearing large chunks out of the Wolf Oak. It swayed, its voice faltering for a moment in its pain, but then it called out to the forest around it. The trees responded, lending their strength to it, and the Wolf Oak grew taller and stronger still, and the storm roared in futile fury as it beat itself to pieces against the protector of the forest.

The moon reappeared as the last of the storm clouds rolled past, revealing the silver Wolf Oak before him. It stood straight and tall, unmarked by the storm. Ice trickled down his back. This wasn't right. An elf stepped from behind the tree, her hands outstretched toward him.

'**Is it not beautiful?**' the Shadow Monarch asked, Her eyes black with frost fire.

Konowa stumbled backward, tearing his eyes away from her to look at the silver Wolf Oak. The tree began to bend, its silver bark flaking, revealing the thick, black ichor underneath. Branches twisted in on themselves as their leaves brittled, their edges shearing into jagged points. Its voice called again to the forest, but it was no longer calm and caring.

'**Why do you resist?**' She asked, looking back lovingly at the stunted tree. '**I saved it, and I can save you.**'

Konowa's voice barely made it out of his throat. "Do you not see what you have done? It's an abomination. It should be destroyed." He kept moving backward, but no matter how fast he walked, the scene before him remained in place. His breath misted in front of his eyes and he began to shake. The Shadow Monarch began coming toward him, her hands reaching out to him, her fingertips alight with cold, black flame.

Her hands drew closer, the flame rising with each step. Konowa reached for his saber but found his own hands too cold to open. He looked back as She leaned forward to touch him—

He was flying high above the trees. It was a glorious, wonderful feeling. He spread his wings and sailed higher on a warm updraft. The wind thrummed along his feathers in a luxurious sensation of freedom as he realized he was a sreex.

Martimis. He was Martimis. It was such a pleasant surprise that he accepted the sudden transformation and reveled in the simple joy of it.

He was free. He looked down at the forest below and already it was dwindling to nothing. The wind infused him with a matchless energy, and he knew that if he wanted, he could fly to the top of the sky and wheel among the stars. But even as he contemplated the idea he knew that he would not.

The answer was literally stuck in his craw—he was flying the message from Rallie to her editor in Calahr. The need to do it made him wonder if magic compelled him, but all he could sense was a constant sadness. Konowa wrestled with the concepts daily, but a sreex? This was a dream unlike any he had ever experienced. It seemed as if he was really flying, even as he was dimly aware of being asleep on the ground hundreds of miles away.

The sadness Martimis felt was strong. Instinct told him things were changing. Prey ran tantalizingly into the open as he flew overhead, but he would not hunt. He only accepted food from *her* now. It was safer that way.

Dark clouds loomed off to the east and he banked away, letting his body slip through the air in perfect freefall before righting itself and once again riding the warm updraft that let him conserve his energy. Movement caught his eye and he turned to look behind him. There was a cool pain in his breast that should have meant something to him, but he was a sreex, and it did not hamper his flying, so he ignored it.

He pumped his wings and lifted his head and howled, letting the sound fan out through the air. This was freedom. The clutter of life that littered the forest could not reach him up here. He momentarily opened his feathers wide to let the sound of his own call vibrate over his skin. He could find prey as small as a swallow this way, but there was nothing to find. He was thankfully, mercifully, alone.

He turned back to his course and flew on, his thoughts simple and clear. Rallie cared for him, protected him, and all too rarely, let him stretch his wings and fly. So he flew to the place he must go, opening his mouth to let the wind cool his throat, and did not see the closing shadow of claws and teeth and hunger from a cold, distant past.

. . .

He wasn't dead, but sometimes he wished he was, if only to get some rest.

It called to him in his dreams every night, and even though Viceroy Faltinald Gwyn knew it shouldn't be, it was.

It had no mouth, nor heart, nor even a brain, yet he heard its cries, and more to the point, he understood them. Night after night it cried out, and he had no way to escape it, not unless he destroyed it, and that was something he would not do, for it was power, power untapped, and he had uses for it.

At first, he ignored the plaintive calls, not believing they were real. Then he found the body of one of his retainers crumpled at its feet and he knew otherwise. To ignore it was to invite mayhem throughout his palace in the capital of Elfkyna, and finding good servants was not easy. So the Viceroy tossed in his sleep, tormented by a voice that should not exist.

The silk sheets of his canopied bed twisted about his body. He dove deeper into sleep, invoking a mind trick he had picked up from a blind fortune-teller. He imagined a black tear in the air in front of him and stepped through, conscious as he did so of the slowing of his heart. It didn't help—its calls following him relentlessly. He created tear after tear, each one smaller and darker than the last, his heart barely beating, his breathing all but undetectable, yet still its calls followed him through to the other side. He had never plunged this deep into the abyss of his mind and it both thrilled and terrified him even as plaintive cries reverberated throughout the maze of his subconscious calling him back.

The Viceroy gave in to the inevitable and swam back up through the darkness of his mind. It was a slow, thick process, but he was strong, and the voice was a beacon guiding him with unwavering purpose. He became aware of his own body, felt his heart resume a steady beat, air pour down his throat as his lungs refilled and he was back in his bedchamber in his palace. He sat up at once and wrenched the sheets from around his naked body, disgusted to find he was covered in sweat. He shot a withering glance around the room, taking in the cool blue glow cast from several radiant gemstones set in wrought silver chalices. Their purpose, beyond luminescence, was to moderate the temperature in the room, keeping it cooler than the steamy air that plagued this land. It took him another moment to realize that they were performing as they should, and that the sweat that beaded his bald head and pale skin was induced by a magic far beyond the gem's simple spell.

It was calling him again.

It was hungry.

Gwyn slid out of bed and moved smoothly across the cool marble floor of his bedchamber to the red oak door set in the stone wall at the opposite end of the room. He placed his right hand on the burnished brass doorknob and felt the vibrations of energy pulsing on the other side.

It was several moments before he turned the knob. When he did, he did so with a quick flick of his wrist and strode into the room as if greeting a hundred heads of lesser states, no matter that he wore nothing but the armor of self-righteous belief in his own powers.

The air in the room hit him with physical force, heavy with cold and something colder still. There were no lanterns or luminescent gems, and the only window was shuttered with iron bars, yet he saw clearly. The single object that stood in the center of the room was illuminated by a silvery light of its own making. It was the thing that had chased him in his dreams and would be heard.

The dragon table.

In his service to the Calahrian Empire, the Viceroy had amassed a large fortune in gems, paintings, amulets, and every kind of native bauble and finery that he'd wanted, but this was something else again. That it had been the previous Viceroy's spoke volumes, especially now that that elf was transformed from the dead into Her Emissary. Clearly, the table was far more than simple wood.

He watched it carefully. It stood silently, as all tables should, yet in his mind it cried out to him with thunderous force. Its leafy dragon head shimmered, the claws of its carved feet clutching the stone like meaty prey, and he had the unsettling feeling of prey being stalked.

"Enough!" he barked, and the voice in his head went still. He walked around the table, trailing a hand along its edges, feeling the depth of its need. Knowledge. It craved information the way he sought power.

"Knowledge is power," Her Emissary hissed.

To his credit, the Viceroy started only half as violently as he had the last time Her minion had paid him a visit. He composed himself as best he could, achingly aware of his nakedness, and turned to face the shadowy specter of his visitor.

"These parlor tricks of yours are growing thin," the Viceroy said, staring down his nose at the twisting shadows at the other end of the room. "You might try knocking one of these times."

"She grows impatient," Her Emissary replied.

The Viceroy felt his face flush and was surprised to realize anger was replacing fear. "I am not some ox to be led about by a nose ring. I am the Viceroy of the Greater Protectorate of Elfkyna."

"So was I."

The shadows that made up Her Emissary surged toward the table, snaking over and around it. A voice screamed in the Viceroy's head, sending him reeling into the cold stone wall.

"Stop it!" he yelled, clutching his temples as the scream rose to a crescendo then suddenly abated into a contented murmur. He took his hands away and shook his head. The shadows coalesced back into something resembling an elf, a black limb gently stroking the edge of the table. The room was still cold, and Gwyn was still scared, but something had changed.

"You will feed again soon, my ryk faur," Her Emissary said.

The voice was jagged steel in his ear, yet there was a hint of something else. A lesser person would have understood immediately, but the Viceroy prided himself on being above the need for affection and other weaknesses.

"Your *ryk faur?*" he asked. "You were an elf of the Long Watch?"

"Fool! I am dyskara, I am one of Hers."

The Viceroy had not until that moment realized the Shadow Monarch's minions bonded with Wolf Oaks as well. *Interesting . . .*

"I don't understand; what happened?"

The shadowy form said nothing. He wondered if it hadn't heard him and was about to repeat the question when it turned its head toward him.

"She demands sacrifices for the good of all . . ."

The Viceroy himself had said something like that in countless nego-tiations on behalf of the Queen of Calahr, but only now did he realize how chilling those words could sound.

For a moment he considered turning from this path, aware that he was committing treason if he went any further. But was it really treason? As the ruler of the Calahrian Empire he would forge a mighty alliance with the Shadow Monarch, creating an unassailable force in the world. The things he could do with that power . . .

"She has nothing to fear from the Imperial Army. No aid will flow to Luuguth Jor to impede your work there."

"You make claims rashly, Viceroy."

The shadows that made up Her Emissary's shape bowed low over the table. The temperature in the room began to fall and soon the Viceroy was shivering.

"Unlike you, I have seen to it that nothing will interfere with my plans."

"Like me before you, you have failed to account for him."

"You're wrong there," the Viceroy said, shaking his head. "The Duke of Rakestraw has been bought off."

It wasn't laughter, but the sound that echoed off the walls had the feel of it, if laughter were thrown daggers.

"Feed it and see."

He was nonplussed. "What, just start bringing in elfkynan for it to kill? What will that do?"

"You do not yet understand its needs." There was a sudden scrabbling at the barred window. Her Emissary raised a jet-black shadow like an arm and pointed. The iron bars shot from their slots across the room like shrapnel, the metal ringing off the stone walls with terrific force. A moment later something brown and hairy hopped into the room, folding large membrane wings as it did so to fit through the window.

It was a dragon, but unlike any the Viceroy had seen before. Its body was too thick, its neck too short, and its wings too wide for it to be any of the species that populated this land. And then he understood. It wasn't that the dragon was out of place here; it was out of time. It had been created when brutal, primitive savagery had reigned.

That time was here again.

Her Emissary motioned the winged creature to it, and it obliged by hopping up onto the table. The Viceroy cringed, expecting the table to collapse under its weight, but the table held firm. The dragon opened its mouth and dropped a smaller bird onto the table. Leathery feathers shed over the top.

"This is how you feed it?" he asked, inching toward the window where warmer air now blew into the room.

"Watch." The shadows that made up Her Emissary reached out and entwined themselves around the sreex and began pulling the hapless creature apart. Wet, tearing sounds filled the room as blood and bits of flesh spattered the table. The dragon watched the process intently. After a few moments, a small cylinder lay in a pool of blood on the table, directly over the dragon's maw pictured there.

"What is that?" the Viceroy whispered.

Her Emissary ignored him, instead whisking away the carcass of the sreex onto the floor, when the dragon pounced on it at once, diving into the bloody mess and coming up with dripping chunks of flesh that it threw down its throat by flinging its head back and forth in short, choppy motions. The ceiling and walls near the feeding dragon turned progressively redder with each mouthful.

The Viceroy swallowed air and turned back to the table. The tube was open, revealing a thin strip of parchment.

"A message?" he asked, thankful there was reason behind the bloody nightmare he found himself in.

For an answer, inky tendrils unrolled the parchment and laid it flat on the table. As the dragon continued to feed, the Viceroy walked over to the table and looked down. The writing on the parchment was nothing more than sticks and dots.

"It's encoded," he said, feeling a sense of control over the situation for the first time that night. "I spent some time in the Black Room when I first started out in the Diplomatic Corps," he said. This thing before him had once worked for the Royal Cryptology Service breaking codes as well. He leaned forward for a closer look. "I recognize the pattern—it's a Linie cipher, really quite simple to break; I'm surprised you need my help for this."

Her Emissary hissed. The dragon looked up and turned a blood-stained eye on the Viceroy before resuming its meal.

"We care nothing for the message." The temperature in the room grew colder still.

The Viceroy abandoned pretense and wrapped his arms around his body. Not even the warm air coming through the window helped now. His breath began misting in front of him and he knew he had to get out, or he would die in the most absurd way in the middle of this sweltering land. He had made up his mind to run for the door when the top of the table shimmered and the parchment dissolved into its surface. The Viceroy blinked and looked again. Solid wood was changing before his eyes, and he was suddenly looking at blue sky.

He forgot about the cold and bent over the table, an act that felt like leaning over the edge of a cliff.

His vantage point was that of a winged creature. He recognized the plain of Qundi at once, its twisted mass of vines shimmering in a heat he couldn't imagine at that moment. As he watched, he saw a regiment begin marching across the plain, its progression a black line through the twisted green. The image faded, to be replaced by one of nightfall, the same regiment now encamped. More images flowed through the wood and the Viceroy saw faeraugs attack, a desperate struggle, the very strip of parchment being fed to the sreex that now resided in the stomach of the dragon not five feet away.

He saw everything.

"Use it well, and keep it safe from harm," Her Emissary said. A frigid breeze whistled through the room and it was gone.

The Viceroy barely noticed. He gripped the edges of the table and accepted the freezing pain.

"Show me more."

TWENTY-SIX

There's a small village to the north of us on the Olopol River," Konowa said, holding out the folded map for the Prince to take a look.

They were riding at the head of the regiment as it marched across the plain. Konowa had lost count of just how many days they'd been on the move, but it felt like an eternity, and still, it showed no sign of ending. As far as the human, elfkynan, dwarf, or elf eye could see, the plain shimmered with green heat above vines bulging with hidden terrors.

The Prince let his mount's reins drape around its neck and used both hands to push back the shako on his head, revealing a clear line between the pale white skin of his forehead and the now-most-unroyal ruddy complexion of his face. The areas under the arms of his silver-green coatee were black with sweat, and he was constantly fidgeting on his saddle, now denuded of its fur covering. Konowa knew, in fact, that the Prince had developed a rather virulent heat rash, a tale Rallie had enjoyed sharing with him the night before.

Hope it rubs you right raw, Konowa thought, careful to keep his face neutral as he leaned over a little more with the map.

"What? Oh, yes, fine. Can we make it there by nightfall?" the Prince asked, not even bothering to look at the map.

Zwindarra snapped his head around at the map and Konowa cuffed him on the ears. The horses and brindos had grown testy, reacting to the heat and the stress as badly as the troops. The muraphants, on the other hand, had become so lethargic that it took a musket with a blank charge fired at their hindquarters to get them up and moving.

Not even the piece of mountain pressed against Konowa's chest seemed immune. It had been days since he felt even a twinge of cold emanate from the pouch, and he was starting to wonder if he had somehow exhausted its power.

"If we push on through the afternoon I think so," Konowa said, deciding then and there it was better to risk a few more cases of heatstroke than to stay out on the plain another day . . . and night.

There had been no further faeraug attacks, but the temporary camps they set up each afternoon to avoid marching in the heat of the day had been anything but relaxed. The strain, both mental and physical, was taking its toll. The troops grew more sullen and quarrelsome with each mile. Fights broke out over dirty looks. Two more floggings were ordered by the Prince in a fit of pique, and no matter what Konowa said, he would not be talked out of it. The act, predictably, bred even more resentment and tension and created a growing cadre with an ax to grind, spurred on, he knew, by Kritton.

"Very good, Major, we'll press on," the Prince said, sitting up straighter in his saddle.

He made it sound as if it was his own idea, nodding as if the world was in complete agreement with everything that tumbled from his lips. Konowa reasoned that a person brought up to be King probably came to believe that everything was his own idea, even when it was spoon-fed to him.

"They have some very talented weavers in this part of the world, did you know?" the Prince said, turning about in his saddle to look around them and back at the regiment snaked out in their wake.

"Weavers, Colonel?" Konowa asked, wondering if this was the nit's attempt at small talk.

"Weavers, Major, spinners of yarn, makers of cloth. Elfkynan embroideries are famous the world over, and quite prized among the finer households in the capital."

"I can't say as I've seen any, sir," he said truthfully. Zwindarra started as a butterfly flew up from a vine in front of his face. "Bloody idiot," he said, then turned and saw the Prince's eyes narrowing. "Oh, the horse, sir, scared of his own shadow. You were telling me about the embroideries . . ."

The Prince relaxed visibly in the saddle and pulled a hanky from the end of a sleeve, dabbing his brow with it. Konowa got a whiff of perfume and bent forward to adjust a stirrup, taking in a deep breath of the gelding's musky scent to counter the cloying smell.

"I think it's their delicate features, especially their fingers," the Prince said, clearly warming to his subject. He held the hanky in one hand and moved the fingers of the other over it as if playing the piano. "Marvelous dexterity. Tens upon tens of thousands of stitches in some of the larger ones. I've heard rumor that they employ a certain form of magic to make them as ornate as they do. What do you think?"

Konowa looked at the Prince, surprised. "About what, sir?"

The Prince gave an annoyed flick of his head. "The stitching. Do you think they use magic?"

Maybe the heat's frying what part of a brain he's got, Konowa thought. "I really don't know, sir, but I suppose they might, though it seems a bit of a waste, if you ask me. I'd think they'd want to use magic for something more useful."

The Prince tut-tutted him. "You must keep in mind, Major, that we are dealing with a simple people here. The elfkynan aren't as evolved as us humans, or even you Hynta-elves, for that matter."

Zwindarra neighed and stamped a hoof, and Konowa unclenched his fists and let the reins slide through his fingers until the horse's head was back at a more comfortable position. "Very kind of His Highness to say."

The Prince waved away the compliment, completely oblivious to the sarcasm. "It's true." He suddenly leaned over in his saddle, looking furtively around them like a child with a big secret. "They are a simple, earthy folk, swayed by beliefs in things they cannot see. They don't think like we do, Major, which is why the Empire is here. They *need* us. They need our guiding hand to become civilized. The Star of Sillra is the perfect example. I've studied the origin of the Stars for years, you know, talked with the finest scholars and wizards on the subject, including your father, I might add," he said, still casting around to see if they were in danger of being overheard.

"My father never mentioned it," Konowa said flatly. Wizards, royalty, and their intrigues. Ideas born in the flickering shadows of midnight candles and snifters of brandy that invariably sent soldiers like him tramping through some gods'-forsaken land in search of what only the mages and their patrons knew. This time, he knew the what—at least, he thought he did. He looked at the Prince's eager face and felt the cold sharp bite of the stone beneath his uniform.

"Absentminded, the lot of them," the Prince continued, rolling his eyes with a patronizing shake of his head. "But the Stars are real, rest assured. And yet, the elfkynan do not see the Star's real purpose. They think of nothing more than to use it to rid themselves of the Empire, ignorant of the irony! They themselves call the Stars sources of knowledge, yet would use it as no more than a bludgeon." He spurred his horse a little closer to Konowa's. "On the other hand, your father and the other wizards I've spoken to all believe we should claim the Star so that we might use its power against the Shadow Monarch. Again, only seeing it as a weapon, however much more sophisticated their use of it might be."

Konowa couldn't hide his surprise. "You have other ideas?"

The Prince tapped his nose with his free hand. "I do, but it's been difficult to get Her Majesty to understand. This new Viceroy has convinced her and many in her court that the Stars are weapons," he said. His mouth was puckered as if he had just swallowed something sour.

Konowa took the opening before his better judgment could stop him. "Aren't they?"

The Prince was upright in his saddle and looking around as if wanting to strike something. "Untold mysteries lie buried throughout the world, waiting only for a man of vision and destiny to find them. The Empire has a duty to procure the artifacts of time and power and preserve them, to mine them for their secrets, not to destroy them out of hand or turn them into swords to be wielded by simple-minded generals."

The spell dropped, the pieces suddenly falling into place. Konowa looked at the Prince with newfound loathing. "You wish to collect this Star for a *museum*?"

The Prince turned his face to the sun, and for a moment appeared to glow in his own magnificence. "Not just a museum, Major, a temple of knowledge! Can you not see it? A great hall of learning where scholars, alchemists, wizards, artists, and more would come together to study and share their ideas."

"A school, then," Konowa said, fighting back the bile creeping up his throat.

"Precisely! The Queen's advisors hold ever-increasing sway in Her court, and all fear the coming changes. They would simply eradicate every amulet and potion that is of a design they do not understand! Ruwl and the Imperial Army see only weapons that must be harnessed to the Empire's carriage. I favor the witches and wizards more, even though they covet the magic as a drunk does his mead. They are a miserly bunch when it comes to sharing their knowledge, but with the proper encouragement, I will see to it that the world is brought into the light."

"Perhaps they have reason to keep their secrets?"

The Prince shook his head even as he settled back into the saddle and took a deep breath. "Their days of shadowy dealings are coming to an end. When we find the Star, we will have begun the birth of a new age."

"What about the Shadow Monarch, and the extinct creatures coming back?" Konowa asked, marveling at the Prince's ego as he did so.

"Of little importance, really," he said, turning to Konowa and gracing him with a pitying smile. "You, and everyone else for that matter, think we're out here to crush a rebellion and banish the Shadow Monarch to her High Forest. No. The finding of the Eastern Star is nothing less than the coming of a new age of enlightenment. Imagine, Major, a world where men can study in peace and tranquility, guided by the greatest powers ever known. Now *that* is a worthy goal, one that will redeem you a thousand times over."

Konowa grabbed Zwindarra's mane in his hand to steady himself as he felt the blood drain from his face. "Are you serious?"

The Prince laughed—and it was the most frightening thing Konowa had heard since the trip across the plains began. "When we succeed, all of it will fall into place. You and the Iron Elves are going to help me create the greatest repository of knowledge and wisdom ever witnessed in the history of civilization. When we find the Star, we will use it to find the others. Even the Shadow Monarch will bow before me, Her power bent to my will as surely as I command this regiment. If not, then She shall be destroyed . . . although it would be a shame to lose Her wisdom. Do you not see, Major? Our quest is not for a single source of magic. Our quest is to have them *all.*"

TWENTY-SEVEN

A regiment on the march is not a quiet beast.

Metal-banded canteens clattered against wooden musket stocks with each thud of a hobnailed boot. Breath whistled through noses misshapen by barstools and barmaids, and between missing teeth, courtesy of same, laced with wit, pleas, groans, and curses. Spit and matter less liquid flew freely, expelled with a rasping smack of sun-cracked lips, leaving a trail of wet stains and gaining the attention of insects large and small who converged on the sweating mass in a thrumming buzz. The serried rows of soldiers took up a ragged applause in response as hundreds of hands slapped away their tormentors, cursing each and every one.

Accompanied, as the Iron Elves were, by horses, brindos, and a baggage train of muraphants, there was the added sound of creaking wagon axles, the rhythmic friction of jute ropes, the clink of bridles and bits, the swish of tails, the clomp of hooves—cloven and not—and the respective calls of animals as annoyed with their current lot as the soldiers that marched with them.

You'd have to be deaf not to hear a regiment on the march. Or dead.

• • •

The order to halt echoed down the line, and the regiment creaked to a ragged stop. Nervousness washed over the men like an incoming tide.

Alwyn strained to hear some kind of commotion up ahead. It would be dark in another hour or so, and even though the faeraugs had not bothered them again, he still expected to see them every night when the sun went down.

There was no sound beyond a few coughs and a single bellow from a muraphant. The soldiers near Alwyn started to fidget and look around them, scanning the vines for movement. Teeter, a former sailor with a limp, had his pipe lit in an instant. He tilted to the side as if leaning into a stiff breeze, his leathery face beaming satisfaction. Another soldier took off his shako, revealing an apple-sized divot missing from the back of his head. He saw Alwyn staring and glared back, giving him a very rude hand gesture to boot.

"Don't mind Scolly," a third soldier said, his face temporarily hidden behind a large, pink hanky he was using to mop the sweat from his face. When he removed it, Alwyn saw the round, chubby face of a middle-aged man who looked as if he should have been at home delivering milk.

"Alwyn Renwar," Alwyn said, sticking out his hand.

"I know. Poor luck having to flog the elf, but from what I hear, he deserved it."

Alwyn nodded and said nothing.

"Alik Senerson, by the way," the soldier said, shaking his hand, "formerly of the Queen's Tamburian Guards." His face betrayed his offense a moment later in reaction to Alwyn's open-mouthed response. "Not all Guardsmen are six-foot oaks; there are a few normal-sized men in the ranks. I was the pay clerk . . . until a small accounting discrepancy, that is."

"Oh," Alwyn said. "So what's the deal with that fellow over there?"

Alik dabbed at his face again with the pink hanky and nodded toward Scolly. "That miscreant yonder is Scolfelton Erinmoss, son of the Earl of Boryn. Fell off a horse when he was ten and got impaled on a wooden stake. It's a miracle he survived, but of course, he hasn't been right ever since."

Thunder boomed in the distance.

"You smell that?"

The voice startled Alwyn, and it took him a moment to realize Yimt had asked him a question. "What?"

"That stench. That's why we stopped."

Alwyn sniffed the air. There was something, and it was far more disgusting than the current gamey fragrance of the Iron Elves. "What is it?"

There was the sound of boots and Regimental Sergeant Major Lorian came into view. He leaned against his halberd to catch his breath. "Arkhorn, fall out and bring your section with you."

"Yes, Sergeant Major," Yimt said, and motioned for the section to step out of line.

As they marched past the rest of the regiment, Alwyn couldn't help but notice that the other troops were giving them an odd look. It surprised him to realize it was pity. What, he wondered, did they know that he didn't?

The section reached the head of the column, where the smell was definitely stronger. Yimt called a halt and the section grounded their muskets, the sound oddly muffled. Alwyn looked down and saw they were standing in tufts of short, spindly grass. Grass. They had made it through the vines! He looked up and noticed that what he had at first taken for more vines in the distance was a grove of trees on a downward slope. He almost shouted for joy, the hardships and horrors of the journey falling away as if an angel had plucked them from his shoulders.

Then he saw the dirt.

"I could plant me some nice crops here," Inkermon the farmer said, scuffing the earth with his boot. "Got heft, it does, and plenty of vitamins in it, too. The Creator has blessed this land."

"What is that?" Alwyn asked, ignoring the farmer's assessment and pointing his chin to where the officers were grouped in a circle. A hundred yards beyond them the earth was humped, at least two men tall and a few hundred feet across. The mound was blood-red in color and peppered with holes big enough for several faeraugs to jump out of at once.

"Some kind of warren, I reckon," Inkermon said, sucking thoughtfully on the single tooth in the front of his mouth. "Awfully big holes to be water gryphs, though."

This was something new to worry about. "Water gryphs?"

"Sure, you find them along rivers an' such, but it don't look like no warren I ever seen them in."

The first drop of rain fell with a splat on Alwyn's nose. He looked up and was rewarded with several warm, fat drops pelting him in the face and blurring his spectacles as the sky opened up directly above them.

"River?"

"Over there past that grove of trees. Can't you smell it?"

Alwyn squinted through the rain. "I don't see it."

"Course you don't, it's tucked down there below where them trees is at. You got to pay attention to the lay of the land is all. That and the smell. I tell you, with this dirt and that water and the Creator's guiding hand, a fellow could do right proper here."

The rain was now slashing down. Alwyn tried tipping his head forward slightly to shield his face, but as soon as he did, the rain trickled down his back. He looked over at Inkermon. He'd taken a different tack and leaned his head far back and opened his mouth wide, his single tooth glistening a buttery yellow as rainwater splashed into his mouth.

Movement to the left drew Alwyn's attention away. The elfkynan witch and a couple of the muraphant drivers had dismounted and walked up to the front of the column. The Prince waved them over to the group. It was impossible to hear what was being said, but there was a lot of pointing toward the mound. One of the elfkynan took a few tentative steps toward the mound, then started shaking his head and turned around and ran right back past the officers and kept going. Alwyn got a good look at his face as he ran past, and it did nothing to instill hope.

The second muraphant driver began gesticulating wildly while the witch pointed a finger at no one in particular and stamped a boot on the ground. The Prince, surprisingly, seemed amused by it all, while the major just stood there, his left hand resting on the pommel of his saber, his right clutching his chest.

The other elfkynan started shaking his head, too, and the Prince appeared to agree, because he suddenly pointed at the major and everyone stopped talking.

"Look sharp!" Yimt said.

The RSM and Major Osveen left the small group and marched through the rain toward them, talking and looking back over their shoulders toward the large dirt mound. They stopped a few feet away and the major addressed them. Even through the rain Alwyn could see the major was steaming.

"It'll be dark soon, so the quicker we get this sorted out, the quicker we can set up camp. Corporal Arkhorn," the major said, "you know how this works."

Yimt nodded. Water cascaded off his beard like a miniature waterfall, turning the normally black mass a shimmering silver. "Is that witch going to be any help?"

Lorian straightened up and glared at Yimt. "Not at this time."

If the news bothered Yimt, he didn't show it. He patted the hilt of his drukar and pointed over his shoulder. "Fair enough. Once I get inside, I'll light a charge. After that, it's all down to who wants it more." He hunched over his pack and opened the flap, revealing a white gauze bundle the size of a loaf of bread.

The RSM looked surprised. "What are you doing with an artillery charge? That isn't part of an infantryman's kit."

Yimt flashed him a metallic smile. "A soldier never knows what kind of important task those higher up than himself might ask him to do. It's a murky path, trying to divine the thoughts and fancies of your finer thinkers like officers, so I try to be prepared . . . just in case. I call it me head-and-shoulder plan."

Major Osveen obliged. "Head-and-shoulder plan?"

Yimt tapped his head and then his shoulder. "Keeping the one as close to the other as possible."

"See that you do," the major said, a smile he did nothing to hide stealing over his face. "And the same goes for the rest of you. There might be nothing in there, then again . . ."

"Not to fret, sir," Yimt said, taking off his shako and unslinging his shatterbow, motioning for the section to shed their packs and all other unnecessary equipment. The rain bounced off the top of his head and the thin skiff of hair covering it. "We'll be back in two shakes of a dragon's tail. Oh, speaking of tails, that kitty-cat of yours any good for sniffing things out, Major?"

The major looked over his shoulder to where Jir was tapping a large paw into a puddle, apparently mesmerized by the splashing raindrops.

"If he's in the mood," he said, whistling to the bengar and making a hand gesture toward the mound.

Jir looked up from his puddle and twisted his head from side to side as if contemplating the request, then bounded toward the warren and was lost in the rain.

"Right, we'd best get after him," Yimt said, saluting and quickly addressing the patrol. "Until we know better, you get it in your heads that there is something nasty down there and act like it. Keep your yaps shut unless you see something. We'll get closer and then see what we're dealing with."

He looked from soldier to soldier, his glance hard and determined. Alwyn returned it, unable to read anything else in the dwarf's eyes.

"Fix bayonets and make sure they're locked in tight. I don't want it pulling off the first time it gets stuck into something solid."

Alwyn grabbed the bayonet out of the frog on his belt and fumbled to get it in place. Everything was slick with rain and he was keenly aware that he was being watched. He took a breath and tried again, sighing with relief when the tell-tale click sounded.

"Follow me." Yimt took off at a casual walk, his drukar in his right hand, his pack in his left. Alwyn wondered if he would ever be that confident. Who knew what they might find in there, yet Yimt walked toward the mound as if he wasn't the least bit concerned.

They were quickly past the cluster of officers who stood watching their movement as if it were a training drill.

Adding to the surreal quality of the moment, their horses were busy cropping at grass. Alwyn took their calmness as a good sign.

Yimt held up his hand and motioned for the section to stay still.

Alwyn instinctively crouched lower in the grass and felt for the hammer on his rifle, then stopped. With the rain beating down, there was no way the powder would be dry enough to spark. He'd heard of regimental wizards casting spells on powder to keep it dry, but he seriously doubted a spell could overcome this much rain, so it wouldn't have mattered anyway. Still, that witch could have at least tried.

He poked some taller grass to the side with the end of his bayonet and peered through the gap to see what Yimt was doing. It was pointless; the rain made everything a gray blur out past fifty feet. There was no sign of the bengar, either.

Then Yimt came into view, a short, dark figure in the rain, and pointed somewhere to the left, and then he was running, his caerna plastered to his legs like a pair of short pants.

Blurred figures rushed forward on either side and Alwyn stood up and followed suit, straining to see what was happening. The rain now hit his face head-on. He took off his spectacles and jammed them into a jacket pocket as he trotted forward.

A shadow suddenly loomed before Alwyn and he yelped, swinging his musket clumsily at it. There was a dull crack and the musket shivered in his hands, stinging them. A moment later he saw the shadow fall backward in the mud with a soft thud and lie motionless.

Shaking, Alwyn moved forward, the musket held by the barrel with both hands, ready to swing it again.

He'd killed a god. Well, a statue of one at any rate. Alwyn knelt to examine the now-fractured jaw of a short, stocky deity that had been placed on a pedestal that he had not seen. It had once been painted in garish reds and oranges, although only remnants of the colors now remained. He wasn't sure, but it looked an awful lot like a pig, or maybe a boar. Whatever it was, bashing it in the head with his musket wasn't likely to bring him anything but bad luck. He tucked his musket under his right arm and heaved the statue back onto its pedestal, placing the broken pieces of jaw in a neat pile by its feet.

"—ere the hell did he get to?" drifted through the rain, and Alwyn remembered why he was there. He gave the statue a pat on the head for good luck, then trotted off toward the sound of the voice, coming upon Yimt and the others crouched in a semicircle, less than twenty yards from the nearest opening in the mound.

Yimt looked at him, but in the pouring rain Alwyn couldn't tell if he was scowling or just frowning.

"Everyone take a hole," Yimt said at once. "Don't stay at the opening, go in about ten feet, then hold there. Keep your bayonet pointing straight in front of you and brace the butt of your musket in the dirt. Anything comes charging up out of the depths will impale itself."

Before anyone could respond, a high-pitched hiss sounded somewhere nearby. A moment later, a large, dark shape came loping out of the rain. Jir strolled right up to them, dragging a fifteen-foot-long constrictor in his mouth. He held the snake just behind the head and seemed completely unconcerned that it was wrapping its muscular body around his.

The snake coiled tighter around Jir's body, straining to squeeze the life out of the bengar. The sound of scales rubbing against wet fur grew louder. The bengar and the dwarf shared a look, and Alwyn was struck by the feeling of watching two predators assess each other. There was a loud snap as the bengar's fangs bit down and the coils of the snake's body slid from Jir's body. He began to play with it, tossing it into the air as if it were a twig, then pouncing on it and tearing off great chunks of flesh.

"All right, let's get this done," Yimt said, leading them around the mound, dropping off a soldier at a hole as they went by. Soon, only Alwyn was left—Yimt stopped at the next hole and turned to face him, pointing a stubby finger.

"You need to keep your head about you. You don't often get a chance to repeat mistakes out here. Now, if there is anything down there, it's going to come up in one hellfire of a hurry. Hold your ground and shout if you need help, and I'll be there." And then he smiled, his metal teeth glinting briefly in the rain, and Alwyn felt all was right with the world again.

"I'll hold, Corporal," Alwyn said, smiling back at his friend.

Yimt nodded and trotted to the next hole, fifteen yards over. He paused, got a better grip on his drukar, and strolled right in.

Alwyn was at the back of the mound and hidden from view from the officers and the rest of the regiment. The other members of the section had already gone into their holes, leaving him alone outside. His eyes now picked up hints of things he wished he'd not seen. Bits of white bone were scattered between beaten paths of dirt that ran between the holes and over the mound. Something, or somethings, had definitely lived here. The question was whether they were still down there.

TWENTY-EIGHT

Konowa debated going after the troops and leading them into the mound. He took a step forward, then something made him turn. Visyna was walking toward him in the rain. He stopped, unable to keep from staring at her as she moved. She came to an arm's length from him and stopped, staring back at him. For several moments neither one of them said a word. Lightning fretted within rumbling clouds and Konowa tried to find the anger he'd felt after the faeraug attack, but he missed having her this close to him.

"Listen, about the other night," he said, "you have to understand, out here, my men come first."

She nodded. "And you must understand that out here, my land and my people come first."

"Perhaps when we get out of here we could come first," he said, hoping the driving rain drowned out the squeak in his voice. "I kind of enjoyed it when it was just the two of us."

"So did I," she said, stepping closer. "Perhaps we won't have to wait until we are out of here. Rallie and I have been talking. I think you and I have more in common than I thought. We both want the same things." She reached out a hand to touch him, then stopped, her fingers just above his chest. "I will do all in my power to protect you and this regiment. Please, get rid of it."

Konowa hung his head, but the rain sluicing down his collar quickly forced his head up again. "I really wish—"

The sound of an explosion drifted up from belowground. And then the shouting and screaming started.

"Oh, hell."

Alwyn saw yellow, then white, then black. An acrid wind blew past him, followed by clods of dirt, and he turned his head away from the open hole. When he dared to look again, thick, dark smoke was roiling out of the mound in a dozen different places.

"Yimt?" he called. There was no reply. He had opened his mouth to yell again when black shapes began darting out of the smoke.

"Bats!"

The cry went up everywhere as hundreds then thousands of the night creatures flew up from the mound and into the smoke and rain. They formed a growing cloud of whirling wings and high-pitched screeching as they circled the mound.

They moved like a big school of fish in the sky, darting this way and that.

Then they dove.

Alwyn barely had time to switch his grip on his musket and use it as a club when the first of the bats screeched toward him. Their eyes bulged white and milky and their fangs glistened with saliva.

Alwyn swung hard, knocking two bats out of the sky. A dozen more swarmed over him. They screamed and darted around his head, beating their wings in fury against his arms as they tried to get at his face. Everything was a blur of black leathery wings, white eyes, and wicked-looking fangs.

"Put me down, you buggers!"

Alwyn swatted three more bats to the ground and turned toward the sound of Yimt's voice. The bats, dozens of them, were trying to carry Yimt away.

Alwyn took a few steps toward Yimt, but was stopped as more bats began swarming around his legs. The thought of one of these creatures flying up his caerna gave new energy to his tiring arms, and he swung his musket like a scythe. Blood and gristle covered his face and hands and made holding the musket difficult.

Musket fire crackled to life somewhere to the left, but Alwyn couldn't imagine it would have much effect. The regiment didn't have enough musket balls to kill all the bats.

"Lie down!"

It sounded like the witch, Miss Tekoy. Alwyn dove to the earth, curling his legs up underneath him. A moment later, the air thrummed with energy and for the second time in as many minutes his vision was filled by first yellow, then white, then black.

The air went eerily silent. Then it began to rain bats.

Alwyn scrambled to his feet as the creatures began tumbling to earth, their leathery bodies smashing to the ground with sickening wet sounds.

Jir bounded into view and began leaping into the air to grab the bats as they fell, as if it were a game. Several soldiers were doing much the same, only they were trying to catch the falling bats on their bayonets. Alwyn shook his head and turned back toward Yimt, who was struggling to pull a bat out of his beard. A quick snap of the neck ended the bat's struggle and Yimt held it up by a wing.

"So what do we do now?" Alywn asked.

Yimt looked at the bat in his hand, then back at Alwyn. "Dinner."

Visyna knew she hadn't had a choice in killing the bats, just as it had been with the faerangs, but it still made her ill. This was nature perverted. The bats had been driven by far more than anger and hunger. She headed for the grove of trees while the soldiers ran around like little boys. It didn't bother her that the troops were acting like little boys as they did this, she told herself. What did bother her was Konowa. He refused to recognize the danger of carrying a piece of the Shadow Monarch's mountain with him, even as he tried to be more understanding of her concerns.

Life thrummed through the land here, a cleaner, more wholesome energy than what had coursed through the vine-covered plain, but it was clear that Elfkyna was sick. Nothing felt the way it should, and it was getting worse. Her concern about Konowa's affections suddenly struck her as utterly foolish. He was a soldier for an Empire that had subjugated her people and land. She chided herself; she would not succumb to passion when the world she knew teetered on the edge of oblivion.

Her pace quickened and she walked briskly to the edge of the grove, then stopped and looked around. Soldiers milled around several fires and even Rallie was occupied, having accepted the Prince's invitation to dinner in Visyna's place. She stepped through the trees and onto a thin strip of grass that ran around the edge of a small pool of still water as black as the sky above it. She sat down and began to seek.

It was easier this time. Her fingers traced filigrees of light in the shadows before her, creating silvery skeins that spread out through the web of natural life, calling. The pool's surface roiled in response to her efforts, scattering shards of light and shadow like daggers about the grove, but none penetrated beyond the trees, for shadows had filled the spaces between until anyone looking from outside the grove would have seen nothing but darkness within.

"He is a threat."

The grove of trees contained the voice, amplifying it so that it resonated within her body. She shuddered and looked away from the brilliant emptiness of the light as she stood up.

"Konowa means well, but he is confused about the right thing to do." The words came out in a rush, as if saying them fast mitigated the guilt she suddenly felt.

The light refracted into the blackness and the earth moved beneath her feet. It felt as if the very ground was dissolving beneath her.

"He must be stopped."

There was tenseness to the voice Visyna had never heard before. She started to tell the Star of the power Konowa now possessed, but for some reason she couldn't bring herself to say it. "He is stubborn and a fool, but his desire is to protect the Iron Elves. I understand that desire."

"As you did on the plains."

It sounded like a rebuke. "I respect all life, but my loyalty remains to my land, my people, and our rightful heritage. I will do everything in my power to see that you are returned to the elfkynan, but I see no reason that others should die needlessly to achieve that goal."

"Your lack of vision is disturbing. She will bend him to Her will, and I am not strong enough yet to stop it. It is why you were chosen." There was a long pause, and then the Star spoke again. "Perhaps a woman is too weak for this task."

Visyna bristled at the thought. "I will not fail. When the time comes, I will do what is necessary."

"The time is closer than you think. Another will aid you in your task."

Before Visyna could protest, the image of the Star disappeared within a collapsing brilliance that seemed to suck the very vision from her eyes. She reached out a hand to steady herself but could find no tree to grab. She blinked several times, and seeing a faint source of light, took a step toward it. Her foot splashed down into water and she would have tumbled into the pool but for a hand that grabbed her by the arm and pulled her back. Her scream was muffled by another that covered her mouth, and then gently withdrew. Visyna rubbed her eyes then opened them, and the grove and light from the campfires was visible again. She was finally able to look at the owner of the hand still on her arm.

"Private Kritton at your service, my lady," the elf said.

TWENTY-NINE

I t smells of the very bowels of all that is unholy," Inkermon said, holding his nose as he stood in the main entranceway to the mound.

"A bit pungent, I'll admit," Yimt said, holding up a burning brand to look down a tunnel. "Still, beats being aboveground, in my book. Now, let's get in here and set up home before some of the others get the idea."

Alwyn did his best to breathe through his mouth as he and the rest of the section followed Yimt down the tunnel and deeper into the mound. Alwyn doubted any of the other soldiers would be in a rush to claim the mound as a shelter.

As they walked downward the flaming brand revealed a series of masterfully worked words along the walls. Alwyn couldn't read the language, but he sensed their purpose as some kind of protective talisman. The words flowed into shapes, and soon the walls were covered in finely carved reliefs.

Human-like figures of majestic proportions cavorted in a great erotic orgy of limbs and other parts so that it was impossible to tell where one body ended and another began. Unlike the statue of the deity outside, these carvings were raw, unadorned by paint, the naked sandstone taking on an almost fleshlike hue as a result. Alwyn gaped, fascinated and horrified at the same time, as they entered a large room, presumably a bed-chamber, although there was no furniture to be found. Feelings welled up inside him that he had felt before, but as yet had not had the chance to do anything about. He found he was breathing fast and took a long swig from his canteen, trying to look everywhere but at the walls.

Unlike Alwyn, Yimt always seemed at ease and ready to pounce at the same time. There was something about the way he just owned the air he breathed and the space around him that other men respected, and feared, even if they couldn't say why. Alwyn knew some of the why, though, having seen the dwarf in action.

Yimt was combing out his beard with the end of his small, wooden dagger. Every so often a bug would flutter free of the tangled mess and zip off toward one of the flaming brands that were lighting their new, temporary home.

The smell of the cave, for it was hard not to think of it as such, was actually less foul now that they were deep inside it—either that or they were becoming used to the smell. Whatever the case, Alwyn began to think staying the night wouldn't be so bad after all.

"Here," Yimt said, holding out one of his canteens to Inkermon, "have a swig of this, and prepare to lose some money."

Inkermon recoiled and shook his head vigorously. "I'll thank you to keep that vile swill away from me, and not to tempt me with your sinful games of chance." He looked around at the rest of them. "Have you no shame? You sit in a room of decadent, lustful filth, but I will not. I am a man of faith."

At this the dwarf cocked a bushy eyebrow, a feat made all the more spectacular as it disappeared under the rim of his shako. "Indeed? How is it then you come to be part of this jolly band of brothers? My sad story is too long to recount here, poor Alwyn there suffers from the stupidity of youth, no offense, lad, you'll grow out of it, and the rest of these ragged scarecrows," he said, waving a hand at the section sitting around the room, "are highwaymen, robbers, and thieves—all falsely convicted, no doubt, and press-ganged into the service. But what about you, eh? Maybe it's time we all got to know each other a bit better, seeing as we're all one big family now."

Inkermon sniffed and spat on the ground, nowhere near Yimt, then spun around on his heel, bent low, and stomped away up a tunnel.

"Another time then?" Yimt called after him. The other soldiers laughed and sent a few catcalls of their own after the farmer. Yimt waved them to settle down. "All right, let him be. Every man's got a right to think what he will, and that goes for the lot of you, too. But with rights comes responsibility, and one of them is to keep a good chunk of what you believe to yourself."

There were a few puzzled stares, Alwyn's included. Yimt shook his head and gave an exaggerated sigh. "Use what little intelligence you haven't drunk away, lads. Think on it. This army has got more races than a dragon has scales, and each one's got a way of looking at the world different from the next. Take our major up there. Not only is he an elf, he comes from the other side of the ocean. And you know who lives over there, that elf-witch the Sha—"

"Do not speak Her name!" The whole room jumped as Inkermon scrambled back through another tunnel to emerge in the room, a small white book clutched in his hand and held against his breast. "She is a pretender to the throne of the Great Father, creator of the world. To speak Her name is to call Her near. How can you sit idly by while Her abominations crawl over the earth again! Do you not see, the end is near!"

Murmurs rose. Alwyn looked at Yimt, who was sitting very, very still. When he spoke, it was in a whisper that carried around the room like lead shot.

"The only end that is near is yours if you keep talking like that. Your so-called Great Father is a great *human* father who created *man* in his image, not the rest of us."

Yimt slowly rose to a standing position. Alwyn gasped as the dwarf slowly pulled his drukar from its scabbard. Inkermon saw it, too, and held the little white book out before him as if it would ward off the blow.

"You're one of them Pure Order believers," Yimt said, his voice never rising as he took a step forward. "I figured you to be just a puritan know-it-all, but it goes deeper than that, doesn't it?"

"I believe in the One Creator and His vision of a pure, ordered world for the peoples who live in it," Inkermon said, his voice quavering, but his eyes burning with an intensity that bordered on madness. "It is clear that His order is being challenged even as we speak. It is up to His true believers to put things right."

"Is that so? And in that little book of yours, does it mention dwarves, orcs, and folk like that as true believers, too?"

Inkermon sneered. "There was no need to list the lesser races, for they were not created by Him. That is why the world today is polluted with magics and cults and evil. Only He should wield such power, sayeth the scripture!"

Alwyn thought Yimt would decapitate Inkermon then and there, but instead the dwarf actually smiled.

"So you admit your creator was nothing more than a flouncy wizard? Way I hear it, a couple hundred years back, he and a few of his sorcerer buddies went whoring and drinking one night and made the whole thing up to impress the gals in the brothel."

Inkermon sputtered with rage. "Blasphemy! You dirt-born slug! How dare you slander Him!"

The drukar whistled in the air between them and stopped an inch from Inkermon's neck.

The other soldiers were frozen. It was clear to Alwyn no one was going to stop Yimt. He was on his feet and beside the dwarf before he knew what he was doing.

"I think you should put the drukar down, Yimt," he said. The blade hung perfectly still, a black shadow on Inkermon's shoulder. A large vein in the farmer's neck throbbed and Alwyn imagined the blood gushing out, splattering the ceiling.

"The world would be a better place without the likes of him." Yimt's knuckles grew white as he gripped the hilt of the drukar.

"And you'd be hung, and then who would lead our section? Besides, you said everyone was entitled to an opinion, and this is his. I'm not saying I agree with it, because I don't, but if everyone started killing people they disagreed with there wouldn't be many people left, now would there."

Yimt blinked, then turned his head slightly and looked him in the face. Several seconds passed in complete silence. Inkermon's eyes darted wildly between him and Yimt and then down to the blade that hovered beside his neck. Finally, Yimt nodded and slowly lowered the drukar, never looking at Inkermon.

"Go pray to your creator," Yimt muttered, turning his back to the farmer, who scrambled down the tunnel and out of sight.

Yimt looked at each soldier in turn, then at Alwyn. He reached out a hand and patted him on the elbow.

"Ally, not that I'm going anywhere, but if I did, I can't think of a better man to lead this section than you." With that, the dwarf sat down, leaning back against an impressive pair of carved breasts, and began taking apart his shatterbow while the other soldiers hooted at Alwyn as the next king of Calahr.

"Leave the poor boy alone, now," Yimt said, squinting one eye and looking down the right-side barrel of his weapon. "You all know he's got the smarts, lot more than you lot put together."

"What about me, then?" a soldier asked, his cheeks puffing out two enormous muttonchops of brown scraggly whiskers.

Yimt looked over the barrel to his questioner, one eye only, his eyebrow threatening to disappear again under the rim of his shako. "Buuko, you couldn't dump piss out of a boot if the instructions were written on the heel."

"I can read well enough," Buuko said in response, sticking his chest out with pride and hooking his thumbs in his suspenders.

More laughter greeted this, and Alwyn couldn't help but join in. Buuko, not much taller than Yimt and as scrawny as a winter chicken, opened and closed his mouth in apparent outrage, then shrugged and started cleaning his musket.

"Make sure you do 'em right," Yimt said, addressing the entire section. "In a climate like this, the moisture will have your musket rusted away to dust inside a week if you don't get at it every day. As me grandmare used to say, keep your musket and your pecker clean and you're likely to live to a ripe old age."

"She said that?" Alwyn asked, finding a place to sit down between Teeter, who was puffing steadily on his pipe, and Alik, who seemed to be having difficulty holding his musket and cleaning it. Alwyn leaned over and helped him steady it, getting a smile and thanks.

"Too right she did. Full of wisdom, she was. Knew more about this world than you lot put together. Reminds me of a time once a way back. Still gnawing on sandstone and chunks of pottery. Seems there was a young miner who . . ."

Alwyn smiled and began cleaning his musket as Yimt rambled on. It was a comfortable feeling. He let his gaze drift around the room and was amazed that the carvings were losing their effect on him until he saw one in particular that might or might not have included a goat. He grabbed the pricker hanging from a lanyard on his jacket and bent over his musket, working the thin steel needle into the touchhole and digging out bits of dirt. If the hole was plugged there would be no way for the spark in the pan to ignite the charge inside the barrel. It amazed him something so small could make such a difference. He looked over at Yimt and was pleased to realize that went for people, as well.

"Now, who wants to live dangerously?"

Alwyn looked at the dwarf, detecting more than a hint of mischief in his voice.

Yimt dipped a hand into his upturned shako and removed a well-used deck of cards from inside. "Ante up, ladies. Elfkynan siasters are worth twelve to the Imperial sovereign or four colonial mints, nickel-silver, that is, for you shady types that have a pocket full of copper."

THIRTY

huge shadow loomed over Alwyn, and he looked up to
see Private Hrem Vulhber crouched over him. "Corporal
Arkhorn around? I've got last watch and he said he'd donate
one of his boys to stand guard with me."

"I'll keep you company for a bit, Hrem," Alwyn said, standing up and
then looking over to where Yimt was reclining against one of the more
interesting carvings.

Yimt opened one eye. "I was thinking Inkermon could use a little
fresh air, but seeing as you're volunteering I guess it can't hurt. Just do me
a favor and stay out of trouble. Hrem, don't let him shoot an officer out
checking the lines . . . unless you really have to, of course."

Hrem smiled and nodded. "As long as you're down here, I think the
officers can walk about safely up there."

"The insubordination," Yimt said, yawning and stretching. He waved
them away. "Begone then, and do us a favor and don't thump about up
there; some folk are trying to sleep."

Alwyn grabbed his shako and musket and followed Hrem up through
the tunnels and out into the night.

There were no stars in the sky, and a warm mist rose from the ground, limiting visibility to a few feet at best. His need to stretch his legs diminished somewhat, but he wasn't going to turn back now.

They met a weasel-faced soldier as they stepped outside. Hrem made a small noise in his throat and kept on walking, pointedly not bothering to introduce him to Alwyn.

"Pleasant watch, ladies," the soldier called after them.

"Who was that?" Alwyn asked, quickening his pace to keep up with Hrem's huge strides.

"Trouble. Some people are born bad, others get made that way. Private Zwitty's both."

"Oh."

Hrem looked over and clapped a huge hand on his shoulder, knocking Alwyn off balance.

"Not to worry; you listen to the Little Mad One and you'll be fine. I'm sure he's probably told you, but when you have a problem, you face it head-on. A fellow like Zwitty, or Kritton, you always look in the eye and you don't blink."

"Must be nice to be as big as you, though," Alwyn said, looking up at the towering soldier beside him.

Hrem laughed, a delicate sound that made Alwyn smile. He was glad it was dark enough Hrem couldn't see it.

"Your corporal is this side of four feet nothing, but you find me a soldier in this regiment, hell, in this army, who'd have the stones to take him on. It isn't size, Alwyn, it's what's inside that counts."

They walked in silence for a few minutes, carefully picking their way through the camp and down the slope toward the river that Alwyn still hadn't seen. He certainly smelled it, though, a pungent, stagnant odor growing stronger with each step. He was beginning to worry Hrem would lead them right into it when a voice called out to them up ahead.

"Who goes there?"

"It's me, Kess, come to relieve you," Hrem said. He yawned and started to topple backward before catching himself.

"About time, too, I was starting to think you'd forgotten about me down here," Kess said, walking into view to stand in front of them. In the dark and the swirling mist he was little more than a shadow. "Who's this then?" he asked.

"Alwyn Renwar, A Company," Alwyn said, holding out his hand. An arm came forward with a hand on it and Alwyn was relieved to feel real, warm flesh when he shook it. "I couldn't sleep so I thought I would get a bit of air."

Kess stepped forward and Alwyn could just make out a pair of muttonchops and a very crooked nose.

"To each his own, I say. Kester Harkon, pleased to meet you." He pulled back and waved his arm in the direction of the river. "Watch your step down there; it's all mud."

"Will do, thanks, Kess," Hrem said, moving off toward the river.

Kess grunted and walked away. Alwyn followed Hrem by walking through the gap he made in the mist.

"We're not likely to see a thing," Hrem said a moment later. He'd stopped walking and Alwyn bumped into him.

Alwyn looked around and saw nothing but gray swirling mist against a deep-well darkness. "Probably not," he agreed. Would, he wondered, anything see them?

Hrem yawned again. "It'll be dawn soon, and I haven't slept a wink."

"I could stand watch for a bit," Alwyn said before really thinking about what he had just offered.

"You haven't slept either."

"I don't think I can, not right now anyway. Just tell me what to do if a corporal comes to check the sentries."

There was a thud and a deep sigh as Hrem stretched himself out on the ground. "Not to worry, Alwyn. The only sneak you couldn't hear coming was Kritton, and he's not a problem anymore. Serves the devilish bastard right if you ask me."

"Fair enough," Alwyn said, hoping his voice didn't sound as worried as he suddenly felt.

"You're a grand fellow, Alwyn, no matter what they say about you," Hrem said through one long yawn.

"Who says what about me?"

". . . don't you pay it another thought . . . damn fine lad . . . bit of a fragile sort, but tough enough . . . you'll make a soldier yet . . ."

Alwyn wasn't sure if that was a compliment or an insult. Or both. A high-pitched snore rose up from the ground where Hrem had fallen asleep, indicating the conversation was over.

Splash.

Alwyn froze, straining to locate the sound. Everything was silent again. He leaned forward slightly, cocking his left ear toward the still-unseen river. A ghostly whirl of mist sailed past, taking shapes every bit as dire as his imagination would conjure. He gripped his musket a little tighter and peered into the fog, praying the sun would hurry up and rise. The underground village, with all its narrow tunnels and hollowed-out rooms more suitable for large gophers, or dwarves, than men now seemed like the most wonderful place in the world.

I'm just being silly, he told himself, realizing he had been leaning more and more forward as he strained to hear. "I'm an Iron Elf," he whispered, not really believing it, but standing up straight and by sheer force of will turning his back to the river.

Splash.

The vines and the faeraugs were behind them, the regiment was largely intact, and Hrem, one of the biggest soldiers in the regiment, was sleeping just a few yards away. Hell, they even had an elfkynan witch, even if she did seem a bit standoffish. So why did the sound of a fish or a frog (he hoped) set his nerves on the edge of a razor?

More mist whirled past, and for the briefest of moments a shape emerged that Alwyn knew he recognized.

Meri.

Alwyn squinted until he thought his eyes would turn to jelly. He shook his head. He could have sworn the one-eyed soldier had just appeared, but Meri was dead.

I'm cracking up, he thought, though he felt more clear-headed than he ever had in his life. It had to be his imagination. Alwyn wouldn't tell Yimt, or the major. As Hrem had let slip, the other soldiers already thought

Alwyn was a bit off—he could all too easily imagine what they'd think if they knew he was seeing things, too.

Scritch . . . scritch.

Just a duck nibbling at snails on water lilies. He debated waking Hrem. If there was something out there, it was the smart thing to do.

Sreeeesh . . . crack.

A turtle crawling over a small log? A water gryphon eating a turtle on a small log? Alwyn shifted his grip on his musket and rolled his shoulders, trying to relax. It wasn't working.

That's it, I'm waking Hrem, he decided, and turned to find the sleeping soldier.

And then he saw it. The first pinkish-orange smudge on the horizon.

It was magic. Everything seemed different with that first tiny bit of light. The tension dribbled out of his muscles until he thought he'd collapse on the ground in one wonderful mushy heap of relief. It was morning, the start of a brand-new day, and the vines were behind them.

Scritch-splash. He turned, and for the first time saw the river. Tall, bulbous-headed reeds rustled at the river's edge as ducks (and they were ducks, he was happy to see) nibbled around their stalks, diving for seeds that had shaken loose from their pods. It was a beautiful sight.

He looked out past the ducks to the river itself, no more than a musket shot across as the far bank began to take shape through the mist. The smell, which he had to admit he was getting used to, appeared to come from the river itself. As the dawn grew brighter he could make out the oily surface of the brown water and wondered how the ducks survived in it. *Maybe they drink somewhere else,* he thought, taking a few steps closer to the reeds.

Water splashed into the air a few feet away. Alwyn jumped, swinging his musket to bear. The mist was still thick enough that large chunks of the area were clouded by it. He eased the hammer back and held his breath, the sound of his own heart so loud he wondered if a person could break a rib. The mist became thicker again, a reaction to the rising heat of the morning, and it clung to his skin like a thin sheet of slime.

A terrible thought occurred to him. What if the powder in the pan is too wet and won't light? He looked down at the musket as if it had just betrayed him.

He cradled the now-suspect weapon in one hand and felt around for another charge in his ammunition pouch, his fingers brushing the tops of the waxed paper cartridges and feeling moisture on each one. He closed the lid on the leather pouch and decided he'd take his chances with what was in the pan. More water splashed.

"Hrem," Alwyn called. He said it so softly he wasn't sure any sound escaped his lips. He tried again and jumped at the loudness of his own voice.

"Naw . . . tickle me there, Dabina, that's the spot . . ."

Alwyn shook his head. He was beginning to think he'd never sleep normally again, while soldiers like Yimt and Hrem seemed capable of sleeping anywhere, any time.

More ducks were splashing and quacking now and the sun was definitely on the rise, though the area around Alwyn was still murky with shadow. He decided a couple of seed pods lobbed into the tall grass like those hand-sized fireballs the grenadiers used should get Hrem's attention. He rested his musket on his shoulder and walked toward the river's edge to grab some.

The smell again. Stronger.

It was earthy and old, a smell that had never seen the light of the sun. It wasn't the smell of the river, either. It was approaching Alwyn from somewhere in the mist.

". . . Hrem . . ." Alwyn cried, but now that he wanted to shout his voice would only rasp, his tongue dry and immovable inside his mouth.

Something large and ponderous loomed out of the mist—it was a dark blur, but Alwyn knew what it was.

". . . R-r-rakke," he tried to scream, gripping his musket so hard the muscles in his hands burned.

". . . use the feather; no, the purple one," Hrem said, sighing with great contentment.

"*Hremmmm!*" Alwyn shouted at the top of his lungs, pulling back the hammer and squeezing the trigger. There was the distinctive crack of flint striking metal followed by a fizz and then nothing.

The powder didn't light.

The rakke emerged from the mist swinging its arms wildly. Alwyn closed his eyes and lunged forward, waiting for the impact.

A bitter cold wind roared up from nowhere. Alwyn opened his eyes. Meri stood before him, a long broadsword held easily in his hands. The body of the rakke was tumbling down the bank where it rolled into the water and sank from view.

"What's going on?"

Alwyn turned at the sound of Hrem's voice. The big soldier was standing a few feet away, his musket at the ready.

"It was a—" Alwyn started to say, turning to point to Meri.

There was no one there. No sign of Meri. No sign of the rakke.

"A what?" Hrem asked, taking a few steps toward the river before turning back.

Alwyn shook his head. "Nothing. Nothing at all."

Sun rays began to stretch out across the land, chasing away the last vestiges of the night. Alwyn watched the mist burn into nothing, and wondered if his mind would soon follow.

THIRTY-ONE

A gold coin for your thoughts," Konowa said, spying Rallie pacing back and forth near her wagon. Blue smoke hung thick around her as she puffed rapidly on a large cigar. Every few steps she would stop, take the cigar out of her mouth, and look to the sky, visible now that the sun was up and had burned away the mist. It appeared that she was speaking to someone Konowa couldn't see.

"I can't see him, either," Rallie said, sending a cool trickle of unease up his spine as she answered his unspoken thought.

"Martimis, was it?" he asked. He looked to the sky, but beyond a new batch of rain-laden clouds on the horizon, there was no sign of the sreex, or any other flying creature, for that matter.

"Oh, I hope it still is," she said, clamping down on the cigar and walking back to her wagon. She motioned for him to follow.

Konowa obliged and was surprised to see Jir curled up underneath her wagon, his muzzle resting on his paws and his ears twitching in dream. Rallie bent and gave the bengar a scratch behind the ears, and his whiskers fluttered and his hind legs stretched out to the fullest. He never opened his eyes. She stood up, jumped onto the running board along the side of the wagon, and leaned her head back against the wooden cages. The sreexes inside purred in response.

Konowa remained standing a few feet away. "Martimis looked like he could take care of himself."

"Normally, yes, but things are no longer normal," she said, pulling out her cigar and waving it around her. The smoke left a fat trail in the air like a snake through mud.

"Will you send another?"

Rallie sighed and looked at the caged sreexes. "I've sent two more since Martimis. My editor is not the most patient of dwarves—if my reports aren't getting through he'll send Wobbly."

"Wobbly?"

Rallie smiled and closed her eyes. "You'll know him when you see him. Still, I keep hoping that you won't."

"Then it is hope in vain, and you know it," Visyna said, appearing from around the far side of the wagon. She was dressed in a light cotton wrap the color of warm gold and had traded in her riding boots for a pair of woven grass sandals again. Her hair was pulled back and tied up off her shoulders, revealing an enticing amount of bare brown skin, much of which was covered with intricate tattoos of animals and plants in perfect harmony.

"Hope is never in vain, my dear," Rallie said, opening her eyes and watching Visyna walk toward them. "Hope is hope. What is vain is when we do nothing to help it along."

"Then you should convince the Prince to turn this regiment around, now. Going to Luuguth Jor will only result in disaster." She pointedly refused to look at Konowa.

Konowa touched his hand to his shako. "Get up on the wrong side of nature this morning?"

Visyna gave him a withering glance and took a few more steps toward Rallie, showing off a significant portion of smooth thigh in the process as the cloth fluttered and settled about her body again. Konowa found himself remembering the touch of her hands against his skin and allowed himself a small smile.

"I'm glad to see someone is enjoying our plight. Everywhere the world grows strange and the weight of an Imperial hobnailed boot does little to aid it."

He sighed and held out his hands. "Surely you don't blame the regiment? We're on the same side, remember?"

Rallie stood up suddenly, clapping her hands together in obvious annoyance. She set the wagon rocking as the sreexes reacted with throaty screeches that hurt even his musket-deadened ears. Jir growled, and his claws extended, but he slept on.

"It would be best for all concerned that the two of you hurry up and consummate this relationship of yours before someone gets hurt," Rallie said. There was not a hint of humor in her voice.

Konowa wasn't sure who looked more embarrassed.

Just then a soldier came running toward them, shouting. Konowa reached for the acorn against his chest and instinctively willed his senses outward, but the natural chaos of life, annoying but not threatening, was all he felt. The soldier came to a stumbling halt, his shako falling from his head and landing at Konowa's feet. Konowa picked it up and handed it back to the soldier, who quickly put it back on and saluted, his chest heaving as he struggled to breathe.

"M-major! The villagers are back! They have news from Luuguth Jor."

"Show me," Konowa said, setting off at once in the direction the soldier had come from, forcing the winded man to trot after him. Visyna and Rallie followed, their heads close together as they walked, whispering to each other.

A minute later they came upon what could only be categorized as a land dispute in full heat.

"—a right swift kick where the sun rarely graces— Oh, hello, Major," Yimt said, spotting Konowa. He gave him a brisk salute, his elbow just missing the very angry face of the elfkynan male he'd been arguing with a moment ago. "Beautiful morning, wouldn't you say? I was just telling my new friend here, Nobnuts the fool, was it, about the Empire and how lucky they are we've come to this land, bringing them a healthy dollop of good old civilization."

"N'bhat," the elfkynan said, stomping away from Yimt to stand in front of Konowa. He was no taller than the dwarf, dressed in only a simple cloth around his privates. His skin was as brown as bark, and he wore his hair in a single braid down his back. A group of villagers similarly attired, including many women and several children, stood off at a distance watching. "My name is N'bhat, *foloo* of the village. You go now. Go and come back never." It was said with fierce determination, and Konowa admired the elfkynan for it, surrounded as he was by a well-armed regiment of the Imperial Army.

"*Foloo?*" Konowa asked, turning to Visyna. She looked as if she had just taken a drink of frog-bottom ale.

"It means headman," she said, with an edge of contempt in her voice clear to everyone, including N'bhat, who looked both angry and frightened of her. The women of the village suddenly began making warding signs and spitting on the ground. "They are Majazi, a nomadic tribe of elfkynan that follow the fish as they move upstream to spawn."

The Hynta-elves, though not the Long Watch, hunted buffalo, deer, and tarnir in the same way, tracking them from the forest as they moved across the great plains. Konowa figured he could deal with these people as well.

"N'bhat," he said, turning back to the elfkynan, "we have no desire to get in the way of your hunting. Tell me what you've seen and we will leave here in peace."

The elfkynan fidgeted. "You go now. We want no trouble. You go."

Konowa tapped the pommel of his saber. "No one wants trouble, but it has a way of finding you all the same. What did you see?"

One of the women, perhaps N'bhat's wife, began shouting at him and gesticulating wildly, pointing at the way they had just come. N'bhat shouted something back at the woman, the only effect of which was to agitate her even more.

"The sooner you tell me, the sooner we'll be on our way," Konowa offered, keeping a wary eye on the woman, who showed no signs of quieting down. The other women seemed emboldened by her display, and many were holding fishing spears in their hands. This could get ugly fast.

N'bhat threw up his hands at the women and, turning back to

Konowa, sighed and nodded. "There, where siggers live, Luuguth Jor. Terrible things. Go now."

"What happened?"

"You go if I say?"

Konowa resisted the urge to grab the elfkynan by the throat and shake him. "Or maybe I set up a garrison here. I'm sure the ladies wouldn't mind too much," he said.

N'bhat looked startled at the suggestion. "Terrible things. No see, but hear. And more elfkynan come, come to war against siggers." He knelt in the dirt and began drawing.

"Siggers are this many," he said, making a dot with his finger.

He then began making rows of dots in a circle around the first dot, and Konowa's heart sank.

When N'bhat finally finished there were over a hundred dots surrounding the first.

The Thirty-fifth Foot had sent a half company to garrison the fort, approximately fifty men. Fine for showing the flag among peaceful natives, wholly inadequate for what was bearing down on them now.

They wouldn't hold out for long.

"You go now."

If N'bhat was right, that meant a rebel force of at least five thousand elfkynan, not counting what the "terrible things" were.

Konowa waved the headman away and looked to the east. The land rose gently into a series of low, scrub-covered hills. The river wove its way through them, a thin strip of flat grassland to either side. It would offer the regiment a fairly easy time of it after the vines. It was also the quickest route, and one the enemy would be sure to watch.

"We'll have to be vigilant," Rallie said.

She didn't have to read his thoughts—every soldier there saw the danger. Konowa turned. "Do you believe him?"

"Do not trust him," Visyna interrupted. She kept casting a glance toward the women villagers, her fingers moving rapidly.

"He seemed genuine enough," he said, unable to determine what was at work here. "Do you know him?"

Visyna gaped and her eyes narrowed. "Most certainly not! The Majazi are nothing like my people."

Rallie scowled, but said nothing.

"Aren't you all elfkynan? They seem very much in tune with nature, which, as you so often remind me, is a wonderful thing," Konowa said.

"You wouldn't understand," she replied, looking with disgust as one of the village women began breast-feeding a baby in the open.

Konowa considered Visyna's fine garment, the way she held herself, her life as the daughter of a wealthy merchant, and suddenly understood perfectly.

"Major!"

Konowa looked past Visyna and grimaced. Lorian was coming toward him with the Prince.

"Sir," Konowa said, saluting for all present when the Prince arrived.

The Prince seemed caught off-guard for a moment, then saluted and looked around. His jacket was undone and his shako was perched at a precarious angle on his head as if he had thrown it on in a hurry. And then he yawned and rubbed his eyes. The bloody fool had just woken up.

"Major, what's this I hear about finding the villagers? Fishermen, are they? I distinctly smell bara jogg being fried."

Konowa gave Lorian a subtle hand signal and the RSM had the surrounding troops bustled away in a flash, leaving only the RSM, the Prince, Konowa, Visyna, and Rallie.

"A refined nose you have, sir," Konowa said, opting to make this as painless as possible. "Apparently the villagers are nomadic, following the fish as they swim the rivers. This village here is their main dwelling. It was empty because they were away upstream, toward Luuguth Jor. The headman tells me something has happened at Luuguth Jor, though he doesn't know what, and that a rebel army is marching toward it. He estimates their numbers to be at least five thousand troops."

"This is good news," the Prince said, waking up considerably at the news. "Rallie, you'll want to make note of this. This is clearly a pivotal moment. Everything is falling into place. We have ascertained the whereabouts of the rebels." He smiled indulgently at the small group around him and placed his hands behind his back, rocking slightly on his heels.

Lorian stared at the Prince with something close to panic in his eyes. Konowa hoped his own didn't show as he realized that the fool had no idea what to do next. "Yes, sir, a pivotal moment. May I suggest we break camp at once and march on the garrison?"

The Prince stopped rocking and nodded sagely. "Exactly what I was going to say. Yes, we'll march at once and meet the rebels head-on. When those elfkynan see the Iron Elves, they'll run like the cowards they are—no offense, Ms. Tekoy, I know a few of your race to be quite steadfast, almost Calahrian in constitution."

Anger flashed in Visyna's eyes, but she only smiled at the Prince and nodded deferentially to him. *Would have taken my head off,* Konowa thought, then focused on what the Prince had said.

"Of course, sir, but we might want to consider a cautious approach when we get there. We don't know the exact size of the force we're dealing with, and what, if any, additional support it might have," he said, wondering what Her Emissary could be up to. "And there is the matter of whether the Thirty-fifth Foot still hold the garrison."

The Prince's smile vanished, to be replaced by the look of one accustomed to getting his own way. "We *will* find the star there, Major, and we will do *whatever* is necessary to procure it. I will not lead a regiment of skulking pad foots through the shadows. This is the *new* Iron Elves, and will march tall and proud straight at the enemy, and it will be they who turn and run. I do hope that is perfectly clear."

"Yes, sir." Konowa saluted and watched the Prince stride off toward his tent, no doubt to make sure his precious books were packed away properly. Rallie and Visyna were already walking away, still whispering to each other. Lorian turned to Konowa.

"I hate to say this, Major, but I think the Prince is going to get us all killed."

Konowa kicked a small clod of dirt with his boot, sending it rolling across the ground shedding bits of itself until it tumbled into nothing.

"Then it's up to us to see that that doesn't happen. I can't spare you, but grab what horses you can, including Zwindarra, find troops that can stay in a saddle, and send them ahead of us so we aren't surprised by anything nasty."

Lorian shook his head. "It sounds like a wise course of action, sir, but it won't work. The horses are all but done in. Your mount looks all right, and the Prince has a couple that might hold up for a bit, but this weather is taking the wind right out of them. We could still do it—I brought a few of the lads from the Fourteenth over with me—but I spread them out through the regiment to steady the weaker elements. I don't think I want to take them out now just when things are going to get dicey."

Konowa considered for a moment commandeering a few brindos or muraphants, but quickly threw out that idea. "Then they'll have to go on foot. If we get there blind, we're dead."

"A section ought to do it. They'll move a lot faster than the regiment, even on foot, especially with that elfkynan as a guide. If we send them out right now, we should have good warning of what's up ahead. If the Thirty-fifth Foot still hold the garrison, we might be able to squeeze the rebels between them and ourselves and catch them in a crossfire when we get there."

Now Konowa shook his head. "Don't underestimate the elfkynan. For all we know, there could be thirty thousand of them waiting for us, and that isn't counting the star . . . or the Shadow Monarch."

"You really think so, sir?"

Konowa patted his jacket over his heart and looked east at the growing wall of rain clouds. "Lorian, I'm not sure what I believe anymore. All I know for certain is we're going to need every bit of luck, skill, and chicanery we've got, so get N'bhat and get me those scouts."

Lorian saluted. "Have no fear, Major, I know just the lads for this."

Konowa saluted and stood there while Lorian ran off into the bustling camp. If there was something terrible waiting for them, the soldiers Konowa had just ordered to scout ahead weren't coming back.

THIRTY-TWO

Can you keep up or not?"

Three Section, First Platoon, A Company, stood perfectly still, waiting. Corporal Yimt Arkhorn glared up at the RSM, who glared right back, a folded piece of paper in his hands. They were orders signed by the major himself, ensuring the scouting party was not mistaken for a group of deserters when they arrived at Luuguth Jor . . . assuming the fort was still held by the Thirty-fifth Foot. Soldiers got hung for desertion, but that wasn't the issue here.

Yimt spat a sizzling stream of crute into the grass. "I've walked more miles in this army than most of these boys have had hot meals. I was there with General Remdol in the Erimii Mountains when we chased those orcs all the way up Mount Ipk and down the other side, but that ain't the point. I could march to the ends of the earth and keep on going with a change of boots, but not with *him!*"

The smallest of tics twitched under Private Kritton's right eye, but he forced a smile and looked down at Yimt with apparent friendliness. "We've had our differences in the past, Corporal, but if I'm big enough to serve under you now that our positions are reversed, surely you won't mind leading me. I've already forgiven young Renwar there. Leaves in the wind. Can't you do the same?"

Alwyn's blood ran cold as the elf turned his stare to him. This was *madness*. Kritton wouldn't forgive anyone, and even though it was Alwyn who had delivered the lashes, he knew that Kritton really blamed the major, and Yimt.

"I'll show you what I can do," Yimt said, taking a step toward Kritton.

The regimental sergeant major slowly spun his halberd in his closed fist. He motioned Yimt over to one side. "No one is showing anyone anything. You'll do exactly as you're ordered, or you'll lose those stripes on your sleeves and get some new ones on your back!" He seemed to reconsider his next words and sighed, lowering his voice so that Alwyn had to strain to hear what he said next.

"Kritton is a bastard, but he's also an elf, and a sneaky one at that. He knows his way around the wild, he's got eyes like a hawk." Lorian pointed at Yimt and cut him off. "A scouting party is going. Kritton is going to be on it. Now, are you going to lead it?"

Yimt tugged on his beard and looked around the group, his stare lingering on Kritton before looking back at the RSM. "I'll lead the scouting party, but I can't promise what'll happen out there. Things get bloody in a hurry—someone could get hurt," he said, his gaze drifting back to the elf.

"Yes, they could," Kritton said, his smile all teeth.

As much as Alwyn admired Yimt's abilities as a fighter, there was no way he'd make it out there with Kritton. He'd need someone to watch his back.

"I volunteer, RSM," Alwyn said, startling the group.

"The hell you do," Yimt shot back, rounding on him and stabbing a thick finger at his chest. "This ain't no game," Yimt said, turning to look at Lorian. "He's done his share and every last one of us here knows it. I'll get my scouts, but not him."

The RSM nodded as if he agreed.

"That's not fair! If Three Section is going, then I should go, too. You said you needed volunteers and I'm volunteering."

"Who volunteered for what?" a voice asked. Alwyn turned and was shocked to see the Prince standing just a few feet away.

"Colonel! Everything under control, sir," the RSM said, saluting the Prince, who returned it slowly, suspicion obvious on his face.

"Of course everything is under control, RSM, how could it be otherwise? What I asked, however, was who was volunteering, and for what. I do hope it isn't anything like scouting. I made it quite clear that the Iron Elves will not be hiding in the bushes in the face of the enemy." He stared at Kritton the whole time.

Lorian looked suddenly very embarrassed about something. Alwyn saw his chance.

"An advance party, Colonel, to announce your arrival to the garrison to give them time to prepare a proper reception." Alwyn realized he was out-and-out lying to the colonel of the regiment and the future King. He took a quick breath and continued. "Sad fact of the matter is, sir, some of the regiments don't hold to the same standard as others out here. The RSM was just telling us about how important it was that the garrison at Luuguth Jor be on top of their game. I had just volunteered to go with the advance party and help them get everything in order."

"Now *that's* initiative," the Prince said, nodding his approval. "I can see why you would be so eager to volunteer. Yes, we have a duty to all the regiments in the Imperial Army to set an example, but it wouldn't do to show them up too much at first, now would it, men?"

The soldiers gave the Prince a half-hearted "yes, sir."

"Well, don't dawdle around here a moment longer. RSM, get these men on their way immediately. The regiment will move out in ten minutes."

"Yes, sir, at once," he said, saluting the back of the Prince, who was already walking back toward his charger. He was barely out of hearing when Yimt was standing in front of Alwyn.

"Are you trying to get yourself killed?"

The RSM intervened before he could answer. "It's done, Arkhorn, so do what the colonel said and get your boys out in front, *now*. We wouldn't want the garrison at Luuguth Jor to greet the Prince in their undergarments, now would we?" he asked, looking long and hard at Alwyn.

Yimt threw up his hands. "Fine. Three Section, grab your kit and form up. And *you*," he said, pointing at Kritton, "I want you ten yards in front of me at all times."

The elf smiled and bowed slightly, tipping his shako to Yimt. "Whatever you say, *Corporal*."

A single shaft of sunlight fell into the chamber through a crack in the half-shuttered window. Only then did the Viceroy realize he had forgotten to close it after the beast had come last night, bearing another dead sreex in its maw. He watched the light move across the stone floor, revealing the brown, dried blood and bits of flesh left over from the dragon's latest meal.

As the light crawled along the stone, not a single dust mote danced in its luminous path, so cold was the air in the room.

So cold, and so pure.

The Viceroy walked over to the window, opened the metal shutters wider, and looked outside, the first time he had done so in days. The sun was up, heating the coming rain clouds so that when their rain fell, it would be warm and dull, unsatisfying. Everything outside was soft with humidity. The land steamed and bubbled like a festering morass while the elfkynan moved listlessly through it, their tired insolence a palpable smell on the thick, wet air.

It was the smell of rebellion.

An example must be made. Not just one, or even a handful, but dozens, perhaps hundreds. Crush the spirit and the body will follow. But who? The Viceroy pulled the shutters to and locked them, turning back to the table in the center of the room. Here, in this room, it was cold like the top of a mountain in the dead of winter. With the cold came clarity. His mind now dissected ideas, formulated concepts, and discerned purpose with a razor precision he had only dreamed of before. Here, he had the power and the vision to see the coming of a great new age.

He moved toward the table, reaching out a hand and gently brushing it against the surface. The cold bit into his flesh, and he released a long, slow breath of pure pleasure, uncaring of the fact that no mist formed when he did so.

He understood it now, this thing that Her Emissary called its *ryk faur*.

Its needs were simple and immense, and he reveled in feeding it. To feed it was to satisfy his own needs, and in so doing the bond between them grew.

"Show me," he said, placing both hands firmly on the table. The cold enveloped him, peeling away shreds of his humanity a strip at a time and replacing it with something heavier, something stronger.

The air in the room thinned as a skein of ice crept up the walls and across the ceiling. The tabletop remained clear, its surface disappearing as the verdant landscape of Elfkyna swirled into focus, its lush abundance teeming with life, crawling with all manner of beasts, including one many-legged creature he was especially interested in.

The Iron Elves were easy to find, their presence on the ground as obvious as a signal fire in pitch darkness. They marched in a northeasterly direction, following the path of a fat, brown river to a fishing village.

"Luuguth Jor." Its ancient history radiated beneath the tenuous skin of life that existed there. Its memory went deep into the earth, tying it to things far older than even he could yet contemplate. He knew the Star was to be found there. Before, he had cared little if the Star truly was a lost talisman of an ancient magic, but now it mattered more than anything, because it mattered to Her.

He wormed his mind deeper into the howling force of the table's soul. The table shuddered, then calmed. The Viceroy saw the garrison at Luuguth Jor, their fear a palpable taste in his mouth. They were being hunted, though some yet remained. The temptation to reach out and crush them was so strong that he allowed a hand to stray across the surface of the table until it rested above a single soldier. With slow deliberation the Viceroy clenched his fist. At first, nothing happened. Feeling foolish, he began to withdraw his hand; then he saw a shadow move close to the soldier. There was a cold, sharp sting, and the soldier fell into shadow. Amazed, he brought his hands toward each other, encircling the village and the fortress above it.

"You begin to understand. Do Her will. Feed its hunger."

The voice resonated deep within his head, and he smiled that he did not startle.

Shadowy figures flowed across the land, closing in on Luuguth Jor. Voices cried out in pain as the souls winked out, smothered in black screams. The Viceroy placed both his hands on the table and absorbed the cold, and the fear, and was content.

Far below in the manicured gardens of the palace, a worker dropped her shears and stared at the plant she tended. Its leaves curled and blackened before her eyes, falling off the stems and tumbling to the ground. She made a warding sign and ran away, never looking back at the palace, so she did not see the growing black frost that stained the stone around a single, shuttered window.

The light was fading, and as it did shadows grew in length, covering everything in a suffocating cloak of darkness. The sky took on the appearance of slate as the rain clouds threatened another deluge. The air was so wet it felt like breathing through a soaked towel. Sounds that had no visible source started to grow in volume, and none of them were friendly. There was no chittering click of a faeraug or mewling howl of a rakke, yet the blacker it got, the more likely it became that something evil would rise up out of the darkness and attack.

Alwyn immediately chided himself for letting his imagination get the better of him and forced his thoughts to more rational things. Anyone, or anything, watching the riverbank would have a difficult time picking Three Section out of the dusk. N'bhat, the little elfkynan headman, knew this land inside and out and guided them with calm resolve, seemingly unconcerned with the various sounds of life that surrounded them. Yimt, now that he had calmed down, moved like a dwarf looking for a fight, his shatterbow cradled under one arm, a hand resting on the hilt of his drukar. And then there was Kritton. He moved in and out of the shadows as if he was one himself. Alwyn tried and failed to keep him in sight as he trailed the elfkynan. Yimt had ordered them all to remove or blacken anything that would reflect light.

"You'll keep an eye out for me, won't you, Quppy?" Alwyn asked, craning his neck around to look at the wooden cage strapped to his back.

Snoring softly inside was a small sreex—Quopparius, Rallie had said, cooing over the creature as if it was her very own child. Alwyn knew Yimt had made him carry the sreex because he was mad at him for volunteering, but Alwyn didn't mind. Having another living creature so close, and a relatively friendly one, helped—at least a little.

The plan (and on the surface it seemed reasonable) was to give a message to Quppy to fly back to the regiment when they reached Luuguth Jor. That assumed a lot of things, not the least of which was that they would actually make it to Luuguth Jor and have the time and ability to give the sreex a message. There was also the slight concern that Quppy, because he was young and new to this, would not fly back to the regiment at all, but instead head straight for the news offices where it had been trained to fly. Scolly had suggested throwing the animal into a cooking pot as the regiment was marching to Luuguth Jor. Alwyn was determined he would set Quppy free before he let that happen. For his part, Quppy continued to sleep, his wings wrapped around his body, his little muzzle twitching with each breath.

"Isn't that nice—the dwarf gave you a pet."

Alwyn jumped. Kritton walked just inches beside him. "Qupp—the sreex is not a pet, and that's Corporal Arkhorn," Alwyn hissed back, hoping his voice didn't betray how scared he felt.

"For now," the elf replied, and slipped away in the shadows.

Alwyn clenched his musket tighter and vowed not to let Kritton sneak up on him, or Yimt, again.

He scanned the countryside, but saw nothing out of the ordinary. Three Section was moving quickly along the west side of the river, its progress made easy by the low grass and relatively flat land that lined the water and served as its flood plain in the rainy season. In front of him walked Teeter, his seesaw gait obvious even in the failing light, then Scolly, Alik, Buuko, and Inkermon huffing along just behind Alwyn. Nine souls—six humans, an elf, an elfkynan, and a dwarf—to spearhead the Iron Elves, who in turn were the spearhead of the Imperial Army of Calahr, into the deep, dark unknown. It was best not to think about it.

A low whistle sounded from up ahead and everyone stopped where they were. Alwyn knelt on one knee, the grass wet and sticky against his skin, and was glad he'd fixed his bayonet on his musket even if it did make the weapon unbalanced. If something came running out of the dark at him, even Kritton, he'd have a chance. He changed his grip on his weapon and adjusted his caerna, the knitted cloth twirling limply around his legs. He had a strange thought and was wondering what they were supposed to do in the winter, when another low whistle signaled they were moving again. Alwyn stood up and looked over his shoulder.

He could just make out the shadows of the soldiers behind him. Six shadows. Six shadows . . . Inkermon. Scolly. Alik. Teeter. Buuko. Had Kritton doubled back to try to scare him again? He looked again and counted; six. It had to be the elf, or maybe the elfkynan. He quickened his pace and moved around a large bush and saw Yimt, N'bhat, and Kritton in front of him.

Alwyn kept walking even though his legs were shaking so hard he thought he would tip over and tumble into the river with each step. Something was behind them. His breathing quickened, yet he couldn't bring himself to shout a warning. He was still afraid, but it wasn't the same as before. He turned around again and counted one more time.

Five.

He should have felt relieved. He debated saying something, but as on the riverbank, he didn't.

How do you explain to people that you see ghosts?

THIRTY-THREE

The regiment left the small village behind with more than a little regret. The soldiers found the elfkynan very amenable to bartering, especially for sewing needles, brass buttons, arr beans, and mirrors. In return, the troops filled their haversacks with all manner of preserved fruits, a sweet nut the villagers called *wumja*, and delicately woven mesh made of plant fiber that when draped over the head kept the bugs out.

But it wasn't just the vibrant trading that had the troops looking back over their shoulders as they marched upriver, nor even the bare-breasted elfkynan women, who seemed not the least concerned by the stares of the men—they were leaving a small sanctuary of peace and calm and marching into battle.

Fear isn't something one soldier discusses with another. Women, food, officers, and the weather were all acceptable and time-honored topics of discussion, but not how one is feeling, unless, of course, with reference specifically to the approved list. It's not that they didn't feel fear; quite the contrary. It was evident in the way they carried good luck charms and amulets and little glass bottles of potions—some, it was rumored, filled with the urine of the bengar the regiment had adopted as its mascot—the warding signs they made, the laughter that was too loud, or absent entirely. Their very profession put their lives perpetually at risk, yet you would never hear them talk about the dangers, at least, not without waving them off as just part of the job. Even now, when several of their comrades were dead and they marched steadily toward unknown peril where more would certainly perish, they did not talk about the fear they must all be feeling.

It was a contradiction Visyna didn't understand.

Konowa said nothing about it. Even in the forest when it had just been the two of them, it was clear he was still a soldier. He could have gone anywhere, done anything, but without the army, he had been like a lost little boy. And now that he had his regiment back, she wondered if he would ever really want for something else.

For her. She knew he had feelings for her—Konowa was certainly not subtle about that. But whenever talk of the Empire and the natural order and the Shadow Monarch came up, he would pull back, even though she knew he felt much the same way she did.

It angered her that she should care at all. Her people and their way of life were threatened by the Empire and the Shadow Monarch, and Konowa was definitely serving one, and was in danger of serving the other. All too soon, choices would have to be made. Something deep within Visyna told her that when the time came, there would be no turning back.

"This is wrong, Rallie, this is all wrong," Visyna said, readjusting her sitting position.

She was riding with Rallie in the correspondent's wagon, and as a result, having to speak louder than she would have liked in order to be heard over the constant creaks and groans of wood killed and carved into unnatural shapes. Faint memories of the trees and what they had once been remained in the wood, and it saddened her. Why did everything that man touched cause so much pain?

Rallie took a long drag on her cigar and blew out an immense cloud of blue smoke. "When young men march off to battle, my dear, it is never right. The question is: What is to be done to make it right?"

"The Empire must be driven from Elfkyna," Visyna said simply. She felt a presence off to the right and turned to see Jir bound out of cover and pounce on a small rat dragon. There was a squeal and a crunch, and the rat dragon disappeared down the bengar's throat in two bites. She smiled as the bengar's joy and satisfaction radiated out from it. "They are an unnatural predator here."

Rallie nodded as if she understood. "I see. Tell me, who then would the elfkynan ally with to fight the Shadow Monarch? The orcs, perhaps? They've always seemed interested in expanding south. Or maybe the dwarves, if you allowed them mining rights. Or what about—"

Visyna shook her head and waved her hands in surrender. "You've made your point. But surely you see that the Empire cannot stay? This is not their land. They oppress my people and steal our resources. Even now, they send this regiment to steal the most sacred talismans of the elfkynan. How can we continue to work with them?" Her own hypocrisy was bitter in her mouth. She served the very Empire she hated, just as Konowa did. Why did she think she was any better?

"We all do things we aren't proud of, my dear—the key, as I mentioned before, is what one does about it to make it right. And the answer," Rallie said, leaning over and patting Visyna on the knee, "you already know."

"You have more faith in me than I do myself," she said. She knew, though she hated to admit it, that the Empire, as vile and heartless as it was, would not allow the Shadow Monarch to exert influence in Elfkyna or anywhere else in the world, just as Konowa would do all in his power to protect the Iron Elves, and her. It was both comforting and confusing.

Something touched her awareness and she looked up, flowing her senses outward. It was a flying creature, but what exactly she could not tell.

"Oh, dear, here comes Wobbly," Rallie said, motioning skyward with her cigar.

Visyna looked up. A snow-white pelican was laboriously flapping its way toward them, tilting across the sky as if fighting a crosswind, then angling back on course. Jir was captivated, his snout high in the air as he watched the bird.

"It's wounded!"

Rallie clucked and stood up, blowing a large smoke ring into the air.

"No, not exactly." She sat back down and pulled the hood of her cloak up around her head. "Duck."

The bird had seen the smoke ring and was now aiming toward the wagon. Soldiers up and down the line began pointing and shouting until sergeants got them in check.

Rallie peered out from beneath her hood and looked to the sky. "Duck!"

Visyna threw herself down on the footboards as the pelican flew straight at them and kept on going, bouncing off the top of the wagon in a spray of feathers, shooting back into the air, and wheeling about on one wing. Jir crouched in the wet grass, his tail swishing violently. The bird spied the bengar in the grass and squawked, swinging back toward the safety of the wagon, its large, webbed feet paddling furiously as if trying to gain traction. It finally made it to the wagon, crashing down on top of the canvas cover in a flurry of more white feathers.

"The poor thing," Visyna said, getting up and climbing back over the wagon to help the stunned bird. It righted itself and shook its head, the skin under its enormous bill flapping about like an extra wing. It saw her and immediately opened its mouth wide. There was a small rolled leather tube inside. Visyna gingerly stuck her hand into its mouth and pulled the tube out. That's when she noticed the smell.

"Rallie, I think this bird has been poisoned."

Rallie looked back over her shoulder and held out a large wooden canteen to Visyna. "Poisoned, indeed. Quick, give it the antidote."

Visyna handed Rallie the leather tube and took the canteen, unscrewing the lid and sniffing the contents.

"This is beer!"

Rallie cackled and nodded. "Just what the doctor ordered after all that whiskey he's been drinking. He's a happy drunk, but one surly pile of feathers when sober."

The pelican still had its mouth wide open and now made a few screeches to get Visyna's attention. Reluctantly she upended the canteen into the bird's mouth. The pouch beneath its bill filled up, then it closed its bill and threw its head straight back, the beer disappearing down its gullet in one gulp. Satisfied, it waddled over to the edge of the wagon and looked down at the bengar keeping pace. The pelican clacked its bill together a couple of times at Jir and then moved back to the center of the wagon where it flopped down with its wings spread out wide to either side and closed its eyes. Sreexes growled and yipped below it, but it paid no attention to them.

"Is it dead?" Visyna asked, watching to see if the bird still breathed.

Rallie didn't even turn around, instead eyeing Jir, who was now fascinated by a large tortoise off to the side of the road. "Just sleeping it off. Old Wobbly is the canniest courier I've ever seen. Has an ability to find who or what he's looking for no matter where it might be, but only when he's got a bill full."

Wobbly's mouth opened for a second and a wave of fumes rolled out, followed by a deeply contented sigh. Visyna put the top back on the canteen and crawled back to sit beside Rallie, who had put the reins in her lap and was reading the parchment she had taken out of the leather tube.

"What does it say?" Visyna asked, looking over her shoulder one more time to make sure. The pelican was snoring.

Rallie rolled the parchment back up and took a few thoughtful drags on her cigar. "It's from my editor in Celwyn. We're in even more trouble than I thought possible, and I have a very expansive imagination."

THIRTY-FOUR

The rain clouds split like overripe melons, drenching the small patrol in an instant. One moment the dark landscape was quiet, and the next it was as if the very world had shaken loose and everything was in turmoil.

Alwyn wrapped a small piece of oilcloth around the lock of his musket, but he doubted it would do more than keep the rain out. The powder would already be absorbing the moisture in the air and rendering the musket unable to fire. His spectacles were once again a blurry mess, and the pressure of the rain on his skin made him feel that he was marching six feet under water.

He reached around behind him and adjusted the small canvas cover on the cage, looking inside to see how Quppy was doing. The sreex seemed completely unaffected by the rain, the water beading up and rolling off its leathery feathers with ease. He saw Alwyn and gave a quiet growl, revealing his toothy mouth. Alwyn smiled back and patted the cage, careful to keep his fingers from getting between the wooden slats.

Daylight was still hours off and the rain showed no sign of slowing, which meant they'd be walking blind. He heard, or thought he heard, a splash somewhere behind him, but before he could turn there was a flash of movement up ahead. Alwyn pointed his bayonet in that direction and cautiously inched forward, trying to watch where he walked lest he slip and go tumbling into the river, which was quickly growing in size and force.

"—somebody with that thing!"

Alwyn jerked to a stop, his bayonet halfway through Yimt's shako. He pulled it out and grounded his musket, shouting his apology as he did so. The rain fell about them in sheets, making it impossible to see more than a few feet in any direction.

"N'bhat says the river will crest inside the hour. We'll have to swing wide and get away from it!"

Other forms started to appear. Alwyn quietly counted the shadows, praying there wouldn't be one extra this time. There wasn't. Now they were one short.

Yimt walked around the circle peering up into each face. When he was done he shook his head, sending water flying everywhere, not that it made a difference. "Where is Alik?"

Heads shook in the dark. Alwyn remembered hearing the splash.

"I think he might have fallen into the river! I heard something a minute ago. It could have been him." His heart felt sick. He'd liked Alik.

"Show me where!" Yimt shouted, motioning for Alwyn to lead the way. A hand reached out and stopped him. It was Kritton.

"He's gone; forget about him," Kritton said. "We need to move on."

Yimt grabbed the elf by the arm and pushed him away. "We don't leave anyone behind, not if I can help it. Now, form a line, grab the other fellow's belt, and move! Ally, show us where."

Alwyn felt Yimt grab hold of his belt and then he was walking toward the river. He imagined this was what sailors felt like being at sea. Water sprayed his face, the noise drowned out any other sound, and everything seemed to be in motion. He felt forward one foot at a time, sure he would suddenly plummet into the river and be swept away like Alik.

"I think this is the place," Alwyn said, trying to judge the distance from where he had been standing and deciding this was it. He could just see the edge of the river a few feet away. The rain frothed along its surface and here and there dark objects raced by faster than Alwyn liked.

"Now work your way downstream for a bit!"

Before he could say he couldn't see a thing, N'bhat was beside him, clutching his arm and smiling.

"Rain good, bring big fish!"

Alwyn tried to smile but failed. The elfkynan held out his other hand and Alwyn reached out for it, feeling the end of a vine.

"You hold tight, or N'bhat no come back." Just like that N'bhat was gone, diving headfirst into the river and disappearing from sight.

Alwyn screamed and frantically started reeling in the vine, passing it back to Yimt. The vine went taut and Alwyn was pulled forward before he regained his balance. The river was now perilously close. He leaned backward into Yimt and tried to back up.

"Not yet, Ally, wait for the signal," Yimt yelled, pushing back.

There was a sharp tug on the vine, then another. "Now!" Yimt shouted, and now he began to pull. Alwyn dug his heels in and heaved. Slowly, inch by inch, the vine slid back through his fingers as the other soldiers reeled N'bhat in. Alwyn gasped and took in a lungful of rain. He didn't see how N'bhat could still be alive, let alone Alik. A moment later he saw something dark in the water and then N'bhat was crawling out of the river dragging the limp body of Alik behind him. They pulled them another fifteen feet from the river's edge.

"Is he dead?" Alwyn asked, looking down at Alik. All he had on was his jacket and caerna and one sock, everything else having been torn off in the river. His eyes were open and his skin was as white as bone.

N'bhat leaned over Alik's head and listened. After a few seconds he stood up and walked a couple of feet away.

So, Alik was dead. Before that thought had fully registered N'bhat turned, jumped, and landed with both feet on Alik's chest.

Alwyn watched in stunned silence as the little elfkynan jumped up and down several more times. Each time he landed water spurted out of Alik's mouth and his arms and legs jerked up as if attached to strings. On the last jump his arms stayed up, and then batted wildly at N'bhat's legs.

"Help him up," Yimt ordered. N'bhat lightly jumped off as Scolly and Teeter grabbed Alik under the arms and hoisted him upright. Alik was coughing and wheezing, but he was definitely alive.

"Are you all right?" Yimt shouted, grabbing Alik's coat to steady him. Alik coughed a few more times and finally caught his breath.

"I—I think so. One minute I was walking along and the next the ground just vanished and I was in the river. I managed to grab hold of some bulrushes, but I was still going under. That's the last thing I remember until now."

Yimt nodded and let go of his coat. "You're damn bloody lucky. As it is, you've lost your weapon and most of your kit. Let this be a lesson to the rest of you," Yimt said, turning and shouting at the rest of the group. "Keep your eyes open and pay attention! Now, stick close and watch where you step; we're moving on."

Alwyn saw a stick lying in the mud and picked it up and handed it to Alik. "Here, it's not much but its better than your bare hands, you know, in case we find something."

Alik took it and nodded his thanks. And then they were moving, heading away from the river on an angle. Each step away from the water felt wonderful, although the rain continued unabated.

Soon they were walking among low shrubs and climbing up a bit of a slope. Alwyn made sure to keep at least two bodies in sight at all times and stumbled more than once over an unseen plant. After another hour of that, a halt was called and heads counted. This time, there were nine.

Yimt had everyone huddle close together and then draped a section of canvas over them, creating a very small, but temporarily dry, circle of heads. There was a click and a hiss and a small lantern flickered to life, its tiny flame casting a warm glow on a very strange tableau of seemingly disembodied heads.

Alwyn slid the cage off his back and placed it in the center to keep Quppy out of the rain for a bit. Yimt placed the lantern on top of it and clapped his hands together to get their attention.

"N'bhat says we've gone a mile or so to the west away from the river. From here we'll head straight north and with luck should come to a forest at daybreak. Now, because of the rain, the regiment won't be able to follow the river either, so when we get to the trees we'll mark a few to show them our path. N'bhat says his people never go into the forest." Yimt held up his hands to forestall objections. "No, not because there is something lurking in there, just because they're river folk, and they stick to the water. All the same, when we get there, keep your eyes open and stay close." Yimt looked around the circle, taking each face in turn. Alwyn smiled when the dwarf looked at him and Yimt grinned back, his metallic teeth glinting in the flickering light.

And then, they were on the move again. The rain slackened as they went, and now that Yimt had steered them away from the river they were making better time.

Yimt spat a stream of crute and ran his sleeve across his mouth. He looked straight ahead as he walked, his shatterbow still cradled in the crook of his left arm as if it was glued there. "You did a stupid-brave thing earlier, volunteering for this. I'm sure it was because you'd hate to miss out on my cooking, and not on account of that slippery eel of an elf. Been a long time since anyone liked my cooking that much."

They continued walking in silence, Yimt chewing and spitting crute while Alwyn tried and failed to say something back. Yimt was more father to him than his own, a man who had left him and his mother when Alwyn was only four.

"I hear you fry a pretty good bara jogg," he finally said.

The dwarf harrumphed and spat a stream of crute. "Fry bara jogg? Bah, you want to sauté it, then dice it into cubes for a nice soup. I'll show you how when we get to Luuguth Jor." He turned his head slightly and looked up at Alwyn for a second, nodded, and dropped back to fall in step with Teeter.

Alwyn took a deep breath and readjusted the cage on his back. Quppy shook himself a couple of times and settled back down. He unslung his musket and noted with satisfaction that the piece of cork Yimt had told him to place in the muzzle was still there. The dwarf knew every trick in the book, and probably a lot more that had never been written down.

Kritton, Alwyn worried, knew them, too. Beyond telling them to leave Alik behind to drown, the elf had done nothing sinister, at least, not that Alwyn could see, and that was the problem. As hard as Alwyn tried, he was never able to keep the elf in sight for more than a few seconds at a time, his ability to blend with shadows so fluid it defied any rational explanation.

He had never put much stock in the whole magical, mystical connection elves were supposed to have with nature. Mr. Yuimi hadn't seemed all that different from any other cobbler. The shoes he repaired didn't sprout vines or give the wearer special abilities, as Alwyn had found out once trying to leap from one tree to another. Even the major, who looked like every wild elf he'd ever heard about in children's tales, seemed like most officers he'd known—kinder, more intelligent, perhaps, but still determined to see the job done no matter what the cost. Now, Miss Tekoy seemed magical all right. And a witch, which made sense as he thought about it. But Kritton was different. Or maybe it was that all the other elves Alwyn knew seemed good at heart. Kritton had a dark heart; maybe that's what let him blend with the shadows so easily. Whatever the case, he wasn't about to let the elf do anything to Yimt.

The rest of the night wore on in a wet haze. Alwyn wasn't sure which he hated more—marching in the broiling sun or in the rain in the dark. He decided neither was pleasant, but at least you could drink the rain. He lengthened his stride a bit to try to stretch. Sometime in the night he'd developed a painful blister on the heel of his left foot and the skin under his arms felt like it had been rubbed raw. He was so wet he couldn't tell what was skin and what was cloth—not surprising when he looked at the tips of his fingers and saw they were white and wrinkled.

He was still looking at his fingers when he bumped into someone and looked up in surprise. Yimt and N'bhat scowled at him and went back to whispering to each other, pointing to a dark, blurry shape to their front. The sun was just below the horizon and beginning to light the land around them. Three Section closed up and took a defensive posture, facing out in all directions of the compass. A quick head count confirmed there were still and only nine.

"We go back to river now. Flood go down, it safe again," N'bhat said, a slight quaver in his voice.

"And crawl through the mud?" Kritton asked. "I can see the path into the forest from here. We'll be through and into Luuguth Jor before nightfall if we go now. Listen to this river rat and it'll take us three days or more."

N'bhat said something in elfkynan and Kritton responded in Hynta. Yimt told them both to shut up.

"Time is not on our side. We need to get to the garrison as quick as we can, and that's through the forest."

Alwyn didn't need to look to imagine Kritton's satisfied smirk.

"Maybe you get there, or maybe you don't," N'bhat said. "Now that we here, I feel trees not safe no more. Go by river and be safe. Almost as fast."

"You aren't going to listen to this little elfkynan, are you, Arkhorn?" Kritton asked.

Alwyn tried to look over his shoulder, but the cage on his back hit Scolly when he tried to turn so he gave up and looked back out across the shrubs they had just walked through.

"That's Corporal, *Private*," Yimt said, his tone quiet and calm. "And I would strongly suggest you watch your mouth. One of these days, that temper of yours is going to land you in a heap of trouble."

There was a long silence. Alwyn traded looks with Scolly, but he couldn't tell if the soldier was even aware of the argument going on behind them.

"Right, we're going into the forest as planned," Yimt said at once. "Stay sharp—don't get caught looking too long in any one direction and keep your mouths shut."

Scolly looked confused. "Where are we going then?"

Three Section turned and Alwyn saw the forest for the first time. It really wasn't like the forests back home. Everything here was greener and leafier. The path that Kritton could see was barely visible to Alwyn, but it looked wide enough for a cart, though he couldn't imagine who would live out here that had one.

He pointed toward the trees. "See, the forest, there's a path through it."

Scolly squinted. "What, that grove of trees?"

Yimt banged the side of his shatterbow with the flat of his fist. "Just follow us."

"But where are we going? In them trees? I don't like trees." There was genuine fear in his voice.

"What do you mean you don't like trees?" Yimt asked, taking a step toward the soldier. "They're just trees. Kritton," he said, whipping around to look at the elf, "have you been putting thoughts in his head?"

Kritton sneered. "As if they would stay. Besides, it was the elfkynan that said the trees weren't safe, not me." After a moment, he hissed between his teeth and raised his hands above his head. He stood like that for several seconds, then closed his eyes and began to chant in elvish.

"What's this about then?" Yimt asked, turning to N'bhat, who shook his head.

Kritton did this for several seconds, then suddenly stopped, lowering his hands and opening his eyes. "The trees are friendly."

"How do you know?" Scolly asked.

Kritton smiled, and it gave Alwyn no joy at all to see it. "I asked them. The trees will not hurt you."

Scolly scratched his head. "You sure?"

Kritton put a hand over his heart. "Completely. You have nothing to fear from the trees."

This appeared to satisfy Scolly, who began walking toward the forest. Yimt snorted and motioned for the rest of them to get moving. He kept looking at Kritton, but the elf did nothing to provoke him, and after a minute Yimt moved back to the front of the patrol.

Within a hundred paces of the forest the rain began to slacken. By the time they reached the edge of the trees, the rain had stopped and the sun was stretching out the first rays of light across the land. Curses sounded from several of the soldiers, but Yimt quickly quieted them again and just like that they stepped out of the light and back into darkness.

With each step deeper into the forest, the light of the sun grew dimmer, as if night was already descending again. Alwyn knew it was due to the thick canopy of leaves high overhead, but it still sent a tiny shiver down his back. Quppy didn't seem to like this choice of route either, growling and fussing in his cage and beating his wings against the wooden bars. Alwyn had to finally reach around and rap a hand against the cage to get the sreex to quiet down, but even then Quppy still growled.

Following Yimt's advice, Alwyn kept his head on a swivel, looking to both sides of the path and even glancing over his shoulder occasionally to check that their number remained constant.

The sreex started beating his wings against the cage again. Yimt turned and pointed at Alwyn to quiet the bird.

"Darn it all, Quppy, you're going to get us both in trouble," he whispered, stopping and shrugging the straps that held the cage to his back off his shoulders. Yimt motioned for a halt. Everyone stopped where they were while Alwyn tried to calm the sreex down.

"I'd be angry, too, if I was caged up all the time. You want a drink?" he asked, grabbing his canteen and pouring a bit of water into his hand and holding it to the bars. "No? Here, how about a chunk of brick," Alwyn said, pulling out of his small pack a gray block of baked flour that the Imperial Army insisted was a biscuit.

Quppy ignored it, going completely still. His body looked like something carved out of wood. Not a blink, not even the twitch of a whisker.

Water mixed with the brick in Alwyn's hand and a gray sludge slowly seeped through his fingers. It suddenly felt cold, as if he'd dipped his hand in a fast-running stream. He shivered and realized the temperature had actually dropped.

A leaf fluttered down and landed in his palm. It was shriveled, the edges blackened by frost.

THIRTY-FIVE

Mewling cries burst forth all around the soldiers as rakkes charged out of the forest.

It was so sudden Alwyn didn't have time to be scared. He pulled the cork from the end of his musket and ripped the oilcloth from the lock, cocked the hammer back, and fired in one continuous motion. To his amazement the musket worked, the butt slamming reassuringly against his shoulder. A thick cloud of smoke and sparks blossomed in front of him as the musket ball flew forty yards and straight into the stomach of a rakke. He had no time to see if the creature got back up as he scrambled to reload. Other muskets fired and shouts rose from up ahead. The distinct sound of a double roar and detonations signaled Yimt had fired his shatterbow.

"Close up! Close up!"

Inkermon ran past him toward the front, his shako gone, his eyes wild. "The end is here! *The end is here!*"

Alwyn bit into a cartridge and poured the powder down the muzzle, almost stabbing himself on the bayonet attached at the end of the barrel. Teeter walked up calmly to stand beside him, his musket already reloaded.

"Wait until they're close; too many trees out there."

Alwyn looked up and saw what Teeter meant. Rakkes were screaming and calling to each other from behind the cover of trunks. The first volley had obviously surprised them. Alwyn finished ramming the new ball home and brought his musket up to his shoulder again.

"What are they doing?" he asked, swinging his musket back and forth trying to get a bead on one of the creatures. Like the rakke he and Yimt had killed back at camp, these wore the rudiments of clothes. Unlike the first rakke, however, they also appeared to be carrying clubs. Instead of rushing forward, they started roaring and banging their clubs against the sides of the trees, creating a terrible noise and shaking loose a shower of wet leaves that began falling all around them.

Buuko, Alik, and Scolly came jogging up the path to stand near them. Alik was clutching his stick in both hands and looking all around him. He was clearly terrified, and Alwyn couldn't blame him. It'd be hard for anyone to feel brave wearing just one sock and having a stick for a weapon.

"Why'd they stop?" Alik asked, jumping as another rakke screamed and Scolly fired at it. There was a loud crack and a burst of bark and splinters from a tree trunk. The rakke roared and ran a few steps forward, baring its fangs.

"We showed them who was boss, didn't we?" Buuko said, his voice triumphant as he aimed and shot the rakke in the mouth. The back of the creature's head disintegrated and it tumbled to the ground and lay still. "You should have stayed extinct, you dumb buggers!"

"Get your arses up here, now!" Yimt shouted at them, brandishing his shatterbow and waving them forward. The rest of the patrol, including N'bhat, was grouped around the dwarf another thirty yards up the path.

Alwyn took his hand off the trigger and reached down to grab Quppy's cage. Leaves were falling so thickly that it was getting difficult to see what the rakkes were doing. He stopped halfway, his hand hovering just above the cage. From the corner of his eye he caught a movement. He looked up. Something dark and fast slipped behind a tree.

It wasn't a rakke.

"Hurry up, Alwyn, we've got to go!" Alik said, tugging at his arm as the others began walking quickly up the path. "Hurry—" There was a swish and thunk and then silence.

Alwyn looked up in alarm. Alik stared at him, his eyes wide open in surprise. A thin, black arrow jutted from his neck. His mouth opened and closed a couple of times and then he was falling. Alwyn reached out to grab him as more arrows sliced through the air. Buuko screamed. A musket fired, and then another. Something flew by Alwyn's face. He stumbled and fell over Quppy's cage, shattering the wood as the sreex howled and flapped its wings. Alik's body fell on top of him, momentarily pinning him to the ground.

More screams, the sound of running feet, leaves falling everywhere, and only the occasional musket firing. Alwyn pushed furiously to lift Alik's body out of the way and get to his musket. He saw another soldier fall, his legs twitching as he lay on the ground, a black arrow protruding from his back, but he couldn't tell who it was.

He finally lifted Alik out of the way and was reaching for his musket when a rakke slammed it down with a large wooden club, smashing his weapon to pieces. Alwyn yelled and rolled the other way as the club came down again where he had just been. He got up to his hands and knees, scrambling up the path toward the sound of shouting. If he could just make it to Yimt he'd be all right. He saw Buuko's body and musket and lunged for the weapon, swinging around and pointing it at the rakke lumbering toward him. He squeezed the trigger and prayed that it was loaded.

The musket bucked in his hands and the rakke went down without a sound, the club tumbling from its grasp.

Two more rakkes loomed out of the forest, cutting off his route to Yimt and the rest of the patrol. They seemed to sense that the musket was unloaded and moved toward him, their white eyes bulging.

At that moment Kritton appeared, a musket in one hand and a blade in the other.

"Shoot them!" Alwyn shouted, pointing at the rakkes.

The creatures paused and turned. Kritton stood still, looking back at Alwyn. One of the rakkes made to move toward the elf and Kritton simply turned and ran.

Mind-numbing fear turned to rage in an instant. "You coward!" Alwyn screamed, startling the rakkes just a few yards away. The rakkes roared and turned back to Alwyn. It was only after Kritton had vanished that Alwyn realized the blade in his hand had been a drukar.

Yimt. It couldn't have hurt more if he'd been shot.

Nothing mattered anymore. Alwyn rose to his feet, screaming and lunging at the nearest rakke, driving the bayonet deep into its chest. The creature collapsed, tearing the musket from his hands as it died. Alwyn looked at his bare hands. He was left facing a rakke with nothing but absolute anguish. With no reason to care, he jumped forward, placed a foot on the dying rakke's chest, grabbed hold of his musket and heaved. It came free with a terrible scraping sound of metal on bone. He pointed it at the second rakke and saw that the bayonet was twisted. With no time to reload, he spun the musket around and grabbed it by the muzzle to swing like a club.

The second rakke paused and turned to look over its shoulder. Alwyn followed its gaze, expecting to see a gloating Kritton.

An elf stood in the space between two trees. Its face was gray and creased like wind-scoured rock. At first, Alwyn thought it was missing its left ear tip, but then he saw that it was there—just pitch black, like the two wet black eyes that stared unblinking at him, drawing the very warmth from his body.

Alwyn shuddered when he realized it had no eyelids. The orbs were forever open, forever seeing.

Its every feature was twisted, as if a giant's hands had pulled it apart and then reassembled the tattered shreds. It wore an overlapping garment of blackened leaves and oily fur held in place by thin, steel-colored vines wrapped tight around its limbs. Bony hands with fingers like black spider legs held a great curving longbow that looked impossibly to be made of iron.

The elf drew back the bow, its eyes never straying from Alwyn's. A noise like steel on slate pierced the forest as the bow was drawn to its limit, a thin, black arrow notched in place. It turned its head slightly and sighted down the shaft of the arrow.

Alwyn lurched forward. There was a metallic *twang*, the rush of torn air, and the shattering impact of the arrow hitting the stock of the musket.

The musket flew from Alwyn's numb hands as something bitterly cold jabbed him in the chest. He stumbled and fell to his knees. Alwyn reached up with one hand and grabbed the section of arrow that now protruded from his body. It was like trying to hold fire. He began shivering violently. His hand fell away, a strip of skin tearing off as it did so, but he could no longer feel pain.

The rakke sensed its moment and rushed forward, knocking Alwyn to his back. The forest canopy flickered and swayed. Leaves tumbled down like snowflakes, revealing one side then the other; light—dark, light—dark.

The rakke stood above him and raised its club over its head. Alwyn tried to get to his feet, but his strength was gone. He was so cold.

The rakke lifted its head and screamed into the air. It was a hideous, triumphant sound. It lowered its head and the club began to fall when something came in from the side of Alwyn's vision.

The rakke fell apart, cloven in two. A shadow stood over it, a long sword held easily in its hands. A cloak of midnight black shrouded it so completely that Alwyn had a difficult time keeping it in focus, but he knew his savior all the same.

"Thanks, Meri," Alwyn murmured, closing his eyes and letting the cold take him.

THIRTY-SIX

Konowa lurched in the saddle from a blow he couldn't see. He grabbed his chest and his hand closed around the leather pouch.

"Something's happened."

The Prince turned slightly and nudged his horse around a large mud puddle, an act of little value, as mud lay everywhere. The river had already receded to its preflood level, but the ground around it was a sopping mess, and the rain still fell, although not as hard as before. "The open rebellion of northern Elfkyna would certainly qualify, yes, but it's not exactly news, is it, as Rallie's editor sent her the message hours ago?"

"Yes, sir, of course. I was just taking it all in," he said, silently cursing himself for being such a fool. A chill crept over his body despite the warm rain. He looked back over his shoulder at the regiment snaked out behind them and shook his head. "We'll need to get to Luuguth Jor as quickly as possible, but this mud is going to slow us down."

"Then fix it," the Prince said.

"Fix it, sir? I didn't bring any paving stones with me."

The Prince frowned and stood in his stirrups, pulling a highly polished brass telescope from a leather holder strapped to his saddle. The royal cipher was emblazoned on the main tube in skillfully inlaid onyx and ivory and tiny rubies. He opened it to its full length and held it up to his eye like a captain at sea. Perhaps the river beside them was giving him delusions of nautical grandeur.

"The witch turned night into day—surely she can do something about this mud. And tell her to be quick about it. We are losing valuable time." He sat back down, sending a spray of water from his saddle.

Konowa started to say Visyna would never agree to it, even if she was so inclined, as it seemed an impossible thing, but held his tongue. She *had* turned night into day, and his father had once slowed a waterfall long enough to allow an elf of the Long Watch to drag an uprooted sapling to safety before it plummeted over the edge.

"Today, Major," the prince snapped. "Nothing is more important than securing the Star."

"As is keeping it out of the Shadow Monarch's hands and putting down the rebellion," Konowa added.

The Prince waved the thought away like an annoying fly. "Yes, of course. Deprived of the Star, the rebellion will founder and die, and the Shadow Monarch will have lost Her chance." He suddenly slapped his thigh and sat up straighter in the saddle. "And I will have saved Elfkyna in the bargain. This is perfect. Major, we must make all possible haste."

"Yes, sir," Konowa said, touching his heels to Zwindarra's flanks and setting out at a trot back along the column in search of Visyna.

No one called out to him as he rode by. It would have been simple to believe that it was the rain and exhaustion that kept their heads down, but he knew news of the rebellion had spread among them like wildfire. The pretense that they were going to relieve a garrison manning a tiny mud fort in the middle of nowhere—the regiment led by the very Prince of the realm—was too much for even the dimmest of them to believe. And now that they knew a full-scale rebellion was in the offing, they also knew that their prospect of ever seeing home and hearth again had fallen through the ground, along with their morale. Whether the Prince liked it or not, the troops would have to be told the truth, at least most of it.

He spotted Jir first, loping alongside Rallie's wagon. The bengar was covered from head to paw in mud, but didn't seem the least bit concerned by it, nor by the numerous bushes and plants that went unmarked as he passed by. The reason perched on top of the canvas-covered wagon dozing in the rain.

Wobbly appeared to be sleeping it off in the most precarious of positions, teetering forward as if he was about to pitch over and then righting himself with the next sway of the wagon. Jir mirrored each movement, no doubt hoping for an easy lunch. Konowa hoped the pelican had better balance sober than drunk. He'd watched the bird's graceless landing and immediately sympathized with it. He knew what it was like to be a moose among deer.

He whistled at Jir, who turned his head for a moment, then went back to watching the pelican. *Be that way*, Konowa thought, slowing Zwindarra to a trot as he came up to the wagon. Visyna sat beside Rallie on the front bench, the two involved in yet another conversation. He reined in Zwindarra and had him walk alongside, deliberately choosing Rallie's side of the wagon. The horse didn't seem the least bit disturbed by the brindos this time, even reaching out his muzzle to sniff at the closest brindo, which flapped its ears in response.

"And what brings you back our way, Major?" Rallie asked. She smiled at him, and he smiled back. Visyna, wrapped in a green cloak with the hood pulled up over her head, did not bother to look at him.

Women.

"In light of your recent news, the Prince thinks we need to make all haste to Luuguth Jor. For once, I am in complete agreement with him." He waited, but Visyna continued to look straight ahead. "The Prince has asked, and I know it sounds silly, but he has asked if Miss Tekoy might use her powers to assist the regiment in making better time."

Visyna finally turned to look at him, pulling down the hood of her cloak. He'd expected anger and was surprised to see a thoughtful expression on her face.

"What did he have in mind?"

Konowa looked at Rallie, who looked back at him with a knowing smile. "His Highness has asked if it would be possible to dry the ground underfoot so that we might increase our pace. You know, firm it up a bit so the slogging isn't so tough."

"All right," Visyna said.

Konowa had already prepared a comeback and was left momentarily speechless. She had an uncanny ability to catch him off guard. He didn't know why, but he found it more attractive than her looks, as stunning as they were. "I'm sorry?"

"I said I'll do it," she said, calmly crossing her arms and staring at him. "For once, we are all in agreement. The sooner we arrive at Luuguth Jor, the better. However," she said, smiling at him, "I will need assistance."

"Absolutely," Konowa said, smiling broadly. *Now why couldn't the two of us get along like this all the time?* he wondered, ignoring the multiple reasons that suddenly sprang to mind. "Just tell me what you need and you will have it."

"You."

"Now wait just one min—"

"Do you want to get to Luuguth Jor quickly or not?" Visyna asked, making as if to pull the hood of her cloak back up.

"All right, all right, I'll help, but I'm not doing anything . . . strange."

"This is not a carnival trick. Rallie, please stop the wagon," Visyna said.

Konowa reined in Zwindarra, who took the opportunity to sniff the brindo a little more thoroughly.

While the brindo and horse were getting acquainted, Visyna hopped down from the wagon and stood in the mud. The last platoon of soldiers marched by, eyeing them curiously, but again, none called out. A pall had settled over the entire regiment and everyone feared to speak loudly. In moments, they were alone as the soldiers struggled through the mud ahead of them.

"So what do you need me to do exactly?" Konowa asked, trying to be helpful.

Visyna took a few deep breaths and closed her eyes. "Hold me."

Konowa's heart sped up. "Hold you?"

"Hold me."

"You want me to hold you?"

"You were in the forest a very long time, weren't you?" Rallie asked, her smile as wicked as a newly sharpened blade.

Visyna stamped her foot. "We are losing time. Now get off that horse and get over here and hold me."

Konowa kicked his feet out of the stirrups and jumped off Zwindarra, tossing the reins up to Rallie, who tied them off to the wagon. He walked over to Visyna, still waiting for the catch.

"Stand behind me, and hold me around the middle. Whatever you do, don't let go."

Konowa stopped just in front of her. "Look, I know we haven't—"

Visyna grabbed him by the hand and pulled him around behind her. "What I need at the moment is your strength. What the Prince asks will require more skeins than I can weave on my own. Now, hold me, and do not let go."

Konowa looked up at Rallie, who was clearly enjoying this. He shrugged and did as Visyna asked, wrapping his arms around her. Her hair danced in front of his mouth. With each breath he let out the temptation to smell it threatened to overwhelm the real reason he held her in his arms.

"No, not like this. I can feel it even now. You must remove it," Visyna said, pulling away from his grasp. "I cannot do this with that thing touching me."

"Look, if this is all some kind of elaborate game to get me to get rid of it you can just forget it," he said. His hand reached instinctively for the pouch.

Visyna raised her hands. "I give you my word you can have it back when we're done. Give it to Rallie if you like, but you must remove it if this is to work."

Konowa looked at Rallie. "This is no joke. I have sworn to protect this regiment and I will."

Rallie looked past Konowa to the regiment slowly marching ahead of them. "Then you had best make up your mind—time is fleeting."

He reached into his jacket and pulled out the pouch, throwing it to Rallie before he changed his mind. Rallie caught it deftly and set it down on the bench beside her. Konowa took a breath and tried to detect if he felt any different. Nothing. He wasn't sure if he was relieved by that or not.

"Now," Visyna said, pulling his arms back around her, "hold on and do not let go. You will feel . . . things, but do not be alarmed."

She brought her hands in front of her face and immediately began tracing patterns in the air in front of her.

It was mesmerizing. Her fingers moved with supple grace, like swans weaving their necks together in perfect rhythm. The air around them changed, or maybe it was a sound on the air. The hairs on his arms and the back of his neck vibrated, and Konowa heard the natural world. He closed his eyes and slowly, tentatively, let his senses flow outward.

It was a revelation like none he had experienced before. For the first time in his life there was order in the chaos. Everything, all life, made sense. Each living thing had a distinct voice, and each formed part of an infinite web of threads, each unique and yet wholly connected to each other.

"Oh, my."

Konowa opened his eyes at Rallie's surprise. Intricate filigrees of light danced in front of Visyna, her fingers tracing ever-finer skeins of glowing thread. The air shimmered around them and Konowa recognized what he had seen back at the edge of the forest when Lorian had found them. Given a hundred years, the best painters in the world could not hope to duplicate the beauty of what he saw, what he felt. It was as if life was a river, flowing through her, through him, both new and very old.

All too soon, Visyna slowed her hands and the light faded away, and with it, the sense of order and reason to the world around him.

She finally lowered her hands and stood panting in his arms. He realized his breathing was in time with hers.

"You can let go now," she said, her voice little more than a whisper.

He didn't want to. He wanted that feeling back. "I—"

A bugle sounded from up ahead and Konowa reluctantly released her. Visyna climbed back up into the wagon as chaos reigned again around Konowa and he closed his mind to the world. Rallie tossed him the pouch, which he stuffed back under his jacket. The last vestiges of the natural order burned away as the acorn rested against his chest.

"Our path will be quicker now," Visyna said, her voice still sounding a little breathless.

"And filled with more danger, I'm afraid," Rallie said, stepping down from the wagon and walking back behind it.

Konowa exchanged glances with Visyna, then held out his hand to help her down. She chose to ignore it, stepping down on her own, and the two of them walked back to see what Rallie was doing.

"Grab hold of this, will you?" Rallie said as Konowa came around the corner. He reached out and took the edge of the canvas tarp and held it high as she directed. Visyna was directed to hold the other side, and Rallie hopped up into the back of the wagon, crawling in between the row of cages. Jir padded around to watch. There was the sound of a lock being opened, and then a rumbling noise that shook the entire wagon.

Jir was off like a shot. There was the slithering of reins being pulled through and then the sound of hooves disappearing and Konowa knew Zwindarra had bolted as well. A moment later, Rallie backed out of the wagon brushing herself off. "Give a good pull now; Dandy's ready."

Konowa looked over at Visyna, who shrugged her shoulders. They began pulling. The canvas tarp slid off, much to the annoyance of the pelican, who started flapping his wings and squawking as he was pulled along with it. Rallie lifted the hem of her cloak and removed a large metal flask strapped to one thigh. When the canvas finally came off, Wobbly flapped his way down to sit on the back board of the wagon with his bill open wide. Rallie unstoppered the flask and upended its contents into Wobbly's mouth.

As soon as the flask was empty Rallie grabbed the pelican by the middle, whispered something to him, and heaved him bodily into the air.

"Rallie!" Visyna cried, putting a hand to her mouth in surprise.

Konowa half-expected the bird to come tumbling right back down, but with agonizing slowness Wobbly flapped his wings and started to fly. He appeared confused at first, making one complete circle of the wagon, then he veered to the west, although he still meandered through all points on the compass.

"Care to tell us what this is all about?" he asked, watching the pelican fly east, then a bit to the north, before doubling back and heading south. Wherever he was going, he was taking the scenic route.

Rallie's answer was cut off by a shriek from inside the wagon, followed by the appearance of an enormous beaked head covered in fine, ash-gray feathers. The beak, all black save for a tiny silver tip, was more than a foot long and curved like a drukar. It turned its head and stared at them with a pair of brilliant amber eyes. They showed not the slightest inclination toward mercy. A cold warning surged through Konowa's body, but already the threat was gone, as the bird's entire body emerged from the wagon. It shot straight into the sky, a gray and black streak propelled by two silver-colored, sinewy legs. The wagon shuddered and the wind from the bird's ascent blew dirt and straw into their faces. Twenty feet in the air, it opened its wings and they easily spanned the length of the wagon. It beat them once, twice, and was already another fifty feet in the air and angling toward Wobbly. For his part, the pelican squawked and started flapping his wings for all he was worth, leaving a trail of white feathers floating in the wind as he headed due west at a surprising rate of speed.

"He'll never make it!" Visyna said, her fingers already starting to weave a design in front of her.

"Have a little faith, my dear," Rallie said, walking over and placing the sleeve of her cloak over Visyna's hands. There was a strange vibration—it suddenly felt as if there wasn't enough air to breathe. The feeling lasted only a moment and then Rallie was sliding her cloak off Visyna's hands and patting her on the arm. "Dandy would never hurt Wobbly; I just like to keep the old sot honest and put a bit of fire under his tail feathers once in a while. Besides, those two have worked together before. They know what they're doing."

"Care to tell us?" Konowa asked, watching a still-surprised Visyna stare at her hands.

Rallie motioned for him to start putting the canvas cover back on the wagon. "You remember the dream you had about Martimis?" she asked, lifting up an edge of the canvas and handing it to Visyna, who still seemed a little stunned. "It wasn't a dream, not entirely. Someone has been intercepting my messages, and I have an idea who."

"What will those two do about it?"

Rallie pulled a cigar out of her cloak and flicked a flint against a steel bolt head, drawing the sparks into the end of the cigar with a skill that Konowa suspected was more than natural. She took a deep drag and smiled as she exhaled a thick cloud of blue smoke.

"They'll shine a little light on the subject," she said, cackling with mirth and refusing to explain any more.

THIRTY-SEVEN

He was drowning. Alwyn struggled to hold his breath, feebly trying to claw his way to the surface. There was a wavering light far above him, while around him cold, black water squeezed in on all sides. It was freezing, and the harder he tried, the deeper he sank. All his energy was being drawn out of his body and he felt progressively lighter and more insubstantial with each stroke. The light started to fade, and he knew he wasn't going to make it. He opened his mouth to let the water in and took a breath. Warm air rushed into his lungs.

"Jilk noré grina hee dfir," a woman's voice said.

Alwyn opened his eyes. At first, he thought he was looking at a pair of polished amber jewels set in the hollow of a tree. A moment later, he saw that they were in fact eyes, and that they belonged to the face of an elf. He brought a hand up, his fingers smearing his spectacles. Well, they were in place. He blinked and looked again. A woman—an elf woman—knelt over the top of him, peering down with all the interest that the major's bengar had eyed him with not that long ago. Her skin was tanned, like the major's, and her black hair was drawn tightly into a braid that hung down over one shoulder of a garment of green and brown. The cloth, if that's what it was, appeared to change even as he watched it, so that leaves and branches danced across her body as she shifted closer to him. It hurt his head to try to keep all of her in focus, so he concentrated on her face.

That's when the horror of the black elf rushed back to him and he started to scream. The woman reached out and placed a warm hand on his lips.

"You are safe, for the moment. The others fled our presence, heading eastward."

Alwyn took in a few more breaths and allowed himself to relax, a little. This elf was nothing like the creature that had shot him. Unlike the major and Kritton, though, she had both her ear tips. It was then that he realized who, and what, she was.

"You're an elf of the Long Watch." It was like walking straight into a faery tale.

"I am." The woman said something again in elvish, her voice carrying through the air like a leaf floating on a stream.

"What?" It was dark, but somewhere above him a cool light cast its glow through the canopy of the forest. It was the moon. Strange, he thought, that he could see it this well from the forest floor. No sooner had he thought it than the earth beneath him swayed. His stomach lurched with the realization that he wasn't on the ground at all, but high up in the crook of a large branch of a wahatti tree. He carefully turned his head to the side and looked down. The ground was fifty feet below.

He closed his eyes and wondered if he was dreaming. He opened them again and the elf was still there, still looking at him intently. He noticed a leafy section of the tree was watching him, and then gaped when the leaves moved, revealing another elf. He blinked. This elf, a male, he thought, was festooned with leaves and other foliage. Through the leaves, Alwyn could just make out dark-brown bark, which he assumed served as armor, covering the elf's forearms and chest. What Alwyn had taken for branches turned out to be a scabbarded sword and a long, curving bow held in his hands. Without the moonlight, he never would have seen him, and even then it was only because the elf moved that he knew he was there at all.

"I told the others that the *morhar* lives."

"*Morhar?*" Alwyn asked, turning away from the second elf. His head was still foggy. Simple questions seemed best at the moment.

"Tree killer," she said calmly.

"But I—" He was going to say he had never done any such thing when he noticed again the bow carried by the elf. The image of the arrow sticking out of Alik's throat was still vivid in his mind, as was the pain from the one that had pierced his chest. He instinctively reached for the wound. His fingers touched cool, wet leaves wrapping his entire left shoulder and chest. The physical pain was excruciating, the emotional even worse. "What happened to my friends?"

"Some will walk among the trees no more. We buried them in a clearing nearby. The arrows that took their lives were *æri tokma*, fire-forged, as was the one that pierced you. You were fortunate that we were able to remove it before it could harm you further." She pointed to a spot beside Alwyn. Ugly black slivers of an arrow shaft lay on a broad leaf. It was fletched with razor-edged leaves the color of steel and a black ichor oozed from the broken pieces, staining the green leaf. Sharp, angular runes covered the pieces of the shaft, and though he couldn't read them, he felt their menace.

"Where is the rest of my patrol?"

The female leaned forward and helped Alwyn into a sitting position. Searing pain raced through his chest. He gasped and would have toppled off the branch if the elf hadn't held on. When the pain subsided, she offered him some water from a hollowed-out gourd. She kept a hand resting on his shoulder.

"The others are injured, and are being cared for."

Alwyn pushed thoughts of Yimt and the others out of his mind before they consumed him. His skin tingled. Insects chittered all around him, and he was surprised at how loud and clear they sounded.

The male elf suddenly moved, walking across the branch as if strolling down a boulevard. His gait reminded Alwyn of Jir—slow, graceful, and deadly. Alwyn put his hands down at his sides to grab hold of the branch and felt a nest of leaves and soft moss beneath him. He gently rocked from side to side and felt a bit more secure at the sturdiness of his perch. The elf halted beside him and bent to look at him.

Alwyn was drawn to his face, aware he was staring and unable to look away. Unlike the naturally tanned skin of the woman, this one's skin was completely tattooed with a leaf pattern. He turned his head from side to side, studying Alwyn with immense curiosity. Two more eyes suddenly appeared on the elf's shoulder, dark and glimmering, and Alwyn found himself being examined by a small, dark brown, furry creature.

"Is that a squirrel?" he asked, pointing at the animal that perched on its haunches by the elf's left ear, its tiny black nose twitching long, golden whiskers. Two tiny ears swiveled on top of its head as it made a soft, purring sound. Suddenly, the twitching stopped and the animal launched itself from its perch into the air, missing Alwyn's head by inches. It spread its legs wide and previously hidden folds of fur opened up and it glided to the next tree, twenty yards away. A moment later, it was back, landing gracefully on the elf's shoulder. Between its teeth was a still-wriggling snake a foot long. It devoured the snake quickly, never taking its eyes off Alwyn. When it was done, it started purring again.

"Of a kind," the woman replied. She switched to elvish and spoke to the male. He said something back in a language that was not elvish—it sounded like wind rustling through the trees, but the woman nodded as if she understood. The male then turned and simply vanished into the branches around them. The last Alwyn saw of him was a small pair of dark eyes twinkling at him from between the leaves with far more intelligence than any pair of squirrel eyes should have.

"Who was the elf?" he asked.

She paused before speaking, a pained look crossing her face. "He was Tyul Mountain Spring. He is now *diova gruss*, one of the lost ones."

Alwyn wanted to ask what that meant, but sensed now was not the time. "You saved our lives," he said. He'd once overheard the major talking, well, yelling really, with the witch. The elves of the Long Watch cared little for humans. He could imagine what they thought about soldiers of the Empire.

"It was not our intent," the elf replied. "We hunted other prey, leaving our homeland of the Great Forest to cross the vast waters to track them here. We did not expect to find you when we found them. Even then you would have been left to the natural order, but most curiously, Her creatures attacked you though you wear the cloth of the *æri tokma*, and we would know more."

It was not a reassuring answer, and it was rude to look a gift dragon in the mouth, especially when it might breathe fire on you if you did. Curiosity got the better of him.

"What was that thing that shot me?"

The elf's amber eyes flashed, and Alwyn feared he had crossed a line. After a moment, she responded. "It, and the others you did not see, are Her servants. They are no more elves than you."

"Actually," Alwyn said, "our regiment is called the Iron Elves, but I'm not an elf," he hastened to add.

The elf hissed. She drew forth a gleaming, wooden dagger and made a sign of warding. "Then you serve the Shadow Monarch. We were wrong to succor you."

Alwyn felt the life force in the blade, and for a moment thought he heard another voice. "What? No. We've got nothing to do with the Shadow Monarch! We're trying to stop Her from getting the Star. We're not evil, honest," he said, holding up his hands.

"You know of the Star?" she asked, the dagger still held in her hand.

"I haven't seen it, if that's what you're asking, but we've all heard about it. I think that's the real reason we're going to Luuguth Jor."

The dagger vanished, and with it the strange feeling that there had been more than just the two of them there. The elf sat down beside him, one hand still on his shoulder. Alwyn lowered his hands and let out his breath.

"What is your name?"

"Private Alwyn Renwar."

The elf shook her head. "What does your name mean?"

"Mean? It's just my name, it doesn't mean anything," he said, his voice rising a little. "What's yours?"

"Irkila Moon Singer," she said, still staring at him with those deep, brown eyes, "*ryk faurré* of Tall Wind. Why do you live as you do, Private Alwyn Renwar? Why do you destroy that which lives so that you instead may live a life with no meaning?"

That wasn't fair. "Hey, I said my name has no meaning, not my life. And besides, my name does have a meaning, it was my grandfather's."

Irkila sat up straight. "You rob your ancestor of his name? How will he be known in the spirit world?"

"I asked you to watch over him, Irkila, not argue with him," a voice said from above. An elf landed lightly beside Irkila without a sound. She was older, her black hair streaked with gray, her skin lined with fine wrinkles that only added to her look of wisdom and beauty. Like Irkila, she was dressed in a fashion that caused her to blend with the tree so that it was difficult to tell where the tree ended and she began.

"I want to understand, Chayii Red Owl, but he makes no sense. He and his companions wear the cloth of the tainted ones, yet are hunted by creatures of Her making. They search for the Eastern Star, yet do not appear to believe in it. They follow orders they do not understand."

Chayii smiled. "Their ways are not ours. Go aid the children of this home. Many were wounded during the battle, their trunks scarred by metal, their leaves burned by the black frost. I would talk with Alwyn of the Empire."

Irkila nodded and took her hand from his shoulder. The sounds of the forest quieted again, and he shook his head. He watched her walk back toward the trunk of the tree and then simply vanish. It was impressive magic.

"Not magic," Chayii said, "but understanding. Many things are yet shrouded in this, and I seek your light. Will you guide me?"

He started, then nodded, wishing he could go back to a time when the only elf he'd known had cobbled shoes for a living and had shown no interest in reading his mind.

"Then tell me, *Iron Elf*, who is the one you call Meri?"

THIRTY-EIGHT

Alwyn's heart thudded in his chest and for the second time in as many minutes he thought he might tumble from the branch.

"You saw him?"

Chayii closed her eyes and slowly exhaled. When she opened them again her brown eyes stared at him with bright intensity. "I sensed him, as I sense all disturbances in the natural order. He lingers in this world, bound here by something that should not be."

Meri, the elf sensed Meri. That meant he wasn't crazy. "He died a few days ago. We buried him out on the plain of vines, but I've seen him a few times since. I think, well, I think he might be protecting me."

She pursed her lips. "Necromancy poisons the natural order. This is Her doing."

Alwyn didn't like the sound of this one bit. "Look, Miss Red Owl, I don't know what's going on, but I know Meri was a good man in life, and he seems to be that way in death, too. I guess that doesn't make a lot of sense, but then I'm sitting in a tree with elves talking about magic, ghosts, and the natural order, which, to be honest, I never even knew there was one. I wish I could explain it, but I really don't know how."

Chayii smiled at him, and it didn't make him afraid. Before she could respond, a bird cry rang through the trees. It was immediately answered by others. Chayii listened intently, cocking her head to one side and closing her eyes. After a few moments, she opened them again and lifted her face to the moon, trilling a series of notes that Alwyn would have sworn were made by a bird were he not watching her do it. More bird call answered her and then the forest was silent. She turned back to him and the smile was gone.

"It is time for answers," she said, holding a hand above her head. She began to chant and a thick vine uncoiled itself from a branch above and lay in her open hand. Her chanting changed and the end of the vine slithered across her hand and toward Alwyn. He leaned back, but it was already across his legs and moving around his body like a constrictor. In seconds he was securely bound, though not so tightly that it hurt.

Chayii moved beside him and grabbed the leaf on which the arrow rested, careful not to touch the arrow itself. She took hold of the vine with her other hand and her chanting changed again. The branch they were on suddenly bent down, and they were sliding off it into oblivion.

Before he could scream, a lower branch reached up and they landed softly among its leaves, the vine acting as a safety line. The process was continued several more times as they slowly progressed toward the forest floor. When they were still twenty feet off the ground and no branches were left, the vine took their weight and lowered them the rest of the way. No sooner had his feet touched the ground than the vine uncoiled itself and withdrew back into the branches above. Chayii took hold of his arm on his right side and steadied him. The murmur of voices he had sensed before started up again.

"That was . . . that was amazing," he said, looking back up.

Chayii looked up at the tree and sang a short song. The tree swayed in response and then went still. Alwyn could have sworn he heard, or felt, the tree say something.

"No, Alwyn of the Empire, that was life. Come."

She led him a short distance through the forest to a small clearing where his comrades were buried. The moon shone brighter here and he could see clearly all around him. Muskets, Yimt's shatterbow, the rest of their kits, and several black arrows lay piled on a large flat rock beside three mounds of frost-burnt leaves. There were no markers, no sign that the soldiers lying there now had lived at all.

Irkila suddenly appeared and took the leaf-wrapped arrow from Chayii, placing it on the rock with the other arrows. Other elves emerged from the forest. Several were supporting or leading members of Three Section. Alwyn staggered and Chayii motioned for another elf to come and help her.

"Never mind, ma'am, I'll take care of that sack of bones," Yimt said, detaching himself from the elf who supported him to limp over and offer his shoulder to Alwyn. Leaf-and-moss bandages secured with thin vines covered the left side of his head and his right forearm. Judging by the way he limped, Alwyn figured his right thigh must be bandaged, too. More shocking than seeing the dwarf wounded, however, was seeing him alive. He squeezed Yimt's shoulder and fought back tears.

"I saw Kritton with your drukar."

Yimt's upper lip curled. "I lost sight of that bastard after two of those creatures attacked me. If we're lucky, one of them caught up and made a nice meal out of him."

Before he could ask for an explanation, the survivors of Three Section were all brought together. Teeter now limped on both legs. Scolly's left arm was in a sling ingeniously made of a broad leaf, while Inkermon looked completely untouched. Seeing the farmer unwounded angered Alwyn, and Inkermon seemed to sense it, for he refused to look him in the eye. He looked back to the mounds where Alik, Buuko, and little N'bhat lay buried, and something cold gripped his heart.

Without any warning, three elves materialized out of the forest. Their raiment of leaves was similar to that of the elf Alwyn had seen in the tree, but he couldn't tell if one of them was him. The three elves stopped short of the mounds, notching arrows they drew from quivers hidden somewhere among the leaves that obscured their forms. They drew back the strings on their longbows as one and shot an arrow into each mound. Several more elves had arrows at the ready.

"What are you doing?" Alwyn cried, looking at Chayii. When she gave no indication of answering, he turned to Yimt. "Stop them." The dwarf tugged on his beard and said nothing.

The clearing shuddered, as if a stone had been dropped into still water.

A sensation that Alwyn could only describe as cold heat washed over him. Flames of frost began to crawl along the leaves of two of the three mounds, burning them to ash. Chayii stepped forward and began to chant again, her voice louder than before. A wind whipped up from nowhere and began to beat back at the unnatural fire. The air in the clearing chilled and Chayii's breath misted with each word. Black-tinged tongues of icy fire stabbed deeper into the mounds, consuming everything. Chayii's voice faltered, but immediately the other elves added their voices to hers. They moved closer to the whirling, burning leaves, reaching out their hands and grabbing hold of one another. Alwyn and the others were drawn into the circle with them. As soon as his hand touched Chayii's, his mouth opened and he began to speak, but they were not his words:

Ni Unka Ro Jéj
Ne Har Ro Léj
Tokma Ka Æri

Ni Swik Ro Triv
Ne Ull Ro Ulmriv
Tokma Ka Æri

Wih Shir Ser
Ock-al Shir Ser
Ki Rorjer Ka Æri

His voice rose with theirs until he was shouting, and though there was not a word he could relate, the meaning was quite clear:

Flesh and bone,
Wood and loam,
Nothing forged in fire.

Grass and leaves,
Sky and seas,
Nothing forged in fire.

Long we watch,
Forever we watch,
For Darkness forged in fire.

The flames of ice finally faltered and disappeared, but it wasn't because of the elves' magic; there was nothing left for the icy flames to consume. N'bhat lay on his back, his face slack in death, his arms crossed over his chest with one of the arrows in his heart. Beside him, where Alik and Buuko had been laid to rest, the other arrows, blackened and seared with frost, stuck out of bare earth.

"What just happened . . . ? Where are they?" Alwyn asked.

Chayii shook her head. "They walk the world between, as does Meri, as do those who went before. Too late did I realize the strength of the ties that bind you, and bind you to each other, though I do not yet understand how it has happened."

Tears rolled down her cheeks, and there was such sorrow in her voice that Alwyn could barely breathe.

"What does it all mean?"

"It means, Alwyn of the Empire, that you may know death, and leave this life behind, but you are forever bound to serve in the Iron Elves."

THIRTY-NINE

We're doomed, we're doomed." Inkermon kept rocking himself back and forth as he sat under a tree. Yimt looked at him and made a noise and turned away.

"So much for his creator," the dwarf muttered, sitting down on the ground and idly running his fingers through the dirt.

Teeter and Scolly were both sleeping, their snores a source of great interest to the elf who stood guard over them. To a being who could walk through a bed of crisp autumn leaves and not be heard, Alwyn figured, the soldiers must have sounded like a herd of muraphants.

"Do you think Miss Red Owl is right?" Alwyn asked. The moon was slowly sliding down the sky, but dawn was still a couple of hours off. The heat of the forest had returned, but it wasn't as humid as before. Alwyn was trying and failing to direct his thoughts to everything but what he had seen in the clearing and having no success. Even the pain in his chest wasn't enough to distract him.

"What, that we're bespelled and all that? I'm not sure how to break it to you, Ally, but we ain't actually elves. That stuff only works on *them*."

"What about that oath we took in the vines? I didn't say anything, but I think I felt something happen, you know? And I saw one of . . . them."

"One of who?"

"One of Hers—it was horrible. And it had a black ear tip, you know, one of the tainted ones, sort of like Kritton and the major."

Yimt steepled his fingers. "Rakkes come in different shapes and sizes, Ally. You sure you didn't mix up seeing Kritton and one of them beasties? People see all kinds of things in battle when they get worked up."

Alwyn shook his head. "No rakke shot those arrows. And you saw what happened to Alik and Buuko. They're gone . . . but they aren't, not really, just like Meri."

Yimt sighed and rubbed his beard. "Now I'm not saying nothing by this, but you are a bit of a sensitive fellow, Ally. You take things to heart a bit faster than the rest of us. You're the only one that thinks he saw Meri, or this black elf, and for all I know, Alik and Buuko were buried somewhere else and all that stuff out there was just a bit of a show."

Alwyn felt his face flush. "What, you think I'm lying?"

Yimt lifted up the leaf-and-moss bandage on his head and scratched at the raw skin underneath. "Did I say you were a liar? I just said you've seen things the rest of us haven't. Maybe what they say is true, or maybe they're playing at games. Just because they get their wind up about the Shadow Monarch and all that doesn't mean we have to."

"But what about Meri and the others?"

Yimt stopped scratching for a moment. "I'm not saying there ain't no such thing as ghosts, I just don't know that I buy into the rest of it is all. Maybe you really did see him, or his shade. Did he still have that snuffbox in his eye socket? Now if he had that, I'd say it probably was him. I doubt many ghosts go around with one of them tucked into their skull. Good stuff, too, I meant to ask him what brand it was."

Alwyn stared at Yimt. Yimt stared back, one hand still half under his bandage.

"How can you not take this seriously, Yimt? She said we're bound to an eternity of serving in the regiment. An eternity."

Yimt rolled his eyes and patted down his bandage. He looked around and snapped a small twig from a nearby bush. He started rubbing the broken end against his metal teeth. It made a high-pitched noise.

"Whether I take it serious or not doesn't really make a difference, now does it? If it's true, I don't see what getting all worked up about it will do, and if it ain't, then there was nothing to worry about in the first place."

The elf guarding them raised his eyebrows as Yimt dug at something stuck between a couple of molars. Alwyn nudged Yimt and motioned toward the elf.

"What?" Yimt asked. He looked over at the elf, pulling the twig out of his mouth and waving it at him. "Just polishing the silver," he said cheerfully, and went back to brushing his teeth.

"Trees," Alwyn whispered, "they really, really like trees."

Yimt pulled the twig out of his mouth and looked at it closer. "What, this? It's just a little branch, no harm. And that ain't no tree no how, more a really tall bushy weed, if you ask me."

"And what if they see it as a baby?"

Yimt paused in his oral hygiene and gave it some thought, chewing on the end of the twig as he did so. The elf appeared to be gripping his bow rather tightly.

Finally, Yimt pulled the twig back out and jabbed it into the ground. "Grow tall and proud, O weed of the forest," he said, blowing the twig a kiss.

"A most interesting blessing," came Chayii's voice as she leaped down from a tree to stand beside them. "I was not aware dwarves cared for the trees of the world."

Yimt nodded solemnly. "Oh, that we do, Miss Red Owl, that we do. Why, if you'd let me grab my shatterbow over there, I'll show you how nice I've kept the wood polished." He made to get up, but the elf guarding them lifted his bow ever so slightly and Yimt settled back on the ground.

Alwyn cringed. Yimt might just charm them straight into eternal shadow.

"It is a most curious weapon, and well kept, but the mixing of iron and wood has killed its spirit. I am saddened by the loss, as I am for all the brothers and sisters that died to make the other weapons you carried."

"Killed its spirit? Not in the least." Yimt stuck out his chest a little, clearly proud of his shatterbow. "Lil' Nipper there fires as true as the day my aunt bought it, and that was more than fifty years ago. Sure, it doesn't have quite the distance it once had, but after fifty years what can you expect?"

Chayii reached behind her back and brought forth her bow. Alwyn had that strange feeling again that someone, or something, was there with them.

"This was given to me by my *ryk faur*, He Who Brushes the Sky, over one hundred years ago." She flexed the bow in her hands. It bent and then sprang back like a new sapling.

Yimt nodded his approval. "As an admirer of form, I feel safe in saying you're both in fine shape."

They'll find us in tiny little pieces. Before Alwyn could apologize for Yimt, Chayii laughed. She sat down in front of them, lightly jabbing one end of her bow into the earth beside the twig Yimt had just planted. Alwyn noticed the bow wasn't strung and wondered what kind of string the elves might use.

"I will show you," Chayii said, placing her hands in the dirt to either side of the bow and twig.

Alwyn barely jumped this time as the elf answered his unasked question.

"Show us what?" Yimt asked.

Alwyn shushed him and pointed to the twig in front of them. It began to tremble, and then tiny green shoots sprouted from it. They waved about in the air for a moment like a many-headed snake, and then began to grow upward, twining themselves together as they climbed up the bow. When they reached the top they uncoiled from the bow itself so that they hung down straight between the ends, where more green shoots had wrapped themselves. Slowly, gently, they began to tighten, spinning themselves into one incredibly fine string. The vines gleamed silvery green as they spun themselves together, bending the ends of the bow closer together until the vine string was taut. Chayii brought out a small wooden blade and lightly parted the newly grown bowstring from the twig and lifted the bow from the dirt, handing it to Yimt to inspect.

"It's as warm as fresh bread," he said, running his hands lightly over the bow. He placed a couple of fingers on the string and pulled back, grunting in surprise. "That's incredible! If I hadn't seen it with my own eyes, I wouldn't have believed it. Ally, give this a try."

Alwyn looked at Chayii, who nodded her approval. He took the bow from Yimt and immediately felt the warmth in the wood. He felt something else, too, or maybe heard something. Whatever it was, he liked it. He wrapped his fingers around the string and pulled, or rather, tried to pull, the pain in his chest too much.

"The draw weight on that would put Lil' Nipper to shame," Yimt said, shaking his head. "That's some mighty fine magic."

Alwyn handed Chayii back her bow.

"What you call magic we call being one with the natural order. To understand the life around you is to be part of it, and it a part of you."

Yimt nodded noncommittally. "And you're doing a damn fine job of it, too. Now, I hate to be rude after all the help you gave us, especially in saving young Ally there from death's door, but I was wondering if we might grab our kit and be on our way? We've got a job to do and Major Osveen will have my hide if I'm late."

Chayii looked pensive at the mention of the major's name. A lantern went on in Alwyn's head.

"The major is an elf. You don't happen to know him, do you, ma'am?"

She gave a wistful smile that made Alwyn regret asking.

"I did, at one time. It has been many years since I last saw him."

Yimt slapped the ground with the flat of his hand. "He's a wild one, no doubt about it, but a damn fine officer, and I've seen a bunch. You'd think that witch of his would tame him, but she seems to do the opposite. Two of them fight like a pair of razorback dragons in a sack."

Chayii's smile vanished. "Witch? What witch?"

Alwyn tried to catch Yimt's eye, but the dwarf was off on one of his tangents.

"An elfkynan witch, to be exact. Miss Visyna Tekoy, pretty little thing, too. Got some power, put on quite a light show a week or so back. You know, give her a bow and arrow and a set of those fancy clothes you have and you'd be hard-pressed to say she wasn't an elf."

"The elfkynan are not elves," Chayii said. The ice in her voice was crystal clear to Alwyn, but Yimt remained oblivious. "Elves would not leave a forest untended like this. The land grows strange and an illness pervades it . . ."

As Miss Red Owl talked, Alwyn couldn't help but think she sounded an awful lot like Miss Tekoy, but he kept that to himself.

". . . they have forsaken the stewardship that is their birthright. These forests are yet children in this world and should not have been left alone to fend for themselves."

"Children? There must be trees in here hundreds of years old," Alwyn said, looking around him in true awe.

"There are Wolf Oaks in the deepest parts of our home that were there when the light of the first morning rose over the *mukta ull*," Chayii said, a reverential tone in her voice.

"Oh."

Chayii turned back to Yimt. "You said they fight?"

Yimt chuckled and nodded. "The major and Miss Tekoy? Only when they see each other. It was like that when I was courting my sweet Amag. We used to squabble over everything."

Alwyn looked at the dwarf in surprise. Yimt, married? He'd never mentioned anything about a sweet Amag before.

"Does she goad him to act against his better judgment?" Chayii asked.

"Not exactly. More like they both have ideas about what's the right way to do something, and neither one is the same. Always on about the Empire and nature, too. This is evil, that is backward, bit of a bore really. I gather she wants him to be more elfish, you know, like you lot, while he would just as soon polish his musket. He may be an elf an' all, but unlike her, you put a bow and arrow in his hands and I think he'd probably use it to start a fire."

Yimt was going to get them all killed yet. Alwyn watched Chayii, looking for the first sign of trouble, but all she did was sit there. She brought a hand to her face and wiped away a tear.

"He's a good officer," Alwyn blurted out. He was surprised to hear himself say it, but it was true. The major got off his horse whenever he could to walk among the men, checking to see that things were in order, but also to see that they were taken care of. They barely saw the Prince, and too much of their sergeants, but the major seemed to know when to show up, and when not to. Looking back on it now, the flogging of Corporal Kritton didn't conjure up the same dark feelings it had before. If he ever saw that elf again, he'd gladly finish the other lashes.

"Ally's telling you the truth—the major is one of the better ones. In fact," Yimt said, coughing politely and looking again at his shatterbow on the rock in the clearing, "he's expecting to see us at Luuguth Jor. We were on our way there when them rakkes attacked us, but I'm guessing you know all about what's going on. If you'd care to come along, you'd get a chance to see him, and the witch, too. Maybe you could talk some sense into them. Seems like they could be a nice couple if they could see eye to eye a bit more."

"Perhaps they have different opinions on the Eastern Star," Chayii remarked.

Alwyn avoided Yimt's look. The dwarf blinked a couple of times and then sighed.

"That was supposed to be a secret, but as it's out in the open I don't suppose there is much point in denying it."

The elf rose from the forest floor in one fluid motion. "We will accompany you, Yimt of the Warm Breeze. Prepare your men for the road; we travel at once." With that, Chayii walked into the forest and disappeared from sight. Bird calls rang out and the trees around them rustled in response.

"You heard the lady, let's get cracking," Yimt said, jumping to his feet and helping Alwyn to his. "Inkermon, make yourself useful and get Teeter and Scolly up. And you ain't doomed until I tell you you're doomed."

Inkermon quit mumbling and did as Yimt said. Teeter and Scolly were quickly roused, and the survivors of Three Section were soon armed and ready. Alwyn had to sling his musket over his right shoulder. His chest was in agony despite whatever spells or potions the elves must have used to heal him, and he seriously doubted he could make it all the way to Luuguth Jor.

"Drink this," Irkila said, appearing at his side and handing him a gourd. "It will lighten your feet for the coming journey."

"What is it?"

"*Rok har*—tree's blood."

Alwyn backed away. "I'm not drinking blood, I don't care where it came from."

Irkila pursed her lips and called out to another elf nearby. After a short exchange, she turned back to Alwyn with a smile on her face. "My use of your language is not as precise as it could be. I believe you call this 'sap.'"

Alwyn let out a breath and held out his hand to accept the gourd. Other elves were offering the rest of Three Section similar gourds, so it couldn't be that bad. He removed the bark plug from the top of the gourd and took a drink. The sap, and Alwyn was sure it was more than just that, was cool and fresh, a wonderful mix of sweet and tang. Unlike the drake sweat Yimt preferred, this immediately made him feel better without trying to burn a hole in his stomach. He tried to hand the gourd back to Irkila, but she shook her head.

"Keep it and drink from it when you have need. We will not rest until we reach our destination."

"Thanks," Alwyn said. He walked over to where the others were standing.

"I feel twenty years younger!" Yimt said, rubbing a sleeve across his beard as he took another drink from his gourd. "Mix in a bit of twelve-year-old Sala brandy and you'd have the perfect elixir for what ails you. Probably sell it for quite a coin, too."

Inkermon still held his gourd in his hands, not yet taking a drink.

"If they were going to poison you, they would have done it by now," Yimt said, motioning with a thumb toward the elves. "Drink it."

Inkermon shook his head and held the gourd out to Yimt. "No spirits except the grace of the Creator shall pass into my body."

He half-expected Yimt to knock Inkermon flat, but instead Yimt just smiled and took the gourd. "You better keep up or you'll have a gullet full of arrows in your backside along with his grace. Teeter, Scolly, you watch the right side, Ally and me will take the left. The saint can keep an eye to the sky for divine intervention. Them rakkes are still out there, and so is Kritton . . . and some other creatures, too," he added, nodding at Alwyn. "Odds are these elves will see them long before we do, but you keep looking anyway."

Irkila reappeared and motioned for them to follow her. Alwyn put his shako on his head and then turned back to make sure they hadn't left anything behind. The rock in the clearing was bare. Satisfied, he started after Irkila and then remembered the black arrows. Before he could ask he saw them sticking out of the top of Yimt's knapsack.

"They'll see the arrows," he said, grabbing Yimt by the arm and bending down to whisper in his ear.

Yimt paused in the middle of putting a pinch of crute in his mouth. "Who do you think gave them to me? Ally, I know how to mind my manners among the fey folk."

"They gave them to you? Why?"

"Miss Red Owl said something about never leaving a weapon on a battlefield."

"She said that?" Alwyn asked.

Yimt shrugged his shoulders. "Well, that's the gist of it. There was something about dark magic and perversion of nature and the like, but it all adds up to the same thing; don't leave a weapon around for your enemy to find and use against you."

Alwyn couldn't argue with that logic, but he suspected there was probably a lot more to it.

He looked ahead and saw that the elves were already through the clearing and disappearing into the woods. Irkila motioned for them to hurry. He lengthened his stride, surprised at how well he felt. For someone who had just been shot by an arrow, and probably a cursed one at that, he was keeping up. The elves of the Long Watch could teach the army surgeons a thing or two, though he couldn't really imagine a human doctor using leaves and moss.

"Besides," Yimt continued, setting off at a slow trot while readjusting the bandage under his shako with one hand, "I think she might be a bit sweet on me. Did you hear how she called me Warm Breeze?"

To his credit, Alwyn nodded and said nothing, wondering whether it was worth telling Yimt that the elf had politely suggested he was full of hot air.

FORTY

Bodies weren't supposed to have trees growing out of them.

Five soldiers of the Thirty-fifth Foot lay sprawled in and around the mud-walled hut they'd commandeered as a forward outpost on the western bank of the river guarding the route toward Luuguth Jor. Each was impaled by a black sapling of a type of tree Konowa had only ever seen from a great distance until now.

It was late afternoon, and the Iron Elves were still a good two-hour march away from the village and the tiny fortress, but Konowa figured that even if they were only two minutes away it wouldn't matter. Luuguth Jor would be a forest of death.

Storm clouds threatened, but for the moment the sun did its best to burn everything beneath it, and the smell of the dead was strong. Most curiously, however, no flies buzzed around the bodies.

Konowa bent over in the saddle. The trees were excreting a dark ichor that ran over the deformed limbs and dripped off steel-colored leaves.

"What is this?" Lorian asked, kneeling beside one of the dead soldiers and reaching out a gloved hand toward the black sapling that grew out of his chest.

"A new forest for Her," Konowa said.

Lorian's hand froze just above the tree. "Then the Shadow Monarch really is behind all this," he said, looking up at Konowa and then at his ruined ear.

Konowa ignored his stare. He kicked his feet out of the stirrups and jumped off Zwindarra, throwing the reins over the horse's neck, giving him a pat on the withers, and telling him to stay. He walked to where Lorian was examining the body.

It was a corporal, the silver stripes on his jacket sleeve still visible through the mud—and blood—that covered his uniform. He crouched by the body, silently cursing as his knee tried to buckle beneath him.

"It's a *sarka har*," Konowa said, recognizing the twisted wood at once, "a blood tree." His father had told him many times of the High Forest and the fell magic that sustained the trees that fed on life.

"Do you think this happened to the scouts?" Lorian asked, voicing a fear that had been building in Konowa from the moment they came upon the scene.

"If they followed the river and were attacked, we would have seen this," he replied, pointing to the tree. "Either they are still ahead of us or they took a different route. The dwarf's a cagey one—I wouldn't count them out just yet." But Konowa wasn't really sure he believed Arkhorn could save his section from an evil like this.

"I picked them," Lorian said, standing up suddenly, his voice quavering. "I sentenced them to this fate."

"You've been in battle before—you've given orders and seen men die."

"But not like this! What's happening to them?"

Konowa looked more closely at the body of the corporal. The large vein in his neck pulsed slowly, as if the heart still beat, but he knew better. "The tree will feed on the blood of the victim, drawing sustenance until it has consumed it. Whether it also feeds on the soul, I do not know."

That was too much for Lorian. "The *soul!* We have to stop it." He lunged forward to grab the sapling, but Konowa caught him by the arm and restrained him. When Lorian stepped back Konowa let go, then reached out with both his hands and grabbed the trunk. Every midnight fear, every chilling tale told in the dark hours when he was a child, raced through his veins as the cool ichor oozed between his fingers. And then came the anger.

Konowa's rejection in the birthing meadow of the Wolf Oaks flashed in his mind and he clenched the sapling tighter. The acorn against his chest surged with cold fury, infusing his body with its energy. The constant murmur of life evaporated, replaced by the anguished cries of the dead soldier and the voracious hunger of the sapling. Each sensed his presence and dug its need into his mind. Konowa grunted and pulled the tree out, the body jerking as if the strings to a puppet had been cut. Black, clotted earth clung to the roots, which wriggled about in vain trying to find something to latch on to. The smell of death grew worse. The voices in his head grew louder. The fire inside him burned colder still.

Konowa squeezed the trunk harder and forced the frost fire into the sapling. The soldier's screams drowned as the sapling absorbed the burning cold like a sponge, but frost soon began to sparkle along its leaves, and it, too, began to scream. Black flames danced along its length, leaping from branch to leaf, consuming it.

When there was little more than ash, Konowa threw it to the ground, gasping for air. He looked at his hands. The ichor had burned off, leaving them impossibly clean. The voices were gone, the unending murmur of life rushing back into the void.

"Major, are you all right?" Lorian asked, laying a hand on his shoulder. He immediately withdrew it with a shout, his glove covered in hoar frost.

Konowa caught his breath and looked up. "I'm fine. I guess it was cursed after all," he lied, looking back at the pile of ash. Already the heat of the day was returning to his skin, and he wiped a sleeve across his forehead.

"What happened? What does it mean?" Lorian asked, mesmerized by the smoking ash.

"Nothing of importance!" the Prince called out, riding up to them at a canter and bringing his suddenly skittish mount to a halt by sawing back hard on the reins. The horse danced about, refusing to settle. The whites of its eyes showed and the Prince had to constantly pull the reins to keep it from bolting. "I will not have soldiers of the Empire spooked like dumb horses by these things!" he said, finally reaching forward to slap his mount between the ears with the end of the reins. "These men were killed by the rebels. Whatever sorcery is at work is ancillary and of no consequence, and that is all the troops need to know. Our primary goal is the Star." The Prince looked back to the column of troops marching toward them.

Konowa rose, gingerly stretching his leg. The sensation of frost fire pouring through his hands made them shake, and he pressed them firmly against his thighs.

"With all due respect, sir," Konowa said, "the men are not stupid. They have a fairly good idea what we're about, and what we might be facing. I always found it better to level with them. They fight better when they know why." Not that he would tell them everything.

The horse danced around in a circle before the Prince got it under control again. He brought it back close to Konowa and leaned down from his saddle until it appeared he would topple right out of it. "All they need to know is that I am the colonel of this regiment and the Prince of Calahr. My orders will be obeyed or they will swing." He sat up straight again in the saddle. "The rebels will pay for this," he said loudly, so that the passing soldiers might hear. Lowering his voice, he continued. "There's no time to bury the bodies. Uproot the trees, put everything in the hut, and burn it all. *Now.*"

Konowa silently cursed Marshal Ruwl and his father for making him nursemaid this fool. The urge to reach up and grab the Prince from his saddle and burn him instead flashed through Konowa, but he fought it—barely.

"Yes, sir, right away." He saluted and watched the Prince take off at a gallop as the horse tore away from the macabre scene as fast as it could.

"You heard His Highness," Konowa said, making no attempt to hide his anger and his contempt. He motioned for Lorian to look after the body of the corporal while he moved to the next tree.

It was the same each time. The cold would surge in Konowa and the sapling would try to absorb it, while the soul of the dead soldier cried out in fear and anguish. Each time, both were consumed, and it got easier to focus the energy. He was about to burn the hut in the same manner when he sensed Lorian's presence behind him. There was no threat, yet Konowa grew colder as the frost fire raced through his veins. It was as if the world was a blazing white sheet of snow with red slashes of life staining it. The need to purify it, purify all of it, clawed its way up inside Konowa until he could think of nothing else. He turned.

Lorian stared at him with wide eyes and an open mouth. He was holding one of the razor-edged leaves in his bare hand. Frost crawled along the leaf's surface, sparkling like black diamonds. And then the same consuming flame that burned the saplings flared up, and a moment later the leaf was ash, and Lorian's hand, like Konowa's, showed no injury.

"What have you done to us?" Lorian whispered, flexing his fingers as if seeing his hand for the first time.

It felt like a dam bursting. The sense of power and exhilaration vanished, leaving Konowa staggering.

What *had* he done?

What had his father given him? He looked down at the bodies in the hut and for a moment saw the bodies of the elves he had once known.

This was not his birthright—this was his curse.

The sound of marching feet passing by the hut brought him back. Konowa stood up straight and adjusted his uniform. "Get a pound of powder and a length of slow match and destroy this." He didn't wait for Lorian to reply, stepping out of the hut just as Rallie's wagon came by. Visyna was sitting beside her, and both of them looked at him as it rolled past.

He'd expected anger, outrage, even threats. Instead, as the wagon creaked past, the brindos honking and swishing their stubby tails, Jir padding alongside still looking up at the top of the wagon for the pelican, Konowa had to turn away. It wasn't rage he saw in their eyes, it was pity . . . and fear.

FORTY-ONE

Luuguth Jor hugged a bend in the Baynama River, a thick, dark ribbon of water that meandered through the central plains of Elfkyna like a constrictor, curling around the village set out in a brown crescent on its western bank. A dozen squat mud-and-grass huts sat well protected within the small peninsula created by the oxbow of the forever-changing river beneath a small grass-covered hill that rose a few hundred feet behind the village. Vine-lashed piers made of roughly cut logs jutted out into the water below the huts like fingers of a gnarled old hand. It was here that the villagers got into their tiny, flat-bottomed *kios* and paddled out into the center of the river to string finely woven mesh nets to catch ijuk, river turtles, and bara jogg. The catch was then brought back to the piers where the women gutted and filleted the fish, tossing the entrails back into the water to thank the gods for their bounty. The heads of the fish, however, were taken to the top of the hill and burned there, allowing the spirits of the animals to escape in the smoke and be reborn in the river with the next rain. Legend told of a Star falling from the heavens in that place at the very birth of the world. So they followed the ritual, and the fish remained plentiful and their lives peaceful.

And then the siggers came. The soldiers planted a pretty green-and-silver flag on top of the hill and claimed it for the Empire. They labored for months to raise a high mud wall all the way around the top of the hill, festooned it with cactus thorn, and then sat in it, staring out at the river. The elfkynan told the siggers they should not build there, for it would anger the gods. They told them the story of the Star.

And where is this Star? the siggers had asked. Did it fall back up into the sky? The village witch made the appropriate warding signs and warned the siggers that the Star would one day return. The siggers laughed and bought the fish heads from the women and used them to make soup. The spirits would have their revenge one day, the witch had said.

The witch never lived to see the spirits' revenge. A cold black arrow crafted by a magic far older than hers pierced her breast, killing her instantly.

Visyna covered her mouth with her hand as she looked down at the remains of the witch. A twisted black tree grew through her to reach its misshapen branches out to intertwine with the branches of others of its kind dotted all around the village and fortress, forming a U against the river. The trees were already taller than Visyna, their metaled leaves moving menacingly though no wind blew or rain fell. There were hundreds of trees, though it was difficult to tell where one ended and another began. She closed her eyes and immediately sensed their roots crawling deeper into the earth. The land here was changed, far more so than the vines where the faeraugs had sheltered. Her magic would not be sufficient to destroy them.

Not like his.

It was a sobering thought. She opened her eyes and knelt on the earth, placing a hand on the ground. It was like touching cold iron.

"In all my years of reporting, I have never seen anything more foreboding," Rallie said, angling her sketchbook to catch the moonlight as she drew the black forest that now grew where Luuguth Jor had once stood. The two women stood by Rallie's wagon on the edge of the village, while a scouting party moved through the gap in the trees by the river to check out the fortress within. "It fills one with a particular sense of dread, as if winter has arrived early. Great and terrible things are bound to follow. Oh, my, yes."

Visyna took one more look at the dead witch, knowing that could easily be her, and turned away. She was shocked to see a tiny smile on Rallie's face.

"Rallie! Don't you see, Konowa and the Iron Elves are the harbinger of the coming storm. I thought when he felt the natural order, he would finally understand."

"Or when he felt *you*?" Rallie asked. "Do not give up on the major, Visyna. He cares deeply for you even if he has trouble showing it. Love is a powerful weapon, but like all weapons, it depends on how one uses it."

"I know he cares, but he loves the Iron Elves more. He would do anything for them," she said, bitterness lacing her words.

"As you would for your land and your people. The two of you are more alike than either will admit. As soon as we deal with this little matter," she said, waving at the trees, "I see I am going to have to improve my chaperoning skills."

"Little matter? Rallie, the very world hangs in the balance and you talk as if you enjoy it."

Rallie stopped sketching and turned to look at her, all trace of a smile gone. "Of course I do not enjoy this. But I am a reporter of events, an observer of all things, and most importantly, a writer. I suffer from a disease few, fortunately, will ever contract. I need to be where fire burns hottest, or the wind blows coldest. It's there, where the tapestry of the world gets burned and ripped to shreds and another is woven new, that history lives, and dies. Our major, whether it be fate or by his own design, and the Iron Elves, and I daresay, us, too, have become one of those places."

As she talked, her face flushed and the years of hard living seemed to melt away, revealing a youthful, bright soul, yet one tempered by the sadness of having seen more than any person should. Realizing Visyna was staring at her, she turned back to her sketchbook. Her quill hovered above the paper, though, and she tilted her head to the side.

"Pray, my child, that you never catch this disease of mine. It is both pleasure and horror, and while I would not wish it on anyone, I would fight with every ounce of my strength if someone were to try to cure me of it. But enough of my life story," Rallie said, scratching her nose with the feather end of her quill while looking at Visyna. "You were telling me about the Star."

Visyna shivered. "I shouldn't have said anything."

Rallie cackled lightly, turning back to her drawing. Her hand moved with quick, fluid strokes across the page. "Ah, but you did. I had no idea a Star could talk, or that it would be so feeble as to need to hide itself from view."

"I do not know how to explain it; it is a feeling. The Star has been gone a long time, as have all the Stars. It is energy, but still weak after centuries of being gone." Hearing it said out loud made the entire situation all sound a bit foolish.

"Indeed," Rallie said, clucking as she turned over the page and began a new sketch. "And you are *sure* this is the Eastern Star?"

"I was," she said truthfully. "It comes to me when I call. It even warned me of the danger Konowa would become, and we have seen it come to pass. This regiment is cursed. The taint of the Shadow Monarch's evil is upon them."

Rallie shrugged her shoulders and continued to draw. "Perhaps. Then again, power is most often neutral, and can be used for good or ill. It depends on the wielder. I have faith in our major, as troubled as he is. For that matter, I have faith in you. You could have burned the faeraugs to a cinder, but you chose not to. That is no small thing, free will." Rallie paused again in her sketching and cast a sidelong glance at Visyna. "Let me know when you speak to this Star again—I'd love the chance to interview it for my story."

Visyna wanted to say no, then stopped herself. Why not? If this truly was the Eastern Star, why should it be secret? She remembered the touch of Kritton's hand on her skin and more riddles emerged.

"Questions to ponder, my dear, questions to ponder," Rallie said softly, the scritch of her quill across paper starting up again.

Visyna knew it was time she took the correspondent's advice.

"The trees won't burn with just fire, and we don't have enough powder to destroy the entire forest, sir," Lorian said, pointedly not looking at Konowa as he directed his answers to the Prince. Lorian gripped his halberd as if it were the only thing keeping him from falling. "For some reason, the area in and around the fortress is clear. It looks like they killed the soldiers there, then dragged their bodies out of the fort to enclose the fortress and the village. We're completely encircled except for right here."

Right here was a twenty-yard gap between the river and the treeline on the other side of the road leading into Luuguth Jor. They stood in the middle of the road looking up at the destroyed fortress. Konowa waited for the Prince to comprehend the folly of entering the forest-ringed position, but the Prince only nodded.

"We really should pull back, sir," Konowa finally said. "We'd be walking into a trap if we go in there. There's no sign of the Star or the previous Viceroy. He may have already found it."

The Prince sniffed and shook his head. He rested a boot on an overturned drum of the Thirty-fifth Foot, its stretched hide skin torn and covered in the blood of the young boy who had carried it. Oblivious, he looked up the hill, crossing his arms on his knee as he bent forward in what Konowa was sure the Prince thought was a martial pose.

"You see that fortress, Major," he said, pointing to the crumbled walls on top of the hill. His boot heel echoed hollowly on the drum, a ghostly accompaniment to his proud speech. "That will be our bastion. What better place to plant the Colors and make our stand. Raise the banner of Calahr high and let the enemy know that Luuguth Jor is once again in Imperial hands. The Star is here, Major, I can feel it! It's waiting for the right moment to reveal itself. Well, when the Colors of the Prince of Calahr fly over Luuguth Jor, the enemy will be drawn here like moths to a flame. And when they show themselves, they will dash themselves against our defenses and be defeated. This forest," he said, sweeping a hand dismissively at the ugly black growth that even now writhed around them, "shall be their undoing. They'll have to funnel through this gap to get to the fortress, and when they do, we will have them."

"Elfkynan rebels are one thing, but this," Konowa said, looking around at the forest, "this is something else. The Thirty-fifth Foot didn't stand a chance." Bits of uniform fluttered from jagged branches, reminding him of dockside sendoffs as wives and girlfriends waved their handkerchiefs and dabbed at tears for soldiers never to come home again.

"Lack of moral fiber, Major," the Prince replied. "Troops grow soft on garrison duty without a firm hand to keep them in line. Clearly, that was the case with the Thirty-fifth. Obviously caught by surprise, no doubt. Well, the Iron Elves won't be caught napping, not while I'm in charge." The Prince stood up straight and patted Konowa on the back. "Have heart, Major. The trees, as fascinating as they are, are of no direct concern to us." He waved at the forest as if it was just one more exotic bit of flora to be catalogued, an example that would be uprooted, tagged, and carefully wrapped and taken back to Celwyn to be planted in the royal maze. "If this is the best the Shadow Monarch can do, then She is already defeated. Don't you see, the forest has actually strengthened our defenses by providing us with a wall far stronger than those of the fort. We'd be foolish not to make use of Her mistake."

Lorian said something under his breath. Prince Tykkin turned to look at him. "You have something to add, RSM?"

Lorian started to shake his head . . . then stood up a little straighter and answered. "It's just that they're men, sir. This place is cursed, and it has them spooked. They don't understand what's going on. They're simple soldiers, they just want to do their duty and get home again. No one signed up for this." The last part was said staring directly at Konowa.

The Prince, as usual, chose to hear it differently. "If there are cowards in the ranks, RSM, we shall deal with them accordingly. Surely this regiment is made of tougher stuff; surely no little old elf-witch can scare them so."

Konowa could see Lorian was on the verge of saying something he couldn't take back. "What the RSM meant, sir," Konowa said, walking a few paces off to the side to draw the Prince's attention, "is that none of them have ever come up against anything like this before, and it has them excitable, eve of battle and all."

The Prince smiled. "Got their blood up, has it? Good. Still, wouldn't do to have them on edge for too long. We should set them to some task at once, burn off a bit of that energy."

"Very good, sir. I'll have scouting parties sent out at once to determine the likely route of the enemy forces. Perhaps you'd care to oversee the defenses in the fort? It could be that your presence there alone will be enough for the Star to reveal itself," Konowa offered.

"Excellent, Major, excellent. Have my headquarters set up in the fortress at once and then report to me when you've disposed of the scouts. I'll want to go over our defenses in depth," he said, clapping his hands together in conclusion. "Rallie! Someone find Rallie and have her meet me in the fortress. We have some exploring to do." He walked over to his steed, took the reins from a private, and mounted, spurring his reluctant horse through the gap and into a canter up the hill.

Konowa was momentarily speechless. He stared at the trees as they continued to squirm and entwine themselves, thickening the black wall that surrounded the fortress while leaving the gap intact. It sounded like bones being grated in a pestle.

"Has the magic taken your senses?" Lorian asked, coming to stand directly in front of Konowa. "You know as well as I do that retreating into that fortress is a death sentence." His voice shook as he spoke, his eyes slightly unfocused.

Konowa raised a hand and motioned for Lorian to follow him. They walked several hundred yards away from the trees before Konowa stopped. "We don't know who or what might be listening, so from here on out, watch what you say."

Lorian looked back at the trees, a new horror dawning on him. "You mean they can *hear* us? Did you feel that when you burned them?"

Konowa shook his head. "I don't know what they are capable of, but all the same, keep everyone away from the trees." He reached out a hand and rested it on Lorian's shoulder. The man's eyes widened, but he held firm. "If it comes to it, I can deal with the trees. In fact, I suspect you and the regiment will be able to as well."

"I don't want this, Major, I don't," he said, hanging his head. "I'm not one of those that fancies magic and all its dark mysteries. I'm already . . . sensing things, things around me. It's not natural. Rakkes and dog-spiders coming back are one thing, but men turned into trees . . ." The fear in his voice cut Konowa deeply.

"Which is why we have to hold together. What happened to the Thirty-fifth Foot will not happen to us. On that you have my word. I don't fully understand it," he said, his hand straying to his chest, "but we have a power to fight this. You have to trust me."

"I wish it gone. Tell me how to get rid of it."

Konowa realized with a start that there was no answer. "I made a vow when I came back, that I would protect the Iron Elves no matter what, and I intend to keep that promise. When we are done here, I will take this regiment back out of the wilderness, and we'll see what we can do about putting things right."

It sounded hollow, and Konowa could tell that Lorian was unconvinced, but the RSM pulled himself together and nodded.

"I'll hold you to it," Lorian said, saluting, then he turned and walked away. There was a thunderclap followed by a blade of lightning, and a hard rain began to fall.

FORTY-TWO

Konowa stood on top of the hill and cursed the rain.

A thunder cloud ripped apart directly overhead and the rain sluiced down in sheets. Shaking his head, he adjusted the collar of the riding cloak he had put on, a first since their little adventure had begun. It wasn't that he hated being wet, which he did, but the rain was no longer the warm steam bath it had been. In all the years he had lived in Elfkyna, he had never known a rain this cool, and his gaze automatically turned to the twisted forest that now surrounded him.

In the course of setting up camp and sending out scouts and dealing with the whims of the Prince, Konowa had passed through the gap in the trees several times in the past few hours.

Whenever he ventured outside the black ring, the natural chaos of the world murmured in the background, annoying but familiar. Within the ring, however, an eerie quiet prevailed. It was as if all life was muted, held deep within the folds of a thick cloak. It was different from what he had felt when Visyna wove her magic. Then, the murmurs of life had felt right, as if a broken bone had suddenly been mended. Either way, it gave him a peace of mind that allowed him to think.

Rallie emerged from the shadows to stand beside him. She pushed back the hood of her cloak to peer up at the cloud-laden night sky, not the least bit bothered by the rain. Lightning struck one of the trees, revealing the forest for a moment in all its grotesquerie. Gleaming blue flames flared up and then were quenched, the tree a pile of ash. Branches from other trees creaked and groaned as they began to fill the gap.

"I feel like things are slipping out of my hands," he said to her, turning away from the trees to stare at the remains of the fortress. The walls were smashed in several places, the mud brick construction disintegrating further in the rain. Two small five-pounder cannon, so named for the weight of the shot they fired, lay knocked off their wheels, but already troops were working to repair them. A short, squat, four-inch howitzer had also been found and was already declared fit to fire. Fortunately, the guns had not been spiked, and the powder room in the fortress still contained several barrels of dry powder and close to a thousand rounds. Standard tactics were to render an enemy's cannon inoperable, or at the very least smash open his powder kegs and soak the powder, but none of that had been done.

A thick cloud of smoke emanated from Rallie's mouth, only to be quickly torn apart by the falling rain. "Then best not hold too tightly, or you'll lose your grip even faster." She turned her head to the side to look at him. "The scouts are out in force, the guard is set, the Prince and I walked the fortress calling out to the Star with no luck, and the fortress, such as it is, is secure. I suggest you take the opportunity to get some sleep. Things always look better in the morning."

Konowa smiled in spite of himself. "Sleep. I've heard of that. Perhaps later. I should make another round of the sentries—everyone is pretty jumpy." He caught the reflection of steel bayonets as a group of soldiers patrolled the line of trees. The RSM had set a path fifty yards away, but their unease at being even that close to the trees kept pushing their circuit farther away until a sergeant bellowed for the soldiers to hold their bloody ground. Arkhorn would have walked right up to them and started carving his initials in the trunks.

"The dwarf may yet appear," Rallie said, her reading of his thoughts so natural that he no longer questioned it. "But your running yourself ragged won't help one bit. If anything comes up, I'll be sure to have someone fetch you. Besides, little is going to get past Jir," she said, leaning down to rub the fur of one very soaked bengar.

Konowa started, unaware that Jir was there. He held out his hand for Jir to come over for a pat, but the bengar only sniffed at it and stayed by Rallie's side. "He can tell that I've changed," Konowa said, pulling his hand back and letting it rest against his chest.

Rallie spat, a gesture lost in the rain. "Oh, pish," she said, rounding on Konowa and poking her cigar at him so that he had to back up a pace. "You're wet, tired, and feeling sorry for yourself. I'm not about to write that the sub knight commander of the Iron Elves is a mewling milquetoast too soft to handle a little adversity. Get yourself out of the rain, find a nice dry place somewhere, and get some sleep."

"Is that an order?" Konowa asked, allowing himself a half smile. Rallie took a long draw on her cigar, the end glowing bright orange and showing no ill effects from being in the rain.

"Soon to be followed by a kick in the breeches if you don't follow it, and take this mangy ball of fur with you," she said, nudging Jir toward him with her knee.

He started to move off, then hesitated. "Have you seen Visyna recently? I'm not sure, but I think I owe her an apology . . . for something." Ever since he'd met her, Konowa had felt he was letting her down. It was bothering him more and more.

"Apology? No. You are doing what you think best, and though she disagrees with that, she knows you do it from your heart. As does she. My advice," she said, turning and looking down toward the river, "is to get some sleep. Things will look clearer after a few hours of rest."

"Orders are orders," Konowa said, saluting smartly and bowing his head. Cold rain ran down the back of his neck and he quickly brought his head up again. "C'mon, Jir, let's see if we can't find someplace a little less wet." Jir looked up at Rallie, who pointedly turned her back on both of them. Jir seemed to give it some thought, then padded after Konowa, the bengar's olive eyes glinting in the dark.

"Well, it's not much, but at least it'll keep the rain off our heads," Konowa said a minute later, crawling under a half-collapsed cart. The sound of the rain pounding on the wood was loud, but at least it was dry. He removed his shako, adjusted his scabbard, and lay down. After a few seconds, Jir flopped down beside him, the bengar's back pushing up against his. Konowa reached a hand out and let it rest on the animal's fur, giving Jir a pat as he did so. "Almost makes me homesick for our little hut by the stream," he said, the last of his words slurring as he drifted into sleep.

A feeling of absolute tranquility washed over him.

Bloody hell.

This time in his dream, he was Wobbly—at least, he thought he was the pelican. Unlike the clear thoughts he had had the other night when he dreamed about Martimis, this one was fuzzy, as if a cloth had been draped over a lantern . . . or the pelican in question was drunk.

He was flying, if weaving madly across a moonlit sky could be called flying. He felt no fear. In fact, he felt very pleased with the world. He was so relaxed that he started to drift off to sleep. It was a glorious feeling, the wind soft and tender against his feathers. Then the wind got harder, and colder. He opened his eyes and saw the ground rushing up from below. With a terrified squawk, he started flapping his wings again, slowly gaining height as he struggled to stay on course. Konowa tossed in his sleep, his own heart racing. It was amazing the bird had survived this long.

He settled back into level flight, more or less, and then looked around for Dandy. He saw a shadow off in the distance mirroring his course and felt relieved. He opened his mouth and was rewarded with deliciously cool air pouring down his throat. It was glorious.

A tree loomed up before him and he veered to the right. Branches slashed at him as he flew by, trying to bring him down. He squawked and flew higher. Another tree suddenly appeared before him, and again he veered away, only to find another tree in his path. Somehow he had flown into a forest and was now anxious to get out. Twisted black branches thrashed the air around him. Razor-edged leaves flew past him, and cries of insane fury echoed in his mind. He saw the silver Wolf Oak up ahead, its canopy snaking out in all directions, cutting off his escape. Somewhere below he knew the Shadow Monarch waited. He flapped his wings harder and pointed himself skyward even as he sensed the approach of something large and old and filled with malice.

He woke up screaming.

The air was cold, and the Viceroy was naked. Each breath drove tentacles of ice deeper into his lungs. He smiled and prayed for the air to grow colder still.

The Viceroy stood before the table, but not because he had been woken from sleep—he no longer needed that luxury. She provided him with everything now, and through the table he was that much closer to Her power. And it was *real*, visceral power, not like the pathetic force the Queen of Calahr wielded. It pained him to think he could have been so blind, so petty, that he had once dedicated his life to such a hollow power as the Empire.

His new monarch was power incarnate, and through the table it flowed over him like a polar waterfall, penetrating every fiber of his being, until he sensed nothing but what the table itself saw.

And what he saw pleased him as few things could.

The Iron Elves, predictably, had chosen the perceived security of the fortress and Her forest wall around it over the open ground.

It would be their doom.

Even now, the rebellious elfkynan were closing on Luuguth Jor, walking into the trap the Iron Elves had already entered.

Soon, the Star would be Hers.

A flicker of regret caught the Viceroy by surprise, but it lasted only a moment. There had been a time, only recently in fact, when he had wanted the Star for himself, for its power, its meaning.

Now he wanted it only for Her.

He bent closer over the table, luxuriating in the feel of its surface, running his hands across it as he would a lover. *Ryk faur*, Her Emissary had called it, bond brother.

It was his now, and he its.

He traced the approaching route of the elfkynan army. It would be over in a matter of hours. He moved his hands and felt the cold force of

Her power at his fingertips. The temptation to crush the elfkynan and the Iron Elves now was immense, but years of perfecting the art of patience won through, and he lifted his hands from the table.

The elfkynan and the Iron Elves would kill each other, and whatever remained would be cleansed from the face of the earth. The rest of the Imperial Army and whatever fool elfkynan chose to rise up would follow, and Her dominion would grow wider across the lands. It was a pleasure to finally serve a monarch who understood the true meaning of force.

There was the heavy flutter of wings at the window and the smell of blood in the air. The Viceroy never took his eyes from the table, barely motioning for the dragon to bring the latest messenger to him. He heard the table cry out for more, sensing the still-warm blood and the message within. A loud thump reverberated along the table and something brown rolled across it to stop in front of the Viceroy, temporarily obscuring his view of Luuguth Jor. It took a moment for him to understand what he saw.

It was the head of his dragon.

He jerked up, turning to see a short, fat, white pelican perched on the edge of the table, its feet doing a little dance as it tried to keep them from freezing to the surface.

Perched in the window behind it was a raptor of immense size, the silver tip of the bird's curving black beak sparkling with menace.

The pelican opened its bill wide and regurgitated liquid all over the table's surface. The smell of alcohol filled the air, and steam hissed and rose from the table so that the room began to fill with mist. The raptor leaned its head farther into the room, its beak poised just above the table.

Only then did the Viceroy understand the true danger this odd pair posed.

"*Noooooooo!*" he shouted, even as the raptor opened its beak and then snapped it shut. Sparks sprayed out across the table and came in contact with the alcohol. There was a whoosh and blue flames leaped upward, knocking him backward into the wall.

The pelican squawked and beat its wings furiously as it took off from the table trailing singed tail feathers in its wake, flying back out the window the raptor had already vacated.

The Viceroy looked around desperately for something to put out the fire, but there was nothing in the room.

Nothing, except him.

His screams echoed far into the night.

FORTY-THREE

The rain finally stopped, and in its absence, a heavy fog shrouded the night around the black forest. Few of the soldiers knew what a sauna was, but all on the scouting parties outside the ring of trees understood the effect. Sweat and fog mixed, turning their skin slimy with heat. Rubbing one's hands against a sopping caerna did nothing to improve the grip on a slick musket, the bare metal already blossoming with the first tinge of orange rust.

But it wasn't the wrath of a nitpicking sergeant that worried them. Scouts were coming back in with reports of something in the east that the soldiers on the outer piquets could hear for themselves.

An army was approaching.

Konowa stood on one of the short wooden docks that jutted out into the river and peered into the mist. It was still too dark to see anything beyond a few hundred yards, even with the benefit of elvish eyes and a full moon trying to shine through the fog. He stepped to one side as a group of soldiers brushed past carrying an elfkynan *kios*, which they took to the end of the dock. With much grunting and cursing they lifted it down onto several other *kios* that had been lashed together and then planked over, creating a thin, precarious bridge that stretched across the river. It was a tenuous lifeline at best, but it would allow the outlying soldiers a quicker return after doing what they could to slow the advance of the enemy.

He felt something brush against his leg and looked down to see Jir standing beside him. "Get back up to the fortress," he said, gently ruffling the fur on the bengar's head. Jir looked up at him for a moment, growled softly, then slowly padded away, but not before lifting a leg on the edge of the dock.

The sound of soldiers working drew Konowa's attention back to the far side of the river. Over the fall of hammers and muffled oaths the sound of the rebels approaching could be heard. Konowa tried to force his senses out beyond the river, but found he could not. He placed a hand over his heart and tried harder. The temperature around him dropped and tiny shards of frost glistened from his cloak, but still he was unable to detect more than a vague presence. He gave up and turned his back to the river, staring hard at the reason.

The trees now rose more than ten feet in some places, their gnarled branches crooking back on themselves to interlock with the trees around them. Their growth appeared to have stopped, but Konowa knew better. Within the ring of trees, his senses were clearer than they had been at any time in his life. Even now the roots were twisting and stabbing their way deeper into the soil, deeper even than their branches reached skyward.

The dock began to shake, and Konowa knew without looking who it was.

"Getting a bit nippy around here, sir," Private Hrem Vulhber said, saluting as he came to attention in front of Konowa. It took a moment for Konowa to pull his stare away from the trees. When he did, he saw that Hrem was staring at the trees, too.

"The Prince's choice of uniform leaves something to be desired, I'm guessing."

Hrem shrugged, his massive shoulders lifting and falling. He absently brushed at his caerna, still staring at the trees. "I'm more worried about them trees."

"As am I, Private, as am I. How are the troops holding up?" Konowa asked, trying to smile.

Hrem nodded toward the far side of the river and the sound of the elfkynan army. "We can handle the natives easy enough. I was riding rear guard on a wagon train a few months back when we were attacked by a couple hundred of them. Two volleys of musket fire put the fear in them and they ran like rabbits. They're brave enough, and there's no denying they would just as soon see the back of the Empire from their land, but they're not stupid. With those cannons we found in the fortress, we'll more than be a match for them. But they aren't going to be our main problem, are they?"

It marked just how absurd their position was that the impending attack of a substantially larger rebel elfkynan army should be considered a secondary concern. But it was.

"No, I suppose they won't," Konowa said, choosing to play it straight. He reached up and laid a hand on Hrem's shoulder. "But I'll tell you this, I won't let this regiment be destroyed. Not now, not ever."

Konowa had expected the soldier to nod, maybe even voice his agreement. Instead, Hrem gently shrugged his hand from his shoulder. "That's what worries us."

It was insubordination, pure and simple, but the way Hrem said it gave Konowa pause. Before he could ask for an explanation, Hrem bent down by the edge of the dock and grabbed something from the water. When he stood up again he held his hand out, palm up. A little crab no bigger than a silver coin stood there, its tiny claws waving in the air to ward off danger. It was futile. A moment later the crab was enveloped in black frost, then consumed by a dark, cold fire.

"Can everyone do that?" Konowa finally asked, looking around at the other soldiers still working on the makeshift bridge.

Hrem flexed his hand and dropped it back by his side. "Maybe, I don't know. A few of the lads went to see the witch and she told them it was a kind of cold fever and that it would go away in a few days. She did some kind of spell to hurry up the healing and told them it was best not to try it again or, um, stuff might fall off."

"Oh." Konowa wasn't sure if he should laugh or cry.

"They're simple lads for the most part," Hrem said. "They'll go along with that for now. Sometime soon though you're going to have to explain to them, to all of us, just what being an Iron Elf really means."

Konowa was about to say he wished he knew himself when the sound of running boots and shouts of alarm came from across the river. The acorn cooled appreciably and his senses immediately heightened. He ran forward, drawing his saber as he did so, Hrem at his side bringing his musket to bear. They met a soldier hurrying across the makeshift bridge, bent over in obvious pain. His uniform was torn and he was breathing heavily.

The private lifted his head as Konowa approached and struggled to give his report. "They're here, the elfkynan army is here."

There was the unmistakable crackle of musket fire from the far side of the river. He saw the familiar shower of sparks out of the corner of his eye—contact had been made.

"One of their patrols must have stumbled into one of ours," Konowa said, sheathing his saber and looking at the group around him. He spied a corporal he didn't know by name and pointed to him. "You, report that we have made contact, though I'm sure they heard the muskets, then have the two cannon brought down to the river. Private Vulhber and the rest of you are with me."

Without waiting for a reply, Konowa headed back to the dock leading six soldiers. His eyes were more than capable of seeing the precarious planking that had been laid down over the *kios*, but he knew the soldiers behind him would not be so fortunate. He turned to tell them to light a torch and saw that Hrem was already lighting a lantern he had found on a pole near the dock.

When Konowa reached the other side, the first thing he noticed was the heat. It was like diving into a hot spring. The air was thick in his lungs and he coughed and wiped his brow. As he put his foot down on the far bank, his senses blurred, and the clarity he had known within the ring of trees vanished.

"Major!"

Konowa unbuttoned his cloak, took it off, and waited for a jogging Lorian to come to a halt in front of him. "How many?"

Lorian saluted. "It was a cavalry scouting party, maybe twenty, twenty-five. Hard to say in the dark, but it looks like we dropped about half of them. I managed to wrangle three horses, one slightly wounded, but no prisoners. We suffered no casualties."

"Show me."

Lorian led him and the six soldiers on a dirt path through knee-high grass for a couple of hundred yards. The night sky had an eerie glow to it, and it occurred to Konowa that he had no idea what phase the moon was in. From the degree to which visibility improved the further they moved away from the mist surrounding Luuguth Jor, however, he guessed it was probably full.

"There," Lorian said, pointing to a squad of soldiers kneeling in a line to either side of the path. From a distance, the wings of their shakos created the appearance of a row of vultures perched on rocks. They had built a makeshift wall with a few fallen branches of wahatti trees and an overturned *kios*, its hull so rotten that its only protective function could be to their morale.

Konowa motioned for Vulhber and the others to stretch out the line on either side and walked forward on the path to where the first body lay just twenty yards away. Other dark forms dotted the grass, some much larger than others and obviously horses. Konowa stopped himself. Better not to assume anything. He tried to search the area with his senses, closing his eyes momentarily and trying to recall what it had felt like when Visyna drew on the living skeins around her. Everything was jumbled, not that it really mattered. He could hear the sound of the main body of the elfkynan army fanning out in front of them, probably no more than half a mile away. Already the surviving cavalry scouts would be reporting that they had made contact. An attack was not far off. He opened his eyes and knelt to examine the body.

The elfkynan lay on his back, his arms raised over his head, his mouth and eyes open in surprise. He wore a simple pair of thin blue cloth pants, the bottoms wrapped tightly around his calves with red puttees. His feet were bare, as was the custom of most elfkynan. Instead of a jacket, his chest was covered by a length of white cloth wrapped up and over one shoulder, the fabric stained with blood still dribbling out of a copper-coin-sized hole where a musket ball had punched through his heart. The cloth was held around his waist by a broad, flat belt of jute fiber adorned with bits of gems and polished pieces of wood. His headdress lay a few feet away, a wide-brimmed hat of woven grass. Konowa looked around and realized what was missing.

"Where's his weapon?"

There were a few coughs and shuffling of feet, and one soldier bent and retrieved it from the grass. "A *mioxja*," Konowa said, taking it from the soldier. It was beautiful in its simplicity. Two blades of razor-sharp jimik grass were tightly bound to the end of a three-foot-long section of willow. It was more bladed whip than spear.

"Is that all they have?" the soldier who had handed Konowa the weapon asked. "I mean, it's just grass and twigs tied together. I've known blind beggars with canes who were more dangerous." A few of the soldiers laughed and voiced their agreement.

Konowa pointed to the grass hat a few feet away. "Pick that up and hold it out from your body. You might want to cover your face; I haven't tried this in a while."

The soldier looked a little startled, but did as he was told. He had no sooner held the hat out than Konowa snapped his wrist and flicked the *mioxja*. The soldier yelped, let go of the remaining tiny section of hat, brought his hand up to his mouth, and blew on his fingers. This time, the laughter was more subdued.

"Never underestimate your enemy," Konowa said, throwing the weapon to the ground and grinding the blades into the dirt with the heel of his boot. "A *mioxja* in the hands of a skilled warrior can flay a soldier alive with a couple of strokes. In the unlikely event that they get through our musket volleys, don't lean back. Close the gap and get right into them."

"What about the trees then, and the Shadow Monarch, sir?" the soldier who had held the hat asked. He had a weasely look about him, thin and conniving.

"Never mind that, Zwitty," Lorian barked, glowering at the private.

Konowa held up a hand. "It's a fair question. The answer is I don't know. The elfkynan are the enemy before us, so that's who we will fight."

The answer satisfied most of the soldiers, but not Zwitty. "What if the Shadow Monarch gets that Star everyone is talking about? What if She uses it to turn them into more monsters? Then what do we do?"

Konowa shook his head. "Bayonets and musket balls are cure enough for that. Keep your head, and they'll lose theirs. They'll attack at *ceh-gwadi*," he said, staring into the distance. "The ears of the morning. It's a herdsman thing. It's the time of day when the ears of the brindos can first be seen against the lightening sky. Until that happens, they'll keep their distance. They fear the spirits that roam in the dark and believe if they are caught, their souls will be lost forever. So they'll wait until dawn to attack."

"But what—"

"No more questions!" Lorian said, looking hard at Zwitty. He shifted his halberd to hold it in both hands. "Save your breath for when you're going to need it. Back to your posts, and I don't want to see the glow of a pipe or I'll be flaying the stupid bugger with ten of those mojas, and the dumb bastards to either side of him who didn't stop him. Now move."

The soldiers melted away, the sound of their boots stomping through the grass receding quickly.

Konowa followed them, passing through the makeshift line and taking the path back toward the river. When they were out of earshot he stopped and motioned for Lorian to stand close. "On edge?"

Lorian grounded his halberd and let out a sigh, slumping his shoulders as he looked back toward the front. "This is utter madness. The elfkynan aren't stupid. Once they realize we're trapped, they'll cross the river to either side and surround us. We don't have supplies to last more than a couple of weeks, maybe a month if we slaughter the brindos and muraphants."

"They won't have the luxury of starving us out," Konowa said, wiping at the sweat on his brow. His breathing was labored, as if he had just run a mile, not walked a few hundred feet. He needed to get back within the ring of trees and the cooler air. "The Star is a lodestone to them. It's why this forest is here, why we're here, and why they're here. They've taken up arms in open rebellion against the Empire. They can't afford to wait for the Imperial Army to turn back from the orc border and move north."

Lorian lifted his chin. "Or for the maker of this hellish forest to come back."

It wasn't a topic Konowa wanted to discuss. Fragments of dreams kept racing through his head, none of them pleasant. "As I said, we'll deal with the enemy before us for now. I want you focused on delaying the elfkynan on this side of the river. Throw out a skirmish line at first light and have them pick off leaders and shamans if they can see any. Draw the elfkynan straight on, but whatever you do, don't make a stand. Keep falling back to the river. We don't want them trying to outflank you."

Lorian nodded. "With the horses we took, I could do a scout of my own and see just what we're facing."

"You're not in a cavalry regiment now. If you get cut off out there, we have no way to come get you. Keep it simple, no heroics. Just make contact, get them interested in coming straight on, and fall back."

Lorian didn't look convinced, but agreed. "We'll make it back, Major."

"See that you do, and bring the elfkynan with you. I'll have a surprise waiting for them when they get to the river."

FORTY-FOUR

Konowa watched Lorian disappear into the night, then walked back across the makeshift bridge. He let out his breath, enjoying the coolness of the air on the west side of the river. Konowa stepped off the dock and looked around, amazed at how fast things were happening.

Luuguth Jor was all but gone. Soldiers were knocking down the last of the village huts and using the mud bricks to create a series of barricades all along the riverbank. Two half walls of one hut still stood near the gap in the trees to protect the five-pounder cannon and its crew. That a family had once lived within the protection of those walls now seemed a distant and quaint idea. Everything from clay jars to wooden platters was now put to use for a far more violent purpose.

Much the same was happening at the other end of the firing line some fifty yards shy of the *sarka har* that curved all the way down to the river. A recalcitrant muraphant trumpeted its displeasure as it was used to haul the second five-pounder into place. Little of the peaceful existence that had once thrived here remained.

With each step deeper into the encampment, Konowa felt his senses clearing. The sweat on his brow cooled and dried and left him wondering where he'd left his riding cloak. He'd take the cold any day, no matter how it was created. He lengthened his stride and made the short distance up the hill to the fort without need to catch his breath. In fact, he felt amazing.

"I do hope your nap did you some good, Major," Rallie said. She was sitting on a fallen mud block at the edge of the fortress, looking down at the river below. As usual, the hood of her cloak was pulled up around her head, a cloud of blue cigar smoke hanging above it.

Part of the nightmare flashed again through Konowa's mind. "If what I saw was real, then I don't think Wobbly made it. I'm sorry," he said, looking back at the river. Fires burned everywhere as the regiment raced the coming dawn to ready their defenses. Even the tumbled walls of the fortress were being reassembled, the power of the muraphants a significant help in that regard. He took another deep breath and let it out slowly.

"Oh, I wouldn't count the little souse out just yet, Major," she said. "Did you actually see Wobbly killed in your dream?"

Konowa thought about it for a moment. He decided to leave the part about the trees out. "No. The last thing I remember before I woke up was a large shadow coming straight at me—him."

"Then have a little faith, Major," she said, tilting her head back slightly to take another puff on her cigar. When she leaned forward again, her voice had a sharper quality to it. "Tell me, what now?"

Konowa found himself nodding. "Now we wait. The belief in the Star will bring our enemies here, all of them. A trap is a trap for everyone—it's all in how you use it."

Rallie blew out a long stream of smoke and pointed her cigar at the trees. "And how do you suppose the Shadow Monarch is using it?"

It was a question Konowa had deliberately chosen not to think about. "It doesn't really matter. Maybe some rakkes attacked the fortress expecting the elfkynan to have already taken the place and installed the Star. Maybe we scared them off when they heard us approaching. I don't know. What I do know, however, is that by this time tomorrow, the Prince will have the Star for his museum, the rebel force will be defeated and scattered, and the Shadow Monarch will have lost Her chance for increasing Her power."

Rallie's cackle signaled her disagreement. "My goodness, it all sounds so neat and tidy, I could write my story up now and save the bother of waiting to see what actually happens," she replied. "Oh, just a minor detail, Major, but where are these rakkes of Hers that did all this? If She is as eager as everyone else to own this Star, one would think Her forces would be close at hand, perhaps waiting and watching the outcome of the coming battle."

"Let them watch," Konowa said, his hand coming to rest against his chest. "If they try to attack, they will pay."

Rallie suddenly stood up, grinding her cigar out on the stone as she did so. "It seems, Major, that your nap restored a bit more stiffness to your spine than I had hoped. Next time, I'll suggest a warm bath, maybe then you'll have time to consider a little more the consequences of your actions. Good evening, Major." She turned to leave, then paused, looking back over her shoulder. "Should you see His Royal Highness, please inform him I'd like a word. I hope there is one officer here who will listen."

Konowa started to protest, then cursed under his breath and kicked at a weed growing by his feet. She didn't understand.

He moved off aimlessly to explore the crumbled remains of the fortress in more detail, frustrated after his talk with Rallie. It was the same feeling he often had after talking with his father. They always ended up asking questions that pushed him to think about things he would just as soon not. He couldn't explain the forest, or its purpose, or where its creators had gone. He wasn't even sure what his father had wrought by giving him the piece of Her Wolf Oak, or what it meant for the men who made up the Iron Elves—living and dead. All he knew for certain was that he would not lose his regiment again, and if that damned him in the eyes of those around him, it was a price he was willing to pay.

Konowa walked through the fortress, silently assessing it and noting with satisfaction the positioning of the howitzer to cover the far bank of the river. Although it looked much like a cannon, the howitzer didn't shoot on a flat plane, but operated by lobbing a hollow shell filled with black powder high into the sky to then fall straight down among enemy soldiers and horses. The sudden explosion of the shell, even if it fell too far away to cause injury, was often enough to unnerve the approaching force, as no soldier could tell where the next shell would land. Set with a burning fuse, the shell could even be timed to explode while still in the air, but Konowa would be happy if the soldiers-turned-artillerists could fire the gun without blowing themselves up in the process.

Soldiers had piled several chests of ammunition beside the cannon and were building a small wall around it. He made a mental note to talk with the crews before it got light—their shells could become critical.

The remains of the Prince's marquee were set up against the southern wall, so Konowa chose to explore the center of the fortress next. His walk took him to a small inner keep. It was square, no more than ten feet by ten feet, with a flat roof of overhanging timbers. He paused at the wooden door half torn from its hinges, aware of voices coming from inside.

". . . right to be wary . . . suitably impressed with your skills . . ."

". . . be stopped before it's too late—"

"What, or who, must be stopped?" Konowa asked, stepping into the small room.

The Prince and Visyna stood up from the table they had been seated at, the surprise on their faces evidence enough that they had been talking about him. The Prince recovered first.

"You forget yourself, Major."

Konowa threw a quick salute, unable to hide his own surprise. "I'm sorry, sir, I didn't expect you here." His sense of the surreal continued to expand. Visyna and the Prince were the two people least likely to be having a close conversation, of any kind.

"Where else would I be, but where I am? In any event," the Prince said, growing more authoritative as he spoke. "I have been having a most interesting chat with Miss Tekoy. We share a love of nature, did you know? The birds, the bees, even the forest at large."

"Is that so?" Konowa said, finding the notion implausible at best. "Have you ever tried living in one, sir? Not quite as posh as a palace."

"It's all in one's attitude, Major. I think I would get along splendidly if put to it."

"Perhaps you'll find out—the elfkynan are here."

The Prince clapped his hands. "Excellent news, Major, excellent news.

We should have them on the run in no time, and then be able to devote our attention to finding the Star and be on our way."

"Your Highness!" Visyna said, her eyes blazing as she looked at him. "We were talking about the importance of the Star to *my* people."

"The Star is important to many people, my dear Miss Tekoy. In fact, I grow more convinced that it is imperative all such power be placed somewhere it can be studied, learned from, and most important, protected, especially from misuse. I do, after all," he said condescendingly, "share your concern that such power not fall into less civilized, cultured hands," he said, looking directly at Konowa. "Now, Major, was there something that you wanted?"

Konowa nodded. "Rallie has asked if you might see her sometime in the next while. I believe she wanted some more detail on your theories of warfare."

The Prince adjusted his shako and rolled his neck inside the loose-fitting collar of his jacket. "Then she shall have them. I am done here. Miss Tekoy, Major."

Konowa saluted as the Prince left, staring at Visyna the whole time. When the sound of the Prince's boots faded he tipped his shako to her. "Slumming it, are you?"

Visyna huffed, then sighed and sat back down on an overturned crate. "Events move with increasing speed, and I feel I have less and less control over anything."

Konowa walked over and sat down on the other crate, angling his scabbard to the side as he did so. He placed his hands on the small table, crossing one over the other. "For once, we are in complete agreement."

She brushed a hair from her face and her expression softened. He was treated to the smile that had dazzled him back in the forest.

"We always have been, I think. We both want what's right, I know that," she said, looking the way the Prince had gone.

"Did you think you could sweet-talk him into letting the Star stay in Elfkyna?"

Visyna shrugged. "I don't know. But I thought if I could reason with him, he would understand. He understands all right—he understands power, but not the terrible price that goes with it."

Konowa thought he detected a subtle jab in her words. "I'm not like him."

Visyna smiled at him. "No, you're not. In some ways you're worse. He wants the Star the way a child wants a sweet from the market. You, on the other hand, don't seem to want it at all, and that worries me."

"Worries you? I thought you would be pleased," he said. "I have nothing against your people. In fact, I've come to care a lot about one of them in particular." Saying it out loud felt good. He did care about her, and if it wasn't for their current situation, he'd be showing her right now . . . if she let him, that is.

"And I care about more than just my people, too," she said, dipping her head as if suddenly shy. Konowa found himself even more attracted to her. "But look where we are. Her foul trees ring this place in a noose, defiling the land as they dig their roots deep in search of the Star. Yet you still call on that same power with utter disregard for what you will bring down on us all. The earth is changing and the air grows cold with malice. You must—" She caught herself. "Konowa, please, give up Her power and break the oath while there is still time."

He shook his head. "Someone has to look after this regiment. Should I leave that to His Highness? You see what he's like. That is our future King." Even saying the words gave him a chill.

Visyna reached across the table, then seemed to think better of it, pulling her hands back. "But he is not King yet. It's a dangerous world out here in the wilds; much could happen."

Konowa waited for her to smile. She didn't.

"Why, Miss Tekoy, the bengar shows its teeth," he said, only partially surprised.

Visyna looked embarrassed. "I'm not saying you should actually . . . I, just . . . things are not going as they should."

Konowa knew the feeling all too well. "They never do."

A musket fired in the distance. He stood up—it was time.

She stood as well, moving closer to him until her face was only inches away from his. "Give up this power and embrace the natural order. Help me, and your reward will be greater than you can imagine. You won't just be saving my people, you'll be saving your men, and I can save you, if you'll let me."

Her hand came up to gently brush back his hair at the side of his head, revealing the ruined ear. She gasped and drew back her fingers. Frost sparkled at the tips.

"It's too late," he said, turning and walking out of the room.

The pain was overwhelming, and for the first hour the Viceroy actually cried for his mother, a sharp-tongued shrew who had substituted a wicker cane for love in the belief that it was the only way for a child to grow strong. Had she lived to see her son as he was now, she would no doubt have despaired that she hadn't hit him often enough.

Though the pain remained, he forced himself up onto his knees, his scarred arms clutching the edge of the table.

It should have been charred, but his sacrifice had spared it—at a cost.

He staggered to his feet with excruciating effort, cringing at the sound of crisped skin stretching and tearing as he unbent his legs to stand. He looked down on the table, which gleamed as if no flame had touched it, and brushed away the ash from its surface that he knew to be his own flesh.

He saw who had done this, and who would pay. First, however, he needed strength.

He ran his blistered hands across the surface, seeking its depths, seeking Her.

"Help me," he said, his voice a thin rasp, his breathing ragged and uneven. "Help me do your bidding."

A tinge of frost sparkled beneath his hands. Red, swollen flesh froze, then turned black and gray, the surface rough and striated. He held a hand up to this face and flexed the fingers. They curled slowly, creaking like autumn twigs. He carefully moved the rest of his body and found that his movements were slowed by the new, barklike skin, but that the pain was subsiding.

He bent over the table again and focused all his thought on Luuguth Jor.

They would all die.

He placed his hands on the table and called to it, but he was too weak. He could see the Iron Elves, but he couldn't direct Her power through it.

"Then I shall go there and kill them myself," he said, not the least bit surprised by the sound of his new voice.

FORTY-FIVE

A re we there yet?"

The humid night air got a little thicker. Yimt stomped on a six-inch-long centipede crawling across the path, grinding his boot into the dirt with more force than necessary. It was a feeling all the surviving members of the patrol shared. They had been marching for hours through air so wet it felt like breathing through a sopping cotton mask. The elvish tree sap did slake their thirst, refreshing them long after they should have collapsed from exhaustion, but it did nothing to cool the heat, or silence Scolly.

"What about now?"

Teeter frowned and tried to shush Scolly to no avail.

Yimt growled something under his breath and stomped another centipede. Alwyn took a quick look around to see if any of the elves were watching, assuming that they would not approve of one of nature's creatures being dispatched in such a fashion, but none were visible at the moment.

"Well? Are we?" Scolly asked again.

It was, and of this Alwyn was quite certain, the one hundredth time.

Yimt reached for his right thigh, then banged his fist against it. Alwyn knew he was wishing he had his drukar.

The dwarf looked over at Alwyn and shook his head.

"It's not the heat, it's the stupidity."

Alwyn smiled, but it wasn't easy. The heat was taking a toll on him, especially with his chest still throbbing with pain. He took another sip from the gourd and immediately felt a little better. The problem was that his gourd was nearly empty, and they still had a long night of marching ahead of them . . . and Scolly.

"Well?"

Yimt cursed and tugged so hard on his beard that strands of it came away in his hand.

"Scolly, for the last bloody time, I'll tell you when we're there. Do you see any magical stars? Does this look like a fort on a hill by a river?" Yimt asked, waving his hand around at the trees.

Scolly looked around and finally nodded as if he understood, but everyone knew five minutes later he'd be asking the same questions again. He was terrified of the forest. If they ever found Kritton, the elf had a lot to answer for. The trees for their part did not look particularly dangerous, though they were strange. One gray-barked variety had fist-sized orange-and-black-spotted fruit in clusters of three growing right out of the trunk. Then there was the kind Yimt had dubbed "Weeping Whipper" for the thread-thin leaves that dangled over the path, the tips barbed and perfect for getting tangled in beards. It made Alwyn think of home and the great bushy chestnut trees, snow-white birches, and great maples that had harbored nothing more fierce than a squirrel guarding its winter hoard.

"What about now?"

"Oh, that tears it, laddie," Yimt growled, grabbing the stock of his shatterbow and taking a step toward Scolly. Chayii suddenly appeared in front of Yimt and gently placed a restraining hand on his shoulder. With her other, she put a finger to her lips.

Alwyn stopped where he was and motioned for Inkermon and Teeter to freeze. They already had, the elves of the Long Watch having appeared all around them. While the soldiers stuck to a winding game trail through the forest on their way to Luuguth Jor, the elves—two dozen, Alwyn reckoned, although it was hard to get an exact count—had taken to the forest itself, moving between the trees without making a sound, at least not any he could hear. He wasn't sure, but he thought some of them were actually in the branches, too, leaping from limb to limb above them. Every time he thought he sensed something and looked up, however, there was nothing to see but leaves. He checked those, too, praying he would never see another frost-burnt leaf for the rest of their journey, and the rest of his life.

"What is it?" Yimt asked, his whisper barely distinguishable from his regular voice.

Chayii chirped softly to Irkila, who notched an arrow in her long-bow faster than Alwyn could follow. She took two steps off the path and melted into the forest. Alwyn blinked, trying to see where she went, but the leaf canopy blocked out too much moonlight for his poor eyesight. He'd never find her, he realized, when something made him turn.

There, not thirty yards down the path they had just come, standing in a pile of excavated dirt near a gaping hole, was another creature from his granny's bedtime story collection—a korwird.

Alwyn was so surprised he never even thought to unsling his musket. Korwird, like rakkes, were supposed to be extinct.

He squinted and shook his head, trying to get a better look. When he finally did, he wished he hadn't.

It looked very much like the centipedes Yimt had been stepping on, except that this one was twenty feet long and had a pointed snout filled with needle-sharp teeth. Its body was covered in shimmering black and green scales, making its milky white eyes all the more terrifying to look at.

The korwird took a few steps forward. Alwyn's stomach lurched. Each leg moved in rhythm with the other like oars on a long boat, propelling it forward at a quick, jerky pace, accompanied by a harsh, staccato clicking sound. The creature swept its snout back and forth just above the forest path, sniffing the dirt. Large gleaming streams of drool hung from its mouth and dragged along the ground. Wherever they touched, vapor spumed into the air, and Alwyn instinctively knew it must be poisonous.

An arrow sliced through the darkness and embedded itself in the korwird's right eye. The creature reared up onto its back legs and shrieked in pain, spraying its lethal venom everywhere. Several more arrows flew out of the shadows at the exposed belly of the beast, but these bounced off the scales without effect.

Fully enraged and still able to see out of one eye, the korwird crashed back down onto all of its legs and shot up the path directly toward Alwyn. Its body made a series of rapid S movements as it came on, the noise of its many legs as loud as a flight of cicadas. More arrows bounced off the korwird's scales, but none seemed to penetrate. Alwyn stumbled backward, unslinging his musket as he did so. He heard shouts and felt hands grabbing his arm, but all his attention was focused on the nightmare racing toward him faster than he could run. The korwird got to within four feet of Alwyn and opened its mouth wide, ready to take a bite out of his exposed legs.

"Back to the fiery pits with you and walk this earth no more!" shouted Inkermon, stepping in front of him. He held a small white book in his right hand and held out from his body like a shield.

Alwyn wasn't sure who was more surprised, himself or the korwird. The creature backed up several paces, its mouth still open wide, its teeth glistening with venom.

"Back I say!" Inkermon continued, his eyes bulging, his lips flecked with spittle. "Your infernal presence is an affront to all that is good and decent! Your fiendish master has sinned against all that is right and pure! Go back whence you came and trouble us no more!"

The korwird seemed to consider this for a moment, then lunged for Inkermon.

Two muskets fired from somewhere just behind Alwyn. His eardrums rattled as acrid smoke billowed around him, obscuring his vision. He heard two loud smacks as the musket balls found their mark. A moment later, he was able to see the korwird in front of him: one large hole in its neck, another in its back, two of its legs now dangling loosely on its left side. It clutched Inkermon's white book between its teeth, while Inkermon was scrabbling up a tree.

The korwird shrieked, spitting out the book and darting forward again.

As Alwyn prepared to club the korwird with his musket, there was a familiar, heavy twang and two black arrows whistled past him, piercing the upper bone of the korwird's mouth and lodging deep within its brain. Its head slammed to the ground, but the legs on its body continued to move, each thrashing madly, twisting the korwird into a ragged circle.

Chayii calmly approached the body, drawing a slender sword from its scabbard as she did so. The faint whisper of a voice both old and wise filled the air. At first, it filled Alwyn with a sense of peace and kindness, but it suddenly grew to be something far more deadly. The voice roared as Chayii sliced the head of the creature clean off with one fluid stroke. She held the blade up to the moonlight and eyed the edge. There wasn't a mark on it. Patting the flat of the blade, she resheathed it and the voice went silent. Alwyn banged a hand against his ear and looked back at the korwird. The legs had stopped moving and the korwird now lay perfectly still. For a moment, the only sound to be heard was the gentle hiss of its venom eating away at the leaves of the trees around them.

Chayii said something and several elves appeared and went not to the korwird, but to the surrounding trees, carefully applying the same moss they had used on the soldiers' wounds to the damaged leaves.

Yimt brushed past Alwyn, casually grabbing Inkermon by the hem of his caerna and yanking him down from his perch in the tree, and went to stand over the body of the korwird, admiring his shot. "Probably could have used just one, but he was getting a mite too close for comfort." He reached down to pull out the arrows, but Irkila held up a hand. Tyul, the elf Irkila had called a lost one, stepped onto the path, his bow bent back with an arrow.

"It is not safe yet to remove them," she said. She switched to elvish and said something to Tyul, who glided forward to stand directly over the body. The little squirrel suddenly appeared from within the leaves that covered the elf and launched itself onto the korwird. It darted over the body as if searching for something, then stopped and sat at a spot near the korwird's spine, firmly tapping one paw. Tyul released his string and the arrow thudded deep into the korwird's body a mere inch from where the unconcerned squirrel sat.

"There is parity now—remove the foul arrows." Irkila brushed a hand to her eye and turned away.

Yimt raised an eyebrow at her, but nodded and began tugging the black arrows out, using the hem of his caerna to protect his hands. Alwyn turned away as Yimt revealed a bit more than he needed to see as he leaned back and pulled.

"Buggers are in there good," he said, grunting with the strain.

"They are already taking root," Chayii said, coming to stand beside Tyul, who remained motionless over the body. The squirrel wriggled its nose and jumped back onto Tyul to disappear among the leaves.

Chayii pointed to the tips of the arrows at the back of the korwird's head. Ugly-looking fibers sprouted there, plunging into the korwird and through it into the ground.

Chayii and Irkila began to chant, and Alwyn felt the same sort of strangeness that he had in the clearing when he had watched the frost-fire burn. This time was not so dramatic, and after a few moments Yimt was able to pull the arrows free, the roots having disappeared from the arrows. Instead, the two remaining arrows began to take root. The brown shafts shimmered and began to glow as their fletching sprouted new leaves of deep, rich green tinged with gold.

"Grow, strong little ones, and cleanse this place," Chayii said, offering a blessing for the arrow-trees that were now consuming the body of the korwird. She motioned for them to start moving, and Alwyn tore his eyes away from the body. Tyul, he saw, remained where he was, his eyes fixed on the arrows now growing into trees.

"Won't they be tainted by feeding off that thing, Ms. Red Owl?" Alwyn asked, feeling some comfort that the elf was now walking with them on the path.

"Evil or good lies in the spirit, Alwyn of the Empire. That creature is as much a victim of Her power as were the children of this place that were injured by it," she said, pointing to the trees around them. "She delves deeper than the roots, far deeper than is wise, and brings forth from the depths things that should no longer be. Long have we guarded against this, confining Her to the mountain and the High Forest there, but we were complacent, and it shames us that we should have let this peril grow."

"But you can stop Her, right? Your magic is the good kind, and that's always better . . . right?"

Chayii stopped on the path and looked at Alwyn. "Much hangs in the balance, Alwyn of the Empire, and I would not seek to unsettle it by stating that which I do not know." She started walking again, gently placing a hand on his arm to guide him. The familiar murmur of life returned. Alwyn felt a spark where her hand rested on his arm, but Chayii ignored it.

"The elves of the Long Watch will strive with all their power to prevent Her dominion from finding any more purchase in this or any other land. You perhaps do not realize, but Tyul Mountain Spring sacrificed much to offer two children of his *ryk faurré*, Rising Dawn, to mend this place. He will mourn this for many moons, and I fear will go ever further beyond us."

"Irkila told me he was a *diova gruss*, one of the lost ones. What does that mean?"

Chayii bowed her head for a moment, then brought it up and looked at Alwyn. "Once in a very long time the birthing meadow will give rise to a silver Wolf Oak. Their power is great, far greater than their brothers' and sisters'. Too often the elf that is chosen gets lost in the purity of its heart, its understanding of the natural order. When that happens, the chosen one forgets what it means to be an elf, becoming instead a creature of the wild, beyond our recall."

"Is that what happened to the Shadow Monarch?" Alwyn asked.

Chayii stopped, her grip on Alwyn's arm tighter than before. "No," she said, her voice heavy with sorrow. "No *diova gruss* would do such a thing, Alwyn of the Empire, for in saving Her *ryk faur*, She broke with the natural order. That is something those like Tyul could never do, for to no longer be part of the natural order would rob them of the very thing they hold precious above all else, even if it meant their *ryk faur* would die."

Alwyn looked back over his shoulder. Tyul no longer stood in the center of the path, but the image in Alwyn's mind grew stronger and a deep sadness overcame him.

"What if Yimt hadn't pulled those black arrows out of the korwird, what would have happened then?"

"A new forest might have arisen as this land weakens, a dark, cold place to challenge the trees that live here in peace. They have not fought Her power as have the Wolf Oaks of our home, so are not yet strong enough to hold back Her influence. They would have succumbed, I fear, their voices hardened, their sap turned black as shadow."

There was an anger in her voice that caught Alwyn off guard.

"I never knew trees were so . . . well, so alive," Alwyn said, looking around him again at the things he had always taken for granted. Now, however, he actually thought he could feel their energy. It was unsettling.

"Then there is much yet for you to learn. Now, as we walk, perhaps you can enlighten me?"

Alwyn looked at Chayii with surprise. "I'd be happy to, Miss Red Owl. What would you like to know?"

Chayii cast a sideways glance at Alwyn and gave the faintest hint of a smile. "Tell me, Alwyn of the Empire, more of this witch, Visyna."

FORTY-SIX

The sound of sporadic musket fire echoed from the far side of the river. Konowa stood at the river's edge, watching the first rays of sunlight creep over the horizon.

It was going to be a slaughter.

He unbuttoned the top of his jacket in direct violation of Prince Tykkin's uniform code, knowing His Highness was still up at the fortress searching for signs of the Star. No doubt the musket fire would rouse the Prince to come and oversee the battle, but for now, the regiment was his.

The first thing he saw emerge from the mist were the wings on the shakos of the regiment's skirmishers. The soldiers marched in orderly fashion in ones and twos about thirty yards at a time, then turned, dropped to a knee, and aimed at the approaching elfkynan files still a hundred yards behind them. As they did so, those who had fired before stood up and marched past their comrades another thirty yards where they took up position, reloading their muskets quickly but in good order. RSM Lorian directed them the whole time, calmly walking back and forth among the skirmishers, pointing out targets, barking orders, and always reminding them to make each shot count.

Despite the accuracy of the skirmishers' shooting—Konowa saw several elfkynan fall never to rise again—the enemy appeared completely indifferent to the firing, paying it no more heed than they would a few mosquitoes. They continued to march forward at an easy pace, their mioxja held high in the air, their faces lifted to the sky in song. The opposing army, not that it resembled any army Konowa had faced before, looked and sounded more like a very large celebration.

It was going to be a slaughter.

The skirmishers kept up their harassing fire, though they were not completely unscathed. Two wounded soldiers were already making their way back across the bridge, one holding a bloodstained handkerchief to his thigh, the other cradling an arm with an arrow protruding from it. Konowa looked past them and saw another soldier fall to the ground, his musket sliding from his hands. Konowa willed the soldier to get up, but he knew that he was dead. Lorian strode over to his body a moment later and grabbed the soldier by the shoulder, turning him over. He then stood and continued to command the remaining skirmishers. Lorian himself continued to present a tempting target to the elfkynan bowmen, who were in a less festive mood than their brethren, but though the arrows rained around him, the RSM remained unhurt.

Konowa calculated the speed of the skirmishers and the advancing elfkynan and knew there wasn't much time left. The skirmishers would soon be back across the river, the brown water the final barrier between the Iron Elves and the elfkynan wild with the thought of finding the Eastern Star and ridding themselves of the Calahrian Empire once and for all. Konowa closed his eyes for a moment and tried to flow his senses out across the river, searching for the Star. He still wasn't sure if he truly believed it was real, not like the acorn that weighed cold and heavy against his chest, but watching the elfkynan approach gave him pause. *They* certainly appeared to believe in it.

Konowa opened his eyes after a few moments, detecting nothing but the usual chaos. He saw rather than felt the splitting of the elfkynan forces, the bulk of the rebels' army coming straight at Luuguth Jor, while two smaller columns were beginning to bend to envelop the village and fortress from either side. Expecting this, Konowa had deployed two platoons of C Company at the gap in the trees. He would have liked to have done the same on the other side, but with no gap in the trees those troops would be at too much risk of being cut off. Instead, he placed two more platoons from C Company through the gap and facing west. When the elfkynan column got across the river to the north and then swung around the trees thinking they would surprise the regiment, they'd be in for a rude awakening.

An arrow fluttered by Konowa's face just a few feet away, bouncing off a mud brick and coming to rest at his feet. He bent and picked it up, twirling it in his fingers, noting that the fletching was rudimentary at best, the tip just sharpened and not even fire-hardened. He concentrated for a moment and burned the arrow with frost fire in a matter of seconds. There was no screaming in his head, no anguish, only a slight unpleasant feeling of regret that he quickly pushed aside.

"Cavalry, Major!"

Konowa looked up to see a squadron of elfkynan riders galloping hard for the river, then making an abrupt turn and racing parallel to it in an attempt to get behind the skirmishers and cut them off. If it weren't for the tall grass and uneven ground they would have ridden straight through them. As it was, if they succeeded in herding the skirmishers together, the soldiers would be easy pickings for the closing main elfkynan column.

"Hold your fire—wait until the first horse gets to the bridge," he ordered, wishing he had his musket in his hands instead of his saber.

With no resistance, the horsemen continued to race along the bank, their mioxja making a high, keening sound as they waved them over their heads. The lead cavalryman was still a good twenty feet from the bridge when a musket fired from somewhere off to the left. At only fifty yards wide, the river was little more than a big ditch, and hitting a target as large as a horse, even one cantering across their line, was not difficult. The ball struck the rider's front shoulder, throwing him over the horse's neck as it stumbled to its knees.

"Front row, by volley . . . fire!" Konowa shouted, unleashing eighty musket balls at once. There was the staccato ripple of seventy-nine hammers sparking seventy-nine pans within half a second of each other, followed by the sharp crack of balls leaving muzzles, the familiar shower of sparks and expanding plumes of gray smoke that rolled forth a few feet before losing their impetus and beginning to blur and rise into the brightening sky.

The effect was immediate and devastating. Twelve horses took the brunt of the shot, the musket balls punching through their hides. Seven riders were also hit, a musket ball plucking one rider off his saddle with a clean shot in one ear and out the other. Screams of dying and wounded horses and dying and wounded elfkynan filled the air, and following cavalry slowed and bunched as they were forced to navigate through their fallen comrades. It was the moment Konowa was waiting for.

"Second row, to the fore! First row, to the rear, reload!" Konowa shouted, hearing his commands echoed up and down the line as sergeants hurried their men. The hollow rattle of ramrods in musket barrels reminded Konowa of battles past and he smiled, a thin-lipped baring of his teeth that would have terrified anyone looking at it.

"Front row, by volley . . . fire!"

Sixty muskets fired this time, but the effect was unknown, as the smoke from the second volley mixed with the first and with the fog that still hung over the river, obscuring the far side of the bank. A thin gust of wind moved enough of the smoke a moment later for Konowa to see again, and he counted at least another ten riders fallen, along with several horses. Confusion reigned on the far side, and the cavalry were now milling about, unsure whether to press on or fall back. It was time to make up their minds for them.

"The cannon will fire on my command, and don't you bloody well miss . . . fire!"

Twin cracks snapped the air. Loaded with canister shot, little more than a tin can filled with fifty musket balls strapped to a round wooden plug by thin metal bands, all of which sat on a flannel bag filled with powder, the canisters burst apart with the force of the blast as soon as they left the cannon. Their shot tore through the hanging smoke and fog and spread out to spray an area thirty feet wide on the other side of the river. The head and neck of one horse simply disappeared in a red mist. Seven more stumbled and fell, two of them rolling over and down into the river, taking their screaming riders with them. One rider stood amid the carnage with his left arm completely shorn away, a stream of blood arcing out of the gaping wound at his shoulder. Instead of running away, he was shaking his right fist in the air, still clenching his mioxja, and shouting curses at the Iron Elves.

He was either very brave, or very foolish, and either way Konowa admired him, which made it a shame that the trooper would be killed with the next volley. Konowa was about to shout for the first row to fire again when he heard the elfkynan cavalry blow retreat on a horn, its plaintive cry calling the survivors back. The cavalry trooper swayed on his feet, but refused to move, still shouting, though his remaining arm had now dropped to his side.

Konowa's attention was pulled away as the massive frame of Private Hrem Vulhber came into view, easily dwarfing the rest of the soldiers as they picked their way through the dead and dying. Lorian was close behind, still walking tall and shouting orders to the skirmishers even as the elfkynan army pressed down on them. He waved at Konowa and signaled with his halberd that the skirmishing line was still in good order and able to fight. The steel point of the weapon was stained red, mute testament that at least one rebel had gotten a little too close.

Konowa cupped a hand to his mouth and shouted across to him, "Get your men across the river, Sergeant Major! And make it look good!"

Lorian gave a thumbs-up and shouted new orders to the skirmishers. Their controlled retreat suddenly became a mad dash for the river and the sole means across it. A cheer rose from the elfkynan line marching after them, thinking that the siggers had finally broken and were running away.

As the skirmishers jogged back, one of them veered off to the right to where the one-armed elfkynan cavalry trooper still stood and bayoneted him in the back. The elfkynan screamed and fell, the soldier stabbing him again and again until the screaming stopped. The soldier quickly rifled through the dead elfkynan's clothing, then rejoined the troops filing back across the bridge.

Konowa saw the weasel-faced soldier as he stepped off the dock and pointed to him. The soldier looked around for a moment, clearly hoping

Konowa wanted someone else, but when he saw he was it, he marched over.

"Private Gorton Zwitty, Major," he said, saluting.

"Why did you bayonet that elfkynan?"

Zwitty looked confused. "Which one, sir? I put the steel to a few of them heathen. Squealed like little girls, the cowards."

Konowa reined in his temper and pointed across the river. He was aware that Lorian and several soldiers were watching. "The one missing an arm."

"Why did I bayonet him?" Zwitty asked, clearly puzzled by the question.

"Answer the major," Lorian barked, startling Zwitty.

Zwitty shrugged. "I did what the major told us: If they had one of those moja things, get in close and do 'em, so I did."

The futility of it all hit Konowa, and he waved the soldier away. He saw Lorian looking at him and asked the RSM for a report.

"The elfkynan are a mess," he began quickly, his breathing still labored after the exertions of the last couple of hours. His face was flushed, and there was a wild look to his eyes. Konowa recognized it at once, a feeling of indescribable exhilaration at having fought and survived in battle. In his banishment, he had missed it terribly.

"Discipline is poor, more like a mob than an army. And the bastards didn't seem to care one bit as we shot at them. They just kept chanting Sillra, Sillra. Main column looks to be a couple hundred wide and thirty deep, give or take a few."

"Their faith in the Star is strong," Konowa said, feeling the smallest sense of disappointment that it was misplaced.

"It's like they think it will protect them from being killed," Lorian said, his breathing slowing as the rush of battle left him. "I couldn't get a good look at the two wings that went out, so I did a quick scout of my own and counted close to two thousand in the right wing. The left has probably got the same. And you saw their cavalry, brave enough, but not much to worry about on this side of the river. I'd wager three to four hundred at the most."

"A quick scout of your own?" Konowa asked, looking at the still-bloody halberd.

Lorian grimaced, then nodded. "I couldn't see a damn thing where I was, so I borrowed one of them ponies and went for a gander."

Cavalry. Lorian was no different from the Duke of Rakestraw, galloping at everything with no regard for his own safety. Having spent considerable time in the saddle the last few weeks, Konowa was beginning to suspect that it was the horses, not the cavalry troopers, that had more sense.

"Not exactly what I had in mind when I said no heroics," Konowa said, waving away Lorian's protest. "The Duke would not have been pleased if I had lost him his best sergeant." He shook his head and smiled. "Well done all the same. If my math is close, that would give the rebels six thousand in the center, maybe a couple thousand in each wing, and a few hundred cavalry." He paused for a moment, then asked the question they were both reluctant to hear. "What did we lose?"

"Two dead and five wounded," Lorian said simply.

It pained him to lose a single Iron Elf, but their losses were light, and the skirmishers had succeeded in drawing the attention of the elfkynan, who even now were marching toward the river.

"Put them in for a citation. I want their widows to get a full pension," Konowa said, knowing it was cold comfort for the loss of a loved one. "Their deaths won't be in vain."

"If they are in fact dead," Lorian said, hanging his head. Ice crystals winked along the length of his halberd and the blood on the metal point thickened, darkening as it did so. A perfectly rounded drop froze before vanishing in a flicker of frost flames. Lorian never looked up.

Konowa glanced around to see if they were watched, but the preparations to receive the elfkynan attack had all the soldiers' attention. "This isn't the time, Lorian."

Lorian brought his head up as if waking from a dream. He stiffened and saluted. "Of course, Major. I'll see to the defenses," he said, striding back to the pier to oversee its dismantling.

Watching him go, Konowa realized he couldn't put it off any longer. The troops deserved some kind of explanation. He walked over to a pile of ammunition crates and climbed on top of them. Soldiers nearby saw him and began motioning to others. Soon, shouts were going up and down the line that the major was going to speak.

"Soldiers of the Iron Elves! Battle has been joined," he began, cringing at the obviousness of it. He shook his head and lowered his voice slightly, looking down at the upturned faces. Many were smiling, their trust in him absolute.

"Today, at this place, the true measure of your heart will be taken. Blood will flow, nerves will fray, and men will die. Make no mistake, the day will be hard. But know also that as with all days, this one too shall fade into night, and a new dawn will rise."

A few muted cheers rumbled through the regiment, the reminder of the coming battle having a sobering effect.

"Take comfort in the fact that you are the rarest of all warriors to walk the land in any age. You are Iron Elves, oath takers bound to all those that went before. Their strength is your strength. Be not afraid of it, for therein lies your power!"

The cheers were louder now. Muskets were held high in the air, the sun glinting off them like steel lightning.

Konowa tried to think of something else to say, but the regiment continued to cheer, the air growing cooler around them. He abruptly pulled his saber from its scabbard and held it skyward.

"For the Queen! For the Empire! For the Iron Elves!"

They answered as one, their voice a cold, clarion note through a mist-shrouded forest.

Konowa resheathed his saber and stepped down from the crates, smiling back at his men as they continued to cheer. Each one believing the lie.

As he walked along the line, the sound of cheering came from the other side of the river. Konowa paused, trying to hear what was being yelled, but it didn't really matter. The rebel leaders would be telling their troops much the same, perhaps invoking the power of the Star. The elfkynan, like the Iron Elves, would believe the same lie, knowing that they would prevail while others died.

Whose speech, Konowa wondered, had been closer to the truth?

• • •

Inja had been born in the palace stables. The warm, heavy smells of the large animals had filled her lungs with her very first breath. By the time she was four, she could ride any horse in the stables, even the big stallions. At seven it was clear that she had the *limoo sy* about her, the ability to know things that had not yet come to pass . . . as it related to horses. Now at fifteen, Inja could predict within the minute when a mare would foal and which horse was going to develop colic and die months before it happened, giving the stable master ample time to sell the beast at full price to an unsuspecting buyer. She knew the fate of every horse in the stable, including the fastest of them all, Hizurantha.

Inja walked slowly toward the stall of the three-year-old gray gelding, the six-inch blade in her hand growing heavier with each step.

She knew that what she was about to do was a merciful thing. No creature should have to endure what she had forseen for Hizu. It was a fate truly worse than death.

Hizu smelled her coming and whinnied with anticipation, knowing she always brought him a chunk of keela fruit. Inja looked down at her hand and saw only the cold glint of steel. Could she really do this thing? What if she was wrong, what if her vision had been a mistake? The nightmare flashed repeatedly through her mind, as sharp as the knife in her hand.

There was no mistake. Hizu would suffer terribly; she had no choice.

Inja arrived at Hizu's stall and reached out her left hand and pulled back the wooden slide that held the stall door in place. Slowly, quietly, she eased the smooth, worn slat back until it made that familiar thunk sound as it hit its wooden stop. Hizu tossed his mane and snorted and stamped his front hooves.

"I am sorry, Hizu," Inja said, stepping into the stall and reaching up to grab Hizu's halter. The horse obediently brought its head down and sniffed her, looking for the keela fruit. Inja refused to look him in the eye, searching instead for the great vein at the side of his neck. "You deserved better."

The knife in her hand grew colder, and the horror of what she was about to do made her shiver. Hizu sensed something was wrong, jerking his head back up, his breath coming fast, its mist clouding the cold air of the stable. Inja looked at the mist in surprise, and then down at her hand. Frost sparkled along the blade.

"What—?" she asked aloud, turning as a new presence entered the stall behind her. Something incredibly cold grabbed her by the throat and lifted her into the air. The knife fell from her hand as she reached up to pry away the icy grip. Already the cold was eating into her, blurring her vision as it bled the strength from her limbs. She heard the sound of Hizu's screams from a growing distance, and then she was flying, the cold vise around her neck letting go. Her head hit the stone cobbles of the hallway in front of the stall, but she remained conscious for a moment more, long enough to hear Hizu's hooves clatter across the stone and fade into the distance.

The Viceroy of Elfkyna was riding to Luuguth Jor.

FORTY-SEVEN

I n the future, Major, I will be the one to give the speeches to the men," Prince Tykkin said, pacing up and down a small patch of grass twenty yards behind the firing line. He'd ridden the short distance down from the fortress on Rolling Thunder despite the horse's continued skittishness within the ring of trees. No sooner had he dismounted than the horse bolted, galloping back up to the fortress to huddle among the brindos and muraphants. Konowa felt a certain amount of pride that Zwindarra seemed unconcerned by their present environment.

"This is my regiment, not yours," the Prince went on. His face was red, but it was more from being out in the sun than from anger. In fact, despite Konowa's breach of etiquette, the Prince was clearly preoccupied with something else. Chants of "Sillra! Sillra!" washed over the regiment from the far bank as the elfkynan worked themselves into a frenzy in preparation for attack.

"Of course, sir," Konowa said, caring little what the Prince thought. The battle would be over soon and this whole nightmare would be at an end.

The Prince paused in his pacing, shivering and wrapping his arms around his body. He looked across the river and shook his head. "I caught the tail end of it, Major, and I noticed you didn't mention me. Still, it was rather rousing; I'll have to ask Rallie to write me up something like it." He stamped his boots and started pacing again. "This weather is absolutely atrocious. First it's hot enough to boil eggs and now I'm thoroughly chilled."

Konowa felt the cold, too, and found he was getting quite used to it. A thought occurred to him.

"Sir, when I administered the oath to the regiment, you were having one of your discussions with Rallie, correct?"

The Prince stopped again and looked skyward for a moment, pushing the brim of his shako back out of his eyes. He had lost a good ten pounds since they set out, the puffiness of his face having disappeared, the collar around his neck looser. Konowa hated to admit it, but he was starting to look like what a Prince and a leader *should* look like, toughened by the outdoors and bloodied, if slightly so far, by battle. Whether he had any more sense was another matter.

"Yes," he finally said, lowering his eyes to look at Konowa suspiciously. "She was fascinated by my plans to build the Great Library in Celwyn. Said placing the Star there would put it out of reach of almost every miscreant and fool that would try to use it, which was, of course, exactly my plan."

"No doubt," Konowa said, wondering if the Prince had ever taken a moment to consider the phrase "almost every." "Do you recall feeling cold at all that night? A cool breeze . . . frost, even a little?"

Prince Tykkin raised an eyebrow. "What are you getting at, Major?"

Now that Konowa had brought it up, he wasn't sure how to proceed. "Some of the men have reported feeling a bit off, sir. I was just curious if you had felt different of late."

The Prince relaxed and actually smiled. "I never would have taken you for a mother hen, Major, but no, put your mind at ease. I have never felt better in my life. If it wasn't for this blasted cold, I'd say I was near perfect."

So then. The oath *hadn't* affected the Prince. "Very good, sir. The men will be pleased to hear it."

"Of course they will," the Prince said, tapping his chest proudly. "They

serve in the finest regiment in the Imperial Army, commanded by the heir
to the throne. Now, enough about my health. Is everything ready?"

Konowa made a point of looking up and down the line as if studying
the placement of the troops, something he had already done a dozen times
before. "The regiment is ready, sir."

"Good, splendid. Well, very good. Yes, very, very good. We'll stand
here then, shall we?"

Once again, Konowa came face to face with the reality of his situation: Prince Tykkin had no earthly idea what to do with a regiment going
into battle.

"As the commanding officer it would be wise if you oversaw the battle
from the fortress. It provides a commanding view and will allow you to
take in the whole field, sir," Konowa lied. A commander's place was with his
men, right in the thick of it—not that this fool would ever realize it.

The Prince looked back up to the fortress. "Seems rather far away
to direct the regiment," he said. No sooner had he said it than a single
arrow fluttered over from across the river, an impossibly long shot by an
elfkynan archer hoping to take out an officer. The arrow barely penetrated
the dirt two feet in front of them before slowly toppling over. The shouts
of "Sillra!" grew even louder.

"The men know you would gladly risk your life to be right up here
with them, sir," Konowa said, turning slightly so he could keep a better eye
out for more arrows. He noticed that the Prince made sure to keep Konowa
between himself and the river. "But yours is a strategic role, sir, watching
for that critical moment when things hang in the balance. And of course
the Star . . . you'll be looking for the Star."

Mention of the Star reanimated Prince Tykkin and his pacing
resumed, faster than before, heedless of exposing himself to further shots.
"It's close, Major, right at our very fingertips. It's here somewhere, I can
feel it!"

"Yes, sir, I'm sure it is. All the more reason for you to continue searching for it. I'm sure you'll find it soon." The air vibrated with elfkynan
chants.

"You're right," the Prince said. Another arrow sailed in a high curving arc across the river and struck the Prince's shako square on, bouncing off the hat just above his forehead to lie at their feet.

"He's got the right idea," Konowa muttered, looking across the river for the elfkynan archer.

"How's that?" the Prince asked, his voice rising in preparation for another tantrum.

"Always aim at their leaders, sir. You cut off the head and the body falls. They obviously recognize the threat you pose," Konowa said. "Perhaps Rallie will help you with a victory speech for after the battle. I know the men will be looking forward to hearing a few words from you."

"It would be appropriate," the Prince said, and then paused, a new thought clearly dawning on him. "And speaking of appropriate, an officer should be mounted at all times practical, Major. The men need constant inspiration. They need to look up to those that command them. That's why we have horses."

"Not all the horses seem comfortable with the trees," Konowa said, succeeding for the most part in keeping the exasperation out of his voice.

"They'll learn, or they'll wind up in a cooking pot," the Prince said, bending to pick up the arrow. "I expect to see you mounted, Major; no excuses. This battle will be fought properly."

"Very good, sir," Konowa said, knowing it was futile to argue.

"Now," Prince Tykkin continued, turning to head back up to the fortress, "I think I'll go have a chat with Rallie and get her working on my speech. My recent brush with death adds a real sense of weight to things, and it should go over well with the men, don't you think?"

"Almost nearly," Konowa said under his breath, "almost nearly."

In the thousands of years that the Baynama River had curled through eastern Elfkyna, long before the land had been named, it had forever run brown with the silt washed into it from the heavy rains that fell throughout the year.

Until today.

Konowa bent and pulled a wounded soldier away from the bank and paused. The crimson water in front of him frothed with the frenzied feeding of fish drawn to the surface.

"Major! Get down!"

Konowa threw himself flat against the grass as the sound of dozens of ice picks stabbing a piece of tin crackled above his head. The musket volley thrashed the forward line of elfkynan just entering the river thirty yards away, flailing their exposed flesh, exposing briefly the brilliance of white bone beneath. Elfkynan screamed. More slipped under the water, trampled underfoot by those not yet hit, their cries gurgling into abrupt silence as water filled their lungs and they vanished from sight.

An arrow pricked the ground inches from his head, the shaft quivering as if furious it had not found flesh. More arrows whistled past, answered by yet more musket fire, the smoke of the volley rolling over Konowa and temporarily blocking his view of the river. Over it all, the chants of "Sillra! Sillra!" ebbed and flowed like a coming tide, each wave climbing higher and higher onto the beach.

"I've got him, sir," Private Hrem Vulhber said, running through the smoke to grab the wounded soldier from Konowa and heave him over his shoulder. "You shouldn't be out in front of the line like this. You're not immortal."

Konowa allowed Hrem to drag him back over the wall of mud bricks, caring little if an elfkynan arrow hit him in the back as he halted on the edge, looking back down at the river.

"Maybe I am. Maybe we all are," he said, recognizing the feeling of utter futility. The elfkynan weren't going to stop. They surged forward in waves with no concern for their lives. The few prisoners the Iron Elves had taken that day wailed and begged to be killed. It wasn't until Konowa threatened to grant their wish by having Jir eat them, starting at their toes and working his way up, that one thought better of it.

"Paradise! Paradise forever! The Star has returned!"

"What paradise?" Konowa asked, motioning for Jir to take a few steps forward.

The elfkynan's eyes bulged. "Death does not matter. The Star has returned. All who perish in its service will be rewarded in the afterlife." Taking heart from his own words, the elfkynan ran into the open and stepped in front of one of the five-pounders just as it fired a canister shot.

Hrem reached up and pulled Konowa off the wall, dropping him behind it as several more arrows ricocheted off the mud bricks. He looked at Konowa for a moment, then nodded and moved back into the firing line a few feet away. Shouts of "Sillra . . . Sillra" still echoed across the battle, but for the first time, the weight of voice had decreased, the screams growing in volume as yet more elfkynan went to their paradise.

Even the yelling and taunting by the Iron Elves as the elfkynan had first charged the river had subsided into grunts and curses, and more than a few prayers for the poor buggers to stop, to just please stop.

This wasn't battle—this was butchery.

Ramrods rattled in musket barrels, sergeants barked hoarse commands to "look lively," "aim low," the gun carriages for the two five-pounders creaked and groaned as they shook under each blast, and through it all, the screams of the dying never stopped.

There was a boom from the fortress signaling the firing of the howitzer. Konowa looked up and saw the blur of the cannon ball arc overhead before it dipped and slammed into a group of elfkynan. For a moment, nothing happened, the cannon shell sitting half dug into the soft earth, its burning fuse hidden from view. The elfkynan laughed, and one stepped forward to place a foot on the shell when it exploded, tossing several of them into the air.

A private held on to Zwindarra's reins a few feet away, the horse remarkably calm amid all the chaos. It angered Konowa to needlessly risk the animal's life for no good reason. At least he'd been able to get Jir penned up in the fortress under Rallie's supervision. He'd miss that bengar more than a little if anything ever happened to it.

"They're absolutely mad!" Lorian said, riding up on one of the commandeered elfkynan horses. Halting beside Zwindarra, the horse—a dappled, shaggy-looking thing—looked like a large pony in comparison. Lorian dismounted, handing the reins to the private holding Zwindarra's, and walked up to peer over the wall by him. "Little boys with toy soldiers make better battle plans than this."

Konowa stood up and looked over in time to see six elfkynan crawl up onto the western bank in front of their position. They rose to their feet yelling fiercely, their eyes bright with belief as they were unceremoniously cut down by another round of canister shot fired at a range of twenty yards, the smoke of the blast blotting them from sight. When the smoke drifted away all that remained was madly thrashing fins and scaly mouths gulping down chunks of red, raw flesh floating in the water.

"How's our ammunition holding out?" Konowa asked, forcing himself to look away as two more elfkynan crawled onto the bank, one trying to hold his innards in with one hand while waving a mioxja with the other. Two sharp musket cracks told Konowa their fate.

"We're down to twenty rounds a man. I've ordered some of the canister shot cut open and more cartridges to be made, but I doubt there are that many of the dumb bastards left that will need it," Lorian said, sliding down from the wall to rest with his back against it beside Konowa.

"Losses?" Konowa asked.

"Eight dead and another fifteen wounded. Prince Tykkin has made it a priority to examine every wound himself to ensure there's no malingering," Lorian said, motioning with his halberd toward the casualty collection area a hundred yards back of the firing line. From there, the wounded were transported by a muraphant-pulled wagon up to the fortress. Those deemed insufficiently injured were sent stumbling back down to the line. Mercifully, there were only a few seriously wounded so far.

Konowa nodded, grabbing a canteen off the ground and offering it to Lorian. The RSM took a long pull and held it out to Konowa, who grabbed it and finished it off, the bitter taste of gunpowder temporarily diluted.

"I think it's time we let them force the gap," Konowa said, pointing to the one open section in the ring of trees that surrounded their position. A large abatis made of cut-down trees spiked with sharpened sticks lay across the road. They were normal trees, as attempts to use some of the black trees had gone nowhere. No soldier would get close enough to the blood trees to swing an ax. As it was, the abatis proved useful in blocking the growing number of elfkynan who were trying to find a way through. "We need to finish this now. Who knows what else is out there."

"Is that wise?" Lorian asked, cringing as a horse screamed in terror. Both Zwindarra and the elfkynan horse reacted, their ears pricking forward, the whites of their eyes showing. Lorian got up to look over the wall as the elfkynan cavalry made another futile charge. Konowa reluctantly followed suit, watching with sadness as hooves flashed through the red water, crushing skulls as the horses panicked and tried to run away. Unlike their riders, the animals had no illusions of immortality and paradise.

Konowa looked up at the sky and was surprised to see the sun already beginning to dip behind the fortress on the hill. "We don't have a choice. We do it now or we'll be fighting in the dark, and that's something I'd like to avoid."

Lorian finally turned away from the carnage and looked at Konowa. His eyes were rimmed with red, his face grime covered and pale. "Are you sure this will work?"

Konowa felt a cold surge as the acorn against his chest reminded him of what real power was. "One way to find out," he said, moving away from the wall and calling to the Color party. A small, fierce-looking sergeant followed by three large, equally fierce-looking corporals all brandishing halberds marched up with the regimental Color. Both the Queen's Color and that of the Prince were flying over the fortress.

"Sergeant Salia Aguom an' Color party reporting, sir!" the Color sergeant said. He saluted smartly, the flagstaff held comfortably against his left shoulder. He was one of the few siggers with black skin in the regiment, no doubt a volunteer from the Empire's southern conquests in the Timolia Island chain. Konowa knew the Timolia regiments to be fearsome warriors, an ethos developed over centuries of battling the red orcs of Winamaruk for control of the islands. From the battle scars on Aguom's face, it was clear the Color sergeant lived that tradition.

"I need you to fall back to where the wounded are and get the rest up to the fortress, then signal the retreat," Konowa said.

"At once, sir!" he said, saluting and marching away, the three corporals following close behind like a group of tavern strongmen hired to keep the rowdy at bay, which, in a way, was precisely their job . . . just with deadlier intent.

"I hope this works," Lorian said, watching the Color party move up the hill.

"We'll make it work," Konowa said, a growing confidence spreading through him. "This battle will be over shortly."

"And what will happen then, Major?" Rallie asked, appearing behind him and Lorian as if from thin air. A particularly large cigar was clamped firmly between her teeth, its smoke more pungent than usual.

"It will get dark," Konowa remarked, not wishing to get dragged into another conversation he had no answers for. "Where is Visyna?"

Rallie clucked and took the cigar out of her mouth, neatly stepping to one side as two arrows sliced through the place she had stood a moment before. A cannon boomed, the momentary silence after its shot followed by fewer elfkynan screams. "Tending the wounded up at the fortress. She is an angel, to hear the boys tell it. Many lives will be owed to her before the end of the day."

Konowa nodded, surprising Rallie and Lorian. "She'll probably do more good than we will. Tell her that whatever she needs, she gets. I want them given the best care possible."

Rallie and Lorian shared a look. "I will be most happy to convey that message, Major. And I sincerely hope there will be little more for her to do this day, though my heart tells me otherwise," she said, drawing deeply on her cigar as she eyed not the elfkynan army, but the ring of trees that surrounded them.

"Tell her . . . tell her I said thank you," Konowa said, his cheeks suddenly growing hot.

"I will, but make sure you're around to tell her yourself, too, when this is over," Rallie said, patting his arm, then leaving him and Lorian.

Konowa turned and saw Lorian staring at him. "Don't ask. Now, let's get this over with." They took the reins from a very relieved private, who scurried back to find some cover. Konowa climbed into the saddle, very aware of just how high off the ground he was as he looked down at Lorian on his smaller horse. Zwindarra tossed his head but remained calm.

"You volunteered for the cavalry?" Konowa asked, urging Zwindarra into a walk.

Lorian smiled, the first time in a while. "Major, it's the only way to fight. You feel that power of the horse beneath you, the wind in your face . . . it's magical—well, the kind of magic I understand," he added.

"You sound like the Duke," Konowa replied, shaking his head. "I never really have understood the relationship between a cavalryman and his horse."

Lorian nodded toward the fortress. "Some people might say the same about an officer and his bengar."

It was Konowa's turn to smile.

An arrow sliced down between the horses, spooking Lorian's slightly. "Signal the Color party," Konowa ordered.

Lorian tied a thin red pennant to his halberd and raised it high, waving it back and forth. A moment later a bugle sounded. The two platoons of C Company assigned to hold outside the ring of trees began an orderly retreat through the gap. As soon as they passed through, the other platoons started to give way slowly. It was apparent by their steps that they disagreed with the order. They had fought long and hard to hold the gap and had seen some friends die for it. And they were winning. The elfkynan charged and fell back only to charge again, their progress slowed by the mounting pile of bodies that littered the ground in front of the Iron Elves.

"They aren't pulling back fast enough," Lorian said, leaning forward in the saddle toward the gap.

Konowa gritted his teeth, silently urging the siggers on. He understood their feeling, but they had to make this look real.

There was a roar from beyond the trees and a group of elfkynan cavalry charged through the gap, their mioxja whistling as they swung them over their heads. They galloped headlong toward the retreating siggers. The five-pounder closest to the gap fired into their center, bowling over half a dozen horses and sending several more reeling. The momentum of two of the horses carried them another fifteen yards, stumbling into the line of Iron Elves and knocking several down. The soldiers quickly got up and reformed, but the damage had been done. Instead of one single line pulling back there was now a break, and the two halves began to pull apart as they retreated, creating a gap between them. The elfkynan following on foot saw their chance and ran headlong for the gap, seeing a chance to roll up the entire defensive line along the riverbank.

"Follow me!" Konowa shouted, drawing his saber and kicking Zwindarra with his heels. The horse neighed, leaped forward, and came close to unseating him now that he was holding the reins with only one hand.

The elfkynan were pushing the gap wider apart. Smoke bloomed from the front row of the Iron Elves and elfkynan tumbled and fell, but more came rushing through the gap, and there was now no time to reload. Another charge by the elfkynan cavalry would carry them through and behind the soldiers still holding the positions on the river. The acorn against his chest stabbed him with ice, spurring him on. He turned briefly to see Lorian galloping beside him, the point of his halberd lowered like a lance.

"Hold, you bastards, hold!" Konowa shouted, taking Zwindarra straight through the gap and into a group of elfkynan, who threw up their hands in surprise as the huge black horse came at them. Konowa brought his saber down on an elfkynan's arm, severing it at the elbow. Black frost sparkled on the wound and Konowa felt the familiar cold fury grip him. Zwindarra reared and flailed his hooves at two elfkynan in front of them, the sound of his steel shoes against skull bone loud and jarring.

Elfkynan screamed in pain and blood sprayed skyward. A mioxja whistled past Konowa's ear and he turned in the saddle and swung across his body, missing the elfkynan and almost cutting Zwindarra in the flanks. The force of the swing had him toppling out of the saddle, but Zwindarra shifted beneath him and he remained seated. The mioxja whipped the air again, the razor-sharp blades of jimik grass severing one of the wings of his shako. Zwindarra's head shot to the side and he bit the elfkynan in the stomach, lifting the screaming man into the air and shaking him. When Zwindarra let go, the elfkynan's innards lay strewn on the ground.

Konowa urged the horse forward at another group of elfkynan. He bent low in the saddle and stabbed one in the chest, the blade jumping in his hand as it hit spine. The wound began to blacken as frost fire licked around the embedded blade. The elfkynan wrenched himself backward, his shrieks ending abruptly as he vomited black ichor.

Two more elfkynan ran toward him, but before they got within distance of his saber or Zwindarra, Lorian came charging past on his horse and skewered the first on his halberd and rode over the second. An Iron Elf stepped out of the line and bayoneted the trampled elfkynan for good measure. Konowa noticed faint flickers of frost fire on the wounds.

He was still staring at the black flames when something hard struck him in the chest. Bitter cold burst over him and he fell from the saddle, barely able to kick his boots free from the stirrups as he did so. He landed flat on his back, the air rushing out of his lungs as everything went momentarily gray. The arrow that had struck the acorn under his jacket lay shattered a few feet away.

An elfkynan ran toward him, his screams of "Sillra! Sillra!" barely audible in the din of battle. Konowa tried to raise his saber, but his right arm was incapable of lifting a feather at that moment. A great black shadow loomed on top of him and Zwindarra dashed the elfkynan's brains out with a single flick of a front hoof.

The elfkynan charge faltered. Konowa's breath came back in a painful rush and he sat up, his limbs once again responding.

"Reform the line! Reform the line!" Lorian shouted, standing up in the saddle and motioning the troops to close the gap around Konowa. The soldiers began to move toward each other again, still falling back as they did so. Two grabbed hold of Konowa and helped him to his feet. He thanked them and gingerly got back into the saddle, allowing Zwindarra to carry him back toward Lorian.

Now that the gap had closed, the elfkynan attack turned to the new gap opening between the river and the fortress. The cannon covering the gap fired one more time, decimating a group of elfkynan and propelling the rest toward the fortress.

Seeing the fleeing soldiers, the elfkynan were encouraged, believing the Iron Elves had finally succumbed to the pressure.

A tremendous cheer sounded from the elfkynan ranks. Their bloody assault on the river directly across from the regiment slowed as the remaining forces shifted to cross near the gap. Konowa estimated at least a thousand elfkynan were still on their feet, but what he had in store for them would lower that number quickly.

The line of retreating siggers began to wheel to the left, falling back on the riverbank. This created an opening for the elfkynan to surge through between the fortress and the river. If they recognized the killing ground for what it was, they never showed it.

"Are you okay, Major?" Lorian said, trotting up to him on his horse. He reached out a hand, but instead of grabbing Konowa's elbow, he patted Zwindarra's neck.

"Thanks to this fellow I am," Konowa said, leaning forward to give the horse a pat as well.

"He's a fine beast, all right," Lorian said, clearly admiring the horse. "Fights like a real demon."

"Let's hope *they* don't," Konowa said, watching with growing dismay as the elfkynan ran past. Thousands were either dead or wounded, and why? Because they believed in a power greater than themselves, a power they believed would deliver their country from the Empire that controlled it. Konowa brought his hand up to his chest and felt the cold presence under his coat. What, he wondered, was he fighting for?

"Major?"

Konowa grunted an acknowledgment, watching the elfkynan stream past, their euphoria childlike. Once they were within the ring of trees, the trap would be sprung.

Konowa looked up the hill to see the Color party running into the fortress where the rest of C Company waited, along with the supporting howitzer. He looked back and saw that every second man in the firing line along the river had spun about to face the fortress.

The elfkynan were now caught in the middle.

The final slaughter needed only his command.

FORTY-EIGHT

A lwyn walked alone in the growing dark, his eyes searching the path before him for any sign of danger. The others had moved on ahead while he and Miss Red Owl had walked slowly, talking for quite a while about Miss Tekoy and the major. He got the distinct impression that Miss Red Owl didn't entirely approve of Miss Tekoy for some reason, but he thought they were very much alike, though he kept that to himself. Miss Red Owl had finally stopped asking questions and gone off into the forest to visit with her other children for a while. Alwyn wasn't sure if she meant elves or trees.

· He unstoppered the gourd with the tree sap that was a lot more than tree sap and took a drink. The liquid tingled as it went down his throat and the aches and pains of the march vanished. Even the throbbing in his chest subsided. He tipped the gourd up for another drink, but only a drop came out. He shook it. Empty. He considered tossing the gourd away, then thought better of it, knowing the way the elves of the Long Watch felt about trees and such.

There was a rustling in the bushes off to the left and Alwyn froze in midstep, his musket already in his hands. He knew it wasn't the elves. They moved through the forest like fish through water. He envied their skill and tried to imitate their light walk, but in a pair of heavy boots with all his equipment it was a bit like getting a muraphant over eggshells.

The sound grew louder as the source of the noise moved toward the path. Alwyn eased the hammer back on his musket and crouched. He wasn't going to be surprised again. The leaves of the nearest bush parted and out came one pleased-looking dwarf.

"If the elves ask, I was watering the mushrooms," Yimt said, straightening his caerna as he emerged onto the path. He walked up to Alwyn and gently turned his musket aside. "Ally, lad, there are many things a sigger can get shot for in the Imperial Army, but emptying your bladder ain't one of them . . . well, unless you do it in an officer's shako."

Alwyn uncocked his musket and stood up straight, letting out his breath. "I should have known it was you."

Yimt patted him on the arm and the two started walking on the path. "Better to be safe than sorry these days." He looked around them, scratching his head. "The others must be ahead. I left Teeter in charge of Scolly and Inkermon. Mercy, those two are a pair. You see what rank gets you? Put in charge of a group of misfits an insane asylum wouldn't take on account it would give them a bad name."

Alwyn smiled and quickened his pace, forcing the dwarf to keep up. It did nothing to slow his tongue.

"Speaking of not quite right, did Miss Red Owl tell you any more about that leafy fellow and that flying rat? Something ain't right about that little critter. And as far as that elf goes, I don't think the shaft goes all the way up in that mine."

Alwyn looked around, knowing it wouldn't do any good. Tyul could be a couple of feet away from them and they wouldn't see him unless he wanted them to.

"He really, really likes trees—well, at least his one tree anyway. Seems they bond with them for life. That's how they get their weapons and those arrows."

Yimt raised a bushy eyebrow. "Bond with trees, you say?"

Alwyn blushed. "Not like that! It's more a spiritual thing. You know, I think I've been hearing them a little, sort of . . . talking, but not with words exactly. The trees, I mean." He waited for the inevitable rebuttal.

"First, there was poor, old, dead Meri come back to life as a shadow, then there was an elf that wasn't exactly an elf but was like the major only not exactly, and now, now you're hearing trees talking," Yimt said, ticking off the offenses on his hand.

"I'm not crazy, Corporal," Alwyn said, glaring down at the dwarf.

Yimt's shoulders started shaking and before long he was laughing so hard he had to stop walking. Alwyn looked around nervously, but nothing that might want to eat them appeared.

"Ally, you don't know how glad I am to hear you say that. I thought maybe I'd cracked *my* crystal ball," he said, rapping his skull with his knuckles.

It was the last answer Alwyn expected. "I don't understand."

Yimt looked up at him, wiping the tears from his eyes. "Neither do I, Ally, but I've been hearing trees in my head, too. I thought I'd finally gone over the edge, but if you're hearing them, then either we're both a few stones short of a castle, or everything you've been saying might just be true."

The sound of running feet and branches being swatted aside heralded the arrival of Scolly, who came to a halt before them, struggling to catch his breath.

"Oh, now look, laddie," Yimt said, his good humor disappearing at the sight of the soldier, "if you ask me one more time if we're there yet, I swear I'll be lacing my boots with your tongue."

Scolly shook his head and pointed back down the path, still trying to catch his breath. Alwyn walked a few steps past him and then heard it.

"No, Yimt," he said, as the boom of a five-pounder echoed through the forest, "he's trying to tell us we've finally arrived."

Visyna shivered and hunched her shoulders, trying to keep her focus on the wounded soldier before her as her fingers danced through the skeins of life. Musket fire popped and crackled down the hill, intermixed with the screams of the dying. She felt each death like rain on bare skin, each blending with the other until their pain and fear washed away everything else. And yet here she was, tending the very men who were inflicting that suffering on her people.

Her fingers paused, the beat of the soldier's heart palpable in her hands. She could let him die. He was a soldier of the Empire, a tool of oppression and death, and worse, bound to the regiment in a way that frightened her. She had first noticed something wrong when she had tried to help the soldier named Meri in the vines. Then, she had put it down to the general malaise that stalked the land, a vague stain that did not yet pose an immediate threat. She knew better now. This was Her doing, and Konowa had been the means, even if he meant well.

"It's getting cold," the soldier said, his lips pale and trembling. Three fires crackled and sparked around them, their heat doing little to warm the open air of the fortress courtyard where the wounded lay. Visyna motioned for a private standing nearby to put another blanket over the man.

"No amount of covering will warm him now," the man said, eyeing the soldier with the casual disdain of one who knew something about death. "It's that elf-witch that holds all the cards here."

Visyna bristled at the comment and started weaving again, eliciting a cry of pain from the wounded soldier. "I'm sorry," she said, slowing and chiding herself for being so easily goaded. "Shouldn't you be with your company, Private . . . ?" she asked.

He sneered. "Zwitty's the name, and no, on account of my wound." He pointed to his left arm. The jacket was covered in blood, yet Visyna remembered dressing his wound earlier, and it had only been a small cut. "Safer to be here. Besides, the scenery is better."

She ignored his last comment. "The elf-witch you speak of does not hold sway yet. The *sarka har* are still young, their roots not yet long enough to feed them the power they seek."

"Wouldn't matter if they did," he said, winking at her. "As soon as the Prince gets his precious Star, we'll be leaving this place and She can do what She wants with it."

Visyna concentrated on the wounded soldier, blocking out the private's words. She found the faintest of skeins and delicately began to weave them together, slowly creating a strong thread to hold on to the life ebbing before her. There! She felt a clean strength and focused her mind on it. Zwitty was still talking, but she could no longer hear him. All her focus centered on the precious spark of life that yet burned within the man before her. She called on the last reserves of her power and laid her hands on the soldier's body. He gasped, his eyelids shooting open. Slowly, his breathing returned to a more normal rhythm as his face grew less pallid.

". . . do a little of that weaving on me," Zwitty said, reaching out and grabbing her arm.

Visyna spun around and used what energy she had left. There was a shock of ice and heat colliding as she pushed him, and then Zwitty was flying through the air. He landed hard on his back, then clambered to his feet, one hand cradled in the other, a look of surprise and anger on his face. He turned and ran back toward the regiment.

Visyna turned away from him and was pleased to see, and feel, that the wounded soldier was indeed healing. She walked briskly to the far end of the fortress, ducking under the remnants of a half-collapsed roof, and sat down on a small keg. Her eyes closed on their own and she let out a shuddering breath. She wrapped her arms around her body and shivered.

"Do you still serve your people, child?"

Visyna stood up suddenly, swaying as she did so. The image of the Star shimmered before her, its form a shattered mosaic of light and dark. Her weariness vanished in an instant.

"My people are being butchered out there because they believe in you. How can you let this happen?"

"Their deaths are of no consequence when weighed against the greater need."

Visyna felt the color drain from her face. "No. You must stop this!"

"Foolish girl, why would I want to?" The image of the Star curved in on itself. Shadow ate light and ground heaved in front of her, crumbling apart as a black figure emerged from the earth beneath her, and Visyna realized the extent of her mistake.

"Deceiver!" Fury blossomed inside her. She brought her hands up to weave a spell, but she was much too slow.

Her Emissary drew forth a long, black dagger. Frost fire danced along the blade, the air sizzling around it. It had drawn back its arm, preparing to strike, when something small and white flew past her.

The shadowy figure shrieked and dropped the blade, a white feather quill stuck in its hand. Rallie emerged from the shadows, another quill held lightly between her fingers.

"I've always believed, but I must admit it is rather gratifying to see, that the pen is indeed mightier than the sword."

"You!" it roared, ripping the quill from its hand and incinerating it with a black flame. It held out its good hand and the dropped blade flew into it. *"You should not be here. This is not your time."*

"Oh, I don't know," Rallie said, twirling the quill between her fingers. "I usually think I should be exactly where I am at any given moment. You, however, are definitely in the wrong place, and very much at the wrong time."

"Your words are as weak as your weapons. This is becoming Her time, and all those that serve Her."

Visyna gasped for breath as two powerful forces consumed all the life energy around her. The natural order began unraveling and she tried desperately to stitch it back together, even as she realized her magic was woefully inadequate to the task.

"That remains to be seen. In the meantime," Rallie said, preparing to throw the quill, "it's time you left."

The ebb and flow of the competing forces suddenly surged in one direction, and Visyna caught her breath, a pleasant warmth filling the air. The dark figure howled, its form splintering, reforming, then splintering again. Visyna reached out her hands and grabbed some of the threads, giving what aid she could to Rallie to help her banish it.

"You cannot hold us for long. A new forest will grow here before the night is out." The ground shook and Her Emissary disappeared between the cracks and was gone.

Visyna felt sick. She looked down at her hands and saw they were trembling.

She had listened to that thing, taken its advice, done whatever she could to help it. This was all her fault. Everything.

"Really now, my dear, you're getting as melodramatic as Konowa," Rallie said, walking over to give her a pat on the arm. "This is the Shadow Monarch's fault, first and foremost. Our task, and it's a significant one, is to undo the damage."

"I should have seen through it," Visyna said.

"Perhaps, but it is skilled in the art of deception, and you saw what you wanted to see."

"That was the last Viceroy, wasn't it?" Visyna asked, looking at Rallie with a newfound respect.

"Her Emissary now," Rallie said, reaching into her cloak for a cigar. She pulled one out and made no pretense of lighting it, the end suddenly glowing red of its own accord. "It's been looking for the Star for some time, believing, apparently, that it is buried somewhere beneath the fort."

"Do you know where the Star is?" Visyna asked, hope rising in her chest.

Rallie shook her head. "Not that I can find it, but don't despair, my dear, I think it will reveal itself when it's ready."

"What did it mean about this not being your time?"

Rallie cackled softly and blew out a long stream of smoke. "That, my dear, is a story for another time." She flexed her fingers around her cigar and for the briefest of moments filigrees of light flowed from them like gossamer threads caught in a breeze.

Visyna looked at her in stunned surprise.

"Oh, come now, dear, you suspected as much, no?" Rallie said, cocking her head to the side as if listening to something far away.

"Then you are a witch," Visyna said.

Rallie brought her head up straight and clamped down hard on the cigar between her teeth. "After a fashion. I like to think of myself more as the one you least suspect . . . until it's too late. Now, I suggest we get out to the ramparts. We're about to become rather busy, you and I. The trees that surround us are focused on digging for the Star, but Her Emissary may soon decide to redirect their energies."

Visyna nodded, following the old woman, the smoke from Rallie's cigar swirling about them in the darkening night.

FORTY-NINE

M ajor, there!" Lorian shouted, pointing toward the gap.
A group of four elfkynan came walking through,
their pace slow and even. They were dressed in bright
crimson-colored robes and tall white hats that rose to
a point more than a foot above their heads. Each hat bore a shining blue gem
in the center that sparkled with the last rays of the setting sun. All four carried tall walking sticks of a dark brown wood entwined with green vines.

"Shamans," Lorian said, his voice rising with indignation. "These
poor buggers have been throwing away their lives thinking they could protect them from musket balls."

"Don't judge a tree by its bark," Konowa said, the old proverb of his
father's coming back to him. He watched the shamans, looking for some
grand gesture or conjuration, but they showed no outward sign of being
in the midst of battle, or of being in danger at all. Wizards were forever
getting under Konowa's skin.

A group of thirty elfkynan warriors dressed in dark blue robes and
carrying spears followed close behind. As they passed through the trees,
they fanned out in a circle around the first four.

Konowa pushed his senses outward. He came up against something
incredibly vibrant and warm, a feeling so natural and peaceful that it caught

his breath. The four red-robed figures turned as one to look in his direction.

"Magic all right . . ." he managed to say, grabbing hold of Lorian to steady himself in the saddle. The feeling reminded him of the calm he had felt when Visyna had woven her magic earlier. It wasn't the deadening of the voices of life, but a complex harmony that made simple, beautiful sense.

"Major, are you okay? Major?"

Konowa tried to speak, but no words would come to his mouth. The four shamans continued to stare at him, their faces calm, their posture relaxed.

"They've bespelled you," Lorian muttered, shouting orders at once. "Take out those shamans! Front row, by volley . . . fire!"

Most of the troops had not had time to reload, but at least twenty had, and at a distance of less than a hundred yards they couldn't miss.

The sound of musket fire sounded from far away. Konowa knew he should care about it, but found it difficult to do so. He started to urge Zwindarra toward the circle, then gasped, feeling as if he had fallen through ice on a frozen lake. He came to his senses at once, the acorn bitterly cold against his flesh. The air shimmered in front of the circle of blue-robed warriors and then cleared again. Not one had fallen. His siggers had missed. Shouted orders echoed down from the fortress. The howitzer in the fortress boomed, its flight almost straight up as the gunners tried to land a shell within the circle. The shell carried long, coming dangerously close to the Iron Elves by the river, and exploded harmlessly in dead ground, throwing splinters of red-hot metal through the air.

The elfkynan warriors nonetheless decided it was time to find safer ground and moved toward the protection of the four shamans, slipping through the ring of blue-robed warriors. As more and more elfkynan stepped through the circle the warriors moved out, increasing its size until it held more than a thousand elfkynan. Soon, all the elfkynan able to make it to the circle had. Chants of "Sillra! Sillra!" rose in volume again as they called on the Star to finally reveal itself.

The Iron Elves looked to Konowa, waiting. This was far beyond their experiences. Muskets and bayonets were their tools, tried and tested, yet they had failed in front of their eyes. It was an unsettling feeling in the lee of the coming night. Not believing what they were seeing, a couple of siggers actually fired without orders. Both times the air shimmered about the circle and no elfkynan was hurt. Somewhere in the line a soldier laughed. Konowa shared the sentiment. Just minutes ago, the elfkynan were being cut down in droves, the shamans doing nothing to prevent it. Now they stood in a perfect killing ground, surrounded by the Iron Elves, and apparently impervious to harm.

Torches and lanterns flamed to life as the last rays of sunlight dimmed. The regiment was growing restless, and Konowa knew Prince Tykkin would be apoplectic, wondering why Konowa hadn't ordered a charge to finish the elfkynan off, shimmering air or no shimmering air. Something would have to give.

The cold in Konowa told him something now would.

It started with the trees. As the sun disappeared below the horizon, the shadows were stretched to their full length, their shapes a dark, twisted stain on the ground. Frost began to crackle wherever they lay, the grass withering beneath the weight of obsidian crystals sparkling in the twilight. To look down was to see the night sky beneath their feet, and many soldiers and elfkynan alike felt a sudden nausea at a world inverted.

A ripping sound criss-crossed the earth between the trees and then surged upward as sickly white roots stabbed skyward, impaling the many elfkynan bodies littering the battlefield. Red blood turned black as the roots began to grow into new trees, their limbs stretching outward like many-fingered hands, groping for contact with the other *sarka har*.

Konowa swayed in the saddle as the hunger of the trees washed over him. He felt a surge of anger, a hunger of his own to destroy them all, to leave him in peace. The confusion of the world as he had known it, that constant thrum of life just below the threshold of understanding forever poised to overwhelm him, seemed a simple, wonderful thing now.

A musket fired, the ball tearing into a tree with no real effect. The howitzer in the fortress boomed in response, tossing a fizzing cannon shell high into the air, its path easily followed by the trail of sparks it smeared across the sky. The gun crew's aim was better, as this shell landed near the trees to the left of the square. It detonated on impact, and both trees and foes were shattered by the blast, but not enough.

"Hold your fire!" Konowa shouted, his mind racing. Zwindarra tossed his head and pawed at the ground nervously, but still responded to Konowa's commands.

The encircled elfkynan were even more agitated, their cries of Sillra falling away as they witnessed the desecration of their brethren. The four shamans in the center of the circle stood back to back, their eyes closed, both hands gripping their staffs, chanting silently. Konowa expected to see a bright light, a glow, something, but though the wizards continued to chant nothing appeared to happen.

"Major, over there!" Lorian shouted, reining his horse in as it reared and neighed in fright.

Konowa swung around in the saddle to look, but he had already felt it.

Gray, awkward shapes were crawling from the water. The creatures were man-sized, their heads a blunt, eyeless knob with a circular mouth filled with rows of small, pointed teeth. There didn't seem to be a neck, just a scaly tube for a body, studded with spikes and supported on what looked like four short legs.

They were the huge ancestors of the bara jogg that swam the river.

Their progress was slow, their transition from water to land an uneasy one. Konowa cast a glance back at the elfkynan to make sure they weren't preparing anything and urged Zwindarra closer to the river. As he got closer, the reason for the creatures' strange gait became apparent. What he had taken for legs were just four large spikes that flailed and scratched at the ground for purchase, propelling them up the bank and toward the Iron Elves.

Konowa's mind was still reeling when a more familiar and unwelcome sight greeted his eyes. Rakkes emerged from the trees, their hulking forms all but hidden within the shadows save for the glow of their white, milky eyes. They began roaring and beating their chests, working themselves into a frenzy. Konowa figured they had a minute, maybe two.

"Major?"

"There's no point holding the river now. We've got to get the men up to the fortress as quickly as possible. I need you to keep them in check; we'll go slow and steady. No stragglers, no heroics, and I mean it."

Lorian nodded, a gesture mostly lost in the dark. "There's still the matter of the elfkynan between us and the fortress. How do we get by them while keeping those monsters at bay?"

"I don't think we have too much to worry about from them for the next little while," he said. The elfkynan were clearly horrified by the new trees squirming to life and showed no sign of mounting any kind of attack. The Iron Elves were no doubt troubled by the spectacle as well, but discipline would hold them together where others ran. Discipline, and an oath.

"Very good, sir," Lorian said, adjusting himself on the elfkynan saddle, which appeared a bit too small for him.

The howitzer in the fortress fired again, the shell landing only a few yards from the previous one. Instead of exploding, the shell bounced, the ground within the ring of trees hardened with frost. It started rolling toward the square, the fuse still sputtering. A soldier leaped out of line and ran toward the shell. He bent over it and fumbled with the fuse, trying to pull the burning cord out. After two failed attempts, the soldier simply picked the cannonball up and heaved it at the trees, where it exploded a moment later. Konowa didn't need to see his face to know the identity of the only soldier who could toss a cannonball like that.

"If he was a little smaller, Private Vulhber would make one hell of a cavalryman," Lorian said, his voice filled with relief and pride.

"Regiment, load muskets!" Konowa shouted, cantering Zwindarra in front of the line of soldiers at the edge of the river. Muskets were held at the hip as cartridges were pulled from leather pouches, the iron ball bitten from the top of the waxed paper that held the black powder, a portion of which was poured into the pan. As one, the regiment grounded their muskets and poured the remaining powder down the barrel, the musket ball following. Ramrods rattled and banged.

"Regiment will fix bayonets!" The sharp clang of steel on steel reverberated in the cold air, and Konowa smiled at its familiar tune. He would get these men up to the fortress no matter what black horror stood in their way.

"What about the guns?" Lorian asked, using his halberd to point at the two positions at either end of the line.

Konowa spit. "There's nothing for it, they'll have to be left behind. We'll never get the muraphants down here now. Have the gun crews fire double canister shot into those things coming out of the water, then a couple of shots into the trees, and then go. The one in the fortress will have to do."

Lorian spurred his horse to a gallop to relay the message. Konowa watched him go, quickly running things over in his mind. They had close to three hundred yards to cover to get to the safety of the fortress, normally a three-minute march.

Konowa stood in the saddle, resting the balls of his feet on the stirrups. "Cannon will fire on my command . . . fire!"

The night momentarily lit up as twin gouts of sparks burst from the muzzles of the two five-pounders, scattering two hundred musket balls along the riverbank. The huge bara jogg blew apart, their scales no match for the force of the canister shot. More bara jogg still crawling out of the river began feeding on the remains of the others. Konowa was sure no one would straggle after seeing that.

The gun crews were already pivoting their guns to face the trees nearest the regiment, the sizzle of the wet sponge extinguishing the remaining sparks in the barrel before the next charge was rammed in place surprisingly loud in the cool, night air. The quiet was broken a moment later when the rakkes set up a new howl, and some of them began lumbering forward.

"The cannon will fire on my command . . . fire!"

Portfires, the metal sticks holding a length of burning cord called slow-match, were brought down to the touch hole at the rear of the cannon barrel. The flame came in contact with the fuse, in this case a goose quill filled with fast-burning powder, which ignited at once, sending flame directly into the powder charge inside. The guns roared, the force of the shot sending them rolling backward on their wheels. Each disgorged a solid cannonball through the air and into the trees.

The force of the impact uprooted several trees and scattered steel-like splinters into the nearest rakkes, felling them as forcefully as musket shot. It was enough to send the rest scurrying back for a moment, which was exactly what Konowa was waiting for.

"On my command, regiment will form a hollow square and prepare to march. Regiment . . . form square!"

In an open field in daylight the maneuver could be quickly and easily done by a well-drilled regiment. This was not an open field—it was night, the Iron Elves had had almost no time to practice complicated drills, and creatures from nightmares roared and crawled all around them.

Lorian's voice rose above the din, and in turn the sergeants and corporals got their men moving. Konowa directed Zwindarra toward the gun crew near the gap while Lorian went toward the other, each shouting at the men to hurry up. The two guns crews came running in a moment later, a wagon wheel being rolled by each group. Konowa kept twisting around in the saddle, trying to keep an eye on both the tree line and the river.

Everywhere he looked there was a threat. Everywhere his senses flowed he felt the malice and the hunger and knew there would be no negotiation, no mutual retreat. There would be only those not yet dead.

When the last man finally entered the ranks, Konowa and Lorian rode in and the Iron Elves closed around them, facing outward.

Typically, a square was formed to defend against roving cavalry. It allowed line infantry to create, in effect, a miniature fortress with all-round defense, their bayonets a bristling abatis, their muskets a deadly fusillade, and most important, the sense of security that derived from standing side by side with other soldiers, comrades in arms, friends. A square was strong only as long as all four walls held. A single breach would invite destruction.

The large bara jogg, their impromptu meal finished, responded by jerking and rolling their bodies faster up the bank, teeth-filled mouths opening and closing in anticipation of more flesh. The rakkes began to howl again and move forward, sensing the change was in their favor.

"Three hundred yards to the fortress, gentlemen," Konowa shouted above the din, walking Zwindarra around the tight area within the circle. He could see his breath as he spoke, though he didn't feel particularly cold. "Just three hundred yards, a stroll in the park."

There were a few laughs, not as many as Konowa had hoped for. He looked over at Lorian. The RSM sat tall in his saddle, the reins in his left hand, his halberd leaning against his right shoulder. He walked his horse slowly around the inside of the square, nodding approval at what he saw. It was now or never.

"Keep it tight, keep it strong, and don't run! Now let's get out of here. Regiment . . . forward march!"

The square lurched forward. Konowa knew the trouble would come from the rear, which was forced to march backward. Lorian was already on it, shouting encouragement to the men and giving a tap with the butt of his halberd to those who needed a bit more.

They quickly outpaced the bara jogg, who continued to scratch and spike their way forward, the first of them crawling over the abandoned firing position. The rakkes were another matter. Their frenzy peaked with long, drawn-out howls, and then they charged as one, converging on both the Iron Elves and the elfkynan.

Many rakkes held crude wooden blades in their hands, the weapons little more than large, splintered chunks of the *sarka har*. The pieces of wood dripped black ichor, the frost that covered the ground sizzling wherever a drop landed. Konowa had been prepared to let the rakkes get within seventy-five yards before giving the command to fire, but then one of the rakkes let out a great mewling cry and threw its splinter at the square. The soldiers facing the rakke saw it coming and ducked, but those facing the opposite direction did not.

The wood caught one soldier high in the back, running him through and slamming his body to the ground. Black frost began to grow on the wood immediately and soon covered the soldier's body. The square faltered as soldiers turned to look.

"Halt! Face out! Hold your positions! On my command, the outer rank will volley . . . fire!" The muskets sounded like deep ice breaking up,

378 ＊ CHRIS EVANS

the cold air lending a clarity to their violence. Sparks flew and gray smoke roiled outward from all points of the compass. Dull, wet thwacks marked the striking of flesh by iron, and scores of rakkes went down, the rest retreating to a safer distance to howl in rage.

The attack against the elfkynan circle made more progress, the discipline of the native warriors not as strong as the Iron Elves', and the rain of arrows not as lethal. As rakkes charged and threw their jagged missiles, many elfkynan shifted position, breaking the integrity of the circle. Those who strayed or found themselves outside were quickly overcome by fangs and claws and dripping black splinters. The bodies were not consumed by frost fire, however; instead, roots from the nearest *sarka bar* would plunge up from below, impaling the body as a new blood tree began to grow.

"Sir, we have to keep moving!" Lorian shouted, struggling to keep his horse under control. The animal's eyes showed white and it began frothing at the mouth as it chewed its bit.

Konowa knew he was right, but already a new problem was literally growing to make that more and more difficult. "There are a lot of trees between here and the fort—I can't destroy them all myself."

Lorian looked over at the body of the fallen soldier. There was nothing left, just a dull, black stain on the ground where he had lain. "Let's get this over with, then." The sound of spikes and scales being dragged across the hard ground grew louder as the enlarged bara jogg came on. The Iron Elves had no choice but to keep going.

Konowa shouted for Private Vulhber. The giant stepped out of line and into the center of the square. Konowa dismounted and held out Zwindarra's reins. "Take care of him for me; the RSM and I have some work to do." It was a gift any of the soldiers would have treasured, a chance to stay within the protective center of the square. After witnessing Vulhber's heroics, Konowa figured the soldier deserved it.

Hrem looked at the reins longingly, then shook his head. "If it's all the same to you, Major, I'd just as soon not. I've got an idea about what you two are going to do, and I figure a third pair of hands might come in, well, handy."

"Can you control the power well enough?" Lorian asked, dismounting.

"Better than most. Seems only a few of the lads can really work it so far and I'm one of them." There was no joy in the statement, or pride. "That's why I'm still here. I used the frost to slow the fuse of that shell while I tried to pull it out. Still working out the kinks, but I saw what the major did with those trees back at the outpost. I'd just as soon help you and get this over with."

"Words to live by," Konowa said, whistling for two soldiers nearby to come and take the reins of the horses. One of them was the weasel-faced private who had bayoneted the wounded elfkynan. Konowa was tempted to order him back into the line, but a chunk of black wood tumbling through the air and gouging a furrow in the ground in the center of the square got his attention.

"Lorian, Private Vulhber and I will deal with the trees; you stay here and command," Konowa said.

Lorian looked surprised. "I'll burn the damn trees, sir, I'm not afraid of them."

Konowa gave him a quick smile. "I know you aren't, but someone has to keep the boys in shape and I'll be rather busy."

"Then you should stay and I should go with Vulhber. You're an officer, sir, you should stay in the center and command. It's your proper place," he finished.

"I'm no Prince, RSM. I'll lead them back through the trees; you have command of the square. Take Zwindarra, you'll have a better view," he said, taking the reins from weasel-face and handing them to Lorian. Konowa then saluted, forcing Lorian to return it.

"Let's go, Private," Konowa said, sheathing his saber and stepping through the side of the square facing the fortress. "You, too," he said, pointing at weasel-face, who was trying to wrest the reins of Lorian's horse from another private.

"Me, sir?" Zwitty asked, shock registering on his face.

"You'll be our scout. If you see trouble, let us know."

Private Vulhber slung his musket on a broad shoulder and grabbed Zwitty by the arm, propelling him through the square.

"I didn't volunteer!" Zwitty shouted, panic breaking his voice.

Konowa grabbed him by the front of the jacket and jerked him onto his toes. Frost radiated out from the point where his hand held the cloth and up to the collar of the soldier's jacket. "Oh, but you did. As soon as I saw you use that bayonet, I knew you were just the man for the job. Now you keep your eyes peeled and watch our backs, or you won't get a chance to volunteer for anything again."

Konowa released his grasp and the frost evaporated in a swirling mist. He turned and motioned to Private Vulhber. "You'll hear screaming; just squeeze harder."

Without waiting for a reply, Konowa looked back to Lorian, now sitting astride Zwindarra. He waved his arm, then turned and walked toward the first tree.

A howl rose from the rakkes at the sight of the three Iron Elves outside the bristling wall of bayonets. Konowa ignored them, focusing his attention on the tree in front of him. Musket fire from the fortress sounded for the first time, a short rippling burst that was quickly swallowed by the night. A single arrow from an elfkynan archer flitted by Konowa's head, but the acorn against his chest had nothing to say on the subject.

"Regiment . . . march!"

Boots crunched on the brittle ground as the square inched forward again. Konowa reached the first tree, its limbs wriggling frantically at his approach, slashing at the air in an attempt to ward him off. He felt the eyes of many on him and didn't care. Power was what you made of it, and he was getting the Iron Elves home.

He grabbed the *sarka har* by the trunk and pulled. It didn't budge. A surge of cold anger flowed through it far greater than its size warranted. It was trying to overwhelm him, and he felt not just two souls, but many. He squeezed, forcing his power into it, but unlike before, the tree absorbed it with ease. Was the power of the Wolf Oak acorn failing?

The cold seeped into his blood far deeper this time, and he felt something new and unexpected. The screaming softened, beckoning instead for him to join them. A great void opened up somewhere deep within his mind, a pool of absolute nothingness. No chaos, no sensations . . . nothing. The temptation to dive into it weighed down on him like a mountain, and his hands began to slip from the trunk. He had almost let go when the pool rippled and vanished in a storm of light and noise. He blinked and looked over to see Private Vulhber grab a tree.

Konowa concentrated, realizing now that they weren't just attacking a single tree, but the power of the entire forest around them. Every tree was connected.

"Major, look out!" Zwitty shouted as he turned and ran back toward the square.

The shako on Konowa's head was ripped off, a chunk of wood thrown by a rakke just missing crushing his skull. He kept his hands on the tree, not knowing what else to do. There were still dozens of trees between the regiment and the fort. If the square was to maintain its integrity, Konowa had to find a way to remove the trees in its path.

The tramping of boots echoed through the ground. With each step he felt a growing strength. As the regiment got closer the power in him increased, magnified by their numbers, and their oath. He sensed the presence of Iron Elves around him, their closeness giving him incredible power. With a shout that was half growl, he ripped the tree from the earth and burned it in a triumphal blaze of black flame.

A rakke suddenly loomed before him, its yellow fangs dripping with saliva. Konowa didn't even reach for his saber. He took one step forward and drove his right fist into the creature's chest. He felt the ribs freeze and turn brittle, snapping into several pieces as they were driven into its heart, which shuddered and stopped.

More rakkes charged.

"Major, Private! Get down!"

Konowa shook his head and moved toward the rakkes. A hand like an anvil came down on his shoulder and shoved him to the ground.

"Fire!"

Muskets barked directly above him. Bitter smoke stung his nostrils, his eyes watering. He shook off the hand holding him down and stood up. Rakkes lay everywhere, trees writhed and flailed their crooked branches, and somewhere a series of bells were ringing.

"—more careful! That volley would . . . and then what . . ."

Konowa watched Vulhber's lips moving, but only caught a few words. He realized the ringing in his ears was from the last volley. Slowly, his hearing came back.

"—you okay?"

Konowa nodded and moved forward again toward the next tree. "Stay close; use their power," he said, pointing to the regiment behind them.

Private Vulhber shook his head. "There's no point, sir."

Konowa snarled. "Don't go soft on me now."

Vulhber pointed to the trees. "Look."

Konowa turned. Dark figures moved across the ground, long, two-handed swords gleaming like lightning dancing above the ground. They drifted in and out of sight, more shadow than substance, making it difficult to keep them in focus. Their swords rose and fell with untiring violence. Black frost sparked into black flame wherever their swords cut, consuming the *sarka har* in a chorus of screams that echoed in Konowa's head. One of the figures paused, its blade held high above its head. It turned slowly, its gaze sweeping across Konowa like a winter gale.

A voice crawled into his skull from somewhere impossibly far away. *"They are coming,"* the shade of Meri said. *"Run."*

FIFTY

I s that . . ." Vulhber started to ask, his voice choking.

"Get back in the square!" Konowa shouted. He drew his saber and pointed up toward the fortress. "Lorian, get them moving! Double time!"

Lorian raised his halberd in response and relayed the order from atop Zwindarra.

Konowa trotted forward, searching. Rakkes bellowed with unmitigated fury at the sight of the shades, but for the moment were unwilling to challenge them.

The regiment picked up its pace, the men sensing the new urgency. Chunks of splintered *sarka har* still flew through the air, and three more Iron Elves fell, but the protective walls of the fortress were tantalizingly close, and cheers began to rise from the ranks. The rakkes turned their attention on the elfkynan, but though the circle wavered, the four shamans maintained the protective spell around them. Konowa knew it couldn't last, sensing the force diminishing under the intense pressure, the warmth of the spell growing cold, fading.

Konowa waved his saber forward, urging the regiment on, the feel of the cool night air in his hair reminding him that he had lost his shako.

That's when Konowa felt them.

He didn't need the surge of ice against his chest to tell him. It was like a sliver of metal slipped between the eye and the lid. The rakkes grew silent, their chests heaving as they tried to catch their breath. Even the clawing of the bara jogg on the hard earth stopped, their scaly bodies uncannily still.

Shadows slipped through the trees, long, jagged blades held in their hands.

Konowa heard their terrible cries in his head. They all did. The shades of the Thirty-fifth Regiment wailed in terror, their spirits overcome by the *sarka har.* Still, they advanced. They had become unwilling servants to Her will, soldiers in a battle no longer for their lives, but for their souls.

"Fire!"

Muskets punched through the screams. Many shades were hit, a few bursting into writhing pyres of black flame, but most continued, the effect negligible. The first reached the front rank of the square, their blades slashing through the wall of bayonets to rend flesh.

Men screamed as frost fire burst over them. Others hacked and stabbed furiously with their bayonets, but it was like spearing water. The sides of the square began to buckle, the square collapsing in on itself as soldiers backed away from the relentless shadow warriors. The square was moments from collapsing altogether when the shades of the Iron Elves turned from the destruction of the trees and filled the ranks of the fallen in the square.

Now, shadow met shadow.

A howitzer shell hurtled skyward, a trail of sparks scribing its flight against the night. It appeared to get caught in a wind, though Konowa felt none. The shell veered far to the right, coming down not among the shades, but near the trees. The explosion radiated a brilliant white light. Several rakkes were scattered in the blast, their bodies flung about like rag dolls.

Konowa sensed something else then, a pure, exquisite malice that surpassed even the *sarka har.* More figures emerged from the trees, and though they moved as if they were shadow, their bodies were indeed corporeal, if twisted. The ground beneath Konowa swayed, or perhaps it was him, he could no longer tell.

Flame from a torch guttered and flared briefly, illuminating the area in front of him. An elf stood there, its black ear tip an obsidian beacon in the night. It held a longbow ready in its hands. Hunger . . . rage . . . anguish . . . extremes of emotion radiated outward from the elf, all of them driven by something bitter and vengeful. They had been left on the plains to die, mere babies, abandoned by their tribe. Death should have found them; a ravening wolf, carrion birds, a hunting dragon. But *She* found them, and took them for Her own, creating the *dyskara*, the tainted ones.

Brilliant black eyes glittered, searching, hunting. Konowa knew they looked for him. He would not bend his knee to Her, so he would die.

Bows creaked as their strings were pulled back, arrows of dark and wicked creation aimed straight at his heart. Lorian shouted at the regiment to fire. The elf hissed between its teeth.

Powder sparked.

Bowstrings sang.

Musket balls and arrows criss-crossed the open ground. Konowa waited for the impact, wondering what his death would feel like. Sudden warmth spread over him, and he recognized the sensation of elfkynan magic.

They were trying to protect him.

The surprise was still registering in his mind when the arrows hit.

"We've got to get in there!" Yimt shouted, his knuckles whitening as he gripped his shatterbow. They stood at the edge of the forest looking out across the open ground to the unnatural black wall that barred them from Luuguth Jor. Musket fire crackled amid screams and howls, but the dark trees blocked everything except the rough outline of the fort atop the hill.

Alwyn fidgeted with the strap on his musket, his enthusiasm not as strong. He'd still go, he didn't care how scared he was—and he was terrified—but he was in no rush to do it. Surprisingly, Miss Red Owl didn't seem overly eager, either.

"Patience, master dwarf," Chayii said, her fingers gently brushing a strand of hair from her eye. "The *sarka har* have created a wall that is not easily broached. They are preparing a new forest for Her. The ground grows cold as the roots delve deep. A moment's thought now may bear fruit long after."

Yimt's right eyebrow shot up as he stomped over to the elf. "And I think the time for thinking is over. That's our regiment in there, and we're going in. If you folk don't want any part of it, fine, but you aren't stopping us."

Teeter and Scolly nodded while Inkermon stared blankly ahead, his ruined book still clutched in his hand. Alwyn heard many bowstrings grow taut around them. Miss Red Owl glared down at the dwarf, then smiled.

"It is not my intent to stop you," Chayii said, shaking her head slightly. The bowstrings relaxed, but arrows remained notched. "In speaking with the others, it is clear to me that we fight the same foe, and allies against Her will are a welcome boon. Still, a little prudence would not be out of place. How will we get through?"

"We can hack our . . ." Yimt trailed off as his hand grasped only air when he reached for his drukar. He huffed, but finally nodded. "Fine, what do you have in mind?"

In answer, Chayii held out her hand, palm up. The flying squirrel suddenly flew out of the night to land gently on it, swiveling its ears with every musket shot. She spoke to it, her voice the perfect imitation of its squeaking. It twitched its nose and jumped onto her shoulder, waiting.

"It seems, master dwarf, that I have need of a favor," Chayii said. "Is your skill with your weapon as good as you claim?"

Yimt looked suspicious. "You mean Lil' Nipper? You saw what I did in the forest to that beastie."

Chayii nodded. "A good shot from a short distance, but I am talking about a much longer distance now, over the *sarka har*."

Yimt looked past her toward the battle. "I suppose I could get a shot over them from here if I use one of them black arrows. But I can't see what I'm shooting at on the other side of the trees."

"You'll be aiming at the next ball of flame," she said, making a graceful arc with her hand mimicking the flight of a howitzer shell.

Yimt started shaking his head vigorously. "That'd be like threading an orc through a needle. You're the woodland folk. I'd have bet real money that one of your lot could do something like that."

Chayii shook her head. "A few could, though it would be a difficult shot, to be sure. But what we need to do is redirect one of those balls of flame so that it lands among the *sarka har.* We will then have our passage-way."

"It's a nifty idea, Miss Red Owl, but it will never work," Yimt said. "An arrow would never have the power to knock a howitzer shell off course, and even if it did, there's no way of telling where it might land. We could do more harm than good."

"You won't be shooting an arrow," she said.

Alwyn looked from Miss Red Owl to Yimt's shatterbow, then back to Miss Red Owl, where the squirrel was sitting up on its haunches, its eyes wide as it looked up into the sky.

Oh.

"Miss Red Owl, I like the way your mind works," Yimt said, putting it together at the same time. "Is the little fellow some kind of magical familiar?"

"My husband, actually," Chayii said, ignoring the looks of astonishment. "He has a tendency to forget himself on occasion, and it so happens that will work in our favor now."

Alwyn watched Yimt carefully, waiting. The dwarf scratched his beard, clearly thinking this over. Finally, he shrugged his shoulders. "Whatever you say."

Tyul suddenly appeared, his leafy camouflage rustling as he came to stand beside Yimt. He said nothing, only staring at the dwarf, his tattooed face unreadable. Chayii said something to him in elvish, but Tyul gave no indication of listening, his gaze remained fixed on Yimt.

"Maybe he'd like to do it?" Yimt ventured, trying to smile at the elf, but giving up when he got no response. "I mean, no offense, but I've never shot anyone's husband before . . . in this way."

Chayii smiled. "In this case, your weapon is better suited to the task, and he would not touch it though the need is great."

"Okay, then, but just remember," Yimt said, clearly at pains to make sure this was really what she wanted, "I'm only doing this because you asked me to."

Yimt placed the end of the shatterbow on the ground and pulled back on the heavy bowstring, grunting with the strain. He hoisted it up and looked at Alwyn.

"Be a sport, Ally," he said, pointing to a spot a few feet away.

Alwyn dutifully walked to Yimt and bent over, allowing Yimt to rest the shatterbow across his back. The position was painful, and Alwyn hoped he wouldn't have to hold it for long.

"Ready when he is," Yimt said, sighting down the shatterbow. The squirrel chirped once and jumped the short distance to land on Alwyn's shako. He sniffed it, then quickly crawled onto his back and up onto the shatterbow, pausing to sniff different parts of it. Apparently satisfied, the squirrel settled in at the rear of the weapon, all four paws clutching the heavy string, its shoulders hunched high around its head.

Alwyn saw a bush beside him and realized Tyul had moved to stand right beside Yimt again.

"Don't squirm, Ally, you don't want me firing this poor critter . . . elf, into the trees instead of over them."

The bush that was Tyul moved slightly, and Alwyn forced himself to remain very, very still. He took deep, slow breaths and hoped the howitzer would fire soon. As if in response, a familiar boom echoed from within the trees and a moment later a trail of sparks arced skyward.

"Happy landings," Yimt said, and squeezed the trigger. The bowstring hummed, flinging the squirrel into the air.

The vibration of the shot traveled up and down Alwyn's spine. He looked up to see where the squirrel was, but it was impossible to tell. He focused on the howitzer shell instead as it rose higher into the air.

This will never work.

"Your powers as a seer need more work, Alwyn of the Empire," Chayii said.

Alwyn jumped and looked again at the howitzer shell. It had reached its apex and was now falling back to earth. Was it drifting? Alwyn blinked. Yes, the trail of sparks was definitely coming down at a different angle than when it went up. It sounded like thunder and looked like lightning bursting from the earth when it landed. When Alwyn's night vision returned he saw a gaping hole in the black mass that surrounded Luuguth Jor.

"Do you think the little squirrel is okay?" Scolly asked, coming up to stand beside Tyul. The elf didn't answer, instead turning and disappearing into the night toward the opening.

"Load your muskets and fix bayonets," Yimt said. He was already pulling the bowstring back on his shatterbow. "Now let's go find out."

FIFTY-ONE

Focus, my dear, or a lot of people are going to get hurt," Rallie said, laying a hand on her shoulder. Visyna felt an immediate rush, the weariness in her lifting, but not all the way.

"I don't know how much longer I can do this!" Visyna said, trying to ignore the sights and sounds of battle. She stood just behind the crumbled wall of the fort where the remaining Iron Elves fired down at the marauding rakkes. Her attention had to be on the diminishing circle of elfkynan, but it was hard not to watch Konowa and Lorian and the Iron Elves make their way up to the fortress. Shades now stalked the battleground, their blades afire with black flame, and she had no more energy left to deal with them.

Her fingers wove and rewove the fabric of the natural order, mending ever-bigger tears as she fought to keep the elfkynan safe.

"You're doing fine, my child," Rallie said, her gruff voice a soothing lifeline in a sea of noise.

"I could use some help," Visyna said. Thus far, Rallie had done little more than stand beside her, puffing on a cigar and sketching the battle in a notebook.

"Help, I think, is on the way," Rallie replied.

A volley of musket fire rattled and cracked in front of them, the smell of sulfur stinging her eyes. Prince Tykkin strode into view, the wings on his shako flapping as he paced back and forth behind the firing line.

"The Star is here, I can feel it," he said, looking around the fort. Musket fire, arrows, and tumbling splinters of wood filled the air, and blood trees writhed and stabbed their limbs at any flesh that got too close. "A gold coin to the soldier who finds the Star! A hundred gold coins!"

"Go find it yourself, you bloody fool!" a soldier shouted back, but it was impossible to see who amid all the confusion.

The Prince sputtered with rage, drawing his sword, then resheathing it, only to draw it again. "Witch! I demand that you find me the Star. Perform whatever magic you must and you will be well rewarded."

Visyna considered striking the Prince down where he stood, but knew that to do so would be to condemn the elfkynan to death. It was her weaving that was protecting her countrymen.

"Put it away, Your Highness," Rallie said, waving a hand at him. "The girl is rather busy at the moment."

"Very well, then I shall lead a charge myself to finish this battle so that the search can continue. Color party! Prepare to charge!"

Sergeant Salia Aguom looked at the Prince, then over at Rallie. Visyna spared the briefest of looks. Would he do it?

"With all due respect, Your Highness," Rallie said, "that would be tantamount to killing the future King, and I cannot allow that to happen. Your mother would be most displeased with me."

"My mother be damned!" the Prince shouted, walking forward to rest one foot on the edge of the wall. "I will have the Star this night!"

Sergeant Aguom sighed and followed, the rest of the Color party reluctantly forming up with him. It appalled Visyna that men would throw away their lives in such a foolish manner.

A new force washed over the battlefield, its evil unmistakable. Visyna kept her hands moving even as she saw the Shadow Monarch's elves emerge from the trees. There was a growl behind her and Jir loped up onto the crumbled parapet and got down low on his stomach, the hair on the back of his neck standing straight up.

"Rallie, do something," Visyna whispered, wishing she could do more herself.

Rallie frowned, then pulled the cigar from her mouth and whistled between her teeth. Jir looked at her, then turned back to the battlefield, settling his body even lower in preparation to pounce. Rallie whistled again, much louder, and the bengar reluctantly came down from the parapet and padded over to her, his tail swishing in agitation.

Visyna couldn't hear what Rallie said to the bengar, but she felt a tremor in the skeins of power as the woman spoke. A moment later, Jir disappeared back into the fortress.

"I meant to do something to stop this," Visyna said, her frustration boiling up.

Somewhere behind them a muraphant trumpeted, the call picked up by the others. The ground began to shake beneath Visyna's feet.

The muraphants were stampeding.

Soldiers dove out of the way as the animals burst from their temporary corral and rumbled through the fortress and over a low spot in the wall. Out of the corner of her eye, Visyna saw Jir clutching the rear of the last muraphant as it ran past, the bengar's eyes quite wide.

The arrival of the great beasts on the battlefield had an immediate effect. Any rakkes unfortunate enough to be in their path were trampled into oblivion. Visyna saw Jir jump from his ride and momentarily lost him in the confusion. The muraphants kept going, passing between the Iron Elves' square and the elfkynan circle as they made for the remembered gap by the river, their only thought to flee. The bara jogg opened their mouths wide in anticipation and were crushed by the maddened herd. The muraphants kept going, only to be stopped by a new wall of trees that closed the road and their escape.

The bengar reappeared, running straight for the nearest dark elf Konowa, but a rakke blocked its way. The rakke's throat was torn out with a single swipe of the bengar's claws. Jir ran on, but more rakkes moved to intercept him.

Just then another howitzer shell lifted into the night sky, the familiar trail of sparks like a comet crossing the heavens. Visyna sensed something odd, and saw from the corner of her eye the shell alter course to come down among the ring of *sarka har.* White light burst forth and then was gone. The muraphants thundered toward the gap.

Rallie blew out a long stream of smoke, nodding to herself. "No need, my dear, no need. Someone beat me to it."

FIFTY-TWO

S tay close, Ally; same goes for the rest of you," Yimt said. He
jogged toward the gap in the trees.

"Sweet knobby-kneed nuns!" he shouted, turning and running back toward them. He grabbed Alwyn by the cross-belts
and heaved him to the side as muraphants burst through the gap in the
trees and into the open.

Alwyn got up spitting dirt and cautiously peered into the gap. The
elves of the Long Watch slipped through with ease, their bows humming
as arrows streaked across the field.

"Okay, let's try that again," Yimt said, his voice a little quieter than
normal. He led them through the wreckage of the *sarka har* and onto the
battlefield. Alwyn gasped as he stepped through the trees, both at the cold
and at what he saw. Of all the nightmares he had had or would ever have,
nothing would match this.

Bodies, of all kinds, littered the ground. Bara jogg of immense size
heaved themselves over the earth, consuming anything that lay in their
path. Shadows flitted in and out of sight, blazing swords of ugly black
flame spraying hoar frost with every thrust and parry. A branch on one of
the *sarka har* stabbed down at Alwyn, its razor-edged leaves slashing the arm
of his jacket, but not the flesh beneath.

"You must be alert to the dangers around you," Chayii said, suddenly appearing at his elbow. She held a long, thin sword in her hand and used it to cut the branch off with a quick flick of her wrist. Black ichor sprayed from the tree's wound, and a scream sounded somewhere in Alwyn's head. He looked down at the gleaming wooden sword, still amazed that something made of wood could be so sharp. The weapon glowed warmly, its surface polished smoother than marble, the deep browns of the grain pulsing with energy.

Something distant tugged at Alwyn's consciousness and made him turn. It was as if the world had suddenly been connected, each thing, each emotion, a tiny piece of an immense puzzle, and all connected to one another. There were no words, but he understood the threat.

Fifty yards away, one of the black elves stared at Chayii. It obviously sensed the power in the weapon and knew it for what it was. It hissed *Hynta-reig*, and Alwyn knew, in the way he had known back in the forest, that the words meant the elves of the deep forest, *the abandoners*. He felt the long-borne hatred that coursed through the elf as it pulled back the string on its bow. So great was its fury that it failed to see Yimt aiming his shatterbow at it.

The shatterbow fired first. The elf was taken in the chest by two black arrows of its own making. The fingers holding the string went slack, loosing the arrow even as the elf fell lifeless to the ground.

Alwyn reached out for Miss Red Owl and pushed her forward, stumbling after her. The black arrow tore through the leather cartridge pouch on his hip, the cloth of his caerna, and finally the flesh beneath. He felt his thigh bone break as he hit the ground, a scream blown from his lungs.

"Ally's hit!" Boots thudded on the ground, hands grabbed him and rolled him over. He was aware of slashes of light and crushing darkness. Elvish words drifted through to him and he latched on to them, understanding they were a lifeline. The sound of his blood pumping roared in his ears. The pain in his leg dug a little deeper each time. A voice whispered in his head, calling him, seeking control.

"I'm sorry, Yimt, I'm so sorry," he said, not knowing why. The pain and the cold were consuming him. He looked down at his left leg, at the black arrow stuck there, high above the knee, its steel-leaf fletching already growing as the shaft pulsed with his blood. A tourniquet was cinched tight around his upper thigh, but he could feel the cold trying to seep beyond it and into the rest of his body.

"Nothing to apologize for, lad," Yimt said, leaning over him, the end of his beard just inches from Alwyn's face. The dwarf turned and looked at someone nearby. "Do your magic! Get that thing out of him! You did it before!"

Chayii came into view, shaking her head. "It has already taken root, and he is still weak from the last one. To try to reverse it now would put too much strain on him. I fear he would not survive."

Yimt's face turned bright red. "This ain't no time to be worrying about trees over people! I put two of them black arrows into that korwird and you countered them; this is only one."

Chayii turned her head quickly toward Yimt, anger bright on her face. "Would you have us shoot him with an arrow in the other leg? No, master dwarf, the arrow is now part of him. This is no choice I make, it is as it is. The korwird was dead when we culled the *sarka har*. To cull this one would be to cull Alwyn as well, sending him to a fate worse than death."

"Then I'll take care of it," Yimt said, reaching out to grab the arrow. "Scolly, Teeter, hold him down. Inkermon, you believe in that creator of yours so much, I want a prayer, and a damn good one." He paused, thinking for a moment, then looked back at Alwyn. "Ally, lad, this might hurt a bit, so try not to scream too much."

Alwyn tried to protest, but his throat was locked, his mouth clenched against the pain. He closed his eyes and prayed for unconsciousness. It eluded him. The irony of it brought tears to his eyes and he started to laugh.

"No!" Chayii said. "To rip it out would kill him. The sapling and his leg are one. There is no way to separate them. We must end his misery before he is beyond us."

Alwyn opened his eyes. Everything was growing distant as the cold infused him. He managed to utter two words. "Do it."

Yimt looked at him with genuine shock.

He turned to Chayii, who nodded. "It is the only way," she said. Alwyn noticed that she still held her sword in her hand.

Alwyn turned his head away as hands gently held his arms and legs. He heard Yimt gasp, and looked back. The dwarf was shaking his head in disbelief.

"No. There is another way," Meri said, holding out a shadowy hand.

Konowa bared his teeth and smiled at death as the arrows struck, their dark runes that branded their shafts guiding them unerringly for the heart. He expected excruciating pain, agony, but after the sound of the arrows piercing flesh he felt only a cold dread as the horror of what happened hit him.

They hadn't aimed at him.

"M-major . . ."

There was a sigh, and an animal scream, and the sound of two bodies falling to the ground. A temporary gap in the square revealed the terrible truth. Lorian and Zwindarra sprawled on the ground, the black shaft of an arrow protruding from each chest. He heard a bowstring pulling taut and turned back to see the elf nearest him taking aim again, and this time it was at him.

A dark blur pounced on the elf even as it released the string. The arrow leaped from the bow as Jir's teeth sank into the elf's neck, snapping its spine. Time seemed to slow for Konowa. He heard the high-pitched twang of the bowstring and a strange after-echo, the sharp cracking of teeth on bone, saw the arrow rotating on its axis as it sped toward him. The acorn against his chest thrummed with energy, but there was nothing he could do with it except watch his own destruction.

The Star. All this death and waste for an idea. Even now, it compelled man and beast to horrible acts.

The arrowhead had reached the edge of his jacket just above the acorn, the very tip of its sharpened point penetrating the cloth, when a second arrow hit it obliquely at the same point, shattering the two shafts and sending the splinters flying off to the side, leaving Konowa unscathed. He blinked and looked down at his chest, expecting to see an arrow there.

He looked up, turning to the right. A leafy bush stood improbably in the middle of the battlefield. He blinked and looked again, and the bush was gone.

A growl brought his head back to the front in time to see three rakkes converging on Jir. Konowa screamed his battle cry and charged. Before he had covered half the distance the rakkes were all down, two with arrows through their necks, the third with Jir's jaws around it.

Konowa felt the power of the acorn increasing and knew the regiment was close. The fortress was now less than a hundred yards away. The shades of the Iron Elves continued their battle with the captured souls of the Thirty-fifth Regiment, an ethereal combat that swam in and out of his vision. Rakkes still roamed the field, their charges coming closer as the regiment expended the last of its ammunition. Black arrows raked square and circle alike. In the course of the battle, the two entities—once mortal enemies, now both prey—had moved closer together until they were now little more than twenty feet apart.

The elfkynan broke. Chants of "Sillra! Sillra!" were replaced with screams. Their circle disintegrated and the survivors ran, hunted by shadow, claw, and frost fire.

A group of rakkes charged to within yards of the square when arrows cut into them from all sides. These weren't random shots, but well-aimed strikes that hit eyes and throats and hearts, bringing the creatures down quickly and with skill. Konowa recognized the archers by the talent of their shooting even as his senses blurred with the power of the bond-oath between elf and Wolf Oak.

The rakkes panicked, howling their confusion as more arrows cut into their ranks. A few muskets fired as well, an odd sound after the silence of the square when it fired what Konowa thought was its last round. Konowa thrust his saber into the chest of the nearest rakke, the frost fire turning it into a burning, screaming pyre. All this death. The futility of it gave strength to his arm, and he swung his saber with abandon, severing limbs and heads, skewering bodies so violently that he was forced to place his boot on the chest of one rakke to pull the saber back out.

Jir stalked around him, a black demon of claws and teeth, ripping into the rakkes, exposing the blood and the bone beneath. The dead piled up around them, their frenzy unmatched. Konowa let the cold take him, giving himself over to its power. His saber arm was cold, black death. His eyes gleamed with frost. They would pay. He would destroy them all.

A shade of the Thirty-fifth Regiment appeared in front of Konowa and he cut it down, his saber equally effective against shadow. Nothing could stand up to him. He heard the twang of a bowstring and felt the arrow slicing through the air. He reached out with his senses and burned it with frost fire. The feeling was glorious. Another group of rakkes massed for an attack. Konowa spread the fingers of his left hand wide and slowly squeezed. Frost and flame burst over the rakkes, their screaming pitiful as they tried to run. Konowa squeezed his hand tighter and then opened it with a yelp. A white feather quill stuck out of the top of his hand.

"I think that's more than enough," Rallie said, striding toward him. Visyna, the Prince, and the regimental Color party followed.

Konowa looked around him. The battlefield had changed. The bara jogg were crawling back to the river, while rakkes and black elves vanished into the *sarka har,* the limbs of the trees embracing them. Elves of the Long Watch spread out across the wreckage, their oath-bond weapons tiny sparks of warmth in a cold, dark sea of Her power.

Black flame danced along Konowa's saber and frost radiated out in all directions from beneath him. His breath misted and hung in the air, a swirling veil muting everything around him. With a single thought he burned the quill in his hand. The power coursing through him was wonderful and terrible.

Konowa flowed his senses outward, searching, and found a source of power searching in return. He turned and saw a tiny sapling pushing up through the frost, but unlike the *sarka har,* this tree grew proud and straight and shone with a brilliant red glow. Konowa looked closer. It looked like a Wolf Oak, only more . . . perfect. The buds on its thin branches began sprouting leaves, and as they unfurled it was clear to see they were unmistakably in the shape of a star. Without a word he walked over and stood above it. He looked up to the sky, searching the darkness for a sign, but he already knew what he had found.

This was the Eastern Star returned.

FIFTY-THREE

When Hizu finally collapsed beneath the Viceroy, he was still a day's ride from Luuguth Jor. Disgusted, he jerked his boots from the stirrups and awkwardly stood to his feet, pulling the long green cloak he had chosen to wear tighter around him. It crinkled with the sound of the hoar frost that lined its interior, a glorious sensation against his new flesh.

He stood over the horse's head and nudged it with his boot. Pink, frothy bubbles blew from its nose and the one eye he could see was rolled back, the cornea shot through with blood. Forcing his knees to bend, a motion he was still relearning as he sought to work the joints where his flesh had been reborn through Her beneficence, he crouched over the dying animal and laid both hands on it, commanding it to rise as he had commanded Her forces to kill.

Black frost spread across its body like ink spilled from a jar. The horse neighed once, twice, and blew dark streams of blood from its nose and mouth. He stood up and waited, watching the eye turn cloudy as the fluid from the animal's mouth changed from red to gray to black. Much faster than even he had recovered, the horse lurched to its hooves, leaving strips of flesh frozen to the ground where it had lain just a moment ago. It turned to him and opened its mouth wide, its sound now rumbling from deep within frost-burnt lungs.

Now this, the Viceroy thought, *was a horse.*

Warm water trickled down her throat. Inja remembered and opened her mouth to scream. A harsh, rasping sound echoed in her ears.

"Easy now, girl, I don't look that bad."

Inja closed her mouth and opened her eyes. At first, all she could make out was polished metal and locks of red hair in the lamplight. She was still in the stable, but now lay on one of the straw-filled mattresses for the help, a blanket over her body. She shivered and clutched it tight around her. Her vision cleared, and she made out a man wearing a shiny metal helm and cuirass—a cavalry officer. Several others stood around her bed, their expressions a mix of sorrow and revulsion. Most curiously, a white bird sat on the foot of her bed, its bill tucked under one wing. It appeared to be snoring.

"Who . . . are . . . you?" she asked, each word a challenge.

"Ah, of course, we haven't been properly introduced." He stood up from beside her bed and doffed his helmet, the long horsehair plume brushing her exposed arm resting on top of the blanket. "I am the Duke of Rakestraw, Colonel Jaal Endrehar, knight commander of Her Majesty's cavalry in Elfkyna. And these gentlemen are my staff," he said, motioning with a gauntleted hand at the group, who bowed and nodded toward her. "We received a message that we should pay a visit to the Viceroy at our earliest convenience, and found you lying on the floor . . . injured."

His voice was deep and rough, but kindness gave it a gentle, soothing quality, and his smile, despite the many scars on his face, outshone the lanterns. Inja brought her hand up to her throat and felt the skin there. It was scarred, and freezing to the touch. "I am Inja, my lord. I work in the stables. I was here when the Viceroy came," she said, understanding now why some of the officers turned away. "He took Hizu and left. I knew what would happen, but I couldn't stop him." At the thought of Hizu, Inja began to sob.

"Oh, now, don't do that, darling. I'm sure they can't have got far. We'll track the bastard down and get Hizu back," the Duke said, looking at his officers.

"Hizu is dead; worse than dead. The Viceroy has changed him, as he has been changed." *And as I have been changed*, she didn't add, bringing her hand up to her throat again. She couldn't stop shivering. The Duke gently took her hand in his and brought it back down to the bed. One of his officers threw a shabraque over her, the lamb's wool thick and heavy.

"I don't understand," he said, still smiling at her.

"Then I will show you," she said, pulling herself up using the Duke's hand. She pulled the shabraque around her like a shawl. The movement woke the bird—a pelican, she saw, which flapped its wings a couple of times then hiccuped and tucked its bill back under a wing.

Inja took a couple of steps and would have fallen if the Duke hadn't put a hand around her waist.

"Easy now, Inja, I think you should rest," he said, trying to place her back on the bed. "We need to get a fire going to warm you up."

Inja shook her head. "No, you must see. He will kill many more. It is the table," she said, pointing up toward the palace.

The Duke stopped trying to sit her back down. "Maybe you'd better lie down. Tables can't hurt you—well, not unless they're being thrown at you," he said, trying to make her laugh.

She shook her head. "No, you are wrong. It is not merely a table. The soul of something dark lies within it. It remembers—it remembers when it was a tree, and it is angry."

"Oh, now, I know a thing or two about the Wolf Oaks and the Long Watch and that, ahem, bonding they do, but I never heard of an oath bond with a piece of furniture."

"You mock me!"

The Duke smiled and ducked his head. "I apologize, but are you sure you don't mean a crystal ball, or maybe a book of spells sitting on the table? I think I know the table you're talking about, carved to look like a dragon? Bit garish, but hardly evil."

"I know of what I speak! It *is* evil. He uses it up in his room. Can you not feel it?"

At this the pelican looked up, suddenly interested in its surroundings. The Duke looked at his officers, who shrugged, clearly unable to sense the forces at work around them. "We've been riding for the better part of three weeks; I can't feel much of anything at the moment."

"Then I must show you, now." Without waiting for his reply she broke free from his arm and stumbled out of the stable. The Duke quickly caught up with her, holding out his arm for her to use for support. She heard the clatter of spurs on the cobblestones as his men followed.

Inja led them into the palace and up the many stairs toward the Viceroy's bedchamber. The Duke all but carried her the last few flights, her strength ebbing as she got closer to the room. Cold seeped into her bones, a deep, insatiable probing that began to tunnel her vision, even as the Duke kicked open the outer door to the room.

"It's freezing in here!"

Sabers scraped free of their scabbards as the Duke's men went to the inner door, the wood patinaed with black frost. Shoulders and boots hammered the door, which groaned and then tore from its hinges. A rush of bitterly cold air flooded the room.

The Duke gently handed her to another officer while he stepped into the inner chamber. He carefully crossed to the barred window, taking a wide path around the table in the center of the room. He flung open the bars, letting the warm outside air in. The pelican landed on the sill, staring in at the table with great curiosity. A glint of silver and the shadow of something much larger flew past the window, but the pelican seemed undisturbed by it.

The Duke turned back to the table, which seemed to shimmer as the air got colder. He stepped closer, leaning over to look at its surface. He suddenly stood up, his saber whistling from its scabbard.

"That sneaky bastard. This thing is like some huge crystal ball." He motioned for his men to stay back. "She's right, it is magic. If I'd known that I would have dug my spurs into it good."

He looked again. "What the devil?" the Duke shouted, his face going white with rage as he gazed at the surface.

"What is it?" an officer asked, his saber poised.

The Duke pointed to the surface of the table. "That's the Viceroy, and he's heading to Luuguth Jor. Damnation! We'll never get there in time." He looked back at the surface and his face grew grim. "Konowa and his boys are up against it, and there isn't a thing I can do about it."

Inja walked unsteadily into the room and stood opposite the Duke, the table between them. The pelican followed her steps intently. "It's very cold in here, my lord. If there were any fuel to burn, we could have some heat."

The Duke of Rakestraw lifted his head and looked at her from across the table. He had the most wonderfully dangerous smile she had ever seen.

FIFTY-FOUR

I t was only a tree, Konowa told himself, a living piece of wood. It was nothing. How could it possibly be one of the Stars? Thousands of elfkynan had given their lives believing its lie. Tens of thousands, maybe hundreds of thousands, were flocking to its legend, fomenting rebellion in the hope they could win their freedom, deceived by a simple tree.

And Iron Elves had died, his men, his soldiers, and for what?

It was only a tree. It should have burned when he grabbed it. Konowa felt his hand close around its slender trunk, and then he was flying backward, a bolt of lightning leaping into the sky, turning night into day. A new, brilliant Star shone down from the heavens, bathing the battlefield in clear, red light.

Konowa landed on his left shoulder and rolled to a standing position. His left shoulder throbbed and he brought his right hand up to rub it and stopped as he saw that his saber was broken in two. All he held now in his hand was the hilt and a foot of jagged steel. He looked up. A single, spiraling beam of light now blazed between the Star above and the tree below. Heat spread from it in ever-expanding waves.

Steam rose from the ground, and the air grew heavier, wetter. Konowa squinted, shaking his head. A figure stood in the light, its robes flowing in the rushing energy being released. It reached and patted the sapling, then moved past it, though the light from the Star followed it. He sensed a new power unlike anything he had felt before.

"Welcome back, little one," Rallie said, looking up to the sky and smiling.

A blast of cold air cut through the heat, and Her Emissary rose from the earth, its form muted. *"Give me the Star and save yourself."*

Rallie looked amused. She pulled a new cigar out from beneath her robes and held it to the light, her eyes twinkling as the cigar end glowed to life.

"Give it to you? It's not mine to give," she said.

Konowa looked around in amazement. All eyes were focused on Rallie and Her Emissary and the blazing Star above them.

Her Emissary took a step forward. A bowstring released and a musket fired at the same time, but each shot passed right through its chest. Its laughter sounded like brittle rocks falling down a mountain. It drew forth its dagger, black flame curling around it like a living thing.

"Impressive," Rallie said, a white feather quill suddenly appearing in her free hand.

"Not even your weapons can harm me now. The sarka har delve deep. Her power will be absolute here, and the Star will fall to Her domain."

"You truly don't understand the power of the quill, do you? This one isn't for throwing," she said as she pulled a sheaf of paper from another fold in her robe. She held the quill over the paper, poised to begin sketching.

Konowa couldn't understand Rallie's game, but it didn't matter. He felt the truth in Her Emissary's words even as the warmth that had originally emanated from the light between the sapling and the Star began to wane. He shifted his grip on his saber and prepared to charge.

"There's no need, Major, Her Emissary will be leaving shortly. It should be quite an exit. I hope I can do it justice," she said, tentatively sketching in a few outlines.

"I will have the Star now!"

It took another step toward Rallie, the flames on its dagger leaping higher into the night.

The air sizzled and sparked between Her Emissary and Rallie. The acorn burned with cold anticipation against Konowa's chest, infusing his blood with shards of an ancient, dark power. This might be the Shadow Monarch's gift, but Konowa would use it to smite Her Emissary and damn the consequences. And this time, he wouldn't just kill the bastard, he'd annihilate it completely. He began to lift the broken saber, then found his arm unable to go any higher. He tried again to no avail.

"Major, if you please," Rallie said, her drawing becoming more vigorous. "I really do need to concentrate."

Konowa looked up and for the first time saw the sketch on Rallie's paper. It showed the tableau before them, but it wasn't still—it was moving. Light and shadow raced across the paper in a furious ebb and flow as Her Emissary and Rallie fought on a plane normal vision could not comprehend.

"Your parlor tricks won't hold me for long," Her Emissary said, taking another step forward. The very air appeared to bend around its body.

"They don't have to," Rallie said, suddenly turning the paper over with a flourish and beginning a new drawing.

Konowa caught a quick glimpse of the Duke of Rakestraw, a table, raised sabers, and a lit match.

Her Emissary stopped, its head cocked to the side as if listening to something. Then it shrieked.

"If at first you don't succeed . . ." Rallie said, drawing deeply on her cigar, the end glowing with red fire.

"My ryk faur!" The form that was Her Emissary wavered and then shattered into nothing.

Rallie nodded with satisfaction as she finished her sketch. "Not my best work, but I think my readers will get the general idea. Now," she said, putting her paper and quill away and looking lovingly at the young sapling, "what are we going to do with you?"

"You're going to give it to me." The Prince spoke up, stepping forward and holding out his hand. He cast his gaze around the battlefield and raised his voice. "I claim this prize in the name of Her Majesty the Queen, ruler of Calahr and all the lands of Her Empire."

Visyna's eyes flared, and Konowa knew it was only a matter of time before the situation got out of control.

"Your father should not have given you Her power, Konowa Swift Dragon."

The voice cut through the raised voices and for a moment everything was calm. It had been ten years since he heard that voice.

He turned to face Chayii Red Owl of the Long Watch. A squirrel perched nonchalantly on her shoulder, its fur smoking slightly.

"He was looking out for me, Mother," Konowa replied, his head swimming with emotion. "Without it, we'd all be dead."

Chayii walked up to him, stopping just outside the ring of frost. She traded a look of recognition with Rallie and then turned to him. "And with it, what are you then, my son? Long has it been since I saw you, and I would hold you to my chest as a mother would her child, yet you would burn me with Her poison." Tears welled up in her eyes as she looked upon him. She cocked her head to one side and then looked directly at Visyna. "And *you*. You are a weaver of the stuff of life. I feel it as I feel the land here cry out in its pain. Why did you allow this to happen?"

Visyna's mouth opened and closed several times. Konowa felt a throbbing at his temples.

"The Star must remain with its people here in Elfkyna," Visyna said at last. "It must be left here, where it was planted. This is where it is meant to be, to cleanse this land and destroy Her foul craft."

Chayii nodded at Visyna. "The witch is right."

"No, she is not!" shouted Prince Tykkin, banging his fist against his scabbard. "The Star will go to Calahr. I want that sapling dug up at once. Regiment! Ready arms!"

Bayonets leveled, their points glittering with frost in the predawn light. Elven archers notched arrows. Cold surged through Konowa.

"M-major . . ."

Konowa turned. He was amazed to see the dwarf, Corporal Arkhorn, making his way over the battlefield with several members of his patrol, carrying a wounded soldier. *They had survived!*

When they got closer Konowa saw that it was the young private who had flogged Kritton. Alwyn, that was his name, Alwyn Renwar. It mattered to Konowa that he remembered his name, especially when he saw that the young man was missing a leg, the stump wrapped in leaves and moss. Worse, however, was the shadow that cloaked him, marking him both human and shade.

"It's good to see you again," Konowa said. He paused before he went on. "What happened to the others? Private Kritton?"

Corporal Arkhorn shook his head. "Dead, or some version of it. Except Kritton. He ran off and we haven't seen him since."

Konowa wasn't sure what to think about that. Kritton was many things, but a coward?

"He'll be caught, punished, and shot," the Prince said, waving his hands in the air. "All of you will do well to remember that."

For answer, the dwarf gently laid Alwyn on the ground with the help of his patrol, then stood up and looked past them to the edge of the trees. The shades of Iron Elves stood arrayed in a line, their two-handed swords held in front of them. Behind them sat a dark figure on a horse, the shade's halberd ablaze in black flame.

"Lorian," Konowa said. The pain was too much. He felt his head spinning.

"The Star can break the oath, Major," Alwyn said, grimacing with each word. Konowa took a deep breath and looked at him. "It can break it for all of us."

"To use the power of the Star in that way now when it is still young would be too damaging to it. You know the danger in that. It would be like Her silver Wolf Oak only a thousandfold more terrible," Chayii said, pointing at the *sarka har* around them. "It must remain here to fight this. We will need its power." She looked down at Alwyn, a sad smile on her face. "I am sorry, Alwyn of the Empire, but the land's need is greater."

"This is preposterous!" Prince Tykkin said. "Major, I remind you of your duty. The only need that matters here is that of the Queen, who, may I add, would be most appreciative to have the Star. You would be a wealthy elf."

Konowa tried to imagine piles of gold and silver. He shook his head.

The Prince drew his sword. The metal was dull and gray and no black flame or frost marred it. "The Star is mine and I claim it now. Color Sergeant! Bring me that tree!"

Sergeant Aguom's eyes went wide, but he stepped forward anyway, slowly walking toward the sapling. Jir padded silently to stand beside the tree, his tail swishing menacingly. Konowa looked around him. He saw Private Vulhber, his towering frame easily recognizable among the soldiers. He wasn't looking at Konowa, or the Prince, but up into the night sky, as were all the Iron Elves.

Konowa felt a cold gaze on his neck and turned back to see Lorian and Zwindarra staring at him. He saw Meri, too, and elves he had known and thought lost forever. This was his chance to set them free, the dead and the living.

"Wait," Konowa said.

Sergeant Aguom let out a sigh and halted, still several feet away from the tree. The Prince looked as if he was about to step forward, but Konowa stopped him with a look.

It felt as if a mountain was pressing down on Konowa. He felt all of their stares, knew all of their desires, and knew that whatever he chose, many would hate him for it. He found himself drifting back to his banishment in the forest, before he'd found Jir.

In his entire life he had never felt so utterly alone.

He sensed the rising of the sun behind him and knew it was time. There was only one real choice.

Thoughts of his time in the birthing meadow came back to him. He saw the Shadow Monarch there, cradling the silver Wolf Oak, desperate to save it. He understood the desire and he understood why he could never give in to it.

"The Star must stay here where it belongs."

The first ray of sunlight stretched over the horizon and infused the sapling's leaves with a warm, pulsing light. The Star in the sky faded and disappeared even as the tree began to glow, its leaves flashing like a thousand shooting stars.

Then the tree burst into flame.

FIFTY-FIVE

Something tugged at the Viceroy's mind. He slowed the horse to a canter, trying to make sense of the feeling. A scream all too familiar to him tore through his head, sending him reeling. The horse reared and screamed as well, gnashing its teeth at nothing until they splintered, and still the scream did not end.

The table! Its pain was beyond measure. This was nothing like the fire of before. Worse, he was not there to protect it. Thoughts of vengeance and the star fled his mind as the screams grew in intensity. He fought to control the horse and managed to turn it around, digging his spurs deep into its sides, and galloped back toward the palace.

Fear and agony lent speed to the horse. The miles merged as all sense of time blurred into nothingness. He rode with screams echoing in his mind until he screamed, too, the pain as real as if it were his own. He rode with complete abandon, his hands clenched so tightly around the reins that the leather melded into his new flesh. The horse beneath him never tired, its gait as manic as the look in its eyes. The ground rushed past, the horse moving much faster than any horse the Viceroy had ever ridden, the animal's speed a raging hunger that ate the miles with savage appetite; yet it was not fast enough.

It was the smell that first assaulted his senses as the Viceroy pulled up in the rear courtyard of his palace, a thick, dry smell that overpowered the wet stench of the horse beneath him. He ripped his hands from the reins, barely feeling the sting of raw flesh exposed, and ran into the palace, climbing the steps to his bedroom four at a time.

He entered his bedchamber and saw the shattered door. He crossed to it and stepped through, his limbs shaking with fear and rage. He took two steps into the room and stopped, the horror of what he found too great to allow him to approach any closer.

Her creation, Her Emissary's *ryk faur*, his power . . . was now but a single-leg upturned with a white doily draped over the clawed foot. Resting on top was a small potted fern. A rustle of wings at the window made him turn, and he saw the white bird.

"Looks much better, if you ask me," the Duke of Rakestraw said, walking up to stand in the doorway behind him. "Gives the room a more homey feel."

The Viceroy tore his eyes away from the pelican and spun on his heels, his hands already clenching as he prepared to rend the very soul from the Duke's body. Before he could, something large and heavy hit him in the stomach, knocking him to the floor.

He looked down to see a large bag of ashes and charred wood spill on the flagstones around him.

"Thought you might like that, bit of a souvenir," the Duke said, casually strolling into the chamber. Several more soldiers of the Duke's cavalry stood equally at ease near the door, hands resting on saber hilts and pistol butts.

The Viceroy lurched to his feet, the hood of his cloak falling away as he did so.

The Duke turned back to him, his scarred face dominated by a wide grin. "Well, well, well, I see the table wasn't the only thing that got fried."

"You will pay for this!" the Viceroy shouted, stumbling to his feet, calculating the odds of killing them all. He was tired from the ride, it would be a close-run thing. *"I will destroy you!"*

The Duke stood a little straighter at the sound of his voice, but he did not back up. "You could try, but I think it'd be the last thing you did. By the way, that horse chase you sent me on worked out better than I thought. Not only did I round up enough horses to pay off all my debts with a tidy sum left over, I even had a bit extra to pay you back for your kindness," he said, waving a gloved hand toward the plant. "It was the very least I could do." The grin grew fiercer.

"When I got back and you weren't home, I found lovely Inja here, who was kind enough to show me around your accommodations. What, I said to myself, can I do to thank the Viceroy, and then Inja had a wonderful suggestion."

The Viceroy turned his glare on her, and she backed up a step. She, too, would suffer.

"No need to thank me," the Duke said, giving the fern a pat as he walked back out of the room, "it's what friends do." He paused at the door, one hand resting on the pommel of Wolf's Tooth, the other taking Inja gently by the arm. "Another thing friends do, Viceroy, is look after one another."

From the open window came the sound of the Viceroy's horse screaming in anger, followed by a volley of musket fire and a heavy thud.

"What was that?"

"That," the Duke said over his shoulder as he led Inja away, "is what you do to sick creatures. Worth keeping in mind, Viceroy."

Long after the echo of the Duke's horses had faded, the Viceroy remained standing in the middle of the room, his rage and despair pinning him to the spot like the weight of a hundred mountains.

Finally, his need to make the Duke of Rakestraw and the elfkynan stable girl pay propelled him to move.

He brushed the ashes from his cloak and turned and looked at what remained of the table. It took him a moment to feel the change in the air; it was growing colder. He leaned closer and saw the leaves of the fern slowly turning white, then black, as frost fire consumed them. He reached out a hand and touched the leg, but it felt as dead as the room around him.

"I don't understand . . ." the Viceroy said.

"You will," said Her Emissary, a dark shadow rising from the ashes, its anger flaming to life in the black dagger in its hand. *"You will."*

The screaming lasted all night.

FIFTY-SIX

The sun rose like a glowing ember caught high on a morning breeze, casting its light on the ruin of battle. The Colors were blown full out from their poles, their ends snapping as a strong wind picked up. Konowa stood in the middle of the battlefield, looking at what he'd done.

Everywhere, the trees burned. Their black limbs slashed the air in a futile attempt to put out the flames that consumed them. Screams filled his head as the *sarka har* died, their dark need extinguished in a blaze of pure, red light. The sapling towered above them all, now a great tree, its limbs reaching high into the sky. The Star was now a bridge between the earth and sky, a tree coursing with power so pure, so elemental that the very air around it thrummed like lead crystal.

The acorn against his chest beat with the rhythm of his heart, its cold need satisfied, its oath unbroken. At the very edge of his understanding, Konowa heard another scream. It confused him at first until he understood it wasn't a scream at all, but laughter.

The Shadow Monarch was laughing.

The Iron Elves stared at him in silence. Konowa had consigned them all to a fate none had asked for. In trying to save them, he had doomed them all.

In choosing to destroy Her forest here, Konowa had condemned the souls of the Iron Elves.

The enormity of it threatened to crush him where he stood. All he had ever wanted was a chance to make things right for the regiment and the soldiers he commanded.

Visyna had seen the truth, but he hadn't listened to her. He thought he could control the power, bend it to his will, but in the end all he managed to do was Her will.

The Shadow Monarch had deceived them all. She'd allowed Konowa's father to escape with the acorn from Her silver Wolf Oak, knowing the wizard would bring it to him. And she counted on Konowa's thirst for redemption, and like a fool he had allowed that desire to blind him to the truth.

The Shadow Monarch had never wanted the Star.

She wanted Her children back.

She wanted the Iron Elves.

Konowa raised his hand and let it brush the top of his ruined ear, feeling the scar that marked Her curse. He looked at the burning forest.

In the fire and the heat, a new purpose rose from the ashes.

A cold, merciless smile crept across Konowa's face as black frost began to sparkle along the shattered remnants of his saber. So the Shadow Monarch wanted Konowa and the Iron Elves for Her own. So be it. Konowa would show Her just how deadly it could be to get what you wished for.

All around him, the trees screamed as they burned.

ACKNOWLEDGMENTS

I began taking riding lessons in the course of writing this book. I wasn't charged for the added bonus of learning how to fall.

I saved a fortune.

Still, each time I dusted myself off and climbed back into the saddle, I realized that writing a novel is not all that different. You are going to make mistakes. You are going to wonder why you ever embarked on this in the first place. You are definitely going to become intimate with entirely new types of fear. And you are going to feel an exhilaration unlike anything else.

Still, anyone who tells you writing is as easy as falling off a horse has never suffered the added indignity of being sat on by the same horse. When that happens, and it will, you'll want friends around. When they stop laughing, they usually help you up. I have such friends, and their support and advice—and laughter—throughout the writing of this novel saved me on more than one occasion, and for that I am in their debt.

My best friend, my brother, Michael, is always there for me, and always will be. You demonstrated just how deep fraternal bonds can go by reading every draft of this book and always finding something encouraging to say, even if it was to compliment me on my bold choice of black ink on white paper.

Deb Christerson, friend from the beginning, a writer of amazing vision, and a most kind and generous person. Hereafter and forever more, the dandelion beer is on me.

Shelly Shapiro, a brilliant publishing maven and writer by profession, and a life coach by choice. I will be eternally grateful that you aren't professionally licensed to give advice or I'd never be able to pay you back.

Karen Traviss, Clarion classmate and trusted companion on this long and winding road, gifted writer, and patron saint for those in harm's way. You are an inspiration.

Chris Schluep, my American brother, fellow editor and writer, co-commiserater and lighthouse forever guiding me back to calmer waters when I set sail into a storm.

Bill Takes, wise beyond his years, who kindly and repeatedly offers me some of the soundest advice I've ever received (even if I don't follow it) and the epitome of class.

At Simon & Schuster's Pocket Books I want to thank my editor, Ed Schlesinger, for his exceptionally keen eye and unflagging energy, which has kept me going, and Deputy Publisher Anthony Ziccardi, comrade in arms from the old days, for taking a chance on something new.

My agent, Don Maass, for representing the very best of me (while sweeping the rest under the carpet).

Special thanks to a true American hero, Col. Robert W. Black and his wife, Carolyn; Edith Dunker; Owen Lock; Steve Saffel; everyone at Stackpole Books for their encouragement along the way; Jeff Young; and the very helpful staff of the New York Society Library.

I'd also like to acknowledge the many historians who have inspired me over the years, first as a student, then historian, editor, and now writer. It would take a whole other book to truly bear witness to what I've learned from their words, and in some cases, advice, so I will simply name them here with my unconditional thanks: George G. Blackburn, Christopher R. Browning, Terry Copp, Bernard Cornwell, Len Deighton, Richard Holmes, John Keegan, Rudyard Kipling, T. E. Lawrence, George MacDonald Fraser, Barbara W. Tuchman, and Gerhard L. Weinberg. If you haven't read their works I highly recommend that you do, but be forewarned: doing so may cause you to embark on a writing adventure of your own.

And finally, my grandfather, Robert James Whitson, who's up there somewhere smiling right now saying, "that's my grandson," and my parents, both for their unwavering love and support—even after I told them I was tossing my academic career—and for instilling in me that single, unquenchable spark of sheer bloody-mindedness to never give up.